Also by Rebecca Kenney

Gilded Monsters
Beautiful Villain
Charming Devil
Ruthless Devotion

CRUEL ANGEL

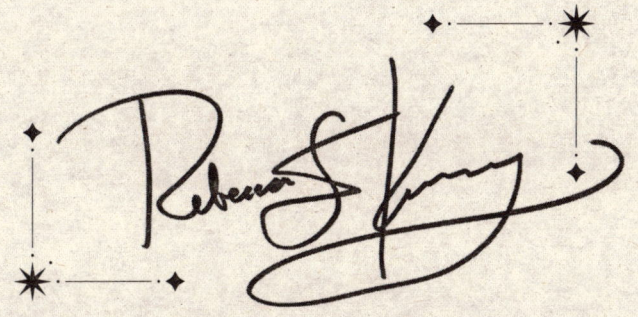

CRUEL ANGEL

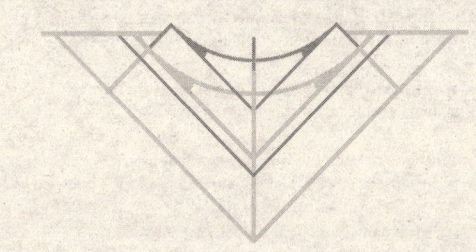

REBECCA KENNEY

To everyone who loved the Phantom for his darkness and Raoul for his light and wanted Christine to have the perfect symphony of both.

Copyright © 2026 by Rebecca F. Kenney
Cover and internal design © 2026 by Sourcebooks
Cover design by Stephanie Gafron/Sourcebooks
Series design by Regina Wamba
Cover images © wabeno/Shutterstock, Ocean Three/Shutterstock, photopsist/Shutterstock, rawf8/Shutterstock, Severage Sanpe/Shutterstock, Retouch man/Shutterstock, Fadaway Creative/Shutterstock, Labutin.Art/Shutterstock, LedyX/Shutterstock, Khakimullin Aleksandr/Shutterstock, Jag_cz/Shutterstock
Internal art © Arra Labadan
Chapter header image © Stefan Ilic/Getty Images

Sourcebooks and the colophon are registered trademarks of Sourcebooks.

All rights reserved. No part of this book may be reproduced in any form or by any electronic or mechanical means including information storage and retrieval systems—except in the case of brief quotations embodied in critical articles or reviews—without permission in writing from its publisher, Sourcebooks.

No part of this book may be used or reproduced in any manner for the purpose of training artificial intelligence technologies or systems.

The characters and events portrayed in this book are fictitious or are used fictitiously. Any similarity to real persons, living or dead, is purely coincidental and not intended by the author.

All brand names and product names used in this book are trademarks, registered trademarks, or trade names of their respective holders. Sourcebooks is not associated with any product or vendor in this book.

Published by Sourcebooks Casablanca, an imprint of Sourcebooks
1935 Brookdale RD, Naperville, IL 60563-2773
(630) 961-3900
sourcebooks.com

Cataloging-in-Publication Data is on file with the Library of Congress.

The authorized representative in the EEA is Dorling Kindersley Verlag GmbH. Arnulfstr. 124, 80636 Munich, Germany

Manufactured in the UK and distributed
by Dorling Kindersley Limited, London
001-358646-Apr/26
CPI 10 9 8 7 6 5 4 3 2 1

Cruel Angel contains descriptions of blood and blood drinking, vampires drugging victims, queerphobic comments by side characters, voyeurism, memories of childhood trauma, sibling death, claustrophobia, mild bondage, attempted sexual assault, murder, gore, and violence.

Music has the power to make one forget everything save those sounds that touch your heart.

—Gaston Leroux, *The Phantom of the Opera*

1

.. 🌹 ..

THE GOD RAISER

"It's Lloyd-Henry, right? Or do you prefer Lloyd?" The therapist welcomes me with a smile.

"Lloyd is fine." I'd prefer my true name, but no one has spoken it aloud in centuries.

"Come on in. I'm Dr. Jekyll." His voice is low, soothing. Designed to put people at ease, to lower their resistance.

I know that sort of voice all too well. If I had enough time with this doctor, I could charm him into doing anything I wanted. And I won't lie—it's tempting.

But I'm not here to exercise my powers today. I'm here because I could use some fucking therapy. I've tried almost everything else to cope with what's happening to me.

This is my final stop before I go to *them*. This man is my last chance. The best in the business of healing minds…or at least the best in Nashville, Tennessee, where fate has led me. No, "led" is too gentle a word—I was discarded here. Cast away like a piece of garbage.

"Have a seat wherever you're comfortable." Dr. Jekyll glances down at his clipboard as I drop into an armchair. "You mentioned you're feeling a lot of stress from work. Do you want to maybe talk about that a little bit?"

"Sure."

"Okay. Tell me about what you do."

"I manage a lot of projects, a lot of people." I prop my ankle on my knee and try to look relaxed. "Lately I've been letting things slip. I've been...failing."

The word tastes bitter in my mouth, but it's time to say it.

"Failing." The doctor leans back in his desk chair, tapping his chin with the end of his pen. "That's a strong word. What's an instance where you believe you failed?"

What would he say if I told him the truth? That I've been working tirelessly for decades—no, centuries—to become Earth's ruler and protector, the balm for all its ills? I have allies throughout the world, research in progress to find a cure for that greatest of evils—death. Vampirism, soul-infused portraits, necromancy, the return of the gods—each strategy was one piece in a plan, a gear in a great machine that should still function, even if one part is fractured.

And yet somehow, each piece has managed to contort itself into an unrecognizable, unusable shape. The vampire factions turned on each other, then rebelled against me. The first god I raised didn't possess any power; he needed more of his fellow gods at his side before he could do anything useful. So I summoned a second god, but he was ruined by the interference of the vampires. Disappointing, to say the least.

Oh, and I've died twice—once quite recently. *Let's talk about that, Doctor.* Let's explore how it feels to be shot in the head and ejected from my body into the Afterworld, where I waited in the dark until a necromancer dragged me back into my body again. It took me weeks to recover, and yet I still managed to keep my plans in motion.

But I'm on the verge of giving up. I'm so fucking tired. Coming back from death the second time wasn't good for me, and I'm terrified that I'm...unraveling. My insides feel different, ill fitting. Sometimes they *writhe*. I can see the bubbling and surging of my essence under my skin, and when that happens, I'm compelled to take a different form—raven, wolf, crow, stag, anything but a human shape. I'm less and less comfortable as a man, and the only time I can find any peace is in beast form.

Maybe I've been alive too long.

Dr. Jekyll's calm voice penetrates the churning cloud of my thoughts. "It's all right if you can't think of a specific instance right now."

"I think I'm trying to do too much," I reply. "I've always preferred to set things in motion and let others do the work while I observe them and nudge them in the right direction as needed, but lately that hasn't been working out for me. It's so hard to find good, hardworking, self-motivated people."

"So you feel you've been counting on people who aren't reliable. They've broken your trust."

"Yes."

"Typically, we can't control how other people act." Dr. Jekyll gives me a sympathetic smile. "They may hurt us or disappoint us, and there's not much we can do about it. What we can work on is our reaction...how we respond. And that's where stress management comes in. Let's talk about some ways you can cope with the pressure you're feeling. Have you tried meditation?"

I stare at him. "Meditation?"

"Sure. Meditation and mindfulness can be very helpful tools to—"

"I don't want to fucking meditate."

Dr. Jekyll's eyes widen slightly at my tone. "Well, there are other techniques, but let me explain what I mean by meditation. There's so much misinformation out there..."

He continues, but I'm barely listening. I'm staring at my hand, where my veins are arching up like inchworms, stretching the skin. All through my arm, I can feel that writhing, squirming sensation, the contortion of a soul that doesn't belong in this body, in this world.

"You seem very agitated," interposes Dr. Jekyll. "Do you want to talk about someone who betrayed you?"

Betrayal...

Dorian. I betrayed Dorian.

For the greater good, for a larger cause.

Something twists violently in my chest, and I gasp.

"This was a mistake." I rise from the couch.

"Lloyd, let's talk just a little longer," pleads the doctor.

"Do you see this?" I hold out my hand, where the veins and tendons are knotting and coiling under the skin. My very bones ache until I can hardly stand upright.

"Good god," mutters Dr. Jekyll. "What is that?"

"You can see it?" I confirm. "I haven't lost my mind?"

"I can see it, and I think you need a different kind of doctor," he falters.

"Usually, I have more time between episodes." I pull my hand close to my chest. In a moment, the small bones will begin to disconnect from each other, and I will have to transform or watch my body disassemble itself. "It's happening at shorter and shorter intervals now. Do you think meditation will help, Doctor?" I laugh, shrill and wild.

The doctor rolls backward in his chair, putting distance between us. "What's happening to you?"

"I'm *shifting*, motherfucker. I came to Nashville because there are other shifters here, and I thought perhaps I could ingratiate myself to them. But I've been sick, as you can see, and I haven't had the time." My spine rolls involuntarily, and I grit my teeth, forcing out my next words. "They're a close-knit group, not easy to penetrate. But I may have to go to them and beg them to help me, to cure me. I thought I would try this first—mind over matter, you know."

"That's not really a thing," murmurs the doctor.

"I should have known it wouldn't work. You humans pretend to know the mind, but the chasms in your knowledge are vast, and you are confidently wrong about so many things—aagghh!" I grimace as my shoulder pops. "Open that window, will you?"

"Look, I'm not just a therapist," says Dr. Jekyll. "I was premed and biochem once, before… Well, that's not important. Maybe I can take a blood sample, figure something out to help you—"

"The window," I gasp.

He hurries over to it, but the latch barely budges. "It's an old building," he apologizes. "We never open the windows because there aren't any screens—"

"Hurry!" I roar.

He wrenches one last time and manages to shove the window wide, just as I lurch forward and transform into a raven. I soar past him, cawing with the sheer relief of being out of that body.

Maybe I had it wrong. Maybe I was never meant to save the world from itself. Maybe I should leave humanity behind and become a beast or a bird forever.

If that is my path, I will first have to make some arrangements for Cernunnos—my useless, pathetic, lost puppy of a god—before I disappear. And perhaps I will go to the Shifter Collective in Nashville, just once, to ask for their help. Imprisonment or death at their hands can't be worse than my current torturous existence.

I wheel in the sky, cawing again for the benefit of Dr. Jekyll, who is gaping at me from the window far below. Perhaps I'll give him a vial of my blood before I take beast form forever. He can amuse himself studying it.

Higher I rise into the sunny air. I've seen beautiful cities, but this one is unmatched for its mystical energies. I sense the power of the ancients everywhere, traces of the muses, the leannán sídhe, lingering in the blood of everyday citizens. A resurgence is occurring, new powers unfurling and old ones awakening.

But for once, my heart doesn't thrill at the thought of being a part of it all. For once, I'm not energized by the possibility of the future, but exhausted.

After millennia, I believe I have finally grown old.

2

THE PHANTOM

In the City of Music, I am haunted by the cries of the dead.

The souls of deceased humans usually find their way into the Afterworld, but occasionally, some are misdirected, left behind as unsettled echoes, doomed to rove the world, out of sync with life.

The lost spirits can sense my former status as lord of phantoms, god of the Afterworld, but many of them don't understand that I no longer have the power to grant them safe passage. I cannot guide them or give them rest. My lack of response infuriates them, so I have become a locus for their anger, the eye of a howling hurricane of wretched souls. I rarely know a moment's peace.

I've been abandoned by my summoner, the one who raised me from my cursed sleep. He is a hybrid creature, a blend of shapeshifting púca and wicked gancanagh, love-talker and soul-eater. I was his goal, his hope, the next step in his complex plan…and yet he was foiled in his purpose, cheated when his enemies trapped me in this form. I'm not the powerful ally he wanted. With my memories blurred and my powers reduced to a mere flicker of the inferno they once were, I'm useless to him. Useless to everyone.

The feeling of being unwanted and outcast is familiar to me. I was always hated by the other gods, most of whom still sleep, bound to earth and darkness.

One of the gods is awake, though. I can sense him distantly, can feel the incessant dirge of his wrathful mourning for the glory that once belonged to the Tuatha Dé Danann. He feels me, too, and he despises my existence. I try to shut him out of my consciousness, like I do with the ghosts.

Left alone in this subterranean lair while my summoner pursues his goals elsewhere, I wait and I wander, empty of purpose, tortured by voices. I meander through dripping tunnels and forgotten halls, aching and angry.

"Stay here," my summoner told me before he left. "Stay away from humans at all costs. If you must go out, remain in the shadows and wear this." He handed me a white mask, designed to cover every feature except my mouth and jaw. "You're disgusting without it."

I could not answer him. For weeks after being trapped in this form, I could barely move, and I had trouble speaking my thoughts. The blond vampire who locked down my powers possessed a compulsive voice, a mental control I've never seen, not even in the days of old. A magical mutation of sorts. I still hear her voice in my head sometimes—a low, sinuous threat, a golden chain, deceptively beautiful and horribly irresistible.

Thanks to the echoes of her voice, the sneering rebuke of my summoner, the distant roar of the sea god, and the cries of the merciless dead, I am going mad.

The only time I feel the slightest relief is when I listen to music. In my subterranean dwelling, I have a radio—my summoner called it an antique—and I listen to it with the volume turned all the way up to drown out the wails of the ghosts. There is something called a record player as well, and a few boxes of records my summoner purchased from a shop somewhere in the city. He said they were cheap, that no one wanted them anymore. I cannot fathom such disregard.

Music is a mercy. It tears my emotions out of my chest and lets them soar in midair, exposed and soothed at the same time.

I began with the radio and the records, but they did not provide enough variety for my voracious appetite. Before my summoner abandoned me, he left me a few treasures to ensure my survival—a laptop, a phone, and a plastic rectangle called a debit card, apparently connected to a vast supply of human currency. The laptop sits on a desk, plugged into a yellowed socket in a wall of bare brick. Through it, I have discovered a world full of music... and other possibilities. I can purchase food and clothing for this body, and I can have them delivered to the old service door at the end of the canal.

With the laptop, I can investigate any subject as deeply as I desire. I can access a vast library of music composed within the past several decades. Most of my days are spent devouring music, studying its structure, reveling in its ascendancy beyond scientific rules into a realm of creative magic.

And yet despite having all this at my fingertips, I feel empty, haunted, hollow. There is an aching void inside me, as deep as the chasm in which I dwelled for centuries. I am always searching for new music, for a song that will perfectly express everything I feel...and for the perfect voice that will serve as the balm to my wretched soul.

3

CHRISTINE

"You gotta pay your dues if you want to make it in this business."

When you live in Nashville, you hear that statement almost every day, and I'm sick of it. I don't want to pay my dues. I'd like to be able to pay rent for a decent apartment instead of having to live in the shitty back hallway of the New Orpheum Theatre.

Today, the person telling me to "pay my dues" is Carlotta Vanetti, a curvy woman in her midtwenties with flawless makeup, acrylic nails, and a cascade of caramel extensions. She's standing in front of my desk, tapping those glossy nails on the varnished wood while I pull up our events calendar to see if the New Orpheum has availability for her birthday party.

The New Orpheum Theatre isn't *just* a theater. It's a sprawling industrial complex that has been mostly renovated and features a bar, several dance studio spaces, a chapel for weddings, and a gigantic ballroom for receptions and parties. Then there's the theater itself, decorated in a decadent gothic style, draped in suffocating crimson velvet and gleaming with electric candelabras. The building also houses green rooms, dressing rooms, storage rooms, and "residences," which is a fancy word for tiny studio apartments that the owner, Firmin Richards, rents out to cash-strapped twenty-somethings like me.

My studio apartment is a severe downgrade from the beautiful suburban mansion I grew up in. In fact, it's barely worthy of the word "studio," more like a closet with a mirrored wall at the end to make it seem larger. The toilet is located in the tiled shower stall. I don't have a sink, so I have to spit my toothpaste down the shower drain. I'm pretty sure none of it's up to code—like much of the work that's been done to the New Orpheum—but Mr. Richards has a business partner with connections in city government, and somehow, they've been able to weasel their way through the inspections and obtain every permit they applied for.

They've cut corners everywhere, and eventually, it will start to show. But until then, it's my job to make sure the books stay full of high-profile events—like Carlotta Vanetti's masquerade-themed birthday party.

"I'm fortunate to have connections in the music business," she says confidentially, leaning over the top of the lobby desk. "Not to mention plenty of natural talent. I've performed in a bunch of shows, and I could get more roles if I wanted them. In fact, I might be starring in this new musical by a young composer who grew up right here in Nashville. It's going to be big. I just know it. I have a gut instinct about these things, and it feels like fate, like the part was written for me. But that's all very hush-hush. Nothing's settled yet." She mimes zipping her lips.

How considerate of her to brag about her connections and prospects to an aspiring singer with neither advantage.

"I won't tell a soul," I say through a dazzling smile. "And it looks like you're in luck. We have an opening for the end of October."

"Perfect! Thanks, doll." Delicately, she plucks at her hair with her long nails, tucking a loose curl back into place as she purses her lips. I've lived in Nashville long enough to tell when someone's lips have had a little plumping assistance, and hers have definitely been overfilled more than once. Whatever makes her feel good about herself, I guess.

After taking her information and her deposit, I assure her that our event coordinator will be in touch soon with more information.

"That's great. And you keep chasing those dreams." She flutters her hand at me before stalking across the wide lobby and flouncing out through the theater's rotating door.

Why did I tell her I wanted to be a singer? Mindless chitchat, I guess. She asked what part of the city I live in, and when I said I live *here*, I saw the slight lift of her eyebrows, the surprise, the judgment. Maybe I wanted to convince her—and myself—that this job isn't the end goal for me.

Maybe I'm tired of being unseen, unheard, and ignored, but honestly, it's my own fault. Dancing onstage has never been a problem for me as long as I'm in a group. I could dance backup all day, every day. But singing for people? Nope.

Sure, I've pictured myself belting out jaw-dropping notes for an adoring crowd and hearing them cheer for me. I dream in cotton-candy colors, but the reality is a sour gummy worm, dust coated and too hard to chew. No matter how low the stakes, even on the tiniest stage in the smallest back-room bar in Nashville with the most accommodating audience, I just can't make myself sing in front of anyone.

My struggle with performance anxiety is nothing new, but

since my parents were killed, it's gotten worse. If I try to sing in public, I go into a full-blown panic attack or I projectile-vomit. It's infuriating. I'm pissed off at my own brain, at my parents, at the whole world. Yeah, I could use some therapy, but who's got the time or the money? Not me, that's for damn sure, because per fucking usual, my parents screwed me over one last time from beyond the grave.

I shouldn't have been surprised. My parents were always more loyal to the Progeny cult and its leader, Wolfsheim, than to their own blood. When Wolfsheim summoned his followers to fight for him, I told my parents not to go. But they were devoted fanatics, dedicated to his cause. Mom was upset with me for even suggesting they ignore a command from their "progenitor," and she refused to speak to me the morning they left.

But my dad pulled me aside into the study where he kept all the trophies of his music career. He used to sing and play bass guitar in a band before he switched to being a talent manager. It always weirded me out a little, seeing old photos of him in his heartthrob days, surrounded by girls begging him to sign their pictures, their arms, their boobs, anything. That was before I was born, though. When my mom got pregnant, he quit touring and shifted the focus of his career.

On that last morning, he spoke quietly, reassuringly. "Don't worry about us. Your mom and I will be fine. This is something we need to do."

I opened my mouth to protest again, but he shook his head.

"Listen...if anything should happen to us, stick with the Progeny. They'll take care of you."

"I don't want them to take care of me," I told him. "I'm an

adult, Dad. I keep telling you, I'm ready to be on my own and fend for myself."

"That's not up to you," he replied, a hint of sternness in his voice. "You have a responsibility as a Chosen female to marry within the Progeny and keep our bloodline pure—"

"God, do you hear yourself?" I exclaimed with an incredulous laugh. "I wish I could convince you to let go of all this Progeny crap. We could do so much on our own, just the three of us. Why don't you and Mom understand that?"

His face darkened. "Why don't *you* understand that after everything we've devoted to this cause, everything we've sacrificed, we *can't* just leave it behind?"

It was the first time he'd expressed anything akin to regret. Silence hung between us, the kind of silence only penetrable by months of family counseling.

After a long moment, I whispered, "I just don't want to lose you."

Dad sighed, pulling me close until I could hear the double thump of his heartbeat. "I'll make you a deal. If anything happens and we cross to the Afterworld, I'll come back and haunt you."

"Screw that," I mumbled against his shirt. "Send me a guardian angel or a muse, something that grants courage. Something that might actually be useful."

"Hey." He pushed me gently back and clasped my shoulders. "You'll find your courage one day. You were born to sing. All you need is the right teacher to give you confidence."

I swallowed the sob sticking in my throat. "So if you die for Wolfsheim, you promise to send me a supernatural mentor from beyond the grave?"

"I swear, I'll send you the best one I can find. Protection and inspiration...a guardian angel of music."

I couldn't help laughing a little, even as I brushed away tears. Mom's voice rang through the house, yelling that they needed to get on the road. Dad gave my shoulders one last squeeze, picked up his leather bag, and walked out of the study.

I never saw either of them again.

It's been over a year, and there's been no ghost, no muse, and no guardian angel. Another disappointment from my disappointing family. Proof that the Afterworld they believed in doesn't actually exist. This life is all there is, and after death...nothing. If I can't manage to pull myself together and go after my dreams, I'm going to languish here at the New Orpheum Theatre until I die, and my life will have been entirely pointless.

"Christine!" Meg's excited voice comes from the doorway behind me, snapping me back to reality. "Was that Carlotta Vanetti?"

I'm grateful for the interruption. A few more minutes in that mental space, and I would have dissolved into hopeless tears.

I clear my throat and straighten my spine. "Yeah, that was her."

"Shit," Meg says reverently. "Mr. Richards is going to be thrilled about this. Did she just *walk in*? No appointment?"

"Yup. She wants to have her birthday party here in October. Some kind of masquerade deal with spooky Halloween vibes."

"That's so awesome!" Meg hops onto the desk and literally kicks her feet. She's tiny, with the frame of a birdlike ballerina, gorgeous bone structure, and dark eyes. Her dad is from France, her mom from China. They moved to the States six years ago, but the marriage fell apart shortly afterward, and Meg ended up in Nashville with her mom. Mrs. Giry teaches in one of the New Orpheum dance studios, and they live in a slightly larger version of my apartment at the end of the same hall.

Mr. Richards says the New Orpheum is a haven from the world—a place where struggling artists and creatives can take refuge and get on their feet. I think he's just hungry for cheap labor. He takes advantage of people with no other options.

Meg expertly pulls her glossy black hair into a bun, her gaze fixed on me. "Are you all right? You seem sad."

I've never told her about my last conversation with my dad, and I can't bear to mention it now. Unfortunately, I have another reason to be depressed.

"I got the call today. It's done. My attempt to contest the will has failed—no more appeals, no more hope. My parents' life insurance money, their house, *everything* goes to that cult they were in. I don't get a cent. And I still have to pay the estate attorney, even though he did fuck-all to help me. It's a lower fee than it would have been if I'd won, but still."

"That's so wrong." Meg's brows pull together. "And you can't appeal to the cult members or whatever? Maybe they would give you something out of human decency."

Human decency—I almost laugh, but I'm too heartsick. "No chance of that. Not after I took them to court and called them a bunch of shit-sucking vultures. I'm utterly broke. I'll be staying here for the foreseeable future." *Probably forever.*

"Well, I'm selfishly glad about that part. I'd hate to lose you." Meg reaches over to pat my shoulder, then jumps lightly off the desk. "Are we going out tonight?"

"Will your mom let you?"

"Please." She rolls her eyes. "I'm twenty-two."

"Yes, and? Your mom hates it when you go out with me."

"True." She winces. "But that's mostly because you tend to disappear in pursuit of one-night stands, and then I have to find my own way home."

"Fair enough. I'm a terrible friend."

"Hey, women have needs, and I'm cool with you getting yours taken care of. I know the deal when we go out. Though I do worry about you sometimes, not gonna lie—so many weirdos out there, and when was the last time you got checked out for STDs, babe? No shame, I just want you healthy as well as satisfied." She reaches for the back pocket of her skinny jeans, but of course her phone isn't there. She loses it constantly. "Oh shit...I just remembered. I might have a shift at the Leroux tonight. When I find my phone, I'll check the schedule and text you, okay? Oh, and I just heard about an open audition for a brand-new musical. It's not till next month, but they're looking for dancers and chorus members. You should come with me. You could—"

"Maybe." I feel bad for cutting her off, but the spicy, prickling sensation behind my eyes tells me I'm close to bursting into tears. I need to end this conversation *now*. I can't let Meg know how broken I am over everything.

Despite knowing the court case was probably a lost cause, I'd hoped that a judge might take pity on me and rule in my favor. But the Progeny's lawyers were too good. Their numbers were decimated in the battle that cost my parents' lives, but they are intent on rebuilding, and my parents' assets are part of that effort.

Meg doesn't take offense at my abruptness. She watches me for a moment, and her bright gaze softens. "All right, well...let me know if you want to come to the audition. I'll text you the details just in case." She kisses the top of my head and saunters off.

I shouldn't leave the desk for another half hour. That's when my shift ends. But it's either flee the desk now or melt into a puddle of snot and tears right here in the glorious lobby of the New Orpheum, beneath the arched ceiling, in the glow of the brand-new chandelier. It's late afternoon, the lull right before the Leroux bar and restaurant opens, and it's rare to see anyone in the lobby at this time of day. I can risk stepping away a little early.

After setting out the sign that promises my return in fifteen minutes (not likely), I escape through the door behind the desk, cut through the back office, and slip into the gloomy hallway beyond.

This titanic building used to be a mill. In fact, it went through several transformations into various types of mills and factories before Mr. Richards got his hands on it and decided to pour his dead wife's fortune into the place.

The Richardses were friends of my parents—not part of their cult, thankfully. After my parents passed, Mr. Richards offered me a job. I was hesitant, because his stare has unsettled me since I was about eleven, but I was also desperate. The situation here at the New Orpheum seemed perfectly suited to my needs, and I couldn't pass it up.

Sometimes I work the front desk, sometimes I serve tables at the Leroux, and sometimes I help out with backstage tasks when there's a production. Basically, I do whatever I'm told, and in return, I get a free place to stay, free dance classes whenever I can fit them into my schedule, and a tiny paycheck that covers food and clothing expenses if I'm really, really careful.

God, I miss having money.

As I move deeper into the New Orpheum, the gilded, classical-style decor of the front-facing spaces gives way to dingy brick, cracked plaster, and stained concrete. The back half of the huge building hasn't been renovated yet. Bulbs flicker in cobwebbed sockets, and the thin carpet cloaking the hall smells faintly of moisture and mouse droppings. Beyond the residence hallways, the rest of the building is closed off...or at least there are signs and caution tape to that effect. I don't pay attention to the tape or the signs. Despite the occasional cockroach or mouse, I actually prefer the back rooms or the empty levels above the fourth floor. I've heard there are lower levels, too, but I've never figured out how to get down there. Once, I discovered a door that might have led to the basement, but it was double padlocked.

My favorite place in the whole complex is an abandoned concrete stairway in the unrenovated part of the New Orpheum. The acoustics there are phenomenal, and my voice seems to carry for miles. I tested it once, with Meg's help, to see if my voice would reach the public areas of the building. It didn't, so I feel comfortable singing there. It's the only place I can really let go.

I left my post five minutes ago. By now, I should have had a quick cry in the lobby bathroom and returned to the desk, but a few sniffles won't relieve the cataclysm in my chest or the agony clawing at my insides, shredding my soul into reckless ribbons. Mr. Richards pays me little enough. He can deal with me taking off early *one time*.

I push a creaking door halfway open and squeeze through the aperture into an even more decrepit hallway. Electricity is spotty here, limited to the few bulbs that still tremor to life when I flip a switch. I love the gloom and the shadows that cling to the walls, encroaching upon each globe of light. I head deeper into the dark, soothed by the absence of the poisonous sun.

A few of the rooms back here are wallpapered—faded patterns featuring glorious sprays of leaves or birds of paradise. I pause in one doorway, distracted by the flash of my own reflection in a gilt-edged mirror. That mirror should be thick with dust, but there's a band of smooth glass through the grime, as if someone swept a hand across it to clear the filth. My reflection is ghostlike—dark hair pulled back halfway, white blouse, black eyes. "Nightmare eyes," my father used to call them, because my pupils are so black they're indistinguishable from my irises. He dubbed me his "little nightmare." I liked that better than the other title my parents gave me: *Our Chosen*.

The knot in my throat swells suddenly, an unbearable ache, and I run forward blindly through door after door until I burst onto the landing of the abandoned stairway and catch the metal railing to keep myself from pitching forward into the dark.

Somewhere below is the locked door that leads to the basement. Somewhere far above is the exit to the roof of the building, a place I've only visited a few times in the months since I arrived.

The stairwell door clicks shut behind me. My gasping sobs echo, each one carried above and below, elongated by the resonance of concrete and metal.

But I don't really want to cry. I need deeper relief.

Inhaling through my nose, I blow out a steadying breath. Then, by the dim glow of the emergency lighting, I slowly mount the stairs to the second floor as I let the first notes slip from my throat.

It's an old song from the '70s, one my mother loved. "Dream Weaver," by Gary Wright. I give it a different cadence, a modern sound. My voice glides through the notes, mysterious and languid, ghostly and smooth. In my mind, I hear the delicate accompaniment of a piano, a complement to the first few wistful bars, and then the crash of drums and the crest of passionate strings as I let myself go. I pour everything I have into the lyrics, sucking in quick, desperate breaths between phrases, flooding the empty air with the brilliant violence of the song. It's a disconsolate wish, a dream of heaven from an angel in hell. I feel the tension rushing out of my body, the purging force of music easing the ache in my heart.

As the song climbs, so do I. I reach the second-floor landing and pause, listening to the notes soar into the darkness.

Few people have heard me sing, and I've never had lessons. But I've lived in Nashville all my life, moving in musical circles with my parents, and I know, objectively, that my voice is good. In mere seconds, I can go from the smoky, sultry tones of a lounge singer to the pure, delicate notes of a light-lyric soprano.

Every note feels incredibly intimate, like my soul is a dandelion that I'm plucking seed by seed, blowing the fragile fluff from my palm into the cruel maw of the universe. Being perceived so fully is more than I can stand, and yet I don't know how to sing any other way. That's why I can only sing when I'm alone.

I haven't auditioned for anything, not even as a backup dancer, since my parents were killed. Since they *volunteered* to fight for Wolfsheim. Since they surrendered themselves to the will of a monster.

I wonder if they were afraid when they died. I wonder if death hurt, if it surprised them, or if they slid gently into the reaper's arms.

Clutching the railing, I begin a new song, Blue Öyster Cult's "(Don't Fear) The Reaper." It's a wandering dirge, a mourning plea, a sacrifice to the echoing darkness.

And from the depths of the shadowed staircase, a voice materializes—a faint, elusive harmony threading with my song.

I stop singing, a ragged gasp in my throat.

Someone is here. Someone's listening.

My first instinct is to run. Not because I'm afraid of physical harm but because this was supposed to be my secret place, my haven, and the idea of someone else being here is abhorrent. Will I lose this, too, along with everything else? Am I to have nothing for myself?

My jaw clenches, and I hold my ground. Waiting.

But I can't hear anyone. Not a footstep, not a breath. Not a sound except the sizzle of an ancient, dust-covered light bulb.

I must have imagined that harmony.

Tentatively, I continue the chorus, listening with all my might, sliding through the phrases, crooning, "Come on, baby..." like I'm tempting the singer to reveal himself, if he exists.

The voice joins me again, clear and masculine, blending seamlessly with the melody, matching my pitch and tone to perfection. I almost stop singing again, but the voice is so lovely that I can't help myself. I want to hear what he'll do next, how he'll complement the notes. It's genius, really, the way he harmonizes—finding unexpected depths and heights to enrich our strange duet. At one point, he hits a note that seems fucking impossible for any human male, even the best countertenors.

The second I end the last phrase, I run down the stairs, all the way to the bottom, to that double-locked door. No one is there.

I run back up, breathless, my skin stippled with chills despite the effort of climbing the stairs. Floor by floor I search, yanking open any door that isn't locked, peering down gloomy hallways.

Finally I return to the second-floor landing, sweaty, panting, and frustrated. No sign of anyone anywhere. If there was someone in this stairway playing a joke on me, he must have run off while I was hunting for him. Which disappoints me a little, because even if he was a weirdo prankster, he had an incredible voice.

As I step to the railing again, a faint male chuckle echoes through the air. I gasp a little, fingers tight around the railing.

So he's not gone.

The voice that accompanied me was ethereal, disembodied. Ghostly, or…angelic. I can't help thinking of my last conversation with my father—how he promised to send someone to me from the Afterworld.

But it's been well over a year. Surely if such a place exists, and if communication was possible, Dad would have sent me a message sooner than this.

Besides, I don't believe in ghosts or angels. Or at least I don't believe in them when I'm spinning on an office chair behind the front desk, poking at the useless paper clips in the little dish beside the pen holder. Disbelief is easy then. Not so easy when I'm standing on a darkened concrete landing with cool air wafting past my cheeks and the echoes of an ethereal voice stirring my mind.

And then there's the tiny fact that I've lived among supernatural beings all my life. I know things that most people don't.

"Who are you?" I say aloud.

The question shivers in the air, taut and invisible.

No answer.

"Are you…a ghost?" I venture. "Some kind of phantom? Or… an angel?" God, I sound ridiculous.

"Angel?" The voice laughs again, a deep, hollow sound this time. Impossible to pinpoint its source. It seems to emanate from everywhere and nowhere.

"Did my father send you to help me?"

"Your father," the voice murmurs. "He is dead. You were singing for him."

"No," I say quickly, bitterly. "Not for him or for my mother. They made choices, and they suffered the consequences. They sacrificed everything for an eternal future, and they lost it all."

"And you…" The voice swirls around me, distant and soothing. "What future do you desire? You sing well. Not without flaws, but I hear so much potential. If you would only let yourself truly *sing*."

I'm on the verge of a *fuck you*, but he's right. I was holding back just now. And I could probably use some pointers on technique—breath support, phrasing, lyricism, all that crap.

"I do need a teacher. I want to improve, but I don't have the confidence to sing in front of anyone."

"Confidence comes through mastery." The way he speaks is old-fashioned, elegant, precise, and despite the undeniable sexiness of his voice, there's a wraithlike quality to it that sends chills over my skin.

"I can't afford singing lessons," I tell him. "I can barely find time to keep up with my dancing."

"Ah, you're a dancer. Of course you are. With a voice like that, your body must obey the call of the music."

"I guess so." I never really thought about it like that, but it's true. For me, music and movement are intimately connected.

When I'm listening to a song I love, I can barely hold myself still. I feel as if I want to accentuate the melody with my limbs, illustrate every phrase with the lines of my body.

"Tell me your name," he says.

"Christine."

"Christine." The consonants bounce crisply from surface to surface throughout the stairway. He whispers it then, intimately soft, an echoing hiss. "Christine."

A tremor, half terror and half delight, runs through my body.

"Come back tomorrow around this time," he says. "You'll sing for me again, and I'll teach you how to master your voice." There's a faint clang, like a metal door closing. I think it came from somewhere overhead, but it's impossible to be sure.

"What's your name?" I call into the darkness. And then, because I can't help myself— "Are my parents all right in the Afterworld? Are they happy?"

My voice drops as I ask the last question. No need to shout—I suspect he isn't there any longer. I'm not sure a ghost or an angel would know the answer, or that I'd want to hear it even if he could tell me about my parents' current state of existence. But the question plays in my head anyway, over and over, with a bitter addition of my own.

Are they happy? Because they don't deserve to be.

4

THE PHANTOM

When she sings, the chaos of my mind is quiet.

The first time I heard her was weeks ago. I was restless, aimless, my mind churning endlessly with the doleful dirges of ghosts. I wandered farther than I usually do during daylight hours, and by the will of the Morrigan, I heard her sing.

Her voice is bliss. Like clear rain, like warm earth, like the brilliant sun above and the liquid lake below. I knew I would risk anything for the exquisite pleasure of hearing it again, so I returned to the stairway over and over, wishing that she might be there. I never saw her, but sometimes I was fortunate enough to hear her. Other times, I returned to my lair unsatisfied.

After weeks of this, I became conscious of the powerful urge to sing *with* her. And still it took me days before I yielded to the impulse. I feared I might drive her away.

But she didn't run from me. She was wary, of course, but not afraid. At the end of our brief conversation, I opened the door for future encounters. I must wait and see if she walks through it.

I have never given a lesson in music. But that voice—that pristine, perilous voice—is too precious to lose. I must enjoy it as often as possible. Which means I will have to teach myself how to instruct her properly. The golden-haired vampire may have shut down most of my powers, but my mind remains intact. I am a god, with superhuman intelligence and an almost infinite capacity for learning.

The vampire's directive has dimmed my memories, though, specifically the ones related to my past existence and the use of my powers. I can barely recall what transpired the first week after I was put into this body, nor can I remember what my original goal was once I rose from my enforced slumber. But now, for the first time in ages, I have clarity. I have a purpose.

I will be Christine's angel, and I will teach her to sing.

For the next hour, I pace along the brink of the canal that runs beneath the New Orpheum Theatre, gnawing my lip, pondering how best to pursue this task. If I am to become this young woman's teacher, I must know more about her. I need to know where she resides. I must understand why she is so reluctant to perform. The humans in the videos on my laptop seem all too eager to put on a show for swarms of screaming fans. Some of the singers don't even possess superior vocal qualities, merely a flair for the dramatic. But the young human who sang for me today—she has raw talent. All she needs is a little polish and the courage to sing from the deepest places of her heart.

As usual, a few dozen ghosts are drifting through my lair, moaning and muttering, with the occasional intermittent wail. Until now, I've never spoken to any of them, not wanting to encourage their presence, but it occurs to me that they might prove useful. Perhaps they, like me, would appreciate a purpose—a goal to achieve.

"You there." I point to a pale, forlorn-looking female spirit with a long dress and a flowered hat. "What's your name?"

The ghost halts mid-wail. "Me, sir?"

"Yes, you."

Her eyes go vacant for a moment as she struggles for words. "I think it's Agnes, sir."

"And you." I turn to a dark-skinned man in a bloodstained dinner jacket who is constantly mooning about and sucking on a cigarette in a silver holder. "Your name?"

He bows to me, an impressive feat since he's floating in midair. "Benedict, my lord."

"The two of you will follow a young woman named Christine. She just left the rear stairway. Follow her until midnight, and when you return, tell me everything you've learned about her."

The two ghosts don't question my orders or demand anything in return. They simply whisk away obediently, leaving me to wonder why I didn't think of this sooner. If I am to be haunted, the least the spirits can do is serve me, their rightful master.

I raise my voice, addressing the remaining ghosts. "The rest of you, spread out through this building. I have learned some of its secrets, but I need more. I want to know every passage between the walls, every dark corner, every neglected hallway where someone might pass unseen. Learn it all, and bring the information back to me."

The ghosts linger for a moment, whispering and muttering, but when I snap, "Go!" they scatter in a frenzy of frightened obedience.

For once, my lair is blessedly quiet, and I am alone.

I wander among the things I have collected—forgotten pieces

of furniture from the lower storerooms of this building, cast-off items I have discovered during my midnight strolls through the neighboring streets. I have been watching a show about reclaiming old pieces and transforming them into objects both glorious and useful, and I've made several such attempts, with varying degrees of success.

I am especially pleased with one of my finds—a giant rectangular mirror, heavier than a human male could move alone but no challenge for my godly strength. The mirror's frame is encrusted with elaborate carvings that delight my soul in a way I don't quite understand. They are beautiful, and I'm beginning to comprehend that I love all things that are beautiful. Perhaps I always have, and I spent so long slumbering in the dark that I'd forgotten.

Standing before the mirror, I survey myself. My form is familiar, a replica of the aspect in which I walked among humans long ago. My body is beautiful, and so is my face—with one notable exception.

Gingerly I remove the mask I'm wearing, one of several I've collected in different colors and styles.

On the right side of my face, open red gashes score the flesh, wounds that haven't healed since they were inflicted by the wicked little artist who created this body for me. And those wounds aren't the worst of it. If I leave the mask off for more than a few seconds, dark tendrils will begin to creep from the cracks in my flesh, writhing into the air like living worms. They spiral outward, sprouting tiny leaves, growing thicker and longer with every second until I smash the mask back into place.

The moment I cover my scars, the vines burst into dark dust and disappear. Despite how easy they are to dispel, they unsettle me deeply. They remind me that though my body may appear human, I'm far from it. I am no longer Cernunnos, god of death, nor do I fit into any of the human roles I most admire—composers, connoisseurs, patrons of the arts known for their power and good taste. With my limited powers and this grotesque face, I'm left to exist as a masked wraith—a phantom ravenous for everything I cannot possess.

When I feel like this—maddened and unsatisfied—the only thing that helps is playing music. I've collected numerous instruments, but my favorite is an upright antique piano I purchased from a place called eBay. I tuned it myself after watching instructional videos on the laptop.

Learning to play the piano was the work of a few days, and I like to amuse myself by mimicking the style, speed, and skill of the world's most talented pianists. There's a piece called "Rush E" that some of them find particularly challenging but which serves as a light exercise for me.

I seat myself on the padded bench and slide back the piano lid. This time, when my fingers find the keys, they don't ripple into the melody of the *Hammerklavier*, "La Campanella," or any of my familiar favorites. The girl's voice lingers in my mind, liquid and thrilling, steeped in the deepest longing. My fingers drift into a new pattern, a trickle of notes in tribute to that voice, to words softly spoken in the dark. *Are you an angel?*

"Christine," I murmur, and I play a delicate little melody, as crisp and lovely as her name.

Until now, all my musical endeavors have been mimicry of others. But after this encounter with her, something in my mind is unlocked, and I am not merely imitating, but *creating*. The wonder of it astounds me, and I laugh, plunging headlong into a flood of wild melody that is *mine*, that is *new*, never before heard upon the whole earth. My fingers fly with frenzied grace over the keys, hammering and thundering, rippling and dancing. By the end of the madness, I'm sweating, my chest is heaving, there are tears in my eyes and laughter on my lips.

For the first time since I came back to life, I am healed. I am happy.

The satisfaction only lasts until the echoes fade. Panting, I stare at my trembling fingers. When I glance at the clock on top of the piano, I realize that hours have passed. I was lost in the whirlwind of my mind, and I don't remember any of the music I created.

"My lord," breathes a voice by my ear, and I leap up with a cry of startled rage. The ghost Agnes flits backward swiftly. "Begging your pardon, sir."

"What have you learned?" I growl.

"I know where she lives…the Christine girl," Agnes says. "If you come with me, I can show you, take you there by secret paths. There's a passage behind the rooms, and you can see her through the mirror. Come, come, we must hurry. She's getting ready to leave."

"Leave?" I frown. "What do you mean?"

"She likes to go out most nights." The ghost arches a disapproving brow. "She enjoys drinks and men. At least that's what I overheard. Some of the other dancers and theater employees talk about her behind her back. They say she's a little slut."

A burst of concussive power surges out of my body, blasting the ghost back several feet.

She wails and cringes. "Forgive me, sir! I was only repeating what they said!"

My reaction surprised me nearly as much as it did her. I'm not sure how I released so much magic at once, nor could I control it, which is unsettling.

I straighten my shoulders and beckon imperiously to the ghost. "Lead on then."

Agnes sails ahead of me along the walkway by the canal and up the stairs at the end. We mount a few flights and take a circuitous route through the building. The ghost pauses at a pile of boards and debris slanted against the wall, and when I bend to look behind them, there's a space just large enough for me to slip through if I bend low and angle my body to the side.

The passage beyond was clearly not meant for common use. It's a gap between walls, with clusters of pipes and wires running through it, making my progress difficult. Despite my height and the breadth of my shoulders, I manage to navigate each obstacle.

Dust rises into my nose. I suppress a cough, shielding my lower face with my sleeve as the ghost leads me onward. The lack of light isn't a problem for me; I can see better at night than normal humans, and Agnes gives off a faint glow of her own.

The passage widens slightly. We walk past cramped apartments, each one visible through a pane of glass. "Two-way mirrors," says Agnes. She doesn't whisper, but since her voice is only audible to me unless I dictate otherwise, it makes no difference. I, however, have to be cautious that I don't stumble and make a sound that might betray my presence.

Some of the rooms are occupied, mostly by women, and when I spot two beer cans lying on the floor of the passage, I begin to understand why such mirrors were installed. Someone did it on purpose so he could amuse himself spying on unsuspecting women.

As lord of the dead, I'm familiar with the lustful proclivities of humans. When I first awakened, I had to bargain with the nearest human and arrange temporary possession of her body. Shortly afterward, I had the delicious experience of residing in her body while she fucked her lover in a church sanctuary. I felt everything—not just the carnal thrill of her orgasm but the passion flowing through both of them—the fierce love, the reckless devotion. I tasted something like it once, long ago, when I pursued the Morrigan, the goddess of fate herself. I lured her into my bed and, with that conquest, won the hatred of all the other gods.

It was a calculated move, an alliance of both pleasure and purpose. I did not love her.

Nor is this grimy passage a testament to love. Its walls are sprinkled with the fetid release of a pervert. I can practically smell the stale reek of his lust in the air.

"Here," says Agnes from up ahead, pointing to the next mirror wall.

Quietly I move in beside her and look through the deceptive glass.

The young woman in the room is facing away from me. A short, tight leather skirt hugs her round ass, and dark brown hair swings against the smooth, bare skin of her back.

"I guess you'll have to do," she mutters, holding up a red shirt for inspection, her voice muffled by the layer of glass between us. Sliding the shirt over her head, she adjusts it before turning around.

She isn't wearing anything beneath the silky material. Her breasts form two delicate points against the fabric.

My mouth is dry as bones. Perhaps I should not be watching.

But I *am* the god of death after all. Surely that gives me some right to observe fully clothed humans from the shadows.

I drag my gaze up to her face.

She's beautiful. Full, blood-red lips that match her shirt. White skin flushed faintly pink across the cheekbones. Dark eyes beneath black lashes.

"Christine?" I whisper to the ghost by way of confirmation.

I must have whispered louder than I thought because the girl startles, her dark eyes flaring wide. All the color drains from her face. After a second, she breathes a single word. "Angel?"

Fuck…

But I'm saved from answering by a quick rap on the door. A pert young woman with shiny black hair bounces into the room without waiting to be invited. "Are you ready, Christine?"

"Almost." Christine casts a wary glance around her room before turning to her friend. "Hair up or down?"

"Down, of course. Men like it best that way, and if you're looking to get laid, loose and long is the way to go."

"Right." Christine sprays something onto both palms, flips her head over, and shakes her fingers through her glorious dark hair. My jaw tightens, and blood rushes to my groin. Perhaps I am no better than the beer-drinking lurker.

No—I *am* better. My interest in Christine revolves around her voice and her music. It's purely an artistic connection. This momentary physical reaction is a base human instinct, not worth indulging.

"You got condoms?" asks Christine's friend, sliding a pink stick across her lips to give them a shocking level of gloss.

"I'm prepared. Don't worry."

"Shit, I don't have my ID or my phone!" Christine's friend exclaims. "I'll run back and get them. Meet you in the lobby?"

Christine smiles indulgently, affectionately. "Of course."

Her friend breezes out of the room. Facing the mirror, Christine casually hikes up her short skirt and adjusts the black, lacy panties she's wearing underneath.

I swallow so hard, I nearly choke on my own tongue. I'm dramatically erect now, my cock pressing heavy and tight against the front of my pants.

"Feeling all right, sir?" murmurs the ghost at my elbow.

"Quiet," I hiss.

Christine must have excellent hearing, damn her. She hastily pulls her skirt down and leaves the room at once with a nervous backward glance over her shoulder.

"I must follow her," I tell Agnes. "What's the fastest way out of here?"

"This way, sir." Agnes leads me along the passage, through a concealed door in a storage closet, down a flight of steps, and along another hallway until we come to a side door. The door yields easily when I open it, but I suspect it will lock behind me when I leave. It's no matter. I know other ways to get back into the theater.

Before exiting, I turn to Agnes. "You have served me well this evening, and I may need you again. Remain close by."

"Of course. Happy to serve the god of the dead." She straightens the brim of her flowered hat.

"Such service deserves a reward. Take my hand."

Cautiously, she brushes her wispy fingers against mine.

Frowning, I concentrate for a moment, sorting through the

powers I can still access. I siphon a pulse of focused energy from myself into the ghost, mentally shaping the magic to suit my intent.

"You now have a limited ability to interact with small physical objects," I tell her. "Books, drinks, windows, light switches, that sort of thing. Enjoy it."

"Thank you, sir," she breathes. "Thank you!"

With a nod, I shove my way through the side door of the building and into the night.

A few dozen hurried strides later, I reach the front corner of the New Orpheum Theatre. I linger in the shadows, waiting for Christine and her friend to appear.

They leave the building together, talking in low tones. Their heels clip against the sidewalk as they head toward the parking lot.

I pace slowly after the girls, keeping my distance, wondering if I'm dressed casually enough not to draw attention to myself. I'm wearing black pants, a long-sleeved cotton shirt, and plain black loafers. Fashion is one thing I struggle to understand. There seem to be no rules, and yet people judge clothing choices harshly.

Why am I concerned about my clothing choices? If anything is going to attract attention, it's the goddamn mask covering my face.

I should turn back. And yet I prowl after the pair like a guard dog, my eyes darting from side to side along the street, evaluating possible dangers.

In the corner of the parking lot, beside a streetlamp, three men sit astride beetle-black motorcycles. One of them notices the girls and jostles his friend's arm. All three ogle the two women in a way I deeply dislike.

The first man wolf whistles, and the second shouts something about a "fine ass." The girls ignore him and proceed to a car that

I presume belongs to Christine, as she is the one who unlocks it. I have limited experience with motorized vehicles, but even I can tell that this one is old and probably unreliable. The passenger door squeaks loudly when Christine's friend opens it, the driver's side window seems to be permanently stuck a few inches open, and when Christine tries to start the engine, it wheezes and coughs several times before finally giving in with a rattling growl. The tailpipe releases a loud bang, and rust sifts to the pavement as the car chugs away, leaving me behind.

I don't approve of Christine's method of transportation. She should drive something safer, something sleek and beautiful.

Now that the girls are gone, I stalk toward the men on the motorcycles, the ones who whistled and shouted. I do not speak. I simply stare, a low growl rumbling in my chest, threat radiating from every pore. I may not be able to access most of my power, but I have enough to infuse the very air with the fear of death.

"What you lookin' at, motherfucker?" says one of the men. He's belligerent, but I hear the sharp edge of fear in his voice.

"You're hella creepy, brah," squawks the second man.

"Let's go," suggests another.

After a moment's hesitation, the leader nods. "Yeah, this mofo ain't worth our time."

They gun their engines and roar out of the lot. A smile tugs at the corner of my mouth. It feels good to instill fear in mortal hearts again.

My anger momentarily suppressed my lust, but the moment my mind returns to Christine, I am ensorcelled by the memory of her long, toned legs and those black lace panties. I could almost see through them, just enough to imagine what lay underneath…

Christine is gone now, out of my reach, headed into the city. She is looking for someone to fuck. And that makes me angrier than I have any right to be.

Tomorrow, Fate willing, she'll meet me in the stairway again. I should return to my lair and prepare some sort of lesson for her. No matter whose dick she wets tonight, I will still possess her voice... her soul. She's too frightened to sing for anyone else, so that part of her will remain mine to treasure, mine to cultivate, if she will allow me to teach her.

Still, the idea of some leering idiot shoving himself inside her body unhinges me more deeply than I care to admit. I hate the grating distress it causes in my soul, almost as much as I hate the lack of control I experienced tonight when my body responded to the sight of her. I should not be so weakened or obsessed by the thought of touching mortal flesh.

I retrace my steps to the New Orpheum, descend to my lair in a storm of raw fury, and thunder my rage through the piano keys.

Music offers relief, solace, salvation. In the distant past, I enjoyed it, but I feel it so much more intensely now. There is more variety in this era—countless instruments and genres and musical styles. A vast world in which I can immerse myself when, like tonight, life seems untamable, and happiness flutters just out of reach.

5

CHRISTINE

Nashville.

It's a whistling, whooping, hell-raising, bass-thumping, guitar-twanging, sequined city, served with a side of creative despair. I love it best at night, when the streets swell with people looking for a good time and the neon lights reflect in the dazzled eyes of tourists. I love the sway of leather fringe, the stamp of handcrafted cowboy boots on polished floors, the hands lifted in blissful adoration of the music, the droplets of drinks spilled while dancing. I love the swerving hips, the crooning voices, and the raucous bands.

Whenever I feel the urge to escape the New Orpheum, I go to Lower Broadway, the pounding heart of the city's nightlife. That's the only Nashville many tourists ever see, but as a local, I'm also acutely aware of the grungy back streets lined with dilapidated housing and the railroad tracks where grifters go to inject the money they've scraped together during the day. I know about the century-old houses bought up by developers and ripped apart to make way for the pristine mansions of wealthy people fleeing California and New York. I know about the farmlands that stretch for miles around the outskirts of the city, and I know they are the heart of Nashville, too.

But those peaceful lands and quiet fields aren't what I need when I come out at night. I need the tourists, the strangers, the wanderers, the people who are easy to extricate from the crowd, the ones who won't be missed for a night. I refuse to prey on the addicts and the unhoused, so I thread my way through the visitors instead. These people have money to burn. They're here for bars with no cover charge, for free music and dancing, for flirting and sex and cheap drinks. They won't be much worse for wear when I'm done with them.

Tonight, Meg and I are meeting up with a couple of other girls. It's best that way. When I disappear, they can give her a ride home.

I'm sure Meg thinks I'm a nymphomaniac, and it pleases me that she doesn't judge me for that or treat me any differently. She simply accepts the way I am. Perhaps she wouldn't be so accommodating if she knew what I really do to the men I seduce.

"There they are!" Meg waves to a pair of girls in crop tops, miniskirts, and cowboy boots. She makes introductions. The tall one is Gabriella—ebony-skinned and elegant, with soft dark eyes and intricately braided hair. The short one is Jaz, curvy and luscious, her pale arms covered in elaborate tattoos. I'm not sure where Meg meets all the people she seems to know. She makes friends more easily than anyone I've ever met.

Music is pouring out of the nearest doorway, so we wedge ourselves through the elbows and shoulders into the steamy heat of the crowd. The smell of the packed bodies is dizzying for me. I can feel my gums swelling, my lips twitching back. I waited too long this time. I should have gone hunting sooner. But I've managed worse cravings.

I've got this under control, I tell myself, over and over, as I lift one hand and bob along with the crowd, pretending to be transported by the jaunty vibe of the music.

And truthfully, it helps. Music distracts me, at least temporarily—gives me a hit of dopamine that's just powerful enough to tide me over. Drinks help, too, so when Gabriella jostles her way back to our group with her hands full of cocktails, I take one gratefully.

I can't get drunk, though. Got to keep my wits sharp if I'm going to find a mark.

Sometimes I picture myself as a ranch hand, singling out a calf, cutting it from the herd, flinging the lasso, jerking it tight with a cruel *snap*. Down he goes, and I'm on top of him, tying his legs before he even knows what's happening. He'll get to run free, but not until I'm ready.

While I scan the bar for the right mark, I keep jiving to the music. The sheer amount of talent in this city never ceases to astonish me. In Nashville, world-class singers and musicians play in random bars, dives, and pizza joints for tips. Published songwriters, master guitarists, skilled vocalists, and talented drummers mingle with the tourists. You could bump elbows with somebody famous and never know it.

"Too hot in here," Meg calls. "Too many people."

I nod, understanding. She's small, so she can feel overwhelmed more quickly amid densely packed bodies. We sidle out of the bar with the other girls and head up the street, past a group of guys embroiled in a heated debate, past a middle-aged couple holding hands, past a dozen shrill bridesmaids and one boisterous bride.

The next bar we duck into is quieter. A scruffy man on the stage is crooning a beautifully desolate country song.

Meg and Jaz head to the bar for more drinks, but I stand still, entranced by the timbre of the singer's voice.

"What is it, do you think?" I say aloud, almost to myself. "What makes this city so passionate about music?"

Gabriella swirls the ice in her cup. "Started with the Grand Ole Opry, I guess."

"Maybe. But that doesn't seem like enough to explain the way music *feels* here—like it's *alive*. Like it possesses people's entire souls and feeds off them. And sometimes it grants their wishes, and sometimes it just...gnaws them down to bones, bit by bit, starving them with hope."

Gabriella crooks an eyebrow at me, and I laugh a little.

"Sorry, I can get weirdly philosophical sometimes."

"It's okay." She smiles. "My daddy used to say that music is a language. Some people like the way it sounds, but they don't bother learning it. Some people learn just enough to get by. Some people master it. And then others—they're born knowing it. It's in their bones and blood. It's their mother tongue. Lyrics, instruments, voice, dance...however they choose to express it, they feel some kinda way about music, and other people just don't get how deep the connection goes."

"That's beautiful," I say. "Your daddy sounds like a wise man."

"He was." She closes her lips tightly.

"My parents passed away last year."

"Then you get it."

"I do."

We're quiet for a moment, listening to the first few bars of the guitarist's next song, which is more up-tempo and gets a few people dancing. Then, impulsively, I ask, "Do you believe in muses?"

"Like for inspiration?"

"Yeah, like people or...or spirits...who inspire artists, actors, singers, that sort of thing."

"I guess, maybe." Gabriella purses her lips. "I'm a violinist, and I know that since I met Meg, I've been extra inspired."

"Is that so?" I nudge her arm playfully, and she breaks into a huge, shy smile.

I'm tempted to push for more information about how they met, but at that moment, Meg and Jaz call to us. When I turn around, I spot a lean, good-looking guy with a five-o'clock shadow, tight jeans, and the hungriest eyes I've seen in a while. He's sipping a beer, eyeing the women nearest him like he wants to gobble them up.

"I'll see you all later," I tell the girls. "Be bad, and have way too much fun." After throwing Meg a wink, I sidle toward the hungry-looking guy, and a greedy light flares in his eyes as I approach. "Hey, cowboy," I say softly. "Buy me a drink?"

Boys never expect girls to drug them. Makes my life easier.

They're used to being the predators, the hunters. They never see it coming.

I use the same strategy every time. Get them talking, let them touch me. Pretend to be drunk and horny. I lure in the guys who would totally bang an inebriated chick and never think twice about whether she was able to fully consent. That way, there's no guilt when I take what I need.

I never sleep with them, at least not while they're drugged. That would be crossing a line, and though I've crossed many, I won't do anything sexual with someone who can't consent—which is more than I can say for most of these assholes.

Each time I finish with one of my marks, I talk to my parents in my head. *See how smoothly that went? I'm an expert at this. You didn't have to keep me so close or hold me so tightly. I can control it. I'm fine on my own.*

I'm like a kid riding a bike, lifting their fingers off the handlebars, feeling the rush of potential danger, the surge of perfectly balanced control.

Look at me, Dad. No hands.

Ever since they died over a year ago, I've entertained the vindictive hope that they're watching me. I want them to know that I rejected the Progeny, that I fought tooth and nail to have their will overturned. Even though I lost, I want them to know I defied them.

And yet I still crave their approval. It doesn't make sense, but I want them to admire my spirit, my self-control, and yes, even my rebellion. I want to know they still love me.

Until today, I didn't really believe they could see me. I wasn't sure if their souls still existed somewhere in the Afterworld or if they'd been erased, annihilated completely from existence.

But ever since I heard that ghostly voice, first in the stairwell and then in my room, I'm haunted by the lingering hope that maybe they *can* see me. Maybe they still exist somewhere. Maybe they're still thinking about me. Maybe they've forgiven me for going against their wishes, and maybe they sent the Angel with the beautiful voice to be my teacher, my guardian, my muse.

Or maybe I'm going out of my mind for real.

Licking my lips clean, I give the unconscious man's face a light pat. This one was cute, but he talked too much about the wrong kind of politics. Too brash, super misogynistic.

Carefully, I fit the lid of my wine tumbler into place so not a drop of its contents will spill inside my purse. As a precaution, I slip it into a resealable plastic bag.

The man mumbles faintly as I rise from the motel bed, straighten my clothes, and hitch my bag over my shoulder. I nudge my toes into my sandals and tug the straps around my heels. Then, as an afterthought, I drag the scratchy motel blanket over the man.

"Sleep tight, douchebag," I say softly as I leave the room.

Getting home can be a problem sometimes. I try to arrange these liaisons within a decent walking distance of wherever I happened to park my car, and usually that works out okay since Nashville is so densely packed with places to drink, play, and fuck. If I end up too far from my car, I sometimes "borrow" my victim's vehicle and leave it in an alley. But doing that is risky, and I have to watch out for security cameras.

Walking at night in certain parts of Nashville might give some girls pause, but not me. One time, a few guys surrounded me and told me to my face that they planned on taking turns with my holes.

Things went badly...for them.

I had to burn the clothes I was wearing that night. So much blood, and I couldn't get it all out, which was a bummer because the outfit was really cute.

This time, my walk to the car and my journey home are uneventful. I use my employee ID to get in the side entrance of the New Orpheum. Typically, I don't encounter anyone on these little return trips, but tonight I almost slam directly into Mr. Richards, who's exiting a storage closet.

He startles and huffs an uneasy chuckle. "Miss Daaé! Didn't expect to see you out and about at this hour."

"Same to you." I peer past his shoulder into the closet, but it's dark, and there's no sign of anyone in there. Whatever he was doing, it wasn't a romantic tryst.

"Oh, um...I was taking some inventory," he says hastily. "I'm not just the mastermind of this place—I like to stay involved in every aspect of the business."

Since when? I want to say, but I only nod, even though I could swear Mr. Richards has never done inventory in his life and wouldn't know how to begin.

"You, uh...you seem to be out a lot in the evenings," Mr. Richards says. "Living that party lifestyle?" He gives me an oily, awkward grin.

I shrug. "Sometimes."

Mr. Richards leans in confidentially. Beneath his cologne, I catch the acrid smell of beer and body odor. "You know, I gave you this job as a favor to your daddy, bless his heart. He would have wanted me to look after you and make sure you're on the right path. I could never take your daddy's place, but I hope you know you can come to me with anything."

On the surface, it's a nice offer. But when he ends the speech, he reaches out and touches my upper arm, rubbing up and down lightly. I don't miss the flicker of pleasure in his eyes at the feel of my skin.

"Thanks." I step sideways and retreat down the hall toward my room. "I should get to bed."

"Of course." His gaze chills slightly. "And Miss Daaé, let's not party too often, all right? I like to employ people of good reputation."

"Sure thing." I flash him a bright smile and stalk away as quickly as I dare.

He can't prevent me from doing what I want on my own time, can he? If he gets strict about my late-night comings and goings, it will ruin everything.

He's my employer and my landlord. He has all the power here, and as much as I hate it, I need to keep him pacified. Despite the low pay, this job is ideal for my situation. It perfectly suits the schedule I have to keep, plus I get free dance classes. I hardly ever have to leave the theater during the day. I don't want to lose friends like Meg—people who accept me without prying into my past. And the back stairway is possibly haunted by some sort of ghost muse my father sent to encourage me, a mystery too new and fascinating to resist.

I can't lose this place. Which means I'll have to either be more careful about my nighttime excursions or come to some sort of arrangement with Mr. Richards.

After work the next day, I head for the off-limits area of the building, specifically the stairway with the brilliant acoustics. I'm fairly sure I hallucinated the gorgeous male voice and his offer to coach me. When I reach the second-floor landing, I hesitate, wondering if I'm making a fool of myself.

Softly, I begin to sing "Green Finch and Linnet Bird" from *Sweeney Todd*, one of my favorite musicals. Ever since I moved from my childhood home into the dark, damask rooms of the New Orpheum, that song has possessed new meaning for me.

But I am no trapped bird. I have chosen to be here in this cage, because for now, the door remains open. I only hope that if the door ever begins to close, I can dart out in time.

The last notes leave my tongue and linger in the air.

I crane my neck and look upward, past the rising flights of shadowed steps into the blackness beyond. From here, it seems as if this stairway is positioned at the center of the universe, a twisting spiral in a great dark void, where I am pathetically small and utterly alone.

The place remains awkwardly quiet. No one was listening. I was singing only for myself, as usual.

I'm turning to descend the steps and head for my room when a silken male voice slithers through the silence. "Beautifully done, Christine."

My stomach flips over, and I seize the railing. "Angel?"

"You faltered a bit toward the end. Time your breaths more carefully, and breathe from your diaphragm."

"Dia-what now?"

"Diaphragm. The muscle right beneath your lungs. Imagine there's an elastic band around your waist, and as you inhale, you're forcing it outward."

"Oh...I've heard singers mention breath support. Is that what you mean?"

"Yes." The word floats around me, its echo once again making it impossible to tell if the voice has any physical source. "Lie down for me, Christine."

My entire body tingles at the gentle command, uttered in that beautiful voice. "Why?"

"Breathing practice."

Swallowing hard, I lie face-up on the smooth, cold concrete of the landing.

"Place your hands on your stomach," he says. "If they rise when you breathe in, you're doing it correctly. Practice in this position, and then we'll try it while standing."

He guides me through several breathing exercises, which include hissing, snatched breaths, and nose breathing. After several minutes of practice, I already feel better acquainted with my lungs and their actual capacity. Then he tells me to stand up and instructs me to sing while I focus on keeping my shoulders level and expanding my lower ribs and stomach rather than my chest.

It amazes me that I've been around music and singers all my life, and yet I never heard anyone explain proper breathing technique, nor did I ever explore the topic myself.

"Sing it once more for me," the Angel commands. This time, I employ what he taught me, and my voice is stronger and clearer than ever. When I finish, he says, "Well done."

"I have dance class in half an hour," I say reluctantly. "Before I go, will you sing with me again?"

Silence, and then he says, "Let's try 'A Little Priest' from the same musical."

"You know it?"

His laugh echoes delicately through the shadows. "I have devoured every song I could find, melody, lyrics, and all. We'll do the abbreviated version, since you're short on time."

The duet is saucy and wicked, and though I can't do a Cockney accent for the life of me, I give Mrs. Lovett's part a Southern twang that makes the Angel laugh through his lyrics more than once. The cautious part of my brain, evolved for self-preservation, keeps muttering frantically about how strange it is that I'm performing a duet with a disembodied voice. But I suppress the worries with all my might, because *this*, singing with someone, is new for me, and I'm loving it. I haven't felt this confident since...ever.

When the song ends, I thank him, and I run. I have barely enough time to get back to my room and change before heading to the dance studio.

When Mrs. Giry guides us through stretches, Meg gives me a sidelong glance. "Your face is flushed," she whispers.

"I was doing some exercises."

"Exercises? Right before dance class?"

"You know me. I'm all about the fitness." I turn and face the mirror wall, watching myself grip the bar and sink into a stretch.

"Fitness. Right." Meg's reflection winks at mine. "Did you burn some calories last night with that hottie? He wasn't my type, but I gotta say, he did have a nice ass."

"Um, yeah. He was delicious. What about you?"

She shrugs. "Danced with a couple guys, made out with Gabriella."

"Oh my god!" I exclaim in a loud whisper, but then I catch Mrs. Giry's eye. She's glaring at both me and her daughter, so I shut my mouth and focus on warm-ups.

But even as I go through the motions, I'm already thinking about my next lesson with the Angel.

For the next month, I go to the stairway every day, usually around five thirty in the afternoon. Some days, I can't make it until six, seven, or later, and on weekends when the New Orpheum is hosting events or when I'm serving in the bar, it could be two in the morning. But no matter when I show up, the Angel is always there. Always waiting.

He seems to favor musicals for our work together, though he adds in some pop and indie songs here and there. At the end of each lesson, he and I sing a duet he has chosen. If I don't know the words, he'll sing it first—both parts. He can clone his voice somehow and sing harmony with himself, which is incredibly eerie and beautiful at the same time. That ability clinches it for me—he's a supernatural entity. It makes me feel closer to him, even though he won't tell me his name or anything about himself. Maybe there's nothing to tell. Maybe he has always been a muse, and I'm just the latest in a long line of creatives he has coached. It piques me a little, the idea that I might be one of many students...nothing unique, nothing special.

One Friday, Meg swings by the front desk to ask me if I want to go out with her and a few of the dancers from our jazz class. Lately, her mom has been way cooler about her going out, and we're taking full advantage of Mrs. Giry's new-found permissiveness.

"Just us and the girls from class? What happened to Gabriella?" I ask.

Meg flushes slightly and shrugs. "I dunno. She got needy."

"Needy, or was she just trying to get closer to you?"

She squirms. Looks away.

"This is what you do, Meg," I tell her. "You're the quintessential bolter, like the Taylor Swift song."

"Since when do you listen to Taylor Swift?"

"Since fucking always."

"Well, I'm not a bolter. I just don't want that kind of relationship right now."

"I call bullshit. You're scared, and because you're scared, you're letting a gorgeous, smart, emotionally intelligent girl slip right through your fingers."

"You're one to talk," Meg mutters.

"Come again?"

"You heard me." She shoots me a challenging look. "Planning another one-night stand if we go out?"

"I thought you didn't judge me."

"I don't. Be cool enough to return the favor."

"What I'm doing isn't judging, it's friending."

She rolls her eyes, but she laughs, too. "Fine. I'll ask Gabi to come along. Will that make you happy?"

I tap my lips as if deep in thought. "I suppose. For now."

"Cool. And in return, you keep your eyes open for someone you might want to sleep with more than once. Like a guy with a fuckable brain, not just a fuckable body. Deal?"

"A fuckable brain? That sounds grotesque."

"You know what I mean. We're leaving at seven. Dress cute." Meg shakes a finger at me, then flounces off.

Work ends at five thirty, and then I take a quick shower. I'd planned to do laundry last night, but my lesson with the Angel ran long. We were working on a piece from *Rent*, and time got away from us. I think he would have gone on all night if I let him. Anyway, my failure to do laundry for two weeks means that after my shower, I discover I have no clean underwear. Not even my scratchy emergency thong or a threadbare pair of the granny panties I sometimes use when I'm on my period. The panties bin in my drawer is completely empty. And everything in the laundry bag *smells* because it's been sitting there getting infused with the sweat stench from my dance clothes. I have no option but to go commando in a short skirt and hope for the best.

I pull on the clothes and do my makeup more hastily than I normally would for a night out. Maybe I should take more time getting ready, but I'm desperate to squeeze in a lesson with the Angel before I meet up with Meg and the others. For some reason, I can't bear to go a single day without hearing the Angel's voice. He speaks in my dreams sometimes, with the smooth, sexy tones of a 1920s crooner, and I'm always sorry when I wake up to silence.

"Today, we'll work on strengthening your pelvic floor," the Angel tells me. "You must learn to use your entire body to support the resonance of your voice. Engaging your abdominal muscles and exerting light downward pressure on your pelvic floor will help you extend and enrich the sound you produce without making you run out of breath too quickly."

"Oh. And how do I strengthen my pelvic floor?"

"There are a number of methods. We'll try an exercise first. Lie down, spread your legs slightly, and bend your knees."

A simple enough request, and yet his voice is so decadently sinful that my mind immediately goes to some very naughty places. I arrange myself in the position he requested, on my back, knees bent. I can feel the chilly air of the stairway like a ghostly breath between my legs. Of all the days to run out of underwear...

Can the Angel observe me while in his spirit form? What if he likes what he sees? Can ghosts get turned on? And why am *I* aroused by this? God, I need sex. When I go out tonight, I might actually have to sleep with the guy I choose before I drug him, just so I can stop fantasizing about my spiritual voice coach.

"Now what?" I say faintly.

"Arms at your sides. Palms down."

Is it my imagination, or does his voice sound nearer, more corporeal? More distinct?

"Inhale," he instructs. "Lift your hips for me."

Oh fuck.

I inhale, but it's more of a gasp.

"That wasn't a good breath," the Angel reproaches me. "Try again. Engage the muscles of your pelvic floor. Lift, and hold that position while I count to fifteen. Breathe steadily. Here we go."

Taking a full, deep breath, I lift my hips and maintain the pressure while he counts, but the delicate trickle of arousal between my legs makes it difficult to concentrate.

About halfway through my third attempt at the pose, my gaze locks on the door leading from the second-floor stairs to the hall. The narrow window in the door has been broken ever since I started coming here. But there's something different about it today.

I lift my head, staring between my bent knees at the window. In the darkness beyond, I can almost make out the deeper black of a shape—maybe a head and shoulders. But I can't tell if I'm imagining it.

Until the blackness moves.

With a startled gasp, I scramble to my feet, tugging down the hem of my skirt. "Angel?"

A few beats of silence, and then his cool voice echoes through the stairway, distant and reproachful. "You seem distracted. Perhaps we should end our lesson here."

"I think someone was watching me."

"Perhaps they were. Does it matter? Are we not working toward the goal of you performing for an audience?"

"Yes, but that's not what I...never mind." Mustering my courage, I stride over to the door and fling it open.

Nothing. Just an empty hallway littered with debris and dust, so dark I can't see very far along it.

I shut the door again. "I guess I'm jumpy today. I'm going out tonight for a drink. That should help me relax. Except I know Meg is going to beg me to audition with her tomorrow."

"Audition?"

"Yes, for a new musical. Meg says they need dancers and a chorus. They're holding open auditions here at the New Orpheum, in the theater itself. I guess the guy who wrote the musical has connections to the building's owners."

"Excellent. Your homework is to audition for the musical."

"What? No...I'm not ready. I've told you, I can't sing for people."

"Then don't sing for *them*," he says softly. "Sing for me."

"For you?"

"I'll be listening. When you stand on the stage, block out everything else, and sing for my ears only. Pretend you're right here, in our sanctuary, and perform the way you do when we're alone."

"That won't work."

"Try. That's all I ask of you."

My palms are sweating at the mere idea, but I don't feel sick to my stomach, which is an improvement. "You'll be there?"

"I will. I promise."

I've only known the Angel for about a month, but he has been present every single day since he promised to teach me. Granted, he's a ghost, which means he probably doesn't have much else to do…but he's someone reliable in my life. Even Meg can't always be there for me—she has obligations of her own.

If the Angel says he'll be at the audition, I know he means it.

He speaks again, his voice swirling around me like a caress. "You've come so far in these few weeks, Christine. You amaze me… you inspire me. This gift you possess—it cries out to be shared with the world."

My very soul cringes. "I think I would hate being famous."

"Fame is irrelevant." There's a tremor in his voice, a fervor he doesn't usually express unless he's singing. "Adulation and accolades mean nothing. The only thing that matters is the power you possess to stir a soul, to move emotions, to alter the course of a heart. Music can do that. *You* can do that. I know you can, because you've done it for me. I am resurrected every time I hear you sing."

Tears pool in my eyes. "That's the most beautiful thing anyone has ever said to me."

"So you'll try," he urges gently.

"I'll try. For you."

Tension vibrates in the air, in the chasm between our voices. I'm trembling as I stand there alone, in a maze of concrete and shadow, goose bumps rising along my arms from the cool air, waiting for something. Waiting for him to speak to me, sing to me… touch me.

What the hell am I doing?

It's been well over a year since my parents died, and I thought I had a decent handle on everything, that I was doing pretty well.

But maybe I'm more vulnerable than I thought, because I am becoming far too attached to a literal ghost.

So when his lovely voice glides into the first few bars of "You'll Never Find Another Love Like Mine" for our finishing duet, it's too much for me to take.

I don't sing with him. Instead, I run.

6

THE PHANTOM

Christine almost caught me.

I let myself wander too close to her, and then, when she lay down and parted her legs, exposing herself to my view, I could not make myself turn away.

I have seen plenty of naked humans during my online excursions, and while they're pleasant to the eye, I don't experience any notable attraction to them. The closest I've come to being aroused by images or videos of humans is when they're exceptionally gifted in the creative arts, brilliantly talented in the areas of music or performance. Otherwise, they hold no sexual interest for me.

Christine is both intelligent and sympathetic as a person. Besides her breathtaking voice, she accepts my instruction with a humble dignity that I find most entrancing. I usually spend our lessons in a state of arousal, and when I caught that first glimpse of her pussy through the broken window of the stairway door, I couldn't help myself. I reached down and pressed my hand against the bulge between my legs.

She performed the pelvic exercises as I instructed, while I rubbed myself lightly through the fabric of my pants, my mind blurred with desire, no thoughts in my head except the pursuit of a pleasure I haven't enjoyed since Cathy's tryst with Heathcliff in the church, so many months ago.

I didn't realize Christine had noticed me until it was almost too late. I had to move quickly. I slipped into a side room, pulled myself up through a hole in the ceiling, and emerged on the third-floor landing. From there, I could cast my voice to any point I desired, and the distorted echoes of the stairwell ensured that she was thoroughly confused about my location.

She must not be allowed to see me. She thinks of me as a spirit, an angel, a phantom. That's why she trusts me with her voice, her soul. If she knew I had a physical body with such desires, she would recoil from me. She would flee, as she did at the end of our lesson, when I sang "You'll Never Find Another Love Like Mine." That song was too poignant, too personal. I should have known better than to venture so close to the idea of a romantic connection between us.

And yet my heart shields the tiniest flame of hope that perhaps, against all odds, Christine might come to cherish more than my lessons.

Perhaps, if I can help her overcome her fears and realize her dreams, she will value me enough to overlook my wretched face and my desolate past.

When I wake up, I am suffocating among thick black vines.

My mask must have dislodged during the night. The tendrils emerged from the wounds in my face and slithered around me, wrapping me tight. I cannot move. I cannot see. I can barely breathe.

Terror blazes through my very bones. This is how it felt, being suppressed under soil, chained by curses, lulled into tormented sleep by the droning of hymns from the cult charged with keeping me bound. The blood of fresh sacrifices woke my spirit in the Afterworld, but I was still only a shadow of myself until I clutched the soul of the necromancer Heathcliff and rode his power out of the darkness into the world again.

But in this moment, I feel as if I never escaped at all.

Panic ratchets up my heartbeat into a frantic rhythm. I have a human body, forged from the magic of the leannán sídhe, but I'm not sure how durable it is. How fast can a human heart race before it explodes? Am I going to die here, strangled by the remnants of my own divine power?

"My lord," calls a faint voice. "My lord."

It sounds like Benedict, the ghost with the cigarette holder.

"I'm trapped," I manage between fear-stiffened lips.

"Breathe slowly, my lord," he replies. "Focus on something pleasant to calm yourself."

Something pleasant. Music, of course, and Christine. I drag in a fragmented breath, then another. The vines loosen slightly.

"Keep breathing," urges Benedict. "Slow and steady. You did this to yourself—you can undo it. Focus on what needs to happen."

His voice is a tether to reality. I cling to it, and to the knowledge that Christine's audition is happening soon, and I promised I would be there for her. I visualize the vines loosening, peeling back from my body, bursting one by one into puffs of black dust.

"I am a god," I whisper sternly. "I control *you*. You do not control me."

Slowly, reluctantly, the vines obey, withdrawing and shriveling into ash, just as I pictured. I fight my way out of the crumbling remnants. My hands are shaking, and my body is slick with sweat. Desperately, I fumble among the sheets until I find my mask, and I fit it into place again.

When I try to stand, my legs give way, and I crumple to the floor beside my bed. "Fuck," I whisper.

"You did it," says Benedict.

I look up at his vague, wispy form, at the satisfied smile on his face. "Thank you."

He nods. "Happy to help."

"I will reward you as I did Agnes, with the ability to interact with certain objects," I say breathlessly.

"I would be grateful. But only after you regain your strength."

The kindness in his tone strikes a chord deep inside me. I could count on a few fingers the souls who have treated me kindly, in this world or beyond.

After a moment, I manage to struggle to my feet. "What news from my theater?"

"Nothing new to report," he replies. "There will be auditions held in the theater today for a new musical. The composer is apparently a relative of Gil Leveque, Firmin Richards's business partner. Should I observe the auditions? Gather information about the composer?"

"I'll be there myself, but you could linger on the theater floor and listen to the comments from the director, the composer, and anyone else with influence on casting choices. And have a few of the other ghosts linger backstage to gather information from those who audition."

"Very well." He drifts away, and I head for the bathroom to shower.

The bathroom adjoining my lair used to be a wretched place, with three overflowing toilets, two broken sinks, and a shower whose drain practically oozed cockroaches, but I repaired and retiled it all myself with the help of several dozen instructional videos. Now it has a luxurious shower, a new toilet, and a gleaming pair of sinks atop a well-stocked vanity. After a thorough application of pest control products and the addition of a rain showerhead, the place is much more worthy of cleansing a god's mortal form.

While the hot water washes the sweat from my body, I mentally review all the pawns I have in play and what the best move might be for each of them.

Three weeks ago, I instructed the ghosts in my service to look for any secrets I could use to control the residents of this place. So far, they've brought back some useful information—a torrid affair between Mrs. Giry and one of her male students, the lighting technician's violent criminal record, the security guard's penchant for watching porn during his shift, the theft of some small valuables by two members of the cleaning staff, and the most useful piece of information yet…the fact that Firmin Richards, the owner and developer of this building, spies on the female residents and the dancers via the two-way mirrors installed at various points throughout the building.

It's surprisingly easy to control humans, even without magic. All I need is my phone, the number of the person I want to blackmail, and their darkest secret, with enough proof to apply the perfect amount of leverage. Thanks to the internet and a few devoted ghosts, I hold all the cards now. If I wanted to, I could bring most of the people in this building to their knees with a few carefully worded texts.

Yesterday, I persuaded the security guard to ensure that Box Five of the theater will be empty and undisturbed during the auditions. It's perfectly situated for my needs—angled for an ideal view of the stage, yet deeply shadowed even when the house lights are on. From there, I can size up Christine's rivals and enjoy her audition.

Shortly before ten o'clock in the morning, I traverse the back hallways of the building, circumventing the residence areas, the dance studios, and the wedding chapel. A black coat with a capacious hood shrouds my form. If anyone should spot me, they won't think twice about my apparel, since the skies opened up this morning and unleashed a heavy autumn rain on all of Nashville and its suburbs.

At last, I reach the theater space and enter by the employees' door, which was left unlocked as I requested. A handful of emergency lights gleam at intervals in the theater lobby and the hallways. I mount the dark steps to the second floor, my polished shoes soundless on the thick carpet.

The door to Box Five is also unlocked, and I make a mental note to reward the security guard for his loyal service. After stepping through and closing the door softly behind me, I walk to the edge of the balcony and survey the silent theater, lit only by the pinpoints of light marking the central aisle and the exits.

From what I've gleaned of this building's history, this space was once a factory floor, now remodeled into a gorgeous theater with tiers of plush seating, ornate wall paneling, gilded cornices, and heavy crimson drapery. The edge of each balcony features carvings of pomegranates, grapes, and swirling leaves, and the ceiling boasts a gothic painting of Hades leading Persephone down to the Underworld.

I take the central seat in the box and lean back, prepared to wait for nearly an hour until auditions begin at eleven.

But I've only waited for ten minutes before light flares onstage, illuminating a swath of the boards.

Frowning, I sit up straighter and lean forward.

A young man appears, rolling an electric piano toward the center of the stage. I'm not sure why the instrument requires so many extra buttons and levers. I prefer a classic piano myself. But perhaps I should invest in one of these modern ones for experimentation.

The light gleams off the man's square-framed glasses and glints on his coppery hair. He adjusts the cord of the piano, then leaves for a moment and returns with a stool, which he sets in place. Slowly, he rolls up one sleeve of his shirt, then the other, exposing lightly tanned forearms while he stares contemplatively at the instrument.

At last, he seats himself on the stool, adjusts a few sliders, and places long, elegant fingers against the keys, his hands perfectly arched. Exquisite technique.

The beat comes first, pulsing like a heartbeat, quickening my breath. Then a faint sound of strings, electronic and elusive but no less effective. His fingers fly across the controls, tweaking the sound, finessing it, exerting his will over the instrument. Then he begins to play.

The melody is good but predictable. In several spots, my brain suggests an alternate chain of notes, a different orchestration, and a key change that would take the song from mediocre to magnificent. I have to bite my tongue and tighten my fists to keep myself from suggesting the changes aloud or from singing the harmony that would perfectly complement his tune.

The man's eyes are closed, and his brows are bent, as if he isn't quite pleased with what he's playing. Reluctantly, I admit to myself that he's very attractive for a human male. He has delicate features and a jaw so crisply cut it looks almost fragile. The glasses give him a look of studious intelligence.

He ends the song with an abrupt clash of frustrated notes and an audible, "Fuck!"

I almost rise from my chair, tortured by the desire to tell him the music is quite good and that he only needs to make a few small changes to achieve greatness.

But a figure emerges from the shadows at the edge of the stage, and a soft voice says, "Don't stop."

A thrill bolts through my chest, and the man on the stool whirls around.

Christine steps forward, wearing a simple white tank top and black dance leggings. Her hair isn't in a neat bun, though—it's on top of her head in a riotous knot.

"I'm sorry," she says. "I didn't mean to disturb you. I'm auditioning today, and I thought if I walked onto the stage first and got comfortable with it, I might be less nervous."

"Of course." The young man leaps up from his stool so fast it spins around. "Please, take all the time you need. I'm just trying to sort out this one bit. It's not working—doesn't have the right impact."

"It sounded great to me." She smiles at him.

He laughs faintly. "Well...thank you." Then he cocks his head. "You look familiar."

Christine nods. "So do you! But I'm sorry, I can't seem to remember your name..."

"I'm Raoul. Raoul de Chagny. And wait, you're Christine Daaé, right? We were both at the same middle school for a year."

"That's it! Seems so long ago."

"I've never forgotten you," Raoul says, so quietly I can barely hear him from my box. "I don't know if you remember, but I was bullied badly that year for giving a valentine to a boy in my class. You were there on one of the worst days, and you defended me."

"Oh my god…I do remember!" exclaims Christine. "That was awful."

"You made it less awful. I had a crush on *you* after that." He gives an embarrassed chuckle. "Until things got so bad my parents moved me to a different school."

"I'm sorry you had to go through such a horrible experience." She's moving nearer to him, being pulled closer by her compassionate heart.

Hatred for Raoul flames in my chest, tightening my throat with its vehemence. I want to bellow my rage at both of them. I want to seize Raoul by the throat and fling him against a wall and roar in his face that Christine is *mine*. I want to hear him panting in terror, feel him break in my hands. I want to know what he sounds like when he screams.

But by some divine exertion of my will, I manage not to move.

"I should tell you…" Raoul tosses a hand through his red-gold hair. "I wrote *Sidewinder*."

"*Sidewinder?*" asks Christine blankly.

"The musical you're auditioning for."

"Oh! Oh god… Of course. I promise I know what it's called." She presses her hands to her cheeks. "This is so embarrassing. I'm sorry. I've never auditioned for a voice role before… I've actually never sung in public before... I'm not even sure what I'm doing here..."

She's falling apart. I groan inwardly, shrinking deeper into my chair.

But Raoul laughs. "Well, I've never written a musical before, so we're both new to this. To be honest, I'm having second thoughts about the score. I'm great at lyrics, but not as good at composing. I had a couple friends help me with the music and the orchestration, but something is missing. I don't know if I'm talented enough to take it as far as it can go."

"I'm sure you are."

"Are you? A few minutes ago, you didn't remember me. And you have no idea what this musical is about, do you?" He doesn't say it harshly, but with rueful humor in his voice.

Christine sighs. "I've made a mess of this already. I may as well not even audition. Clearly, I'm unprepared."

"Hey." When she turns away, he catches her wrist. It's a light graze of his fingers, just enough to make her pause. "I'd like to hear you sing. Please stay."

The look that passes between them is like a broadsword cleaving straight through the muscle of my heart, splitting it in two. I'm hemorrhaging hope, watching my plans bleed out onto the crimson carpet of Box Five. The attraction between them is unmistakable, almost tangible. I can practically smell the pheromones in the air.

"Okay," Christine replies. "I'll stay."

"Good. Thank you. Marj should be backstage by now with the audition forms. Go ahead and fill one of those out, and we'll get started soon. It's so good to see you, Christine."

Fuck him for saying "Christine" in that warm, intimate tone. Her name belongs in *my* mouth, not his.

"Agnes," I whisper, and I feel the immediate response of the ghost as she rushes to my location.

She appears within seconds, adjusting her flowered hat. "Yes, sir?"

"That boy on the stage. I want to know everything about him. Get some of the others to help you, and find something I can use to ruin his life."

"Right away, sir!" she squeaks and darts away.

I lean forward, propping my elbows on my knees and lacing my fingers together. Angry though I am, there's a thread of excitement in the rage. I haven't had a true adversary since the conflict with the vampires at Wicklow. I lost that battle, but I don't plan to lose this one.

On the surface, Raoul might seem like a paltry rival, easy to defeat, but he has an advantage over me with this prior connection to Christine. He is kind, talented, and *human*. If I underestimate him, I might fail, so I must treat him as a serious threat. I must discover what it would take to unravel him down to his core, to lay his heart bare and pulsating before me so I can thrust a blade through it.

And perhaps, when I have him at my mercy, I'll torture him with my alterations to his musical score and show him how he could have been so much better if he had only a shred of my creative genius.

7

CHRISTINE

Maybe I didn't ruin everything. At least not yet.

I screwed up by not researching the musical ahead of time. But they handed out some information about it backstage, and I've been reading the sheet over and over while I wait.

Basically, it's a musical about space cowboys with superpowers, with a passionate love story at its center. The concept seems wild, but in a good way. Flamboyant, dramatic, and romantic.

I bounce on my feet, trying to expel my nervous energy. They're holding the voice auditions first, with the dance auditions taking place later this afternoon. I'm not so worried about the dancing part. I've been taking lessons since I was tiny, and I'm skilled at lyrical, jazz, and hip-hop styles. I pick up choreography fast, too. The part that terrifies me is opening my mouth and singing for strangers whose entire job is to judge me and decide if I'm good enough to sing in front of even *more* people.

Maybe I'd be less nervous if Meg were here, but I don't see her. She'll show up for the dance auditions this afternoon, whereas I was foolish enough to try for a singing role, as if one month of lessons with a ghost could ever be enough to prepare me for something like this. As if I could ever compete with the theater kids waiting all around me, the people with training and plenty of achievements to list under the "Prior Experience" heading on the audition form.

If by some miracle I do get a part, there will be practice and rehearsals, and my schedule is already filled with work, dance classes, and nighttime escapades with random men. How will I ever squeeze in rehearsal time?

This was a mistake. I shouldn't be here.

I crumple the *Sidewinder* info sheet in my hands and turn to flee, but I nearly collide with a set of heavily perfumed boobs that are trying to escape the red dress that's barely covering them. A familiar cascade of caramel locks drapes over one of the boobs, and with a growing sense of dread, I look up into the flawless face of Carlotta Vanetti.

"Watch where you're going!" she exclaims. "Arabesque, do my nose."

Arabesque, a person with huge false lashes and a shiny aqua jacket, whips out a compact and powders Carlotta's nose obediently.

She waves them away and frowns slightly, scanning me up and down. "I know you. How do I know you?"

"I'm the girl from the front desk," I reply. "The one you spoke to when you reserved the New Orpheum for your birthday."

"Oh, of course. You work here. Perfect! I need a sparkling water, preferably San Pellegrino. And a chair with a cushion. If I sit on plastic, the toxins mess with my tone." She strokes her throat.

For a moment, I actually consider fetching her what she wants, just to be able to escape this situation. I used to have more fight in me, but I spent it all surviving the trauma of my childhood, then trying to get my family fortune back from the Progeny cult. I'm done. All that's left are shreds of my willpower and scraps of self-worth.

I'm already turning, yielding to Carlotta's will. But the Angel's voice speaks in my memory. *The only thing that matters is the power you possess to stir a soul, to move emotions, to alter the course of a heart. I am resurrected every time I hear you sing.*

I can't disappoint him. He'll be out there, listening to the auditions, waiting for me to come onstage and sing for him. He might be invisible, but he's the only one who really sees me. I won't give up, not after trying so hard to improve myself.

"I'm not working right now," I tell Carlotta calmly. "I'm auditioning."

"You're auditioning? Okay." She laughs. She fucking *laughs*, and not in an apologetic way but in an aw-how-cute-that-you-think-you-have-a-chance kind of way. "Good for you. Break a leg." And she flounces off with her assistant, loudly critiquing the backstage aesthetic and trying to find "a good place to go live."

Just like that, my fight is back. Hell yes, I'm auditioning, and I'm going to be brilliant just to spite her. I step away from the group and turn my back to everyone else. I breathe deeply from my belly, slow and steady, and I do the vocal warm-ups the Angel uses at each of our sessions.

When I close my eyes, I swear I can almost hear him running through the warm-ups with me, his voice chasing mine up and down the octaves. I feel the shiver of delight when he dips into the bass range, and I thrill when he soars into the higher registers with me. I've never heard a voice like his, so versatile and vibrant. Such purity of tone in those high notes, such fervency behind every phrase. I think I might be addicted to his voice, because it's always there, in my head. The duets we sing at the end of each lesson linger in my mind for hours afterward.

Was he once a voice teacher, now a ghost? Or is he a muse, a spirit birthed to inspire artistic endeavors? Whatever his story is, I'm one hundred percent sure he has made me better, not just technically but emotionally. Before I encountered him, I didn't realize how much I needed someone to take an interest in me, not for my tragic past or my pretty face but for my voice. I craved a constant in my life and a goal to work for. He provides both.

When my name is called and I step out onstage, I won't be singing for Carlotta, for the casting team, or even for Raoul, no matter how kindly he treated me earlier.

I'll be singing for the Angel.

8

RAOUL

It's agony listening to some of the auditions. Most of the voices are decent, but during a few of the performances, I genuinely want to cover my ears. How can these people truly believe they can sing? What lies have their families fed them in the name of supporting their dreams?

I hope to god Christine can sing. She certainly has a lovely speaking voice, not to mention the lithe body of a dancer.

Seeing her here, at the auditions for my musical, was a complete shock. She's been enshrined in my heart for a long time, ever since she defended me during that awful year in middle school. Over Christmas break, I'd realized I liked boys as well as girls, and after watching far too much *Glee*, I told myself things were better for my generation, that people were more accepting, that tolerance was a thing. When February rolled around, I mustered my courage and gave a paper heart to Damian, the smartest, cutest boy in my class. He'd always been cool to me, so I thought at most I might have to endure some mild rejection. Nothing ventured, nothing gained, right?

I was wrong. So miserably wrong.

His entire personality seemed to change in the space of a minute, and from then on, I had no friends. Sickening names were muttered behind my back whenever I walked through the halls. People jostled me, bumped my lunch tray, cut me out of conversations. The teachers did nothing, and the bullies grew bolder.

They cornered me one day at dismissal when most of the teachers were busy. I remember their mouths vomiting slurs, their hands cuffing my face and tugging my jacket. One of them kicked my shin.

And then Christine burst into the group, her face blazing like an avenging angel. She scattered the boys, scolded them viciously— *hissed* at them with her teeth bared. She grabbed one boy's coat and hurled him away from me, and when she let go, the fabric had five distinct cuts where her nails were. I remember thinking it was odd for a middle-school girl's fingernails to be that sharp.

"Raoul." My codirector Marjorie bumps her elbow against my arm.

I return to the present, suddenly conscious that the woman onstage has ceased caterwauling and is looking at me expectantly.

I clear my throat. "Yes, thank you very much for coming in today. We'll be in touch."

She nods and ambles off the stage.

"Next we have..." Marjorie peers at the next paper on her stack. "Carlotta Vanetti."

"You should really wear your bifocals, Marj," I tell her.

"Fuck that." She chuckles and takes a large gulp of her coffee.

"Carlotta Vanetti?" exclaims Gil Leveque from my other side. His family are distant cousins to the de Chagnys, and he's a partner in the management of the New Orpheum Theatre. My sister,

Philippa, insisted that if I wanted to use family money to back this musical, I must make him one of the directors. So there are three of us directing—me, Gil, and Marj, who is the only one with true experience. She has actually lived in New York and has worked on Broadway musicals.

"Carlotta Vanetti has hundreds of thousands of followers on socials and a killer voice, too," mutters Gil. His hot breath stinks of cigarettes, and a droplet of his spit hits my ear.

Jaw tight, I shift slightly away from him.

"She's got a bit of an attitude," he continues. "But she's fucking hot, with a great rack. And real talent always comes at a price. She's our lead, Raoul. You can be sure of that."

"So you've cast her already? Before we've heard her sing?" I raise an eyebrow.

"Carlotta fucking Vanetti." His eyes bulge, boring into mine, as if I should be awed by the very name. "She'll bring so much visibility to the show. We need her."

"Visibility is great, but influencers also come with a lot of risk, especially if they're easily pissed off," Marj counters. "If something doesn't please her, she could go on socials with her complaints and rally her followers to tank the show."

"I appreciate both of your perspectives," I tell them. "Let's table this until we've heard her sing, okay?"

"Fair enough," says Marj.

Gil grumbles, "Fine. But I'm telling you we need her."

"Noted." I raise my voice and call, "Carlotta Vanetti."

She saunters to center stage with a brilliant smile, dressed in a low-cut red dress and white leather boots. I have to admit, she's striking, and she commands attention with her very presence.

Right from the start, she fixes her attention solely on me, barely giving Gil or Marj a second glance.

"Good morning," she says brightly. "I'm Carlotta Vanetti, and I'm the star you've been looking for."

The statement throws me a little, and I fumble over the first few questions, which only seems to inflate her confidence. Her dazzling grin and her laser focus on my face unsettle me. She's like a predator, and I'm the prey, the elusive prize she's determined to get. I can feel my cheeks heating, my anxiety kicking into high gear along with my fight-or-flight instinct. With me, it's usually flight.

"So…Carlotta…" I shuffle papers around in an attempt to look busily professional. "What are your thoughts on the musical's female main character, Eugenie?"

"Well, she's a strong, independent woman who doesn't take shit from anyone," says Carlotta. "She's ready to kick some ass and take names. Whatever she needs to do to reach her goals, she'll go for it. Nobody's getting in her way. Let me tell you, I relate to this girl. She and I are the same. If someone disrespects me, they're gonna regret it."

"Wonderful." I force a smile. "All right, I think it's time for you to sing for us if you're ready."

"I was born ready, darlin.'"

She doesn't introduce the song, just snaps her fingers at someone in the shadows. The person—her assistant, I assume—trots onstage after her and sets up a huge, purple boom box bedazzled with silver stars. Our pianist, Sam, glances questioningly at me, and when I nod, he sits back to watch.

Before the music begins, I place a mental bet with myself that she'll do "All That Jazz" from *Chicago*—and when I'm right, I can hardly keep a straight face. I've never seen anyone dance to "All That Jazz" in cowboy boots, and it's a vision I won't soon forget.

She's talented. A powerful dancer with a strong voice. Well-trained, obviously. But I'm uncomfortable with her take on Eugenie, and I don't know that she'd be open to critique if I asked her to portray the character differently.

Carlotta goes well over the two minutes we allotted for each audition song. I wonder if I should stop her, but I can't bear the thought of confrontation. I clear my throat faintly a couple of times, but she doesn't take the hint until Marj, who has no qualms about confrontation, lifts a gaunt hand laden with rings and waves it imperiously at Carlotta with a loud, "That will do, thank you! We'll be in touch."

Carlotta's showgirl smile falters, her stage veneer cracking just enough for me to glimpse the offended rage beneath, but she pulls herself together, blows me a kiss, and stalks offstage. Her assistant scrambles to collect the boom box and then scurries after her.

"Thanks, Marj." I exhale with relief.

"Oh honey, I'm from the Bronx," she replies. "Anytime you need a bitch shooed offstage, I'll shoo. But you gotta grow some balls if you want to be in this business. You're not just the writer. You're one of the directors, and you can't let the talent push you around."

"Note to self: Grow some balls."

She chuckles. "You're a sweet kid. Loads of talent. But you need that backbone, okay? Gotta have some grit on you."

"Thanks." I neaten the stack of papers on my desk and pick up the next sheet. A little thrill runs through my stomach when I call, "Christine Daaé!"

I half expect her not to appear; she seemed so skittish earlier.

But she walks to center stage with her shoulders back and her head high, each step so graceful anyone could tell she's a dancer.

Marj leans forward, eyes narrowed, pen tapping her lips. I've come to recognize that pose—it means she's interested. Gil shifts in his seat, licks his lips, and grins, surveying Christine with a different kind of appreciation.

"She's one of our in-house dancers," he murmurs to me. "Hot little piece. Orphan."

Orphan seems like an odd word to use for a grown woman, and an out-of-date one at that, but I don't challenge him on it, or on the "hot little piece" comment, though angry heat creeps beneath the back of my shirt collar. I'm a coward for not wanting to offend him, but he's vital to the realization of my dream and the production of *Sidewinder*, so I let the misogyny slide. I just sacrificed Christine's honor on the altar of my ambitions, and I hate myself for it. In fact, I'm so busy hating myself that I forget to ask her any questions, and she stands there awkwardly smiling.

"Miss Daaé," Marj intervenes, glancing at the audition form in front of me. Bless Marj's heart, she's worth her weight in gold. "Why do you want to play the part of Eugenie? And what's your interpretation of the character?"

"She's a woman of great strength, of course," Christine says. "That's obvious even in the synopsis. But there's a vulnerability to her, too. She's not always strong, and I love that, because no one is *always* strong. We all have weak moments when we make mistakes and do the wrong thing. What's important is what we do next. I love how this character isn't afraid to ask for help and brings others around her who complement her strengths. I'd love to portray her and learn from her."

Marj glances at me, her mouth slightly tilted at the corner, one eyebrow raised. It's as good as a gold star from her.

As for me, I feel stricken, unmasked, deeply and uncomfortably perceived. Christine gets it. She gets the character…and me. Because, let's face it, all characters carry a splinter of their creator inside them, some bloodied shard of the writer's soul.

"Sing for us." The words jerk out of me abruptly. "Sam!"

The pianist sits up straight, hands poised on the keys.

Christine walks over and hands him the sheet music. "It's quite short. This is 'I Saw Him Once' from *Les Misérables*."

The song title surprises me so much that I say "fuck" without meaning to. "Sorry. Go ahead."

It's rare to meet anyone who knows about that song, much less someone who would audition with it. "I Saw Him Once" was a short piece sung by the character Cosette during the first English production of *Les Mis* in London. After that, it wasn't performed or recorded again. It's a beautiful little song, like a tiny gem lost in a forgotten cave.

Christine returns to the middle of the stage. She hesitates, and for a minute, her face turns so pale, I think she's about to vomit. Her fingers are visibly trembling. She scans the shadowed theater behind me like she's looking for someone. Then her fingers curl into fists, and she closes her eyes, inhaling through her nose.

"What's she waiting for?" Gil whispers loudly, but I shush him.

After another long breath, Christine glances at Sam and nods.

The moment she starts to sing, I am transported, transfixed by her clear, pure soprano. It's like listening to light itself. On the lower notes, her voice possesses a golden richness, and I know instinctively that she could sing in multiple musical genres and sound just as captivating in each one. Her phrasing could use a little work, but there's a wild, winsome longing in every note that transports me outside myself into a heaven where only two things exist—music and *her*. As she spreads her arms, palms up, and lifts her face to the stage lights, I'm reminded of the avenging angel who rescued me in that middle-school hallway.

Forever isn't long enough to listen to that heavenly voice, and when the last note ends, I'm ready to get down on my knees and beg her to accept the part. I think I might die if I can't hear one of my songs from her mouth.

"We'll, um..." I clear my throat, trying to drag my thoughts back down to earth, to reality. "We'll be in touch."

Christine smiles at me.

And I fall in love with her.

No—I fucking *leap* into love with her. Or maybe I've been in love with her since that day, and the love has been dormant, like bulbs under the soil, waiting for the sun to warm them so they can unfurl and burst into bloom.

She's gone. Disappeared backstage.

I have to see her again. Her email, her phone number—they're both on the audition form. I grip it with my sweating hands.

Marj pokes my arm with a long nail. "You seem smitten."

When I don't speak, Gil interjects. "Her song was too short. But she's pretty, and she can dance. I say we use her for the chorus."

"We'll go through the options later after we've heard everyone," Marj counters. "If there's anything I've learned in thirty years of show business, it's never to decide until you've seen the whole bunch. Sometimes, the best one will pop up right at the end."

But though we see and hear plenty of talent throughout the rest of the day, no one compares to Christine. When she appears for the dance auditions that afternoon, I am feral for the way she moves.

Some dancers are technically perfect, and some possess not only the skills and training, but also an extra sizzle of passion in every sweeping movement. Christine is the latter. She dances like she's on the brink of madness, like she's holding back a stunning amount of power, like there's a suppressed fire coursing through that slender body. She doesn't just perform the steps—she interprets them. Every flowing gesture, every arch of her spine, every extension of her leg is clean, crisp, beautiful.

I can't get enough of her dancing, and I desperately want to hear her voice again. She's brilliant, compassionate, charming—a fucking muse. And it maddens me that neither Marj nor Gil seem as enamored with her as I am. I try not to gush about her when we're sitting at the Leroux bar afterward, talking through the auditions over drinks.

"What do we think about Carlotta for the role of Eugenie?" says Gil.

"I'd thought of her for Ovina," Marj counters.

"Then who's our star?"

"That one with the nose ring, Chanel," says Marj. "Raoul, what do you think? Chanel or Carlotta?"

I take a deliberate sip of my drink. "I can see Carlotta as Ovina—or a version of Eugenie, but she's more bold and brash and saucy than I'd imagined. And Chanel...I don't think she's a strong enough dancer. To be honest, I'd prefer casting Christine as Eugenie."

"The Daaé girl?" Gil chuckles. "She's sexy, sure, but we need a star with a big personality, not some mousy little virgin with a pretty voice."

"Okay, I'm done." Marj gets up and gathers her things, bracelets clinking on her wrists. "I've had about as much of you as I can take for one day, Gil."

"Come on, Marj, you know I'm right," he calls after her, but she only flutters her ring-laden fingers at me as she breezes out of the Leroux.

Her words echo in my head. *Grow some balls, Raoul.*

"You're wrong," I say quietly.

"What's that?" Gil says, smiling even as his brows bend.

My heart is beating insanely fast, and my palms are sweating again. But I speak a little louder, despite the panic racing through my veins. "I said you're wrong. And you should show Miss Daaé more respect. The comments you've been making about her are not appropriate."

Gil gives a short, incredulous laugh. "Sure, okay. So you're one of *those*, huh? A male feminist? The kind that can't just hang with the guys? Good to know." He gulps his drink, slams down the glass. "I think Marj had the right idea. Let's get some rest and talk about this tomorrow. Think it over, Raoul. You'll come to the right decision."

He rises and pushes in his chair.

My hands are shaking, so I hide them under the table. "And the right decision is doing whatever you want?"

He grips the back of the chair and leans down, his voice low. "Let's put it this way. You're lucky to have the New Orpheum for your little musical. And we're happy to support you as a favor to your sister, so long as this arrangement remains mutually beneficial. I'm a patron of the arts, sure, but I'm also a businessman. I didn't get where I am by being politically correct or ignoring the bottom line. I know you're this dewy young artist, and you want to be true to your creative side or whatever the shit, and I respect that, I do. But when it comes to marketability and turning a profit, you should listen to the big boys. Okay, son?"

He claps a heavy hand on my shoulder, then strolls out of the bar.

I'm sweating so much that my glasses have slid down my nose. I push them back up with trembling fingers.

At least I said something. Defended Christine. And it had the effect I feared it would.

I have to walk a fine line with Gil Leveque, or I'll lose everything I've worked for. If he tells my sister I haven't been cooperative, the musical will be the last of my worries.

Philippa lets me have some freedom—as long as I do exactly what she wants.

She's like Dad. If I told her that, she'd consider it a compliment, when in reality, it's the worst condemnation I can deliver. Even now, several years after his death, I can't shake the sound of his voice or the piercing insistence of his eyes. *You're not trying hard enough, Raoul. You're shaming the family, Raoul. You need to change. I'm doing this because I care about you, about your future in this family. This is for your own good—*

My heart rate is skyrocketing. No, no, no—I can't have a panic attack right here at the bar. I grip my knees as tightly as I can, feeling the material of my slacks, the bones beneath. I focus on the clink of glass, the gurgle of liquid being poured. The faint jazz being played over the speakers. And I haul in deep breaths, picturing my heart, imagining its pace slowing to a steady, normal pulse.

This time, it works.

Swallowing the rest of my drink, I shove together the papers on the table and straighten the stack. Maybe we should have done online applications, but I have this weird obsession with doing things old-school, on paper, whenever I can. Now I've got to cram this mess into my laptop bag and tote it all home. Then I'd better go for a run to release the anxiety that's currently buzzing in my veins and knotting my muscles. If I don't purge the tension, I'll go to a very bad place.

Besides, a run is a good excuse not to go home just yet.

When I leave the New Orpheum, it's dark, and a chilly fall breeze whisks crunchy leaves across the sidewalk. The New Orpheum is a massive building with what seems like acres upon acres of parking around it. In the gloomy distance, I spot other buildings, like monumental gravestones, relics of an era when mills and factories kept this city alive instead of microphones and guitars. Those buildings haven't yet been renovated.

I wonder if Firmin Richards and Gil Leveque plan to expand their empire throughout this neighborhood once they've finished outfitting the New Orpheum. That could be why Gil is so keen to turn a profit with my musical. I wonder if he knows the statistics about new musicals, how few of them break even, much less earn extra money.

I try not to think about the numbers too much. For me, it's all about the music. The songs in my head demand to be heard, they *scream* to be heard, and if I don't bring them into the world, the muse will find someone else. That's how it feels anyway. Like I'm one failure away from never being able to write another song.

When the anxiety spikes in my stomach, I quicken my pace and yank open the rear door of my car. I keep a gym bag there for random runs, and changing in the back seat, under cover of the tinted windows, is normal for me. Slinging my laptop bag onto the floor behind the passenger seat, I strip off my work clothes and shimmy into running shorts and a moisture-wicking T-shirt. My feet welcome the comfort of sneakers instead of the leather shoes I wore all day.

Within minutes, I fling the car door open again, emerging as someone entirely different from the Raoul of the audition table. My key fob, phone, and earbuds accompany me. Everything else stays locked in the car.

I don't head for the well-lit street. Instead, I jog across the parking lot toward the abandoned buildings in the distance.

To most people, it would seem foolish, I suppose. I could twist my ankle on a bit of rubble, trip and fall onto a chunk of debris or some broken glass. But I'm sure-footed, and my whole body wants to *run, run, run* to escape the anxiety gnawing on the inside of my skin. I jam my earbuds into my ears, flood my brain with music, and plunge into the dark.

Once I cross the huge parking lot, the nearest building rears up like a specter, like a warning. I turn and jog along its front, peering up at the partly boarded windows. Several of them are broken, and loops of white spray paint decorate some of the bricks. The graffiti is so worn, I can't read it.

The front of the building has a couple of recessed areas where the shadows thicken, and as I pass one of them, my eye catches a sudden movement. A tall figure wearing a long, billowy coat.

At the same moment, the wind carries a scent to me—dark and damp, like the rich green moss clinging to the hollows of an ancient forest.

My heart takes a flying leap into my throat, and at the same time, instinct kicks in, adrenaline zinging along my bones. I don't change direction or quicken my pace. At a steady jog, I aim for the corner of the building.

When I risk a glance over my shoulder, I don't see anyone.

I'm imagining things. There's no one out here. I probably saw a tarp blowing in the breeze. I'll jog a little farther and then head back to my car.

My feet strike the pavement in time with the beat of the song flowing through my earbuds. Motion is relief. Motion is music. I was wrong to be worried, because I'm alone, utterly alone. Running alone is the purest freedom and— Wait, something is wrong. There's an off-kilter beat, a tempo that is neither the music nor my footsteps.

I pluck out one earbud, and there it is—a scuffing, repetitive beat behind me. Heavy footsteps that are not mine.

With my heart hammering violently, I whirl around.

The figure stops. He doesn't try to hide that he was chasing me.

He's big, wearing a black coat with the hood thrown back. A white mask conceals most of his face except for a full mouth and a square jaw that could belong to a 1950s movie star or some caped superhero.

"What do you want?" My voice sounds weak. Clearing my

throat, I try again, deeper. "What do you want?" No, *fuck*, that sounded *so* fake. That was so much worse.

The black-clad figure emits a low, menacing chuckle. He advances, and I swallow hard, because while I'm almost as tall as him, he's much wider in the shoulders.

I retreat slowly, tucking both my earbuds into the pocket of my shorts. I should run for it. But something about the guy's stance makes me think he's waiting for me to do just that. I get the feeling he'd love to chase me down.

The man in the black coat angles to the right, and I shift slightly to the left as I continue my retreat. Too late, I realize he's cornering me against the wall. My back hits the bricks, and I freeze.

The masked man surges forward and slams both palms against the wall on either side of my head, effectively caging me. Threat pours off him in waves so heavy, I can almost taste it. His scent is overpowering—ancient forests, damp leaves, and the dry darkness of bones sunk in soil.

"I don't have any money on me," I manage. "But my wallet is in my car. I can get it for you."

His voice is rich, smooth, and dark, like black coffee. "I don't need your money."

"The hell you don't," I say breathlessly. "Everyone needs money. Except the billionaires. Eat the rich and all that. Except half the reason we want to eat them is because we want to *be* them, am I right?" A faint laugh cracks from my lips. "You are what you eat, I guess..."

"Do you always talk nonsense?"

"No." I wince. "I'm a—I'm a writer, believe it or not. I'm good with words—the written kind, not so much the spoken kind."

Cautiously, I lift my hand, careful not to let it brush against his chest, and I nudge my glasses back up my nose.

The stranger's gloved hand darts up and plucks the glasses off my face.

"I need those!" I protest. "I'm basically blind without them."

The man inspects my glasses from all sides, then slides them carefully back onto my face, his gloved fingers tucking the earpieces behind my ears. Something about the gentle brush of those leather-clad fingers against my temples sends a panicked thrill through my chest. He's so close now that in spite of the gloom, I can see the faint gloss of his black, wavy hair. His eyes glint through the holes of the white mask.

"You want Christine Daaé for the lead role," says the man.

"This is about Christine?" I frown. "Yes, I want her to have the lead, but it's not up to me."

"Who then?"

"Gil Leveque, the co-owner of this place. I can't put on the play without him, and for some reason, he's set on Carlotta for the lead. Fuck, why am I even telling you this? Who are you?"

The mouth beneath the mask curves upward a little. "Say 'fuck' again. Like you mean it this time."

"What?" I gasp, and it's almost a laugh. I don't understand this guy, and he seems truly dangerous, but I can't help feeling a kind of frenzied excitement that I'm in this position, trapped by a stranger who is probably drop-dead handsome under that mask.

Before I realize what's happening, he takes both my wrists, lifts them, and pins them against the wall. His voice is rough, commanding. "That word has a raw kind of power in this age, but it is overused. When you say it, you should mean it. Again."

"Fuck," I manage through my dry lips.

"Deeper, like this," he growls. "Fuck."

I'm panting, my skin on fire and my dick at full attention, tenting my shorts. If he shifted forward even a little, he'd feel it. I desperately want him to close the distance.

When I'm in writing mode or when I'm polishing up a song, I barely think about sex. I might jerk off now and then, hastily, like I might swallow a glass of water or eat a sandwich, purely to satisfy my body's basic needs. But as far as indulging in sex, really enjoying it with a partner…it's been months. And between Christine's lithe feminine grace and this guy's dominant male energy, my bisexual ass has had way too much stimulation today.

I fix my gaze on the two eyeholes of the mask. Jaw tight, a vicious need driving the words, I grit out a challenge. "Fuck me."

He lets go of my right wrist. Grabs my jaw instead, his fingers compressing the bone almost painfully. "But you care for Christine."

It's true, and I don't feel like justifying or explaining it. "Yes."

"Christine belongs to *me*," he snarls, crushing his body against mine. "Her career must progress. She will have the lead role—I will ensure it. But know that if you attempt to thwart my plans, or if you try to take her for yourself, I will bring down ruin upon this theater, and your name will be forever linked to tragedy and misfortune. Do you understand?"

"Yes." I writhe against the weight of his body, but the instant I move, I go still again, electrified by a swift thrill of pleasure. I felt the grind of a hard dick against my own through layers of fabric.

His shoulders are heaving under the black coat, his jaw clenched beneath the mask. For a moment, we are suspended, taut cords of tension vibrating between us—and then he tilts his head and takes my mouth in a bruising kiss.

It lasts only a second, and then he whirls away and stalks off into the night. I could swear I see pale mist swirling around him, like the shadows of restless ghosts.

9

CHRISTINE

I don't know if I got the part, but I'm so proud of myself.

I owe a bit of gratitude to Carlotta, honestly. Her presence galvanized me with enough strength to walk out onto that stage. And when the moment came for me to sing, when I felt the familiar roll of nausea in my stomach, when I thought my vocal cords might have dried up completely, I heard the voice of the Angel in my head, saying, *Sing for me*. I imagined him sitting out there in the audience, ghostly and invisible but listening with all his heart.

He promised he would be there, and I was so eager to hear his opinion of my performance that I declined Meg's invitation to have dinner and drinks with her and Gabriella after auditions. Instead, I drove to the nearest gas station, purchased a cheap bottle of red wine, and rushed back to the New Orpheum, to the stairwell where the Angel and I have our lessons.

I expected him to be waiting for me, as excited to discuss the audition as I was. But even though I sang for him, called for him, and waited for him, he never responded.

Now I'm sitting on the second-floor landing, halfway through the bottle of wine, wondering if maybe I fooled myself into thinking I did a good job. I lift my plastic cup for another swig, only to find that it's empty. Time for a refill.

After pouring a generous amount of wine into the cup, I check my phone. It's nearly ten o'clock, and no Angel. Tomorrow is Sunday, which means I don't have work until late afternoon. I might as well head back to my room, finish the bottle myself, and binge-watch something on my phone until I fall asleep.

Maybe the Angel's task is done. He gave me lessons, encouraged me, prompted me to audition for the first time, and now he's finished with me. He's gone off to be the muse for some other struggling artist or singer.

The thought makes me irrationally angry. A desperate panic swells in my chest, quickening my breath into frenzied gasps. I slam down my cup, sloshing the wine, and I jump to my feet, fists clenched.

"No!" I scream into the echoing stairwell. "You can't leave me, you asshole! You can't leave me here, in this place, alone... I won't allow it. I can't bear it." Tears race down my cheeks, and I dash them away furiously. "You can't just *decide* I don't need you. That's not your choice to make. I want something on *my* terms for once, something that's *mine*, that no one can take away from me. You, this, *us*...it's all I've got. It's everything."

I sink down again, limply, slumped against the railing.

"Don't leave me," I whisper. "Don't do this. Not yet. Not like *them*."

For a while longer, I sob and I drink, first from the cup and then straight from the bottle, until everything blurs and fades. I'm dimly conscious of my face pressed to cold, wet concrete, of my eyelids weighed so heavily that I can't open them, not even when I'm lifted and I seem to float through cool air and darkness. There's a sliding sound, and then I land on a soft surface that smells familiar, like peach-scented lotion. My bed. I curl up into a ball, and a blanket drops over me.

Soft, warm lips brush my temple. The kiss feels good, and though I can't manage to open my eyes, I smile. The strange sliding sound happens again, and that's the last thing I remember until I wake up the next morning.

I don't return to the stairwell that day or the next. In fact, a whole week passes, and though I want to visit the Angel again, I don't. If he's still around, he needs to know that I'm angry with him for not meeting me after the audition. And if he's gone, I can't bear the thought of calling for him again and receiving no answer.

Maybe a normal, undamaged person would be more likely to grant second chances. But I grew up with parents who were anything but normal and made startling, traumatizing choices all the time without consulting me, even when those choices directly affected my life and my well-being. I'm heartbroken over the one reliable person in my life just...disappearing. Especially when I needed him to celebrate with me over my successful audition.

What if my perception of the whole thing was twisted? What if I sang badly, and the Angel was so ashamed of me that he left? I haven't heard anything from Raoul de Chagny or the other audition judges. I know it can take weeks to decide on casting, but I'd hoped Raoul would at least text me to hang out. But maybe I misread that, too. Maybe he isn't interested in me, as either a singer or a friend.

I've struggled with depression all my life. It's like I exist on the edge of darkness, on the brink of a ravine with a sludgy river at the bottom. One misstep can trigger a downward slide, and if I don't claw my way out with all my might, I'll be sucked into that river, pulled down into the thick, black mud. It will close over my head, pushing me lower and lower, crushing me down until I can't breathe or swim back up.

I've drowned in that river many times since the age of eight, when I endured my parents' first great betrayal. Sometimes, the drowning lasts for days or weeks—or months. Against hope or understanding, I've managed to resurface every time, and I've struggled back up to some semblance of normal. But I live with the fear that the next time it takes me down, I won't survive.

I've thought about borrowing or stealing medication, but I wouldn't know the right dosage for someone with my...complicated anatomy. I can't go to a regular doctor for a prescription. They would do tests, and the medically impossible results would land me in someplace worse than a mental health facility. And I absolutely refuse to go to a Progeny physician. My mother would have taken me if I'd asked, but I kept the dark times a secret from her as best I could. Not too difficult, with my parents so busy whenever they were in Nashville, not to mention their abrupt departures for long trips.

The only hope of surviving my depression is me. So when I start to lose ground, I kick my feet, hoping for traction as they slide in the mud. I hang on by my fingernails. I fight to stay out of the pit.

I practice my dancing whenever I have free time because movement helps and music unlocks me in a way nothing else can. If I don't keep moving, I will go still and silent. My limbs will be too heavy to lift, and the darkness will descend.

I eat protein, take generic-brand supplements, and hope they'll do something good for my body. I focus on my work.

Most of all, I fight the pull to go out every night and lure men into dingy motels. In this mood, I'm not sure what I would do to them. Could I stop myself from going too far?

Instead of hunting, I stay in my room and drink more than I should, trying to drown the predatory urge.

I'm in a really bad place a week after the auditions when an email comes through with the casting selections for *Sidewinder*.

The moment the notification pops up on my phone, my stomach pitches horribly, and I have to leave the front desk and run for the bathroom to throw up.

The sickness isn't just nerves. I've waited too long to hunt, and I *need* to go out tonight. But I'm scared to, because whenever I hunt in this depressive state, things get messy. My inhibitions are already low, and my brain desperately craves dopamine, serotonin—all the things.

But if I don't hunt soon, everything will get much worse.

After flushing the toilet, rinsing out my mouth, and walking back to the desk, I screw up my courage and open the email.

Carlotta Vanetti got the role of Eugenie. I'll be dancing and singing in the chorus. Beside my name, in parentheses, are the words "understudy for the role of Eugenie."

I'm disappointed and relieved at the same time. Yes, I wanted the triumph of scoring the lead role, but did I really want all that pressure? Did I want to be in the spotlight, with an entire audience focused on me? I might be a good singer, but I have no training as an actor, and Carlotta does. They made the right choice putting me in the chorus. And that little parenthetical note, that I was chosen to be her understudy, soothes any lingering wound to my pride.

This is good news. This is the relief I've been needing, the lifeline to drag myself up out of the sludge. Or it should be. But depression doesn't care about good news. Only time will tell if this is enough to lift me out of the danger zone for a while.

For now, I pretend it's enough. I pretend I'm happy.

After work, I put on makeup and a cute outfit, and I give the mirror wall a beautiful, brittle grin while humming the lyrics to Taylor Swift's "I Can Do It with a Broken Heart."

I consider going to the stairwell to see if the Angel is there, to tell him I'm in the chorus for *Sidewinder*. But the thought of hearing his voice again is almost as painful as the idea of sharing the news with empty air. I'm not sure I can handle either a confrontation or another disappointment.

I don't tell Meg I'm going out. I've barely seen her this past week. She's been distracted, and with good reason: She and Gabriella are officially dating now. I'm thrilled about it, but it feels like I've lost someone else.

I leave the New Orpheum at nine o'clock. Before I start my car, I sit in the dark and read through the casting email again, noting the rehearsal times. It's a heavier rehearsal schedule than I was expecting. I'll have to switch around some of my shifts at the bar or drop them altogether, which will mean fewer tips. The chorus part is a paid gig—not much, but almost enough to cover expenses—*if* I didn't have the private loan that I took out to pay the estate lawyer.

The email states that in a month, we'll be hosting a preview performance of the musical for some potential patrons, investors, and critics. That seems way too soon, but who am I to judge the timeline of the theater business? I guess the upcoming showcase is the reason for the intense rehearsal schedule.

My brain is so preoccupied with logistics that I barely remember the drive into downtown Nashville. I come to my senses in a parking space along a dark street with neon lights glowing up ahead, marking the beginning of Lower Broadway and its dazzling nightlife.

I flip down the visor, check my makeup in the mirror, then slide out of the car and lock it. I didn't bring a large bag tonight, just a small crossbody one with the bare necessities.

I wander past the bars and restaurants, waiting for something to draw me in…a laugh, a scrap of melody, a cheerful roar of voices. This city is all about instinct, about flowing with the mood, submerging yourself in the music, following the whisper of the Nashville magic.

Or, you know, going wherever the drinks are cheapest.

I know the magic when I hear it—the rippling twang of a bass guitar plucked by skillful fingers, the melodic croon of a male voice, lighter than the Angel's, but with a pathos that tugs at my soul. I turn, boots striking confidently on the sidewalk as I stalk into the tiny pizza parlor. There's a stage to the left, strung with soft golden lights. Blue neon letters behind it spell out the words "Tupelo Pie," and the phrase melds itself with the image of Raoul de Chagny, perched on a worn barstool, cradling a guitar.

A couple of guys flank him—percussion and another guitar—but I barely notice them. I'm entranced with the gleam of the lights on his coppery hair, with the dark fringe of his lashes, and with the tiny crease between his brows as he bends over the guitar like a diligent lover. The long fingers of his left hand slide along the instrument's neck, pressing just firmly enough in all the right places, while his right hand flicks gently yet decisively at the strings.

The way I want to *be* that guitar right now...

He's singing. His voice is warm, lilting, exquisitely sorrowful, an aching delight.

Every cell in my body unites in thundering urgency, my hunter's instinct entangling eagerly with my music-worshipping soul.

He's the one I want tonight. I *need* him. I won't be able to think of anyone else or pursue anyone else.

Fuck my life, fuck the parents who condemned me to this existence, and fuck Raoul for being the ultimate prize, the delicious sustenance my primal brain craves.

I try to turn around and walk out the door, but I physically *can't*. With growing dread, I realize that I haven't just waited too long. I've passed the point of no return. My inhibitions are being drowned, submerged beneath the ravenous craving that floods my mind.

Inside, the predator is awake, but outwardly, I still know how to behave. I sway with the music, I smile, and I drift ever closer to the stage until Raoul looks up and notices me.

His green eyes light up, and he strikes a wrong note.

Oh, he's so fucking doomed, and he doesn't even know it.

Somewhere in the back of my head, my rational voice is yammering, *Don't do this, don't wreck this, there's no way you'll get away with feeding from him, he'll find out what you are, and everything you've worked for will be lost.*

But I don't listen. I stay put and smile at Raoul until his number is over. While the crowd claps, while he lifts his hand and grins and thanks them, I head for the exit, glancing back at him over my shoulder. The look I give him is unmistakable—the look every woman gives a man when she wants him to follow her for salacious purposes.

Once I'm outside in the cool air, I suck in a shattered breath. He'll follow me, I know it. There's an alley a few steps away—the perfect spot.

Don't do this. You only take strangers, never people you know, never men who would be missed, who would remember it, who could find you. Don't do it, it's too risky, you're not thinking clearly...

I snarl at myself, fangs emerging. Too late to back out now.

At the corner of the alley, I wait for Raoul to emerge. When he does, he'll see me here, and he'll follow me into the dark.

But before he appears, a pair of arms wraps around my body and yanks me backward into the shadows.

I don't scream. My whole body trembles with a vicious, violent joy, because this attack is an excuse to *kill*.

The stranger drags me deeper into the alley, my back to his chest. I struggle just enough to fool him, and I wait for the right moment.

The moment his grip loosens, I spin around, fangs bared. My senses collect the information I need in a split second—tall man, black coat, white mask. Lightning-quick, I leap on him, my legs ensnaring his waist. I seize a fistful of his black hair, jerk his head to the side, and plunge my fangs into his throat.

His blood hits my tongue like a rich, hot tidal wave, and my eyes roll back. I can't help the guttural hum of delirious satisfaction that rolls through my chest. I swallow and swallow, taking several gulps before I realize that something's wrong.

This blood—it's like nothing I've ever tasted. Like the bold flavor and fizzy sting of soda when you've been drinking water for days. Like cocaine when all you've ever had is a joint. His blood buzzes in my throat, thrills in my stomach, and races along my veins. My brain is expanding, unfolding throughout the whole universe, streaking into kaleidoscopic realms that keep opening up to me in dazzling glories of shape and color.

His blood isn't smooth and quiet. It screams, it howls, it carries ghosts in the torrent of its power. It roars in my head, pounds in both my hearts—the human one I was born with and the secondary one that developed when I became a vampire. I have a second stomach, too, where the blood is rerouted when I'm feeding from someone. My smaller heart's job is to pump liquid from the blood stomach into the regular cardiovascular system. It's hard at work now, going wild at the influx of this new blood, thundering and swelling until I think it might explode.

With me clinging to him like a parasite, the man backs up, staggering against the wall of the alley. I'm dizzily aware of the movement, but I can't make my jaws unlatch from his throat. As terrifying as the rush of his blood is, my entire being is ravenous for more. I need every last drop. And he attacked me, so I have every right to drain him.

I bite deeper, moaning with frenzied pleasure. He tenses, and then gradually the rigidity eases from his muscles. His arms close around me, holding me in place.

Faintly, from the far end of the alley, I hear Raoul's voice. "Christine?"

The man I'm drinking from slides down the wall until he's sitting on the ground, so the two of us are concealed behind a garbage bin. Raoul calls again, more uncertainly this time. He doesn't come down the alley.

I should be able to smell the garbage and the other distasteful odors of the alley, but the only scent filling my nostrils is the fragrance of my attacker. It's stronger than when he first grabbed me, or maybe I'm just more attuned to it. He smells like a lush forest, like tiny flowers in the deep shade, like rain refilling a woodland stream. Like darkness and silence.

I remain latched to my attacker's throat, sitting astride him, drinking my fill while he yields to me. Groggily, I realize that he should be fighting back. It's odd that he isn't.

I shift my weight against him, and he hisses sharply, a distinct hardness rubbing against my center, between my legs. The heated haze in my brain intensifies, and I slide my fangs out of his flesh. After a second's hesitation, I trace the wounds with my tongue. My saliva will heal him within the hour. I owe this stranger that much, because he saved me from wrecking my career, ruining my cover, and losing the one man I could possibly see myself dating for real.

He's still cupping my body with his hands, holding me against him. His masked head lolls aside, his ravaged throat exposed. My night vision is better than the average human's, and I can see everything I did, the messiness of it. I tore him open, and I fear that he will bleed out before the healing is complete.

Leaning forward, I lick him again and again...and again, because *fuck*, his blood is so damn good. I've never tasted anything like it. I've fed from guys who had narcotics or coke in their system, but this guy must be on some kind of designer drug. I can't get enough. Dazzling heat rolls through my body in endless waves, and a quivering warmth intensifies between my legs.

Without thinking, I let my hips roll, rubbing myself against the stranger's bulge.

He lets out a ragged groan, and I shiver with delight at the sound.

My mind isn't my own. That's the only possible reason for what I do next.

I reach down between us, where the heat is most urgent, and I tug his zipper down, just an inch, in invitation. Then I rock back, waiting for him to make the next move.

With one gloved hand, he unzips his pants and pulls himself out. He's thick, uncut, smooth. I curl my fingers around the shaft, relishing the heat of him.

My claws are still out, and he hisses through his teeth behind the mask. He has every reason to be afraid, but that doesn't seem to be stopping him: He wants this, too.

I stroke him once, eliciting a low, tormented rasp from his throat. Then I reach under my skirt, pull aside my underwear, and settle myself back into place astride his hips. I guide him inside me, nudging his cock head between the wet lips of my pussy, sinking slowly onto him.

I've never done anything like this. I've always insisted that my victims take me to a cheap motel at the very least, and I don't fuck them. But this one is different. Mesmerizing. Delicious. My eyes drift blissfully shut as I sink down all the way, wholly full of him—his blood, his cock. I need his cum, and then I think I'll be sated.

My lips find his throat again. I prod the wounds with my fangs, teasing out a little more of that addictive blood. I'm drunk, I'm high, I'm out of my mind, and I tell myself that's why I cling to his shoulders, my mouth sealed to his neck, while I lift my hips and fuck myself on him.

His gloved hands grope beneath my skirt, finding my ass, grasping both cheeks. I let him take over, lifting and lowering me in a swift rhythm, using me like a toy to get himself off. It's so fucking hot, I can hardly breathe. I tuck my nose beneath the corner of his jaw, reveling in his scent. The edge of his mask grazes my cheek as he works me up and down.

I sheathe the claws of my left hand and tuck it between my legs, rubbing my clit while he fucks me. I'm whimpering through my fangs, through blood-wet lips, drenching his cock in my helpless arousal. It's the messiest I've ever been, and it's everything I need.

When I come, it's like a firework in my brain—the kind where each separate streak of glittering gold bursts into its own shining explosion. I scream faintly, and I bite him again, tearing his flesh cruelly. He comes inside me with a convulsive jerk of his body and a hoarse cry of pain and pleasure mingled.

"I'm sorry," I whisper, bathing the jagged wound with my tongue, selfishly savoring the fresh rivulets of blood that stream down his throat, soaking the collar of his coat. "For what it's worth, I hope you don't die."

He doesn't speak, but his cock flexes inside me again. It feels good, and I squeeze around him in response. He gasps, then releases a long, slow sigh of relief.

I cling to him a moment longer, letting myself enjoy the fullness of cock in my pussy and the richness of blood in my belly. My second heart is hard at work, pumping the fresh supply through my veins. His blood sparkles through my limbs and glistens in my brain. It's absolute bliss.

But I can't stay here. My predator self is receding, and my rational self emerges with concerns about where I am and what I've done. Reluctantly, I lift myself up, letting his length slide out of me. I stand up, swaying for a moment on trembling legs. Cum is dripping down my inner thigh, so I scoop it up and smear it across the front of his coat. Then I reach into the little purse at my hip, take out a wet wipe, and clean the blood from my mouth and chin. My fingers are shaking.

I ball up the wipe and tuck it into a tiny side pocket of my bag. After a quick fix of my underwear, I look down at the masked man. He's still breathing. Panting, really.

I'm starting to unravel, to panic, but I can't let him know that. I keep my voice as steady and casual as I can. "Well, this was a pleasure. Do I need to kill you, or can you keep this quiet?"

He lifts one gloved finger to his lips, a silent promise that he won't tell. Since I don't want to kill him, I'll have to believe him.

"Good boy." Swaying a little in my boots, I manage to walk out of the alley and down the street. I'm still buzzed on the blood I drank from his veins. My panties are damp, and I can still feel the phantom shape of his thick, warm cock inside me.

What did I just do? That wasn't me. I don't have sex with strangers in alleys. It's not that I'm worried about STDs. Vampires don't get them, or if we do, our bodies eradicate them almost instantly—a perk of having special regenerative cells. And I'm not worried about pregnancy either. A vampire's fertility window happens way less frequently than a human's, so I should be fine in that regard.

My lack of self-control tonight worries me. I waited so long to hunt that I couldn't stop myself from fixating on Raoul. I'd have attacked him once I got him in the alley. I might have even drained him dry. I was lucky that masked stranger intervened. Biting my attacker was only natural—I was in hunting mode, nearly out of my head with the blood-craze. But screwing him? That was something else entirely. I don't fuck where I feed. And I certainly don't feed on guys who are conscious.

What if he remembers my face? It was dark, but it's possible he was able to make out my features. And he heard Raoul call my name.

Shit...why did I let him live? Since when do I trust anyone else to keep my secret, much less a stranger?

My steps slow as I come to terms with the unfortunate truth. I need to go back and kill him.

I don't want to. The only people I've ever killed were the wannabe gang rapists who cornered me in that alley several months ago. I've come close to murder a few other times, but I've always managed to avoid it.

I turn back, still warring within myself—my moral code against self-preservation. A herd of laughing, drunk girls teeters toward me in their cheap pink cowboy boots, so I step back and lean against a building until they pass.

My attacker's blood left me feeling stronger than usual, as if I could lift a truck or a whole-ass building. It's more than enough strength to take down one masked man.

But I still can't decide if protecting my identity is worth the murderous stain on my soul.

Suddenly, a pickup truck pulls to a halt near the curb. The passenger window rolls down.

"Christine!" Raoul's bright smile is like a bolt of lightning, a shock to my wicked heart. He's popped up twice tonight. It's like fate, like something out of a rom-com—or maybe a horror movie.

"Are you stalking me?" I force a smile.

He laughs. "You're the one who came to watch me play."

"By accident. I didn't know it was your show. I just heard the music, and I..." The memory of his soothing voice and those delicate chords vibrates through my mind. "I was kind of obsessed."

"The way you looked at me...I thought you might want to, um...talk."

Is he blushing? That's too fucking cute.

"I did," I admit. "And then I got to thinking it might be weird if you and I...*talked*...since I'm part of the cast now."

"Right." He winces. "I guess that could be perceived the wrong way."

"For sure. But I'll see you Tuesday night, yes?"

"Yeah. Hey, can I give you a ride somewhere?"

"My car's just up here. I'm good."

"All right then. Good seeing you, Christine." His voice lingers over my name, turning it warm and golden.

Impulsively, I take a step toward his car—and at the same moment, the breeze swirls against my back, whisking my hair past my cheeks, flowing toward him.

Raoul's nostrils flare, and his handsome face tightens, his eyes wide and alert. His gaze locks with mine, half confusion, half challenge.

My heart flutters with the foolish terror that somehow, he *knows* what I did in that alley. But he couldn't possibly know.

He stares at me a second longer, and then a car honks as it swerves around his truck.

"Sorry!" he calls to the other driver, then says tersely, "I should go."

He guns the engine and roars away without another word.

I return to the alley, still uncertain what I plan to do. But when I reach it, the masked man is gone.

10

THE PHANTOM

Abhartach. A fragment of the Old Tongue surfaces in my mind.

It means vampire.

My Christine is a blood drinker, like the wretches who defeated me in the Wicklow church.

How did I not see it? How did my ghosts not notice any clues about her nature?

She's very good at hiding what she is. And it makes sense now—her appetite for men, her frequent trips into the city to lure them.

Earlier this evening, I watched Christine through the mirror in her room. I have observed her daily for the past week. Ever since I became preoccupied with Raoul and failed to meet her on the night of her audition, she has been avoiding our meeting place. But I could not bear to be apart from her for too long, and my ears were hungry for even the barest murmur of her voice, so I've been lingering in the passage behind the walls.

I spotted Firmin Richards in the passage once, from a distance, as he leered through one of the mirrors, dick in hand. Instead of confronting him myself, I summoned one of my most terrifying spirits—a woman with a partially crushed face and a tangle of wild hair. I made her temporarily visible to humans and sent her streaking toward Richards. Somehow, he managed to avoid screaming aloud, though the smell of his urine lingered for a while after he fled.

I don't think he'll be back. Which means I have the run of the secret passage and unfettered access to a view of Christine's room whenever I like. For a human, it might be wrong to spy on her, but I am a god. Why should I not indulge myself by watching a single human girl? I deserve some fragment of personal pleasure amid this desolate existence. If she is unclothed, I turn away. But I see no harm in observing her while she lies on her bed with her phone.

While watching Christine this evening, I realized she meant to go out. The amount of makeup she puts on when she's hunting for men is far more than she usually wears. My whole being revolted at the thought of someone else being close to her, touching her, or kissing her mouth. Unbearable. I could not allow it, so I hurried to her car and concealed myself in the back seat before she arrived. I was concerned she might see me, but she seemed too distracted to notice much.

When she arrived in the city, I followed her at a distance, and through the window of the restaurant, I saw her staring at Raoul while he played onstage. I read their faces, and I knew she planned to fuck him. Which I could not allow because, as I informed him, Christine is mine.

Once she emerged from the restaurant, I intercepted her impulsively, without planning my next move. I had some vague idea of keeping her in the alley until Raoul lost interest and left.

But my darling Christine, my sweet-voiced singer, my

teachable ingenue—she turned on me, transformed into a thing of fangs and claws. She drank me down, fucked me raw, and left me sitting here, propped against a clammy brick wall, with cum on my coat and my dick exposed.

I'm already healing, thanks to my nature and her tongue, but when I move, pain spears through my injured throat. The agony is oddly bracing. It clears the fog of sated lust from my mind.

Her body sucked a violent orgasm out of me, and I feel washed clean. Exhausted and satisfied beyond belief. And in the wake of that pleasure, I'm more certain than ever of one all-consuming truth.

I need her. She must be mine, *only* mine, forever.

And that copper-haired bastard, with his innocent green eyes and his delicate beauty and his poetic soul—he must leave Christine alone.

My ghosts, lingering near her desk, read the casting email as soon as she opened it and informed me of its contents. I was disappointed that Raoul did not make her the star of his musical. I will have to make sure he and everyone else in the New Orpheum Theatre understand who is truly in charge. Over the past weeks, I've been attaching strings to the puppets I need, and now is the time to tighten those strings and make the marionettes dance for me.

It begins with Firmin Richards. He deserves lasting punishment, and he will receive it, but for now, I need him for two things: money, since I'd rather not depend solely on the account Lloyd-Henry left me, and the reservation of Box Five for my personal use in perpetuity. In exchange, I won't publish the evidence of Richards's voyeurism and perversion.

I pull myself together and leave the alley, but getting back to my lair takes a while, since I have no previous experience summoning a ride. I hate downloading new apps and learning how to use them, and I despise interacting with all humans except for Christine and Raoul. It's not that I *like* interacting with Raoul. It's simply that he is surprisingly interesting. He's a rival I might enjoy toying with for a while before I finish him off.

The driver who picks me up looks very uncertain about the mask situation. Before getting into the car, I turned up my coat collar to conceal my bloodied throat, but I think he caught a glimpse of it, because after the first greeting, he says nothing else, and he keeps darting nervous glances at me in the rearview mirror.

"Stop looking at me," I command. "Watch the road, drive me swiftly to my destination, and our transaction will be complete. As long as you do your part, I will have no reason to harm you. Your reward will be five stars and a thirty percent tip."

He stops looking at me after that, and when I reach the New Orpheum, I add the tip and the rating.

I take my usual route into the building through the side door. Locks are no trouble. All it takes is a sizzle of power from my fingertips, and I can bypass any card reader or lock humans can devise. Even fingerprint scanners and facial recognition are no match for me. It's a minor triumph, a mere vestige of my former power, but it gives me a deep sense of satisfaction. I am no longer bound to the dark, locked away, chained below. I am free, and no one can prevent me from going anywhere I choose.

When I reach my lair, I strip myself and discard the mask I wore tonight. The coat will have to be cleaned. Fortunately, I have two others in a similar style.

Benedict and several other ghosts are lingering above the canal, murmuring to each other, but when I arrive, Agnes floats over to me, her pale, wispy fingers fluttering over her mouth. "Why, sir, what happened?"

"Nothing." Snatching up my favorite half mask, I fit it into place and stalk past her to the bathroom. I lean over the sink and bathe the blood from my throat and collarbones. The wounds that Christine left are gone, the skin as flawless as if they never existed. I run my fingertips over the place where she bit me, faintly disappointed that her sharp teeth left no scars.

The weight of what happened crashes upon me like a boulder, like the ponderous bulk of an entire mountain. I grip the edge of the sink, my head hanging low, my gaze fixed on the water running endlessly down the drain.

I did not want my first sexual encounter with Christine to be so crude and hasty. The act should have been thoughtful, magnificent, exquisitely beautiful, performed upon a luxurious bed bathed in candlelight. I feel as if I've lost something perfect, some ideal to which I clung, and now I must acclimate to a raw, gritty reality I can hardly bear.

I wanted her to fuck me. I joined willingly in the act. But I'm angry with myself for yielding to impulse, for rushing into a liaison that I did not plan. When I ruled as the god of death, nothing occurred without my control and command. Even my seduction of the Morrigan was a calculated move.

The only event in my existence that I never foresaw was the betrayal of the other gods. Their power was waning, their defeat imminent, and even in the throes of such decline, they found the energy to band together against me, to punish me for impregnating Fate herself and fathering the race of banshees.

My mind recalls that reality distantly, but my new heart, the one beating in a chest forged by unfamiliar magic, has no emotional tether to the Morrigan or to my ancient progeny. Thousands of years have passed between then and now. During my cursed imprisonment, I played no role in the guidance of the dead. Although my existence was linked to the Afterworld, it functioned more or less automatically, and it continues to serve its purpose even without my conscious presence.

I am no longer needed. I no longer rule anything or command anyone except a handful of ghosts who respect me for the deity I used to be.

I turn off the water and stare at myself in the mirror. One half of my face is beautiful, the other half corrupted. I cannot control the vines that writhe out of my skin any more than I could control my body's urges tonight. The panic of that helplessness seizes me suddenly, and with a sharp bellow, I smash my fist into the mirror. My knuckles crush its center, and cracks branch from that spot, fracturing my reflection. Panting, I groan with the agony of my pounding heart.

Somehow, I must find a way to seize whatever power I can grasp, any happiness I can reach. Only then can I conquer this feeling of wretchedness, of loss, of abandonment.

I am alone, alone, alone, and I don't want to be alone. I don't desire the company of ghosts. I crave the touch of fingers, the intimate press of mouths, the voice of someone who is *alive* and utterly devoted to me—as endlessly devoted as I will be to them.

From now on, nothing must stand in the way of my goals: the control of this theater and the pursuit of a true companion. If

I cannot rule the Afterworld, I will rule the New Orpheum. If I cannot feel any emotional connection to my past life, I will have a powerful love in this new existence.

Christine is central to everything. Whatever she is, whatever we did tonight—it makes no difference. Hers is the voice that spurs me to write music, hers the first soul that sang to mine. I will make her a queen, a star of the stage. She will have everything she desires, and when I have given her everything, she will love me.

It begins with the pulling of a few strings. A test of the leverage I've amassed and the power I wield.

After wiping my face with a towel, I return to the main area of my lair and head for the small refrigerator I purchased months ago. I pluck out a tall can of sparkling water, flavored with lime and peppermint. The dance of the crisp bubbles over my tongue is a small delight that instantly puts me in a better frame of mind.

Drink in hand, I lean back against the black satin pillows on my bed. My sleeping area is on a raised platform surrounded by curtains, tied back so I can view the glimmering black water of the canal. "More candles," I demand, and while the ghosts hurry to light them for me, I craft a text for Firmin Richards, demanding my new salary and the permanent reservation of Box Five for my sole use. I send him a video clip I took of his sordid activities, assuring him that I have plenty of additional proof.

That should do the trick. Richards has a family, not to mention a prominent position in Nashville society and a brand-new multiuse development that must succeed, or he'll slip into financial ruin.

Richards replies shortly with a terse assurance that I will have my box. Moments later, I receive a notification that he has sent the money I requested from him.

Now that my salary and my box have been secured, my next step will be to approach Richards's business partner, Gil Leveque, who handles the theater part of the New Orpheum. From what the ghosts told me and what I heard from Raoul's pretty mouth, Leveque is the one championing Carlotta Vanetti for the lead role in *Sidewinder*. He was at the audition table. He seems bullish, headstrong, not as skittish as Richards. To show him who's really in charge, I may need to do more than send threatening texts.

A smile spreads over my face as I realize how amusing this game is going to be.

11

RAOUL

We've been rehearsing for weeks, and *Sidewinder* is everything I feared it would be.

A disaster.

On day one, the entire packet of sheet music disappeared—the whole score for the musical. I gave it to the conductor, and he swears he left it on a table backstage. Yet somehow the whole thing vanished into thin air. I had to reprint it all.

Since then, it's been one thing after another. A dancer twisted her ankle. Mist and smoke drift through the backstage areas. The lights are finicky at best, despite a technician coming to work on them multiple times. Most of the cast and crew claim to have either spotted a floating object, felt a cold spot, or seen an actual ghost. A few of them have quit—not that it matters much, since they're easily replaced. In Nashville, there's always a crowd of eager young talent ready to jump into any available role, even when that role involves a potentially haunted theater.

Carlotta is always late to rehearsals and offers an endless litany of excuses, from a mishap at the salon to a flat tire to ghosts stealing her possessions. This week, she has seemed unusually fragile, probably due to a rumor circulating online that she made insensitive comments to another influencer. I'm not on socials much, but the drop in her follower count was noticeable, even to me.

Whenever she's not singing, Carlotta complains loudly about being targeted, stalked, and harassed. Not a good headspace for my leading lady to be in, but I'm not sure how to fix it. The few times I've tried to encourage her, she has seemed a little too interested in receiving physical comfort from me, so I maintain a professional distance.

I've thought about the masked man in the black coat, but I haven't seen him again, nor have I mentioned him to anyone. I did ask Firmin Richards to hire a couple extra security guards for the New Orpheum, though, and he says he did. I'm not sure I trust his word. He's more jittery than usual these days, always startling and sweating and glancing over his shoulder. He's as spooked as the cast.

The preview performance is tomorrow, and we're far from ready. In fact, I'm actually beginning to believe my musical is cursed...or haunted.

Standing just offstage, I gnaw the end of my pen. I'm supposed to be watching Carlotta so we can finesse her choreography and gestures during this song. But I can't help watching Christine in the chorus. I can't get over the way she dances—like she's *part* of the music, like it's a living entity that's possessing her, moving her limbs, transforming her into the perfect expression of itself. And yet despite how beautifully she dances, I can't shake the crawling sensation that something is with the music. Something is missing. The score isn't everything I hoped it would be, and I'm not sure how to make it better. I had such a strong vision for this musical in my head, but the reality is a sketchy, distorted reflection of my dream.

I've barely spoken to Christine since we saw each other downtown the night I played at Tupelo Pie. I couldn't think what to say after the wind carried her scent to me. Smells are stories, distinctive threads blending to tell a tale, and I couldn't understand the narrative I scented on her that night. I still don't know how to interpret it.

Blood and sex and ancient forests and raw, surging power...

Carlotta's voice shrills on the high note of her solo, breaking me out of my trance. At the same moment, movement catches my eye—something high above the stage, swaying, dropping, then plummeting downward—

"Carlotta, move!" I shout, and I dive forward, shoving her aside just as a piece of the lighting rig crashes to the stage, denting the boards.

Cries of shock rise around me as I climb to my feet and reach out to Carlotta. She knocks my hand aside and gets up on her own.

"This shitty theater is falling apart!" she exclaims. "What next? Is the stage going to fall out from under us?"

I crane my neck, staring up at the catwalk. No one is up there that I can see. "Joe, could you run up there and see if you can figure out what happened?"

Joe Buquet, the stage manager, mouths the unlit cigarette between his lips. "Sure, boss." Unhurried, he saunters off backstage.

I don't like him. He never shows any of the forethought or urgency that a guy in his position should demonstrate. I need somebody capable, proactive, and quick-thinking, but in this, as with almost everything, I had no choice. Buquet worked with

Richards on the renovations for the New Orpheum, particularly the residential section, and Richards wants him to keep him employed, apparently. So I have to make do.

But I'm pissed enough to mutter while he ambles away, "No rush, of course. Nothing urgent, just our star almost getting squashed."

Christine smothers a giggle.

Carlotta's head whips toward her, eyes narrowing. She gives Christine a death glare for a couple seconds before turning back to me.

"So how was it?" Carlotta asks. "Before I almost died? What did you think of the way I moved my hands during the second verse?"

"Oh..." Fuck, I was watching Christine. Thinking about Christine. My eyes dart toward Christine for a moment before I say, "It was good. But we should run through it again once Joe checks everything out and we're sure it's safe."

Carlotta's gaze sears into mine. "You weren't watching me. You were watching *her*." She jerks her head toward Christine. "You're always watching her. Are you two fucking or something?"

"What? No, I would never— I mean, *no*," I splutter, giving the bridge of my glasses a nervous poke.

Christine hooks an eyebrow as if to say, *You would never?*

"We're rehearsing," Carlotta says with vicious emphasis. "You're supposed to be listening to me and looking at *me*. Not that I need your input, because I'm fucking amazing, but the least you can do is show a little interest in the star who is carrying your whole shitty musical on her back! I don't have to deal with this, you know. I can get another role like *that*." She snaps her fingers.

"I'm sure you could," I say.

"Damn straight. Do you know how many directors would suck dick to have me in their show? And you take me for granted." She gives a dramatic sniff and fans herself hastily. "Somebody get me a tissue."

One of the dancers hurries to comply, and Carlotta dabs the tissue delicately beneath her eyes.

Firmin Richards and Gil Leveque hurry onstage at that moment. Richards is sweating anxiously, and Gil looks unusually red in the face when he says, "Raoul, what was that goddamned crash? Sounded like the place was coming down around our ears."

I point to the chunk of metal and glass on the stage. "That fell."

"'*That fell*'?" mimics Carlotta with an incredulous laugh. "That's all you can say? It almost fell on top of me, Gil. While I was singing. I could have been *killed*. And Raoul can't be bothered to even look at me. Someone bring me my phone. I need to film a video about this *right now*. My followers need to know how I'm being treated."

"Oh, now, now, let's not be hasty," drawls Gil, coming forward. "You've had a scare, no doubt about it. The important thing is that we're gonna make sure nothing like that happens again, okay? You're our beautiful star, darlin', and we'd be nowhere without you. Everyone knows that. Ain't that so, Raoul?"

"Of course." I force a smile.

"Of *course*. Can I give you a li'l ol' side hug?" When Carlotta nods, Gil wraps an arm around her shoulders. "Honey, you have every right to be angry, but trust me, we got you. Everyone is here to back you up and support you. Right, Rune?"

He shoots a look at our male lead, Rune Donaldson, who's

handsome in a mediocre thirst-trap sort of way. To be honest, I keep forgetting about him when he's not actively singing. He has a good voice and a decent stage presence, but he's a bit vacuous, not as charismatic as he seemed during his audition.

When Gil speaks to him, Rune blinks and says, "Yeah, no doubt, man. All the support, bro."

"See? We've all got your back," says Gil. "Now show me that beautiful smile. Can you do that for me?"

Carlotta sniffs. "Don't tell me to smile."

"Of course not, darlin'. Only if you want to."

She nods with a haughty flutter of her lashes, then gives him a dazzling, tearful smile.

"Gorgeous," purrs Gil, squeezing her shoulders. "And here's the truth, from me to you—you're the most beautiful woman on this stage and the most talented, too. Ain't that right, Raoul?"

The lie hovers on my tongue. But I can't speak it, not with Christine standing right there, looking like a goddess in dancewear, hiding that exquisite voice.

My eyes flick to her for a mere second. And I'm done for, because Carlotta sees. Everyone sees.

Anger floods Carlotta's gaze again. She throws off Gil's arm. "That's it! I'm done. You can find someone else to sing your precious Eugenie." She stalks away backstage.

Gil glares at me, then hurries after her. Firmin Richards remains where he is, twisting his hands together like he's trying to wring water out of them.

"Whoa, man...can she do that?" asks Rune.

"She has a contract," I tell him. "But technically, she doesn't have to sing in the preview performance, so...yes, she can."

He stares, then scratches his head. "Bro, if she's gone, then... who's gonna sing with me?"

"Christine is the understudy," pipes up Meg Giry, one of the other dancers. "She can sing the lead tomorrow night."

The memory strikes me like a fist to the gut. A solid body in a black coat crushing me against the wall, muttering words of dark intent. *She will have the lead role—I will ensure it. But know that if you attempt to thwart my plans or if you try to take her for yourself, I will bring down ruin upon this theater, and your name will be forever linked to tragedy and misfortune.*

No one person could be behind everything that has happened. It's ridiculous to even consider the possibility. Besides which, no one was on the catwalk when the piece of lighting fell. If the masked man had been nearby, I would have caught his scent.

I thought I smelled him that night when I stopped my car at the curb to speak to Christine. His scent, twined with hers, redolent of lust and blood. Is he her secret boyfriend? An ex? A stalker? Is she in danger?

Richards speaks in a strained voice. "Yes, Christine is the understudy...but is she prepared to sing the role? I know you dance well, Christine, but how is your voice? Have you had training?"

Christine speaks through tense lips, her face paler than I've ever seen it. "I had a teacher for a while. He taught me well."

"You'll have to do. I need to get someone in here to clean this up...can't have glass everywhere... There you are, Joe! Any idea what happened?"

Joe Buquet shrugs, removing his cigarette. "Nah. Screw must have got loose."

"A loose screw?" Richards's laugh carries a tinge of hysteria.

"We can't have loose screws up there with all the lighting and the beams and things!" He waves a hand upward. "Fix it! And fix this floor! And do it as cheaply and quickly as possible!"

"I can get it done quick or cheap, not both," says Joe.

"We have an audience coming tomorrow night," I remind Richards. "We need to impress them."

"Fine. Do whatever has to be done. Just remember I'm not made of money." Richards hurries away, his footsteps punctuated by a string of muttered curses.

The eyes of the cast press on me like prodding fingers. I hate it. I like sitting in a quiet space, crafting lyrics and humming snatches of melody. I wasn't cut out for this. I don't think I like directing.

Luckily for me, my lord and savior Marjorie returns at that moment, carrying a cup of fresh coffee in one hand and a bedazzled phone in the other. She takes one look at the damaged stage, asks a few questions, and orders everyone to head over to the Blue Ballroom for rehearsal while the mess is cleaned up. Everyone obeys except Christine, who lingers for a moment while Marj pulls me aside.

"You look awful," Marj says.

"Thanks. I can always count on you for an ego boost."

"You can count on me for the truth, hon. We'll move the rehearsal to the ballroom for now, and I'll make sure Christine is ready to step in for Carlotta. You go home and get some rest. Smoke a joint or something. We need you relaxed and ready to schmooze our guests tomorrow night." She pats my shoulder and heads up the aisle, on her way to the Blue Ballroom.

She's right, of course. But before I follow her suggestion, I look at Christine, who remains onstage, frozen in place, even though everyone else has gone. Her eyes aren't full of excitement for her first big role—they're fractured with terror, filled with an unspoken plea that I understand as surely as if she'd screamed it aloud. *Save me.*

I cross the stage and take both her hands. They're ice-cold.

"Meet you out front when you're done with rehearsal," I say in an undertone. "Eight thirty? I'll have the car waiting."

A little of the fear recedes from her gaze, and she nods.

We descend the stage steps and walk together up the slanted aisle to the doors at the rear of the theater. We cross the small lobby area of the theater and head down the hall, where I leave Christine at the entrance to the Blue Ballroom.

I continue to the big front lobby on my own. Its carpet is flecked by scintillating shards of light, cast from the crystals of the chandelier, and the glittering spots mirror the excitement in my heart as I consider my plan for tonight.

Christine has never sung for an audience. And even though she auditioned for the lead role in *Sidewinder*, it would be cruel to throw her into that role without first giving her a taste for public performance. She needs to experience the thrill of connecting with a crowd, pulling energy from them, sensing their response to her voice and her emotions. It's a magic like no other. And I intend to give her that experience.

As I exit through the front doors of the building, my phone buzzes in my pocket, so I pull it out and check my messages. There's a text from a number I don't recognize.

> Do not take Christine out tonight. If you do, you will regret it.

My stomach takes a tremulous leap as I type a reply. Who is this?

I told you she is mine.

Fuck, it's him. The hot masked guy in the black coat.

I clamp one hand over my mouth, staring into the distance, trying to figure out what to say next. Should I reply at all? Leave it alone? Call the police?

After a moment's consideration, I decide to try an honest answer. This isn't a date. I'm taking Christine out to sing. I need to get her comfortable with performing for an audience before she takes the lead tomorrow night. Also, you can't claim people as your property.

That's the longest text I've sent in years. I tug on my lower lip with my teeth until he replies.

I have every right to claim anything I want. Where are you taking her to sing?

The Alouette, I answer without thinking.

Why am I giving this guy information? He's a creepy stalker in a mask. I guess part of me wants to pacify him, to reassure him that I'm not a threat. And…shit, I may as well admit it…a part of me is intrigued and wants to keep the conversation going. That night, weeks ago, he made me so hard I could barely think. From what I could tell, the feeling was mutual.

I'll be there, he texts back.

Well...shit. I consider making a change to avoid him, but the Alouette is the best place for Christine. It's a small, intimate venue, mostly unknown, so it'll be easy to get in and secure a spot at the mic. Besides, I know the owner—a family friend. It's not the Bluebird, but that place is overhyped and impossible to get into these days. I much prefer the lesser-known dives and bars around Nashville. The decor at the Alouette is cozy, and the vibe should put her at ease.

And maybe a small part of me wants to see *him* again.

I've got four hours until I need to be back here at the New Orpheum to pick up Christine. Enough time to run home, shower, and change. And smoking a joint doesn't sound like a bad idea. I need to be good and mellow if I'm going to be around Christine *and* the masked hottie tonight.

It takes me half an hour to reach the exclusive Nashville suburb where my family and our closest friends live in sprawling mansions surrounded by smooth, green lawns. Our house has a pair of stone wolves flanking the gate. They're seated atop the wall, looking haughtily down their slender muzzles, somehow managing to appear both regal and wild at the same time. By their very presence, they proclaim to everyone that "rich white assholes live here." One of the first poems I ever wrote was about those wolves and the way I felt whenever the gates parted and we drove between them. I called it "The Wolves Are Watching."

I guide my truck up the long drive. The giant garage has several bays, but I don't bother parking in one of them. I'll be leaving again in a few hours. If I'm lucky, I can get in and out of here without running into—

Knuckles rap on my window, and Philippa's voice penetrates the glass, muffled but insistent. "Raoul."

Shit.

I wave for her to step back. When she does, I open the door and climb out of the car. "Philippa."

"I'm glad you're here."

She's the epitome of professional savagery, my sister. Rail-thin with crisp angles, a seamless bob several shades darker than my hair, and flawlessly tailored clothing, usually of the blouse-and-pencil-skirt variety. Her eyes are a match for mine—two icy emeralds.

"You've missed too many family dinners lately," she says.

"I can't stay tonight. I'm going out with a friend."

"Friend?" She lifts elegant, penciled eyebrows. "What friend?"

"Just someone."

"Man or woman?"

"Does it matter?"

"One of those genders can give you children. The other can't."

I don't bother debating her backward thinking. I've tried that before with no effect. I hop down from the truck and shut the door. "Really, Philippa? This again?"

"We have a responsibility to the family, Raoul," she replies coolly. "To *all* the families. Maybe if you spent any time with us, you'd remember that. We need each other. It's the only way we can survive and thrive in this city."

I step to the side, aiming to move past her. "Look, I came home to shower, get dressed, and relax a little before I head out, so—"

Philippa catches my arm. Her fingers squeeze my flesh so hard, it's agony.

"Dinner's at seven, so you'll have time to prepare for the meal," she says. "Dress appropriately for the table, not for a bar. We'll eat, and then you can go meet your friend."

Her grip never relents. She speaks in the cold, hard, dominant tone I know so well…the tone I can't disobey, even if I want to.

"Be grateful I'm letting you go at all," she adds.

I swallow hard. I know she expects the words, so I force them between gritted teeth. "Thank you."

"Of course, Raoul. I want you to have a good life and pursue your dreams." She releases my arm, and I resist the urge to massage the injured muscle. "Speaking of which, how is your little musical going?"

"My 'little musical' is going fine," I say. "I can tell you more at dinner."

"I look forward to it." Her nod is a dismissal—permission for me to leave her presence.

My face flames as I head inside and hurry to my suite. On the second floor of the house, I have a bedroom, a bathroom, and a giant walk-in closet all to myself. It's a privilege and a prison.

I'm not living at home by choice. I was recalled after college because our father's health was declining. After his death, I stayed because Philippa claimed to need my support as she took on our father's role and responsibilities. After that, she kept inventing reasons for me to stay until at last, we came to the crux of the matter—she wants to control me.

I'm expected to be grateful for the freedom Philippa allows me, like the privilege of producing my musical at the New Orpheum Theater. But I know she's letting me have this just so she can hold something else of mine in the palm of her hand, ready to be crushed by her ruthless fingers if she decides I don't deserve it.

I can't disobey a direct verbal order from her when I'm in her presence, so I try to avoid being around her as much as possible. Her commands hold sway over me as long as I'm on our family's home property, so technically I should be able to do as I please once I leave the gates—but Philippa rules more than this family. Her influence and her spies are everywhere, a sprawling net over this city. And I'm linked to her by a deeper chain, too—one that's fused with my bones and twisted around my veins. A blood loyalty that was imprinted on me ruthlessly since before I could speak.

Defying her over a family meal is out of the question. But I come to dinner wearing a blazer over a band T-shirt and black jeans as a slight form of rebellion. Philippa doesn't comment, partly because she's immersed in low conversation with her fiancé, Conri. Theirs is a match of bloodlines, not love. Still, they seem happy enough when they're discussing business ventures or the latest gossip from the families.

Sometimes, our evening meals involve a few dozen people. Tonight, only a handful of guests are seated along the polished length of the dinner table—two second cousins, my long-dead mother's younger sister, and a couple of other distant relatives by marriage. There's someone at the far end of the table whom I don't recognize. Philippa introduces him briefly as Lloyd-Henry Woodson, an out-of-town guest looking for sanctuary with the Collective. I couldn't care less who he is or why he's here. I just want to get out of this house.

Our maid, Nadezhda, brings us the food in silence. When I pick up my fork, Philippa says sharply, "The prayer, Raoul."

I let the fork clatter back onto the plate.

My sister's eyes flare brighter for a moment. "Say it."

A command. I struggle to resist, but it's like an ant trying to hold a boot at bay to keep from being crushed. The words are already leaking from my mouth.

"To the ancestors, we give praise. To the gods, we give thanks. From the Morrigan, we ask a blessing, that the line of Gévaudan may thrive. To this end, we receive our sustenance."

"So we do," says Philippa, and the others echo the phrase.

The guests chatter among themselves while I'm unlucky enough to be sitting on Philippa's left-hand side, too far away from the others to join their conversation. Not that I'm particularly interested, but it would be better than enduring her never-ending critiques.

As I begin to eat, I feel her watching me. Every bite of the steak falls into my stomach like a blob of hot lead until I'm sure I'm going to be sick.

The worst part of being around her is waiting for the commands, never knowing when she'll decide to give one or what it will be. Whether it will destroy my life.

"You need a haircut, Raoul," Philippa says, delicately spearing two green beans with her fork. "You're beginning to look rather beastly."

Conri snickers.

Philippa takes the bite, chews and swallows, then says, "Have you been practicing?"

"Yes," I lie.

"Don't try to deceive me. You know I can tell." She frowns, long fingernails tapping her water glass. "You're supposing to be doing your exercises every day, like Papa taught you, or you won't make any progress."

"I know."

"It's for your own good. Papa was too easy on you, and I need to set you straight."

I almost snort when she says Papa was *easy* on me. He'd lock me out of the house all night in January, shut me into the little room under the stairs for several hours at a time, force me to eat my meat raw, and try all sorts of exposure therapies, most of which involved either physical pain or endless barrages of cruel words. All for the purpose of making me into something I might never be.

Philippa sets down her glass hard and leans close to me, lowering her voice so our guests can't hear. "Do you know what the others are muttering behind your back, little brother? That you're broken. Faulty. A backward step in the evolution of our species. Useless except as a stud, a sperm donor, and maybe not even then. What if you pass this flaw of yours to your children? What then?"

I stare at my plate, lips pressed tight. I want to talk back to her, but I've learned that's unwise when she's in this mood.

"When they say these things, I defend you," she continues. "I tell them you'll get it eventually. That you're still a worthwhile member of the Collective. But I can't arrange a mate for you until you have some kind of breakthrough. Do I need to call Jean-Luc to do a session with you again?"

"No!" The word jerks out of me, torn by terror. My experience with Jean-Luc was the most traumatizing event of my life. Rather than fixing me, I think it broke something in my soul, created a wound I've barely managed to stitch shut with my music. I can't go through that again, or I'll go mad.

"Jean-Luc thinks you lack the correct stimulus," Philippa says. "If he can find the right trigger—"

"No, Philippa…please." My nails dig into my palms beneath the edge of the tablecloth. "I swear I'm working on it."

"If this musical of yours is distracting you from what really matters—"

"It's not. I promise."

"I'll give you two more months. If you still can't show me results, I'm calling Jean-Luc again. And if that doesn't work, we'll need to take a serious look at your priorities and whether your musical obsessions may be blocking your true instincts."

My mouth is so dry, I think I'll choke if I try to take another bite. "May I go?"

She sighs as if I'm an exasperation, a burden, an endless weight on her mind. "Fine."

I want to run out of the room, but if I'm too visibly eager to leave, she'll call me back, so I rise deliberately, place my napkin on the table, and say a polite "good night" to the guests and Conri.

Bursting out of the beautiful house into the night air feels like an escape from hell. I run to my truck, leap in, and drive it through the open gate, windows down, sucking in lungfuls of the chilly autumn air.

Failure. Disappointment. Useless. Broken.

It's only a matter of time before Philippa takes away everything that matters to me. And if she does—if I can't break free from her—I may as well die.

I turn up the radio, letting the beat pummel my sister's words to the back of my brain where they don't hurt so much.

For tonight, I won't think about my family, my sister, or the

Collective. I'll focus on Christine. I'll soothe her anxiety and show her how much fun performing can be.

If I can't find the strength to save myself, maybe I can set her free.

12

CHRISTINE

I don't know Raoul well, but when he picks me up, I immediately sense that something is wrong. It's odd that I can tell. Almost like I'm attuned to him.

He's smiling as usual, polite and kind as always, and yet there's a forlorn sadness in those pale green eyes of his. Maybe pain sings to pain, grief recognizes grief, and that's how I know he's hurting.

When he halts at a stoplight, I reach over impulsively and squeeze his hand. "Thanks for this. Whatever this is."

He glances over, a naked sweetness and vulnerability shining in his gaze for a second before he conceals it with a broad grin. "Tonight is your first time performing for an audience. Small venue, cozy vibes, friendly crowd, okay? Zero pressure. Just you and me, having some fun with a song or two."

My heart thrills with panic. "And why are we doing this?"

"So you've got a little experience under your belt before tomorrow night."

I swallow the lump of terror trying to crawl up my throat. It's sweet that he's doing this, and honestly, it's a good idea. But that doesn't make it any less scary.

"You know 'The Fighter'?" he asks. "Carrie Underwood and Keith Urban?"

"Of course."

"Yeah, it's one of my guilty pleasure songs. The lyrics aren't really that deep, but—"

"There's no such thing as a guilty pleasure," I tell him. "If a song touches your heart, makes you feel something, that's damn good music. No guilt involved."

He brightens. "I like that. Anyway, I think it's a good choice for us—easy lyrics, simple melody, a crowd favorite. It's low-pressure, not vocally challenging…just plain fun and good feelings. There's one big note for Carrie's part, but you've got it, no problem."

"Okay."

"I just want to show you that performing doesn't have to be this huge scary thing. It can be such a rush, especially when you're vibing with the audience."

I curl my fingers tight and try to breathe normally. "Not sure I believe you, but I'm willing to be proven wrong."

"Sweet." He turns into a public parking lot. "Come on. Let's do this!" He scans the QR code on a nearby sign to pay for the spot, then reaches behind the front seat of his truck to get his guitar case. "This is my favorite baby." He opens the case and lifts the guitar reverently from its bed. "1958 Gibson LG-0, beautiful mahogany. Rebuilt it myself with help from this older guy who owns a guitar shop. We did the frets, nuts, saddle, top braces, back braces, everything. Not long ago, I put in a really nice hybrid system, transducer and mic with a built-in preamp, plus battery pack and volume control…best decision I ever made. It sounds absolutely golden, and it's great for playing live. And I've got this solid-state amp..." His voice trails off, and he winces. "Sorry, I get nerdy about this stuff."

"Don't be sorry. It's cute."

"Yeah?" He grins, hopeful. Adorable.

"Can I help carry something?"

"You can carry the Gibson, and I'll get the amp. It's nowhere near as heavy as a tube amp, but still—"

I grab the amp case and lift it easily.

Raoul's eyes widen. "You're strong."

"I'm a dancer." And a vampire, but my simple excuse seems to satisfy him.

After closing the guitar case, he practically bounds up the sidewalk toward the bar, and I can't help laughing at his puppy-dog energy. He's got the slim build and delicate jawline of a male fashion model, and the glasses add this layer of bashful intelligence to his look, making him even sexier. I think I'm in trouble.

The Alouette has a cozy interior with a colorful, bohemian vibe that eases my nerves a little. The low stage is constructed of warm-toned wood and draped with tattered rugs in various faded patterns—probably a tripping hazard, but nobody seems to care. There's a motley collection of overstuffed couches, small painted tables, and slouchy chairs, perfect for curling up and enjoying good music. In the center, there's a clear space for anyone who might want to dance. Mosaics and autographed portraits cover the walls.

Raoul introduces me to the DJ, Andre, who greets him with a drawling "Whassup" and a fist bump.

"Y'all can go on after these folks." Andre jerks a thumb over his shoulder toward the trio onstage and mutters confidentially,

"They been playin' this sad shit for half an hour. It's melancholy as *hell*, and my people are ready for something cheerful, you feel me?"

"I got you," Raoul promises. "I don't have a drummer tonight. You wanna do a beat for us?"

"Sure, man." At the end of the song, Andre ushers the trio offstage to scattered applause, then lifts the mic to his lips and croons, "Listen up, folks, we got us a treat tonight. My boy Raoul is a kick-ass songwriter and a bona fide magician with that Gibson of his, and he's gonna sing for us along with the beautiful Christine Daaé. This is her first time performing for an audience, so y'all be good now. Let's give her a hand!"

My cheeks burn as Raoul tugs me forward. I step onto the low wooden platform, and he points me to a stool, plugging in his amp before taking the other one. Andre hands me his mic and seats himself at the house drum kit, just offstage.

My primary heartbeat is sky-high, which makes the beat of my second heart all the more noticeable, and even though I've lived with it since I was eight, it's unsettling. My palms turn slick against the hard plastic of the mic.

"Hey." Raoul's voice brings my attention to his face. The stage lights gleam on the black rims of his glasses. "You'll do great. Just keep your eyes on me. Here we go."

He adds a few extra flourishes to the intro, showing off his guitar skills, and I see the crowd start to perk up and take notice. As he starts to sing, he keeps smiling at me, his green eyes shining like he's having the time of his life.

His enthusiasm suffuses the very air, warms me right up, and steadies the trembling of my hands and knees. It's contagious, that smile of his. I can feel an answering smile spreading across my own face. Renewing my grip on the mic, I chime in right on cue. Somehow, the sound of my own voice is reassuring, too. My voice is *my* instrument, the one I've been polishing under the guidance of the Angel. Thanks to him, I'm more confident than ever about what I can do. I've got this.

Raoul gives me a wink and adds a sassy run on the guitar before he sings the next verse. When I join him on the chorus again, I relax even more, because the crowd is jiving and dancing with us, and I can *feel* their energy, just like he said. Our chemistry attracted them, and their response feeds us in a cycle that's nothing less than magical.

When we've finished "The Fighter," we move on to "Shallow." The crowd is singing along with us now, and the way I'm belting the notes would make Lady Gaga proud. It's actually *fun*. I'm singing in public, I'm enjoying myself, and it's all because I'm with Raoul. This is no gloomy, echoing stairwell with ghostly acoustics and a mysterious, masterful voice to guide me. This is hearty, healthy freedom in a room full of laughter and light.

Until Raoul's fingers slip, and he strikes a horrible, disjointed chord. He keeps playing, and the crowd shrugs it off, but when I glance over at him, he's no longer looking at me. His eyes are fixed on something across the room.

When I follow his gaze to the back of the crowd, I spot a tall, broad-shouldered man in a black hoodie, wearing a white mask that covers everything but his beautifully carved lips and his strong jaw. Menace radiates from him—a dark dominance that grips me even from this far away.

Terror blazes over my body like the shock of ice-cold water.

It's the man from the alley. The one who grabbed me. The one I bit and fucked. The one who knows what I am.

He's here.

But why does Raoul seem to recognize him, too?

The people around the stranger seem oblivious, dancing blithely to the music while he stands among them, a towering figure garbed in black. A lot of odd people pass through Nashville on a daily basis—the city is sometimes called "Nashvegas" or the Vegas of the South. Still, the fact that no one is weirded out by a masked visitor sends a chill writhing up my spine. It's almost like Raoul and I are the only ones who can see him.

Raoul glances over at me, and I look at him at the same moment, as if by instinct. He forces a bright grin, a wordless directive to keep singing, so I inhale deeply, using my diaphragm as the Angel taught me, and I pour all my fear and frenzy into the song. Raoul's voice twines with mine, harmonizing so smoothly I could almost imagine I'm singing with the Angel himself. Except the Angel's voice is wilder, fiercer, capable of the richest depths and the most delicate high notes, while Raoul's voice is a golden tenor with the faintest country twang.

We finish the song, and when the crowd clamors for another, I hesitate, my mind blank. Raoul looks uncertain, too. But just as our hesitation becomes awkward, a voice whispers right beside my ear...a voice I know all too well.

"'Nothing Breaks Like a Heart.'"

I whip around, but no one is there.

That was the Angel's voice. I'd bet my fangs on it.

Swallowing, I catch Andre's eye and say, "Should we do 'Nothing Breaks Like a Heart'?"

He nods, and Raoul exhales with relief, strumming the first chords.

My right knee presses Raoul's, the touch grounding me as I plunge into the wild darkness of the song. We keep it up-tempo, and he switches between echoing and harmonizing as I sing my best smoky impression of Miley Cyrus.

Somewhere along the way, I lose my fear of the audience. The only source of terror now is my secret, which the hooded stranger holds behind his silent mask. He's closer now. He glided nearer to the stage before I knew he was moving.

Raoul notices, too, and his voice comes out slightly breathless, a quaver here and there. But I look into the shadowed eyes of the mask, and I sing like I'm serenading the devil himself.

Maybe I am.

I can still feel the crowd—they're frenzied, carried away by the strange energy they sense coming from the two of us. But I feel something else—taut cords of power linking me and Raoul and the stranger in a triangle sharp as a knife, keen as desire. Everything else blurs into a soft watercolor, and the three of us glitter in high definition while the bass thumps and the guitar twangs. I could swear a third voice slithers in the background, between mine and Raoul's, but the stranger's lips are barely parted. It couldn't be him.

The song ends, and I'm left swaying on its edge like a woman on a clifftop, a breath away from jumping.

The Alouette erupts with cheers and applause. Raoul draws me to my feet. We bow, wave, collect our things, and pass the spotlight to another group. They jump right into a jazz-blues number while Raoul guides me past several enthusiastic people who apparently became hard-core fans of ours during our three-song set. One woman waves cash in Raoul's face until he gracefully accepts the tip, and another man won't stop asking if we have a website. I shrink behind Raoul while he suggests the man come see *Sidewinder* when it opens.

Then we're out in the cool evening air, and I can breathe again.

Grit crunches under our boots as we head down the sidewalk toward the parking lot. Neither Raoul nor I say a word, but he keeps glancing back over his shoulder. I risk a look backward once as well, but I don't see the masked man.

Back in the Alouette, I heard the Angel's whisper by my ear. At least…I think I did. Hard to tell, since I hear him in my head sometimes, clear as a bell. I can't help wondering if it's just a coincidence that the stranger showed up right before I heard the Angel…but the Angel is a spirit. A disembodied voice floating in a stairwell. He doesn't smell like a deep forest and carry exquisite blood in his veins and fuck people in alleys.

It doesn't fit. They are *not* the same.

Cautiously, I peer at Raoul, who clears his throat but says nothing.

Okay, so I guess we're not going to talk about the masked man and the fact that we've clearly both run into him before. Fine with me. It'll be one more secret piled up between us. Just as well. Secrets keep people apart, and I need to keep my distance from Raoul de Chagny. He's the director of the musical in which I'll be playing the lead during the showcase. If anyone related to *Sidewinder* saw us out together tonight, there are going to be plenty of rumors racing around the New Orpheum, and the last thing I want to do is feed the gossip mill. It's best that we remain distant friends.

We get into his car and ride back to the New Orpheum in

silence. Only when he pulls up to the curb at the entrance do I finally say, "Thank you for this. It was fun."

"It was." He gives me the ghost of his former smile. "I hope you didn't strain your voice."

"I'll be fine."

"And now you know you can perform for a crowd."

I don't point out that tomorrow night, the audience will be full of critics, that the stakes are entirely different, and that he won't be onstage with me, comforting me with the warm tones of his guitar and his voice. He did something nice for me tonight, and I'm grateful.

I climb down from the truck, and then impulsively, I step back up to say, "I'll be singing for *you* tomorrow."

Raoul's eyes light up again, and I grin at him before shutting the passenger door.

So much for keeping my distance.

As he drives away, my smile fades, because those words felt like a betrayal.

I enter the New Orpheum by the side door and cut through the dance school wing on my way to the residence area.

Back in my room, I drop my bag on the floor and sit limply on the bed, feeling utterly drained.

My weariness tonight isn't exactly physical. Being a vampire means that my body's cells—all except the blood cells—regenerate fast. I'm basically immune to disease, I heal quickly, and I have more strength, speed, and stamina than normal humans do. My vampiric nature is a huge advantage when I dance, and it will ensure that any strain to my vocal cords heals swiftly. But it doesn't keep me from feeling mentally exhausted, and while I need less sleep than most people, I still require at least a few hours to help my brain reset itself.

I tug off my boots and flop back on the bed, trying to banish the masked man from my mind. Instead, I focus on Raoul's lean, earnest face, his lovely green eyes, his smile.

"Raoul," I whisper.

"Simpering fool," hisses a voice.

I sit bolt upright, goose bumps breaking out on my skin.

After a long moment, I venture a whisper of my own. "Angel?"

"That boy is no true devotee of music." The Angel's voice seems to come from the very walls of my room. "He uses wires and electronics and tricks. He is pretty, yes, but ensnared with the fashions of modern performance. Do not let him lead you astray."

"Where have you been?" Angry tears spring to my eyes. "I waited for you that night, after my audition."

"One night." His voice dips low, a menacing purr. "You waited for *one night*, and when I could not meet you, you gave up on me—on *us*, Christine. You abandoned your teacher, abhorred my guidance. You achieved a little success, and now you believe you do not require any further instruction."

"That's not true," I gasp. "Well...maybe it's true that I gave up on you too quickly, but you didn't reach out to me. You're a ghost. You should be able to speak with me anytime. Just like this."

"A ghost," he repeats dryly. "Yes, to you, I'm nothing but a phantom. Your mysterious angel from whom you drink knowledge until you are glutted, and then you abandon me for someone like *him*."

"Raoul is a good person, and he's talented."

"Had I not taught you and guided you, you would never have had the courage to sing for him or anyone else."

Sighing, I tug my knees up to my chest and wrap my arms around them. "I'm grateful to you, of course. But I was angry when you didn't meet me. So many people have disappointed me throughout my life, but I thought I could trust you to always be there. When you weren't, it *hurt*. I thought you were disappointed in me, or that your job as my teacher was done so you left without saying goodbye. I didn't go back to look for you again because I was afraid of more disappointment. Can you understand that?"

"Can I understand the fear of rejection?" His voice is softer now and very near. "Yes, I know that pain."

I frown, tilting my head. "Where are you?"

Abruptly, his voice changes. It seems to come from my bedroom door, then it bounces nearer as if he's sitting at the foot of my bed. "I am here. With you. Always in your heart and in your mind."

The last three words are a whisper in my left ear, and I startle, clapping my hand over it.

"God, don't do that!"

"Ask a question, expect an answer."

I roll my eyes, but I'm too glad to hear his voice again to be angry for long. "I'm singing the lead in *Sidewinder* for the preview performance tomorrow night."

"I know this, as I know everything. I have come to give you another lesson."

"It's late. I can't sing here," I reply. "Do you want me to come to the stairwell?"

"The lesson is a simple one," he says. "Not so much instruction as direction. Tomorrow night, when you perform the role of Eugenie, you will sing it for me. No one else."

A chill travels up the back of my neck. When I told Raoul I

would sing the role for him, we were completely alone, not a soul along the street, no one in the plaza in front of the building. Only a ghost or a spirit could have overheard what I said.

Every time I begin to wonder if he's really a spirit, I'm faced with more proof of the fact that he *must* be. So why is there still a lingering doubt in the back of my mind?

He makes a rough sound of impatience, a harsh contrast to the usual beauty of his voice. "You will sing for *me*, not him. Trust me, I will be watching, and I will know the difference. Tomorrow night, you will reach down into your own chest, seize your soul, and drag it up through your throat. You will deliver it to me on the wings of your voice, and I will accept the sacrifice." His voice vibrates with deadly intensity. "Give me everything, Christine, *everything*, and perhaps then I will deign to be your teacher once more."

Breathing hard through the pounding of my heart, I hug my knees tighter to my chest. The dark possession in his tone thrills me right down to my bones, appeals to some primal, monstrous side of me. I feel my fangs slipping from their sheaths, even though I don't need blood. I manage to keep them from elongating fully, but they swell against my upper lip as I reply, "You're asking me to choose between you and Raoul."

"Yes."

"Why?"

"Because I demand your entire focus, your undivided attention. Only when you fully trust me can I transport you to the peak of your true potential. You can play frivolous songs for drunken crowds, or you can soar to the heights of real excellence."

"Some people do both," I venture.

"This is not a debate, Christine. You must choose. I will accept no compromise. Tomorrow, when you sing the final solo, I will know your decision. Will you belong to the delicate poet, with his dramatic libretto and his mediocre music, or will you belong to *me*?"

His voice fades on the last words, growing more distant, and in the silence that follows, I sense that he has left me again.

But he was there. I heard his voice, melodic and lovely, fragile and powerful, rich with the heat of desire and the pain of rejection. I can't deny it—he awakens a side of me that I keep concealed from everyone else. The passionate ambition I've been afraid to confess, the murderous rage I sometimes feel, the darkness my soul tends to inhabit.

Raoul is light and comfort, but the Angel is a dark, rich violence I can't help but adore. I didn't realize how much I missed him until I heard his exquisite voice again. If I could fuck a voice...

But ghosts don't have dicks.

Maybe angels do. Maybe I should ask him.

Stop it, Christine.

Still pondering our conversation, I prepare for bed. I feel a little odd changing my clothes, because even though I'm pretty sure the Angel left, what if he can see me?

And then I smile, because what if he can?

13

THE PHANTOM

I LEFT HER ALONE.

And then I returned, and I lingered.

Guilt is a foreign sensation to me, but I feel a touch of it as I stand on the other side of the mirror, watching Christine. It must be guilt, this vague unease with my actions. The urge to go elsewhere wars with my desire to stay as close to her as possible.

Now that I know what she is, it all makes sense. The graceful power of her limbs, her superhuman stamina when she dances, the faintly feral quality of her smile sometimes when she thinks no one is watching.

I never thought I would be obsessed with a blood drinker, a nightwalker, an abhartach. Especially not after Gatsby and his vampires defeated me in the church at Wicklow. Ever since that day, I've carried a resentful grudge against their kind.

But Christine dismantled my walls before I knew what she was, and now I am defenseless, laid bare and vulnerable. If she sank her claws into my chest, cracked my breastbone apart, and extracted my heart, I would welcome the invasion. If she plunged her fangs into my flesh again, I would instantly be transported to the farthest realms of bliss.

Even as I watch her, new strains of music unfold in my mind, wave upon wave of fully orchestrated sound. Stunning melodies, heavenly music, and yet none of it seems quite worthy of her.

After our tryst in the alley, I felt our connection had been sullied somehow…but now that I've adjusted my expectations, I realize that seeing the earthier, grittier, monstrous side of her has only deepened my obsession. It has given me something far more dangerous than love itself—it has given me hope. Because if she possesses secrets she must hide from the world, if she has a touch of the monster about her, perhaps she might come to understand me entirely. Perhaps one day, she could see me as I am and not be terrified.

That hope holds me captive as I stand in the dark corridor behind the mirror. It immobilizes me as Christine begins to remove her clothing. She sways her hips as she shimmies down the shorts. Pulls the flower-print tank top over her head slowly, almost theatrically. In her lacy bra and panties, she lifts both arms above her head and stretches, her beautiful body going taut, every lean muscle on display.

My breath catches as I realize she's not simply undressing—she's putting on a show for my benefit. The little devil has decided to tempt her Angel.

When she takes off her bra, I place one gloved hand on the mirror, concealing her chest from my sight. Or perhaps giving myself the illusion that I could touch her.

She climbs onto the bed, and my lungs tighten at the sway of her breasts. I've seen breasts in my forays through the human internet. They seem to pop up at the most inopportune moments. I've never felt anything but mild interest for them. But Christine is someone I know intimately. Her breasts seem designed to drive me to madness. Small yet plump and perfectly sized for my hands. Creamy skin, light brown nipples. I want one of those breasts in my mouth.

My hand curls into a fist against the mirror.

She leans over to the nightstand beside her bed and takes something from a drawer. Then she settles back on the pillows, arches her knees, and parts her legs.

The thing she's holding is small and pink, and it makes a soft buzzing sound as she runs it over the thin material of her panties. Christine's head tips back on the pillows, and her lips part, a faint moan issuing between them. She glides the toy over her underwear with expert strokes, slow circles. A wet spot forms quickly, slicking the delicate fabric to the shape of her sex.

I'm burning alive. Scorched from the inside, my whole body straining as I fight against the desire to touch myself. My cock is painfully swollen, hard as a rock, and my balls ache.

I didn't have much self-control in the alley. Nor can I hold back now, not for more than a moment or two. With shaking hands, I open my pants and take myself out, venting a silent groan as my fingers close around the burning shaft.

Christine is whimpering, lifting her hips off the bed. It's similar to the pelvic exercise I had her perform during one of our lessons...only this time, when she surges upward, she lets out a soft, urgent whine in the shape of a word: "Angel."

I grit my teeth in agony and press my fist harder against the mirror while my gloved hand rubs my cock. It doesn't feel nearly as good as the silken wetness of her pussy.

I could have her again. I've detached this mirror at the edges so it can be shifted aside—that's how I brought Christine back from the stairwell when she drank herself to sleep after her audition. I didn't want to carry her through the main hallways, so this corridor was the best option.

If I slid the mirror aside now, charged into her bedroom, and jerked the panties off her legs, I could bury myself to the hilt in the slippery heat between her thighs. It would feel infinitely better than this frantic rubbing. But once Christine realizes I'm not a ghost but a man with a raging lust for her, she might be frightened. And she would be still more disturbed once she realizes that we've fucked before. I can imagine her screaming, shrinking away from me. Running to Raoul for refuge.

Revealing myself now can only end in the destruction of the fragile connection I've crafted between us. I will show her the truth soon…perhaps tomorrow, after she triumphs onstage and she's flush with gratitude for my tutelage. The timing has to be right—

"Oh god, Angel!" moans Christine, and she pins both thighs together around the little toy, squirming wildly as she comes.

I open my mouth in a voiceless cry as I come, too, sprinkling the back side of the mirror with my release. A hoarse gasp bursts from my throat without my permission, and Christine lifts her flushed face with a cunning expression that tells me she heard the sound.

"Are you there?" she whispers.

I don't answer. I stroke myself once more, then put my cock away and fasten my pants while I watch her remove her sticky underwear and replace them with a fresh pair. She washes her hands, pulls on a loose T-shirt, and climbs into bed. The light switches off, and I'm left in darkness.

The loneliness crushes me like an avalanche. All I want is to lie beside her, hold her, feel her breathing while she sleeps. I want to pull her against my chest and sing my most beautiful melodies softly in her ear. I want to go where she goes, love what she loves, make my entire world revolve around her, if only she will be entirely devoted to me alone. If only she will save me from this wretched solitude. I cannot bear it much longer.

The walk back to my lair feels longer than ever, and when I reach it, I wave aside the drifting ghosts who advance eagerly to make their daily reports. Though I would never admit it aloud, their presence is slightly comforting. It keeps my quarters from feeling so terribly cold and hollow.

"I'm tired," I tell them. "Give me your reports tomorrow." I strip off my gloves and toss them aside, then pluck my phone from my pocket and check for new messages. There are none.

I shower for a long time, then fling myself naked into the sheets, where I writhe restlessly for a few hours. Was Christine able to fall asleep right away? If so, I envy her.

At last, I pick up my phone again and watch several videos of kittens yawning and mewing. I'm convinced they have some sort of magic to charm the unwary. There's no other explanation for the way I find myself smiling as I watch them. Their tiny, fluffy forms and huge eyes seem to unlatch something that has been locked tight inside my chest for a very long time.

I switch to my phone's contacts and scroll through the names of every pawn I possess within the New Orpheum—over a dozen now, each one ignorant of the others, each terrified to disobey me or speak of me lest I reveal their darkest secrets.

At the bottom of the list, under "Z," I saved a number that's connected to the debit card my summoner left me—a backup number to be used to confirm identity. I suspect it's his real number, a way to contact him.

The name on the debit card—Erik Lind—is a false one, of course. I've heard my summoner called both Ian Holcum and Lloyd-Henry Woodson, though he seems to prefer Lloyd. As a gancanagh-shifter hybrid with so many enemies, it makes sense that he would have several aliases. But with the bank account and the other scraps of information he left me, I've built up an entire online presence. For all intents and purposes, I *am* Erik Lind.

Erik is a decent name. Perhaps I should adopt it permanently. I can't very well introduce myself to Christine as Cernunnos, former god of death, now the phantom dwelling beneath the New Orpheum Theatre.

I toy with the idea of contacting my summoner. But a flicker of fear accompanies the impulse—the fear that the one who gave me this identity could take it away. Better to leave him to his own devices while I continue with my plans.

The idea of me, a god, fearing anyone is so repulsive to me that I seek out immediate distraction, scrolling up through my contacts again until I reach "R," for Raoul.

I begin typing a message to him. Simple, succinct. A test to see if he is as sleepless as I am.

Christine sang well tonight.

Almost immediately, he replies. Yes.

You sang well also. Why am I complimenting the bastard who wants to steal my beautiful protégé away from me?

Raoul responds with, Who are you?

A dull question. One you know I won't answer.

Fine, he types back. Why aren't you asleep?

I am thinking of everything and nothing.

He sends back a laughing face, to which I raise an eyebrow and respond, And why aren't you asleep?

A pause, and then he texts, Horny.

I've encountered the word. It means to be preoccupied with sexual desire or need. Can you not view some nude images of women or men and pleasure yourself?

Raoul sends another laughing face. Pleasure myself? You mean jerk off? What century are you from?

I send him a row of skulls.

He replies, Can I call you?

Surprise flutters through my stomach. After giving it careful thought, I conclude that a call won't pose any greater risk than texting.

Very well.

My phone buzzes a moment later, and when I answer, I can hear Raoul breathing quickly, as if he's nervous.

For two full minutes, neither of us speak. We simply exist in silence, linked by the sound of each other's breathing.

"I don't know why I asked if I could call you," he says at last.

"I'm not sure why I answered."

"Goddamn, your voice is beautiful." He sounds reluctant to admit it. He clears his throat and says more forcefully, "Maybe I called to tell you to back off. To leave Christine alone. You scared her tonight."

"What are you, her guard dog?" I ask dryly.

"Maybe."

"If you're the dog, I'm the master."

"Master..." He gives a ragged laugh. "You're a stalker. A bully."

"I am neither and more."

"What do you want from her?"

"Everything."

"Does Christine know who you are?"

"No one knows me completely."

"Yeah." Raoul's tone shifts, a note of sadness in his voice. "I feel that."

"What do *you* want from Christine?"

"Her talent, obviously, for the musical. And...I knew her in school, when we were kids. She protected me once. I think I've loved her since that day."

My jealousy revolts at the idea of a prior claim, but I stay silent, waiting for him to continue. The more weaknesses he reveals, the easier it will be to defeat him.

"I want her," he says quietly. "But I'm not sure she's the only one I want. God, I should *not* be saying this, but...I've thought about you for weeks. Ever since you and I..."

His voice trails off, but I know what he means. I felt the raw heat thrumming between us when I held him against the wall with my body. But I've made up my mind about who I want. It's Christine and no one else.

"Let me be clear—you and I are enemies. Rivals."

"Right." He releases another low, breathless laugh. "Then why does the very sound of your voice make me hard?"

"You're mentally unhinged," I suggest.

"Probably true. Go on. What else am I?"

"You're a talented poet. Your libretto is perfection. A little melodramatic for some people perhaps, but I happen to enjoy dramatic language. I could find nothing upon which to improve. Your skills as a composer, however, are lacking. And you do not possess the genius necessary to create truly remarkable orchestration. The bones of the musical are good, but not great. You have only come this far because of money and prestige, I would guess. Your family is wealthy, and they have influence in the right circles."

"All true." His voice sounds odd, slightly jerky, as if he's making some rapid, rhythmic movement. "Keep talking. Please."

I hesitate, listening to his huffing breaths. "Are you jerking off to my criticism?"

"Please keep talking to me."

I hesitate, trying to analyze the heat flooding my chest, the ripple of excitement in my stomach. My voice, my compliments, and my thoughtful critique have a profound effect on this man. I enjoy power, specifically power over *him*. It cannot hurt to indulge in this strange kind of dominance a little more.

"Despite Christine's talent, your musical will ultimately fail," I continue. "Unless you yield it to someone with greater genius than yourself. But I suspect your pride wouldn't allow you to hand over control to anyone else. You are proud, aren't you, Raoul? Proud yet insecure, because someone has been telling you lies about yourself for years, and you no longer know what to believe. Believe *me*. You sing well, you play well, you compose well, but your poetry—it's fucking godlike."

Raoul chokes out a cry, and I tighten my grip on the phone as my mind paints an image of him coming to the sound of my voice.

"Do you want to know my favorite line in the musical?" I ask quietly. "It's the phrase about 'humans plucking endlessly at the fragile threads of immortal patience.'"

He sobs out a gasp.

"I'm ending this call," I tell him. "And then you will send me a picture of the mess you made. Do you understand?"

"Yes, sir," he whispers.

I end the call and count to twenty before the photo appears. Raoul's bare thigh and a fold of his sheets, spattered with cum. A dark delight surges through me as I murmur, "Good boy."

Then I send him one final text.

> Tomorrow Christine will sing for me, not you. She will give her soul into my hands, and she will be mine.

14

CHRISTINE

After Raoul took me to the Alouette yesterday, I knew there would be gossip. But I didn't expect the palpable chill in the green room when I enter it Saturday evening, the night of the preview performance.

"What is she even doing back here?" someone murmurs half audibly, like they want me to hear.

"They probably wouldn't let her use Carlotta's dressing room," someone else murmurs, followed by a few tittering laughs.

I ignore them and head straight for Meg, who is stretching by the wall. She gives me a smile edged with caution or pity—I can't tell which.

"Big night for you," she says.

"Yeah. I'm kind of terrified."

"You'll do great." But she doesn't sound remotely convinced. And why should she? My only experience singing for a crowd was literally last night, and that ended weirdly to say the least.

"Haven't seen much of you lately," I say as I start stretching. My dance part is nowhere near as rigorous now that I'm playing Eugenie, but I might as well limber up. "Things going well with Gabriella?"

Meg smiles more genuinely at that. "She's so great. Thanks for giving me a little shove in the right direction."

"Hey, no problem."

"And you..." She hesitates, then whispers, "You and Raoul? I heard you sang together at the Alouette last night. Are you two a thing?"

"No!" I exclaim, probably too loudly, but I know people are listening, and I want them to pass my words along the gossip chain. "Raoul and I knew each other as kids, in school. We went to the Alouette to sing together once, as friends, for old times' sake. I'm not into him like that."

At least I'm *trying* not to be, because it could never work between a sunshine sweetheart like him and *me*, a literal woman of the night by necessity. I can handle sunlight for an hour or two, as long as it's not too intense, but it's uncomfortable for me, and I can't endure it any longer than that without breaking out in horrendous blisters. After that comes the nausea, the bloodthirst, the loss of speech, the convulsions. It's an allergy, plain and simple. Same thing happens if I don't drink blood often enough, except in that scenario, the discomfort turns into an obsessive feeding frenzy. If I don't get blood, it progresses to weakness, then seizures, then death.

"You might not be into Raoul, but I think he's into you," Meg says under her breath, lifting one leg straight up and holding it steady.

"It's too complicated."

"Tell me about it. I mean, he's a director, Christine. It could get really messy, especially because Carlotta has a thing for him."

"I've noticed," I say dryly. "She practically salivates for his attention whenever we rehearse."

"Just be careful, okay? She has a lot of influence, and not just online." Meg casts a glance aside, and I follow her gaze. Four dancers are clustered together, watching us, and one of them is filming Meg and me. All four of them are Carlotta toadies, sycophants who pander to her whenever they have a chance. They all believe they can use her to make more connections in the music or theater industries, or both. She probably asked them to spy on me.

"Cut it out!" Meg tells them.

The girl who's filming shrugs, but she doesn't stop.

A scarlet haze suffuses my vision, and I march toward her, heedless of the warning in Meg's voice as she calls my name.

"You wanna pretend we're in high school, drama whore?" I snatch the phone out of her hand. "Fine. I'll bite." I whirl away, tapping her phone screen to delete the video, all while ignoring her shrill curses. "Here." I toss the phone back to her.

"Bitch," she says. "Carlotta's gonna get your ass fired when she comes back. Wait and see."

I give her the middle finger and stalk out of the green room. When I encounter Marj backstage, I impulsively ask if I can use Carlotta's dressing room tonight, and to my surprise, she agrees. But my temper doesn't abate—I fume the entire time I'm getting my hair and makeup done and putting my costume on.

The anger isn't just about Carlotta and her little toadies. It's about last night—how the masked stranger showed up when Raoul and I were having such a good time together. It's about the way neither Raoul nor I talked about him on the way home. It's about the Angel's visit and the fact that I did a striptease and a masturbation show just in case he was watching. It's about the ultimatum he gave me: him or Raoul. I have to choose which one of them to sing for, he said. And supposedly, he will know which of them I chose.

Last night, I was all horny and worked up, but I've been stewing about his ultimatum all day. Now I'm just pissed. I hate being boxed into corners and forced to make choices. Feels like what my parents used to do—hem me in with arguments and repercussions until I was practically forced to make the decision *they* wanted, which meant it wasn't really my decision at all.

"All done!" The hair stylist stands back to admire her work.

Carlotta's dressing room reeks of her perfume. Gives me a headache, but I'm not leaving until I'm called. I have every right to be in here tonight. For the first and possibly the only time in my life, I'm the leading lady.

"Can I have a minute alone?" I ask.

"Sure thing! I got plenty to do." The stylist folds up her kit. "I'll have Petra come get you when it's time."

"Thanks."

When she leaves, I stare at myself in the mirror. I don't look like Christine Daaé anymore. I'm Eugenie, a sexy intergalactic bounty hunter assigned to chase down a rogue space cowboy. In just moments, I'll be stepping onstage, and I'll have to act the part. I'll have to hit all my marks, remember the cues and the lyrics, sing everything as perfectly as I can, inject emotion into the spoken lines, and give plenty of *face* to the audience.

Sure, I've been rehearsing for weeks, but as a chorus girl, not the lead. I won't lie, I've practiced Carlotta's lines in private, and I've watched her closely, imagining what I would do differently if given the chance. But I didn't really expect my chance to come so soon, if ever.

Someone raps at the door, and I call "Come in" automatically even though I'd rather say "Go away."

In the mirror, I see Raoul enter. He's carrying a huge bouquet of flowers.

I smile in spite of myself. "Aren't you supposed to give me those afterward?"

"Consider them a sign of my confidence in my lovely Eugenie." He sets the vase on the right side of the dressing table, then locks eyes with my reflection in the mirror. "Are you all right?"

"I don't know, to be honest."

"You'll do a wonderful job. And remember, it's a preview performance. Everyone expects a rough patch or two."

"Do they?"

"I don't know." He shrugs and breaks into a nervous laugh. "I'm new to this, too."

"Raoul, I'm sorry." I turn around on the stool. "I was so deep in my own head, I forgot what a big night this is for you. Your musical, being performed for the first time."

"It's wild, for sure."

"It's beautiful, all of it."

"You really think so?" Anxiety etches lines between his brows. "Someone said a few things to me last night that made me wonder if it actually sucks. Maybe I should pull the plug on the whole show."

"It's *good*, Raoul." I rise and place both hands on his chest. His heartbeat thumps faster beneath the layers of suit coat and crisp white shirt. I press in closer, listening to that strong, healthy heartbeat that carries the promise of so much rich, red blood...

"Christine?" Raoul frowns deeper. "Your eyes..."

Oh shit. When I feel like feeding, sometimes my eyes go milky white in the middle. It's a really strange effect—one I can usually control right up until the moment I bite. But with my nerves so taut and my mind on the show, my control slipped. I turn away from him and blink. "Um…new contacts."

"You don't wear contacts."

"How do you know?" I walk away from him. "Maybe I do."

After a beat, he says quietly, "So this is going to be another thing we don't talk about."

My heart kicks into a faster rhythm. "I don't know what you mean."

"You know exactly what I mean."

I whirl around, my hands clenched. "You want to do this *now*, Raoul? Right before curtain?"

"No, but I…" He pokes his glasses up on his nose. "You seem off, and it's not just nerves. You're angry and maybe scared. Christine, I'm just going to come out and ask… Is someone stalking you?"

I open my mouth to deny it outright, but I find myself saying, "Not exactly."

Raoul makes an exasperated sound. "What does that mean?"

"I'm being…" I clear my throat and wince as I say it aloud for the first time. "I'm being haunted."

"Haunted?" Raoul crooks an eyebrow. "Look, I've heard the rumors from the cast and crew, but that's all just good theater fun. There's really nothing—"

"But there *is*. I can't speak to what the others have heard and seen, but there's one ghost in this theater who is absolutely real. My father sent him. I call him the Angel. He's the one who's been teaching me, inspiring me. He gave me the confidence to audition."

Raoul blinks at me.

"I know how it sounds…god!" I press a fist to my forehead. "It sounds like I've lost my mind. But I promise I haven't. Raoul, I've heard him. His voice is like nothing I've ever experienced—it's beautiful, musical—"

"Enchanting?"

"Yes. Wait…what?"

He's staring at me with growing horror in his eyes. "Christine, where have you encountered this angel?"

"I've heard him in the back stairway, and…in my room."

"Fuck." He swipes a trembling hand over his mouth and jaw. "Christine, that's not a ghost or an angel. He's a living human with a physical body. I know, because I've seen him, felt him. I've heard his voice, too. And you're right—he's obsessed with you. He warned me to stay away, and I—god, I should have called the police immediately, but I thought I could handle him myself. He didn't seem like a threat, just a really intense fan of yours. I should have known better."

"He's not human," I protest, my heart racing faster. "The way he speaks—it's like his voice comes from everywhere and nowhere. He sings like an angel from heaven—like a literal god. He knows things he couldn't possibly know."

"Trust me, he's corporeal. He was the one in the mask at Alouette last night."

"No." I shake my head wildly, dread carving a hole in my stomach. "No, that couldn't have been him. That was someone different."

He's confirming the suspicion I discarded—that our masked listener, the stranger I mauled in the alley, and the Angel my father sent me are all the same person.

Not my Angel, oh god, not my Angel. Limply, I drop onto a small bench by the wall, piecing together the fragments.

Raoul steps closer. "Christine, if he's stalking you, we need to do something. Should I call off the performance?"

"No!" My voice shrills with panic. "You've got this all wrong, okay? We don't have time to sort it out now. There's plenty of security in the theater, so everything will be fine. We'll talk after the play and decide what to do."

"We'll talk," he agrees. "But either way, I'll be calling the cops. It was stupid of me to let this go on when I knew he was obsessed with you. I let him get in my head."

His cheeks are scarlet, and he won't look me in the eyes. That scares me almost as much as the idea that my Angel and the masked stranger are the same person...and that the Angel has a physical body that is very much male—a body I already fucked, god help me.

Petra pokes her head in at that moment. "Christine, we're ready for you. And Mr. de Chagny, shouldn't you be in your box?"

"I should." Raoul clears his throat and pushes the bridge of his glasses, even though they're already sitting perfectly in place astride his nose.

From the glance Petra gives both of us, I'm sure she's going to tell everyone she saw me and Raoul together in the dressing room, all flushed and agitated. Maybe she even overheard something about a stalker. Just my luck.

But I can't worry about any of that now. Somehow, I have to scrape together my shredded composure, and I have to go out onstage and sing. I have to star in Raoul's musical without letting any of the stress seep through into my performance.

As I walk past Raoul, he says in an undertone, "You're safe, Christine. I swear I won't let anyone hurt you."

I don't answer. When we leave the dressing room, he heads one way toward the stairs and his box, while Petra and I head in the opposite direction.

I follow Petra along the hallway, past stacked chairs, racks of costumes, and pieces of scenery. We pass several empty, darkened rooms, and as I walk, I swear I hear a whisper from the shadows. "Sing for me."

What if the being who worships my talent, gave me guidance, sang duets with me, and bolstered my confidence truly does have physical form? Isn't that what I've been secretly wishing for—that the sexy male voice I love so much could be housed in an equally sexy body? Or even a regular body...just something I could *touch*. Didn't I run away from the Angel that one night because I felt myself falling for a disembodied voice? And wouldn't it change things if the voice belonged to someone corporeal?

And yet...why would he hide? Why lurk in shadows and spy on me? Why let me believe he was a spirit sent from my father? Why did he pull me into the alley that night? He's a creep, a stalker...a terrible, terrible person.

But the things he said to me were beyond beautiful. As if he could see me more clearly than anyone else ever has.

You amaze me...you inspire me. This gift you possess—it cries out to be shared with the world. The only thing that matters is the power you possess to stir a soul, to move emotions, to alter the course of a heart. Music can do that. You can do that. I know you can, because you've done it for me. I am resurrected every time I hear you sing.

Clearly, he worships my voice. And what right do I have to

judge him for a little light stalking when I regularly flirt with men, drug them, and drink their blood while they're unconscious?

Mechanically, I take a bottle of water from one of the crew and drink a few swallows. With each gulp, I pretend I'm washing all those worries away, drowning them inside myself. I count the beats of the music, mark the rise of the curtain, watch the chorus begin their number. And then, on my cue, I walk onstage.

At first, the stage lights are so bright and the theater is so dark that it's easy to pretend the audience isn't there. It feels like another rehearsal, one without Marj telling us to stop and correct something every few minutes. In fact, I'm so immersed in my role that I startle the first time the audience laughs. I doubt anyone noticed my reaction, and I move smoothly to my next mark. When I complete my first solo, the applause is enthusiastic, and I sense the tide of energy flowing from that dark sea of people onto the stage. It fuels me through act two.

I make a couple tiny flubs, but otherwise the scenes go smoothly. Rune plays opposite me, and though he's a bit of an airhead, he's an easy partner to work with. Luckily, he seems to like me better than Carlotta—there's an alertness to his performance that hasn't been there during rehearsals.

I've done well, yes, but I haven't excelled. I haven't triumphed. I haven't reached the heights the Angel spoke of. I'm holding back.

During intermission, I change costumes and submit to being powdered and fluffed. Then, with a muttered excuse, I hurry to a little-used bathroom at the end of a backstage passage, behind several large pieces of scenery that Mr. Richards scored at a discount from some local playhouse that went out of business.

The bathroom I'm hiding in hasn't been remodeled yet. It has a 1950s look to it—a glossy mint-green sink and mustard-yellow tiles. There's a single bulb glowing half-heartedly overhead, flickering occasionally as if it's trying to make up its mind whether to go out. Some of the bathroom stalls have been dismantled along with part of one wall, and there's a random stall door and several large boards propped against the framing at strange angles. The way they're leaning, with the dark gaps between them, it's hard to tell where the back wall of the bathroom actually is.

The place is creepy and probably unsafe. No one comes in here, which is why I chose this spot. Intermission isn't over yet, and I don't appear in the first scene of the third act, so I have a whole fifteen minutes before anyone needs me.

I stare into the spotty mirror over the sink, and I speak the Angel's words aloud. "You amaze me…you inspire me. I am resurrected every time I hear you sing."

Halfway through, he starts speaking the words with me. Aloud.

His lovely voice mingles with mine, and a golden thrill passes over my entire body at the sound. I close my eyes, letting him take over, the words fading on my tongue.

"Tonight, you must give me your soul, Christine."

I still can't pinpoint his voice, can't decide if it's coming from the mirror, the ceiling, or one of the bathroom stalls. It sounds as if he's standing right next to me. I could swear I feel a stirring in the air, like a physical presence, but I see nothing.

"Where are you?" I say desperately. "I know you aren't a ghost or an angel. You've been tricking me. Telling me to trust you while you kept secrets from me and treated me like a delusional fool."

"You are neither delusional nor a fool," he replies. "I never claimed the identity you gave me. I simply allowed you to continue believing what you needed to believe so we could work together. And I'm not the only one who has been keeping secrets, Christine."

He pronounces my name with his usual crisp, reverent diction, as if it's the loveliest word in the world. But there's an edge to his tone, a hint of betrayal.

He knows what I am. Of course he does, because I bit him. That miraculous, delicious, impossibly satisfying blood was *his*.

That thick, hard cock was his.

Speechless with panic, I stare at my own face in the mirror.

"You tore me open," he says softly. "It was my pleasure to bleed for you, to give you everything you needed. I accept you as you are."

A shudder courses through me. I want to cry over those words. I've waited so long for someone to say them and mean it.

"You have done well tonight," the Angel continues in the same gentle tone, tinged with bitterness. "But you are not singing to the best of your ability. If you continue like this, your precious Raoul will have only tepid interest in his musical, and none of these critics will understand how brilliant you truly are. Or you can open your mind, unleash your soul, and sing for me, your Angel, with all the force and beauty you possess. If you do that…if you give yourself wholly to me, I will answer all your questions afterward."

"I want to know how you cast your voice in so many places," I say. "Are you a ventriloquist? Were you watching me in my room? How did you hear what I said to Raoul when I got out of his truck? Why have you stayed in the shadows instead of introducing yourself like a normal person?"

"I will tell you everything, I promise. But first you must yield, Christine." His voice shakes ever so slightly this time, a betrayal of the intense emotion he's trying to conceal. "You must *want* this. Complete honesty between us. No masks or walls or trickery. I want to know you in every possible way. You have to want me just as fiercely."

"And if I do this...after it's over...where should I go to meet you?"

"Return to your room. I'll come to you there."

Someone hammers on the bathroom door. "Christine? Are you in there?" Raoul's voice.

The Angel makes a disgruntled sound. "He follows you everywhere like a lovesick puppy."

"He's worried about me," I answer.

"Christine?" Raoul's voice goes up an octave. "Who's in there with you? I'm coming in!" He bursts through the door, flushed and frantic, with his tie askew. "I've been looking for you. I wanted to congratulate you on the first two acts. Christine, was he in here?"

"No one is here, Raoul." I push past him. "I need my nose powdered again before I go on. You should get back to your box."

He catches my wrist like he did on the day of auditions, when he persuaded me to stay. "Christine. Please don't lie to me."

"I'm not lying." I pull my arm free. "I can't talk now, but...later."

He nods, but there's tragedy in his green eyes. I can't bear it—I can't.

I seize him by the lapels of his suit coat, rise up on my toes, and kiss him.

His mouth is soft, his breath sweet. A heady, tingling sensation suffuses my body as I lean in, forgetting that I intended this to be a quick, comforting kiss. It's so much more than that. Raoul's taste fills my mouth, his tongue sliding over mine. With all my soul, I want to crush him closer, kiss him deeply, recklessly, drink up his air and swallow his blood. His mouth tastes so fucking good…

"Miss Daaé!" Marjorie's clipped tone cuts through my daze. "Makeup!" she calls sharply. "We need makeup over here! Raoul, go back to your box, for god's sake."

Sheepishly, Raoul obeys, with a final glance at me. He looks much less tragic now, and I smile as the stylist tries to correct my lipstick.

I don't know who I am anymore. I don't understand why I crave both of these men so violently. I don't know what I'm doing.

All I know is that my parents would be both very proud of me and very displeased with me tonight. And for once, I truly don't give a damn either way.

When I walk out onstage again, I am something altogether new.

15

THE PHANTOM

Christine sings for me like a woman possessed.

I lean forward in my seat, deep in the curtained shadows of Box Five. My heart is pounding, my eyes streaming tears of the loveliest pain.

This is the Christine I heard in the stairwell—the Christine I knew she could be. She has done exactly what I begged her to do—dragged her soul out through her throat and sacrificed it to me.

She is still confused about what she wants and needs. I know because I stood in the shadows and watched her kiss the young poet. I was angry, but not in the way I thought I would be. I thought I would feel madly jealous over her, but instead, I was strangely jealous of them both. I wanted the kiss to end, and yet I wanted to watch it happen over and over again. For one glorious moment, I pictured myself between them, devouring first Christine's lips and then Raoul's mouth while their hands glided over my body.

Then my anger returned, along with the determination that I must separate the two of them, at least for a while. I must have Christine all to myself without the distraction of the green-eyed poet.

My plan will unfold after the curtain falls. Until then, all jealousy is driven from my mind as I sit in Box Five, weeping silent tears of bliss while Christine sings. Raoul's musical does not end with a chorus number but with a climactic solo, and she is singing it as if the world is ending and no music will ever be performed again.

The orchestra can sense her energy—they are playing better than they have all night, but I can imagine an ideal version of the music, a more worthy orchestration. Vibrant strains of searing melody from the strings, heart-stopping percussion, glorious brass softly swelling behind Christine's voice. I can hear it all in my head, not as Raoul wrote it, but as I would.

My hands lift when she nears the peak of the song as if I'm conducting the piece, eliciting each pure, inhuman, mercilessly beautiful note. Christine turns her face toward Box Five, toward me, and I know the entire third act has all been for me. She is truly, torturously mine.

Her voice drifts away on the final note of the song, and for one scintillating second, the entire theater is dead silent.

Then, a hurricane of applause.

They leap to their feet as one, all of them. Every critic, every guest. A standing ovation for the young woman who stands before them, flushed and triumphant.

I am breathless, motionless, wrung out and bled dry, but I find enough strength to lend my applause.

Christine moves to retreat when the curtain descends. But as it sinks slowly down, she hesitates, sways, and falls headlong.

Her costar catches her. I'd thought him rather useless, but apparently he has the reflexes of an athlete as well as the body of one. The crowd utters a unified exclamation of shock as he carries her offstage while the curtain descends. There's a scuffle in one of the boxes to the left of mine where Raoul sits. No doubt he's scrambling to get out, planning to hurry backstage and be there the second she awakens.

"Agnes." I speak the name low, but with a resonant power behind it that will carry for miles, summoning the ghost from wherever she may be.

She appears within seconds. "My lord?"

"Go backstage. Find out if Christine is all right."

She whisks away and returns in a moment. "She fainted, my lord. She's coming around now."

"Good. Tell the others we're expecting a guest in the lair tonight. I want candles—lots of candles along the mirror passage, leading all the way down to my chamber. And we'll need music. Romantic music, not that annoying business you put on the other night."

"That was disco," she says haughtily. "And you liked it."

"I did not. Off with you."

I stay long enough to see Christine come out with the rest of the cast for the final bow, supported by her costar and one of the dancers. She looks pale, but her smile is triumphant.

Reassured, I rise from my seat and leave the box, determined to exit the theater before the audience does. Since these guests are here by special invitation, they'll be headed to one of the ballrooms for hors d'oeuvres and cocktails. Since she fainted, Christine will have an excuse to skip the reception and go to her room to rest.

I pass two people on my way to the secret corridor in the residence wing. One is a security guard in a corner stairway of the theater. The other is Mrs. Giry. Both of them are my pawns and were told to expect me and ignore my presence. When I pass, I unfurl mist and shadows around my body to enforce the idea of a mystical phantom. I'm fairly certain the security guard pisses himself, and Mrs. Giry shrinks against the wall, clutching the pendant she wears.

I slip through the entrance to the hidden passage and hurry along it until I reach Christine's room. I wait until she appears, darting hastily through the door and shutting it behind her.

She's back in her usual clothes—leggings, a tank top, ballet flats. I notice immediately that the bra is absent tonight.

"Angel?" she whispers.

"Brava, bellissima," I croon, casting my voice into the center of the room. "You sang yourself into a dead faint."

"That was unexpected," she admits. "I'm not used to my body failing me, ever."

"And where is your faithful dog, your precious Raoul?"

"I wish you would stop saying his name in that spiteful way. He's at the reception, enjoying some well-earned praise, I hope. He produced something quite beautiful."

"Beautiful lyrics, yes. Imperfect orchestration."

Christine plants her hands on her hips. "Are you the one who told him he wasn't any good?"

"I never said that," I counter. "I simply pointed out where his strengths and weaknesses lie. Is it my fault if no one has ever told him the truth?"

"Speaking of telling the truth, you promised me answers. I want to see you. Now."

After the glory of this night, simply pushing aside the mirror would be too prosaic. I can't resist a little theatricality, so I let mist unfurl from my palms, filling the hallway and creeping around the edges of the mirror into her room.

I lift my hand, and the ghosts waiting along the passage each illuminate the candles they carry.

Christine advances cautiously and touches her fingertips to the mirror.

"You can see me." Her tone is laced with accusation. "You've been watching me."

I could explain that I was not the one who installed the mirror, but instead of making excuses, I simply admit the truth. "Yes, I have watched you." I curl my fingers around the edge of the mirror and slide it aside, leaving a gap large enough for her to come through.

When I ordered an expensive, three-piece designer suit for tonight, I did not suspect I would be wearing it to meet Christine for the first time. I stand in the swirling mist, my heart thundering more ferociously than I thought it would, fighting the urge to reach up and smooth my hair as Christine steps through the opening.

She turns to face me.

And I find myself wishing for one power I do not possess—the ability to read a woman's mind.

16

CHRISTINE

There he is. The phantom, the Angel, not just in my head but right in front of me, close enough to touch, surrounded by swirling mist and floating candles. A white mask conceals his face, but I can see his eyes clearly. They're a light honey color, practically golden. He's breathing hard, lips tight, a muscle flexing along the hard line of his jaw.

He's nervous.

I almost laugh. And I do smile, a wondering kind of smile, because he's *real*. He is both the masked stranger and the ghost with the beautiful voice. And judging by the candles bobbing in midair and the mist curling around his feet, he is definitely a supernatural being of some kind. Not a vampire, or he would have bitten me back. That's a relief. The only other vampires I'm familiar with are the Progeny, my parents' cult, and I couldn't handle being around any of them.

"What are you?" I ask.

"We can't talk here," he replies. "Come with me."

When he heads down the passage, I hesitate, partly out of

caution and partly because I'm still trying to wrap my head around the fact that this secret corridor exists.

He notices my hesitation and turns back. "I did not create this place, and I've only used it to watch over you." He extends his hand, sheathed in a black glove. "Come, Christine."

Slightly reassured, I venture forward and slip my fingers in his. Why does he wear a mask and gloves? Does he have a facial difference? Scars? Surely he must know that wouldn't matter to me. As curious as I am about his face, I'm more interested in his powers… and his intentions. Does he want to fuck me again? I'd be lying if I said I hadn't thought about it. I'm not scared in the least because I overcame him physically last time, and I'm sure I could do it again.

Unless he *allowed* me to overpower him that night. He could be hiding secret reserves of strength.

"Why did you grab me that night in the alley?" I ask. "Were you going to hurt me?"

His head whips around, and he glares at me through the eyeholes of the mask. "Never. I was jealous, and I simply thought I would keep you there for a short while. Away from *him*. Truthfully, I acted on impulse, without a plan. Since then, I have striven to calculate each move I make."

"Calculation is all well and good," I reply. "But there's something to be said for impulsiveness, too."

He stares at me, and when I give him a little smile, he clears his throat and forges ahead. More candles float above us, near the ceiling, lighting our way. Even when we emerge from the narrow passage into an empty part of the building, the candles mark our path, clusters and rows of them, from pale, narrow tapers to fat, creamy columns dripping wax onto the floor. The mist precedes us, too, shrouding our steps and flowing up the walls like the white froth of ocean waves.

Down he leads me, through doors I've never opened, along steps I've never seen, to lower levels that haven't been used in decades. He flings open a pair of metal doors, and their raucous groan gives way to distant strains of music. I gasp, still clinging to his hand, gazing at the wide space before us.

Between broad stretches of gray concrete, there's a glimmering black canal with a motionless water wheel at the end close to us. I'm not sure how far the canal goes, but I suspect it must empty into the Cumberland River or an underground offshoot thereof.

Banks of candles light the way, softening the effect of the ancient gears and machinery I glimpse in the corners of this subterranean lair. We're coming into a living area of sorts, set apart from the rest of the industrial space by wooden screens and partitions draped with luxurious silk hangings. There's a central space with a record player, a piano, a cello, and a range of other instruments, several low bookshelves stuffed with books, two worn leather chairs cloaked in blankets, an old-fashioned steamer trunk, and an antique coffee table cluttered with sheet music. Off in the corner stands a desk with a laptop on it. To my right is a closed door decorated with swirling vines that he must have painted himself, and beyond the living area lies a raised platform with a gigantic bed on it, half-hidden by a luxurious abundance of black velvet curtains.

This living space was curated by someone with old-fashioned tastes who prizes the patina of age and enjoys all things luxurious and comfortable. He likes textures and patterns, from the plush rugs layered across the floor to the silky shawls and soft woolen blankets draped over the screens and the furniture. The microwave, the small refrigerator near the desk, and the laptop seem to be the only concessions to modern convenience. Even the lamps are old-fashioned, if pricey. I spot a banker's desk lamp with a green glass shade and three Tiffany lamps that look old enough to be genuine.

"This is your home?" I glance from the living area to the cold black water of the canal.

"This is where I live."

"Alone?"

His lips tighten. After a moment he says, "I have the ghosts."

"The ghosts?"

With a sigh, he lifts his hand, and suddenly the entire vast space is filled with ghostly figures, each holding one of the candles. The spirits seem to be from every conceivable time period, and some of them bear grotesque death wounds.

I claw at the Angel's arm, pulling myself tighter against his side and whispering hoarsely, "What the hell?"

"Thank you for your loyal service," he says to the ghosts with another wave of his hand. "You may leave us for tonight."

The ghosts set their candles down and disappear. A shuddering breath of wind passes through the room at their departure. The Angel sends a few tendrils of mist to douse most of the candles, leaving a few of them alight near his living space.

I thought I had seen plenty of strange and supernatural things, but *that* was deeply unsettling. I'm glued to the Angel's side, gripping his arm like it's my tether to existence.

"You're safe," he says. "They know how important you are to me. They would never hurt you."

My breathing slows a little. Guilt etches at my ribs because Raoul promised me the same thing tonight, sweet man that he is, yet I left him alone with unanswered questions and came down here with the stalker he fears is a threat to me.

It's a mess, to be sure. And the only way to untangle it is to persuade the Angel to confess everything.

I relax my grip on his arm to something more like a caress. "Now will you tell me who you are?"

"I should tell you who I *was*, but I'm not sure you're ready to know that. I could play for you first while you recover from seeing the ghosts. And perhaps you would like something hot to drink."

"Or something *strong* to drink," I mutter.

"I'm rather fond of rum."

"That'll do it."

While I sink into one of the leather chairs, he fetches me a glass of rum, the honeyed kind that goes down easily. I sip it slowly as he seats himself at the piano with a flourish and begins to play Piano Concerto No. 2 in G minor, Op. 22 by Camille Saint-Saëns. He flies through it with the practiced ease of a virtuoso, with the violent passion of an obsessed muse.

Even though I was forced to study some classical music, it has never been my preferred genre. But when he plays, it's compulsively addictive. I have to listen, and the longer I listen, the more I crave.

I sense the change when he leaves Saint-Saëns behind and forges into some new place, something wild and uncharted and raw. I'm convinced he's creating the piece on the spot, birthing it straight from his mind through his fingers, and it's more ferociously beautiful than anything I've ever heard. I'm being laid bare, my beating heart exposed to the music, and he's plucking my heartstrings with every haunting interlude, pumping his artistic frenzy straight into my veins with every roaring crescendo.

I have never heard anyone play like this, not even when I spied on my father's clients, not even when I idly browsed music videos online. Those performances were technically great, but this one isn't just flawless—it's for *me*. I gave him my soul tonight, and he's giving me his in return. He's tearing his own consciousness open, transporting me to blissful heaven, crashing with me into the darkness of hell.

By the time he's finished, I'm transfixed, my pulse racing and my drink forgotten.

He swings around on the piano bench and faces me.

For one tense, electrifying moment, my eyes lock with his. Then I grip the arms of the chair and launch myself out of it toward him.

His arms clasp tight around me as I collide with his chest. I kiss him brutally, desperately, hungry for his pain and mine. My tongue lashes into his mouth, and he opens wide, letting me in. His hand clamps around the back of my head, forcing a harder kiss, like he can't get enough, like he's as desperate to be inside me as I am to be part of him.

I don't care what he is or who he was. My hands claw at his shoulders, raking him closer, and I'm hungry, I'm starving, not for blood or sex, but for *everything*, every morsel of the creature who could produce that music.

We tumble off the piano bench and crash to the floor, bruises and pain. He rolls me onto my back, kisses me with a degenerate fervor that makes me want to scream *yes*, but I can't spare any breath. I shove his jacket off his shoulders; he flings it aside.

I don't like the mask. It's getting in the way, and I want to see all of him.

I reach for it, tuck my claws beneath the edge, pry it up just a little—

He freezes, his hands locked around my wrists, keeping me from moving the mask any farther. His mouth is bruised and bleeding. I slide my tongue over my teeth and realize my fangs emerged without me realizing it.

"Do not touch the mask," he growls.

"I'm sorry," I whisper. "I thought we could kiss better without it."

"No."

"Okay."

The magic is broken, the madness halted for now. When he releases me, I get up, putting distance between us.

We stand there, tense and panting like two animals, each waiting for the other to pounce, uncertain if the result will be a mating frenzy or a fight to the death.

"You promised you would answer my questions," I say at last. "About the voice thing and your other tricks."

"I can throw my voice." His words seem to come from behind me, though he's standing in exactly the same spot. "I can also mimic the voices of others reasonably well. I can wield the mists and shadows of the Afterworld, and I can command the spirits of the dead, those who have not yet found rest. In a previous existence, I could do far more. I could take other forms, grow entire forests in a single night, cloak the sun in darkness, and raise great armies of shadow beasts. I could even bring the dead to life. I was the king of all phantoms, the seducer of Fate herself, herald of destruction. I was Cernunnos, the god of death."

He says it calmly, almost casually. My brain short-circuits when he says "bring the dead to life," and I have to hold in a hysterical laugh because if I laugh, I think I might also start to scream.

"God of death?" I say faintly. "That's why you taste so good. It's like drinking pure liquid power."

"You can taste me again," he offers, a hint of eagerness in his gaze.

"You'll tell me all that, but you won't let me take off your mask?"

"It's one thing to know what I am, quite another to see it. The part I conceal is the side of me I can't control." He seats himself backward on the piano bench. "Oddly enough, it was a vampire who locked away the majority of my power. She has the abilities of a leannán sídhe—a voice so dominant I can still hear its echoes in my head." He looks down at his hands.

"Was she one of the Progeny?" I ask.

"I don't know what that is."

"It's a vampire cult, led by a first-generation vampire named Wolfsheim. My parents were absurdly loyal to him and his philosophy. They died fighting his battles, and they left their money and our family home to the Progeny cult. I got nothing. If I'd become part of the cult myself and followed their rules, I could have kept living there, but I don't play well with other vampires."

I don't tell him why I hate the Progeny so deeply. That agony goes back too far, and the loss is still too painful.

I settle into the chair again. "How did you end up here?"

He explains more of his origins to me, along with the fact that his memories of the past are blurred in places. I confess a few things about my parents and the Progeny, but I don't venture too close to my worst memory. I'm not ready to talk about that. And I sense he's holding a few things back as well. Of course he is. He's a literal god.

I believe him, I do. His story explains so much about him that was mystifying to me. But at the same time, he's so personable right now, and this conversation feels so intimate. It's hard to grasp the fact that I'm speaking with an actual deity—or more correctly, one of the powerful supernatural beings known as the Tuatha Dé Danann.

I think I need time to process all of it, to really let it sink in. As much as part of me would like to stay and explore other intimate things with him, it's probably wiser for us both to take some space right now and acclimate to this new phase of our relationship.

With a sigh, I stand up, stretching. "I should go back to my room and go to bed. It's late."

He rises, tall and broad, towering over me. "You won't be going back. Not yet. You need some time away from Raoul. Time to clear your head and understand what you really want."

Alarm flickers in my chest. Yes, I need time away, but not from Raoul. "Angel, I'm going to my room."

"You can have my bed. It's very comfortable. I have all the cosmetics you prefer in the bathroom, in a basket under the sink. There are clothes for you, too, in there." He points to a wardrobe I didn't notice before. "All your size."

My hand goes to my thigh, to the pocket of my leggings where I usually tuck my phone. But it's not there. I must have left it in Carlotta's dressing room or on my bed. *Shit*.

"Angel," I say as calmly as I can manage. "I can't stay here tonight."

"I told you I would never hurt you, nor would I allow any harm to come to you," he says. "Do you not trust me?"

"It's not that I don't trust you. This is about me making my own choices."

"And you will, but Raoul has been confusing you, clouding your mind and your desires. It is time to let him go. He is the writer of a decent musical, nothing more. You need some distance from him so you can understand your true destiny."

A voice echoes from the darkness, and footsteps sound on the concrete beside the canal. "Decent, and nothing more?"

Raoul emerges from the shadows. His dress shirt is askew, half-unbuttoned, and his sleeves are rolled up to the elbows. His fists are clenched so tightly, the sinews of his forearms stand out rigidly. Behind his dark-framed glasses, his eyes burn bright green. They're almost...glowing. Must be a trick of the weird subterranean light in this place.

"I'm hurt, honestly," continues Raoul. "I thought you and I were becoming friends, Angel."

"Only *she* gets to call me that," the Angel replies tightly. "How did you find your way down here?"

"You keep your secrets, and I'll keep mine," Raoul says. "But she is leaving with me. Come, Christine."

He beckons to me, almost imperiously. Something about the gesture rubs me the wrong way. I don't like the Angel telling me I can't leave, and I don't appreciate Raoul coming to fetch me home like I'm a runaway dog.

I take a step back from Raoul, crossing my arms.

"See there," purrs the Angel. "She wants to stay with me."

"Not true," I snap.

He reaches out and draws me closer, his golden eyes glittering behind the mask. "I need you with me, beside me, and you need me just as deeply. Think of the music we'll make, my darling. The piece I created tonight—it was entirely inspired by you. I have never crafted anything so beautiful. Imagine the loveliness we could create—my compositions and your voice. Music to make the gods weep, Christine."

I shouldn't be relenting. I should struggle against his hold, maybe yell something about free will and shit...but when I'm this close to him, I have trouble thinking clearly. I can feel the heat and strength of his body. I can smell the addictive spice of his powerful blood. I remember the music he played for me, how it transcended everything I've ever heard.

"I'll stay," I whisper.

The Angel cups my chin with his gloved hand. He seems about to kiss me, but Raoul makes a sound of distressed frustration, and the Angel's attention snaps back to him.

"You've got her under some kind of spell." Raoul's voice falters as the Angel turns from me and prowls toward him.

Raoul takes a couple steps back. Whatever courage he summoned to come after me seems to have faded. He looks suddenly very young and vulnerable compared to the broad, menacing form of the Angel.

"I told you she's mine," the Angel says. "I want her, and I will keep her."

"You—you can't take people just because you want them," says Raoul.

The Angel tilts his head. "Can't I, though?"

"No," Raoul says more firmly.

"You're a pestilent creature, aren't you?" The Angel's voice lowers to a sinister, menacing purr, and his hand curls around Raoul's throat. "Pretty, yes…but irritating. You say I can't take what I want? What if I decide I want *you*, little poet? What then?"

He tightens his grip slightly, and Raoul gags.

I dash forward, clutching the Angel's arm. "Please let him go."

"He wants to destroy us, Christine. Don't deny it. I heard the two of you talking. He said he would call the police."

"He won't. He's just scared. He's confused—*I'm* confused. Let's all calm down and take some time. We can figure this out. Raoul won't tell anyone about you."

"The fuck I won't," Raoul wheezes.

I roll my eyes, exasperated. "Really? I'm trying to help you."

"I think you're right, Christine," says the Angel with a cold smile. "I think what we all need is a little time to calm down. You stay here, and I'll take Raoul somewhere he can think about his choices. Don't worry, he'll be perfectly fine."

"I'm not staying here," I protest, but the Angel is already striding away, dragging Raoul with him. As I move to follow them, a wall of mist rises between us, a moist cloud blinding my eyes and clogging my lungs. I cough, struggling through it, but I can't see a thing, and I'm nervous about falling into the canal. I have no idea how deep it is, and I can't swim. I may be a vampire, but I'm not sure that renders me immune to drowning.

I forge ahead slowly, step by step, calling out for the Angel and for Raoul. Neither of them reply.

My foot slides off the edge of something, and I vent a little scream, expecting to pitch headlong into black water, but it's only a ridge or a step of some kind. My ankle bends sideways with a loud *pop*.

"Shit!" I exclaim, hobbling forward despite the searing pain. My ankle will heal quickly, but the injury is robbing me of precious minutes.

By the time the fog dissipates, Raoul and the Angel are gone. As I look around, I realize that this level of the building is honeycombed with doors and passages, some hidden behind brick columns, others tucked between monstrous old hunks of machinery in dark corners. If I search for Raoul or try to find my way out, there's a very real possibility I might get lost.

Swearing, I hobble back to the Angel's living area and fling myself into one of the chairs.

The Angel healed well from my bite—there's not even a scar on his throat. When he comes back, I might just rip out his spine. Let's see how fast he recovers from *that*.

17

RAOUL

THE ANGEL—OR THE PHANTOM, AS I'VE DECIDED TO CALL him—drags me down a hallway, opens a door, and flings me inside. Lights come on as he slams the door shut—bright, searing lights whose heat stings my skin.

The room is made of mirrors, so seamlessly joined that when I turn around, I'm not sure which panel is the one with the door. I bang on one of them, but it doesn't sound hollow. None of them do.

The room is too low for a man to stand upright and too narrow for anyone to lie down. I've been in a space like this many times. Except it was dark in the closet under the stairs, and this space is horrendously bright and hot. The entire ceiling panel glows so fiercely I can't look at it.

This can't be happening.

It's been four years since I was last locked in the closet, and perhaps that's why the visceral horror strikes me so suddenly. There's no buildup, no slow endurance before I finally break down—it's immediate. Panic vaults through my throat, acidic bile searing the back of my tongue.

"Don't leave me in here," I call. "Please...please, you have to let me out!"

The Phantom's voice echoes in the room, seeming to come from every direction. "I designed this room for the man who summoned me, in case he returns as my enemy one day. I can fill it with water, too. It's a multipurpose prison and torture chamber—quite genius, really. I'm rather proud of it. The heat isn't high enough to cause you injury, only discomfort. Take some time to ponder your choices while I speak with Christine alone."

"No! No, you don't understand," I gasp. "I've been confined like this many times throughout my life. You'd think I would get used to it, but I haven't. I can't stand it. Please, please..."

"You were confined?" His voice sounds different now. Surprised, maybe, or disturbed.

"Yes. I was imprisoned, locked away, exiled to the dark..." I crouch on the mirrored floor beneath the searing light, sweat coating my skin. My heart is racing so horribly fast that I wonder if it might actually burst this time. It seems to fill my whole chest, my brain, my mouth.

Several seconds pass...or several minutes. It's hard to tell with my pulse screaming through my veins at the speed of terror.

He's not coming back. He really has left me in here alone, in this unbearable box, staring at countless sweating, shaking reflections of myself under the blaze of the merciless lights.

The horror builds, pounding in my head until an agonized, roaring scream rips from my chest. I scream again, but I can't get enough breath for a third scream because I'm panting too fast, too shallow. Black spots dance at the edges of my vision.

A door opens, and the Phantom drags me out into the blessed

coolness and gloom of the hallway. I cling to him, sweat slick and gasping, tears oozing from my eyes. I'm breathing too fast. I can't get enough air.

He drops to the floor, leaning against the wall, holding me while I convulse and sob. I barely understand who it is I'm grasping so tightly. I only know that I made it out of that mirrored box.

"I have been a prisoner, too," the Phantom says, low. "I did not realize... Forgive me."

Light, hurried footsteps sound at the end of the hall, and then Christine's voice reaches my ears. "I heard screaming... Oh god, what did you do to him?"

"I put him in the torture room for only a minute or two," the Phantom protests.

"You're a menace, you know that?" she snaps at him. Then she kneels beside me. "Raoul, it's all right. You'll be okay." She removes my glasses and sets them aside carefully. Her cool fingers slide into my sweaty hair.

When she touches me, the Phantom's arms tighten around my body. "I've got him."

"I can see that," says Christine more gently. "Maybe if we all return to your living quarters and just talk like reasonable people instead of resorting to arcane methods like torture rooms..."

"He isn't ready to walk yet," objects the Phantom.

"Then perhaps you could carry him."

My heart rate is slowing, and the relief that follows turns me weak. I'm not having a heart attack. I'm not going to die. More tears gush from my eyes, soaking the Phantom's vest.

Carefully, he gets to his feet, lifting me as he does so. It's a fucking princess carry, but I'm trembling too much to care. My face rocks against the swell of his bicep as he carries me along a hallway, back to the living space we just left. He strides to the platform where his enormous bed sits, and he drapes my body on top of the covers.

Christine sets my glasses on a ledge on the headboard. "Sit up, Raoul. Just for a moment, so we can get this wet shirt off you."

I let her peel the sweaty dress shirt off me. She removes my shoes and socks as well, and the Phantom summons a misty breeze to cool my body.

"Some water," Christine suggests, and the Phantom brings a glass, then stands with arms folded across his broad chest, watching from beneath his mask while Christine helps me drink.

When I've taken a few sips, I lie back down and turn my face away from her. All my energy is gone; I'm entirely wiped out from the panic attack. I despise this weakness in myself. After all, I came down here to rescue her, and now she's taking care of *me*.

"You didn't explain how you found us," says the Phantom.

"Is now really the time for that question?" Christine asks.

"It's all right." I pull myself higher on the pillows, wincing a little. Sometimes, after an episode of my heart racing that fast, there's a faint soreness in my chest for a while. "I left the reception early and went to Christine's room to check on her. When she didn't answer my knock, I tried the door and found it unlocked. I didn't plan to go in. I just looked inside to be sure she hadn't passed out again. Then I saw that the back wall was pushed aside, a gap big enough for someone to walk through, and I discovered the passage behind it."

"And you followed us? How?" the Phantom persists.

His scent was as strong in that room as hers. It was easy to follow their entwined fragrances. But I can't bring myself to tell them I can track people by scent.

"The drops of candle wax all over the floor," I reply.

"Ah." He seems satisfied by that explanation. "Careless of me. I'll have the ghosts tidy that up."

"The ghosts?"

"Oh, don't worry about that right now!" Christine interjects quickly. "You don't need any more stress."

The Phantom leaves my line of sight, presumably to "have the ghosts tidy up." I feel the beginnings of a tension headache coiling at the back of my right eye, so I force myself to relax, and I close my eyes.

Just for a moment.

When I resurface to consciousness, the first thing I see is Christine curled on the bed beside me, sound asleep. Her head is tilted against my arm, locks of brown hair swirled over the velvety black blanket. Her cheeks glow faintly pink, and the fringes of her eyelashes are so temptingly thick, I want to run my fingertip along them.

The heavy curtains have been drawn around the bed, but we're softly illuminated by a string of tiny lights fastened along the headboard. Somewhere in the cavernous space beyond the drapes, a record is playing, its occasional soft crackle echoing in the subterranean night. A distant voice hums along...faint, beautiful, and far away.

Everything is slightly blurry without my glasses. When I shift my position, I realize my pants have been removed, along with my belt, phone, and wallet. I'm in my boxers under the sheets, while Christine lies on top of the blankets.

Reluctant as I am to wake Christine, this may be my only chance to talk to her alone and find out what she wants to do—try to escape the Phantom, or stay where we are.

I stroke her soft cheek with the backs of my fingers. Her eyes open immediately, and the vicious darkness in them only softens when she sees that it's me. For a second, she actually looked murderous, and it takes me a moment to recover my breath and remember what I was going to say.

"Do you want to leave?" I whisper. "We could sneak away. Or we could overpower him together."

"Where would we go?" she replies softly. "If I go back to my room, he'll only follow me."

"I would take you home with me, but my family is..." I hesitate, struggling for words.

"Complicated?" Christine offers.

"Controlling. Demanding. Dangerous."

She scoffs lightly. "Sounds like mine. Before they died, anyway."

"I'm sorry you had to go through that."

"It's been shit, not gonna lie." She rolls over and stares up at the velvet hangings above us. "My parents always had so many expectations. So many rules. Even about who I could date or marry."

I prop myself on one elbow. "Mine too. That's one reason I can't bring you home. My sister wouldn't let you stay. In her eyes, you're not acceptable relationship material."

"Oh, I'm definitely not."

She flashes a smile, her cheek dimpling, and before I know

what I'm doing, I've leaned forward to kiss that delicious little dent.

Christine sucks in a quick breath. "Damn, you smell good."

"That's a relief, because I was sweating earlier and—"

"Hush, Raoul," she whispers, her nose drifting along my cheek.

"Sure," I say breathlessly. "I can be quiet. Except I tend to talk when I'm nervous."

She smiles—I can feel the stretch of her lips against my throat. "Your heart is beating really fast. Are you scared? This is kind of an enclosed space. The Angel said you got claustrophobic in his torture room."

"Yeah," I admit. "There wasn't even any torture, just mirrors and heat, and I fucking lost it."

"We all lose it sometimes." Her voice is low, melodic, a vibrating purr. "I've killed people, you know."

I gulp, and she draws back, looking startled by her own confession.

"I have no idea why I just told you that. I mean, they were rapist guys who attacked me, so the killing was totally justified, but...god, what am I doing? Why am I dragging you into my mess when you're a *nice* guy, a decent guy? The last thing you need is me and *him* and all this chaos—"

I duck in and kiss her—a quick, soft touch of my lips to hers. Then another. And another. Tiny, teasing kisses until she makes a sound of urgent frustration, wraps her arm around my head, and pulls me in for a long, luscious kiss.

A warm floral scent unfurls from her. I can pinpoint its source, and I know its cause. She's aroused, and that enticing scent is coming from between her legs.

I lay my palm across her lower belly, nudging my fingertips just beneath the edge of her leggings. She tenses and breaks the kiss, panting lightly, but she keeps her forehead pressed to mine, watching my hand disappear gradually beneath her leggings. She's not wearing panties, and my dick twitches at the realization. Her pussy is bare and soft.

My middle fingertip encounters her clit first, and she whines faintly.

"Shh," I warn her, and we both pause, listening. But the music is still playing, and the Phantom is still humming somewhere in the distance.

I move my hand deeper, sliding into the wetness between her pussy lips. My fingertips curl into her slit, and I sink two fingers all the way in. Christine trembles, gripping my shoulder, flushed and overcome by my secret possession of her body.

With two fingers inside, I trace my thumb over the peak of her sex, tenderly coaxing her toward the edge.

"Raoul," she whispers against my mouth. "Raoul...please."

"Trust me." I flick my tongue against hers and pump my fingers faster. Her body is sucking me in deeper, begging for more. My thumb twitches across her clit, and she grinds against my hand, whimpering into the kiss. "You have such a sweet, soaked, needy little cunt," I whisper.

"Oh my god," she gasps through a faint laugh. "I wouldn't have pegged you for a dirty talker."

"Pegging is definitely on the table." I extract my fingers from her opening and swirl the wetness over her clit, rubbing with quick circular motions under her leggings.

"Oh shit." Her grip on my shoulder intensifies to the point of pain, but I'm too focused on getting her off to care about my own comfort. I watch her face for tiny changes in expression, altering the pressure and speed accordingly until she comes with a sharp gasp.

"That's it," I croon, exulting in the dazed bliss on her face. I stroke her more slowly, guiding her through the pleasure. "God, you come so beautifully. Look at you."

She's struggling to stay quiet, so I take my hand out of her pussy, pull her close, and let her bury her face in my chest. Only then do I realize that there's blood trailing down my shoulder in thin rivulets from where her nails have pierced my skin.

She notices the wounds at the same moment and withdraws her hand.

"God, I'm so sorry, Raoul." She rises halfway and bends down, licking the trails of blood and the punctures in my flesh.

I shiver at the touch of her tongue. It's a strange way to clean up, but I suppose she doesn't want to get blood on the Phantom's bed.

When she's done, she hides her face against me again while I lick her arousal from my fingers.

"You're way too good at that," she murmurs after a few minutes.

"I've mostly been with guys, but the two women I've slept with were kind enough to answer all my questions and give me a thorough tutorial on what usually works. Let's just say we practiced a lot—"

Christine clamps her hand over my mouth, cutting off my words. The humming has stopped, and my pulse quickens with dread.

But a moment later, the Phantom continues humming, and we both exhale with relief.

I'm still hard beneath the blankets, but the temporary terror eased things enough for me to rearrange my priorities. Decisions now, sex later.

"So...run or stay?" I whisper to Christine. "I can get us a hotel, a place where we'll be safe."

"He'll find me wherever I go. It's disturbingly sweet and weirdly flattering how obsessed he is." She gives me an apologetic wince. "How unhinged would it be if I said that I want to stay?"

"Deeply unhinged. But I don't really blame you. He's gorgeous."

"Right? And there's something about him...a fragility underneath all the bravado. When he was holding you, there in the hallway, I could only see part of his face, but there was something so tender about his mouth, his body language. A sweetness almost. I can't describe it."

"I believe you," I murmur. "I felt it."

"I want to know more about him. He told me some things, but I couldn't really grasp it all."

"So it's decided, then. We stay a little longer, of our own free will."

"Yes." With a weary sigh, Christine pulls back the blankets on her side of the bed and slips beneath them. She scoots over to me, and I savor the sensation of her body against mine. It's like a dream, the two of us snuggled here in the welcoming darkness, listening to soft music in the night, guarded by a dangerous angel.

When I wake again, it takes me a minute to remember where I am. Beyond the curtains, muffled by their thick drapery, I hear a rippling cascade of notes, the most exquisite piano solo I've ever listened to.

It's *him*, of course. His playing is magnetic, irresistible. I can't stay in the bed—I *have* to go watch him play. The music summons me like a compulsive spell.

Slowly, I ease out of the sheets, careful not to disturb Christine. My glasses are sitting on a little ledge attached to the headboard, so I pick them up and put them on. I emerge from between the curtains and descend barefoot from the sleeping area onto the thick rugs covering the concrete floor of the main living space.

The Phantom sits at the piano, wearing only a pair of black sweatpants. I'm mesmerized, not only by the delicate melody but by the flexing muscles of his arms and hands as he plays. He looks like a masked god carved of pale marble, set into motion by magic. My fingers itch for my phone or my little idea notebook so I can write down a hundred different phrases that describe him in this moment. But both the phone and the notebook were in my pockets.

I suspect the Phantom has hidden my things somewhere, including my phone. He showed me mercy last night, but I doubt he's going to let either of us go easily. As Christine said, he's obsessed with her, and while he views me as a rival, he's obviously attracted to me, too. And I'm hot for both of them. As if this situation needed to be any more complicated.

Now that I'm out of the curtained bed, his dark, woodsy fragrance hits me like a delicious breeze. Never have I been so deeply affected by a scent as I am by his. It's wildly different from anything I've experienced in my lifetime.

Christine's scent is odd, too. It's human, yet it seems to change slightly every few days, and I can't figure out why. It's as if her core scent remains the same, but it's constantly being overlaid with new notes.

The Phantom continues to play while I approach. He's wearing a half mask today, and the beauty-loving poet in me appreciates the sharp angle of his jaw, the way his glossy black hair clings in soft waves around his ear, the strong lines of his throat, and the prominence of his Adam's apple. He has the broad shoulders and tapered torso of an Olympic swimmer, complete with not only a killer set of abs but a row of defined little muscles along his side, visible when his arm is lifted to play.

He has discarded his gloves, and his strong, veined hands move masterfully along the keyboard. His technique and finger placement are unusual, but he plays with a brilliance that steals every question I was going to ask him and replaces my curiosity with a sense of awe.

Suddenly I recognize the melody underlying the chords and runs. It's one of my songs from *Sidewinder*, interpreted in a way I would never have imagined.

He looks up at me, still playing.

There's just enough room on the bench, so I sit down beside him, facing away from the piano. Looking at him. Listening as he transforms my song into something utterly new and far more enchanting.

Fingers still dancing, he leans toward me ever so slightly. I mirror the movement, angling my body so we're nearly nose to nose, facing in opposite directions on the piano bench. His tongue traces his lips briefly, his forearms still moving, but the music is slower now, heavier, richer. My mouth hovers near his while he plays, his warm breath ghosting over my lips.

"Fucking kiss me, poet," he says hoarsely.

I lean forward a fraction and meet his mouth.

The music never stops, but it takes on a fervent timbre, a tender urgency emphasized by the way his tongue surges into my mouth. I bring one hand up to clasp the back of his head, to ensure he can't escape my kiss. My other hand slides over his thigh, between his legs. The song falters, but he persists even when I cup his length through the sweatpants. He's big, but not so big that I couldn't take him in my mouth, or elsewhere.

He groans, the sound humming through my lips and jaw. My answering smile breaks the kiss for a moment.

And then, several things happen at once.

My other hand, wandering through his silky black hair, finds the thin cord of his half mask. And without truly considering my actions, I tug at that cord.

The mask slips from his face.

The music stops with a discordant crash.

The Phantom jolts away from me with a snarl. "Fuck you!" He seizes the mask and claps it to his face. But I glimpsed a handful of deep gashes through his cheek and something...something *moving* within those wounds.

A shudder runs over my body, and he notices the involuntary recoil.

"Are you pleased with yourself now?" His voice is like black ice. "You've seen what you wanted to see? Time to call the authorities and tell them about the monster? Play out the role of the handsome prince rescuing the damsel from a marauding dragon?"

"No, I—"

"You kissed me to put me off my guard." His whole body is rigid with fury, but this isn't just anger—it's pain, deep as any I've ever felt.

I rise from the bench and face him. "I kissed you because I wanted to."

"Liar," he hisses.

"You're the liar." I'm shaking, like I always do during a confrontation. My stomach feels like jelly. "Stop pretending this is only about Christine!"

His lips clamp tight, and a muscle twitches along his jaw. "It was only supposed to be about her. Her voice, my music. I didn't expect *you*."

"Right. I'm always the unplanned one. The afterthought, the disappointment." My lips curl back in a pained sneer. "I know what you think of me and my songs. Yes, I came here to save her from you, but now I'm starting to think she never needed my help. She has fucked you before, hasn't she? That night when she came to hear me play, I could smell you on her—*inside* her. I didn't believe it at first. I thought I was going mad. I don't trust myself because I'm the worst of my kind, unreliable and dysfunctional. I doubted my own senses, but now I *know* it's true. You don't want me? Fine. The two of you just stay here, okay? Stay in your fucked-up stalker fantasy. I'm going home."

"Home, where they lock you up and revile you?" He takes a sudden step forward. "Where they twisted your mind so thoroughly that you came for me while I was critiquing you?"

"It wasn't the critique. It was your goddamn gorgeous voice. And...you said my poetry was godlike."

"I understand you now." He's right in front of me, shirtless, glorious, dominant. "You crave praise, little poet. I can give you that. And as for Christine, she *chose* to have sex with me. She came on my cock like she came on your fingers last night. Yes, I heard the two of you. I *watched* you."

"You fucking creep."

The Phantom wraps his hand around my throat, a light compression, but the threat of his strength is there.

"I don't play by human rules," he hisses. "I am a *god*. I have every right to observe anything I please, especially when it takes place in my domain, not to mention in my fucking *bed*."

"A god?" I choke out a laugh. "God of what? Candles and canals?"

"Delightful alliteration, little poet, but no. God of death, in fact."

"Death, huh? And you're going to kill me now?"

"Kill you, kiss you, tie you to the canal gate and edge you until you scream—I haven't decided yet."

Shock rolls through me in a blazing thrill. I can't decide which fate I'd rather endure.

A rustle of curtains draws our attention, and we both look toward the bed as Christine emerges, flushed and sleepy. "What the *hell* are you two fussing about? I was having such a nice dream..."

She yawns, and I stare, speechless, because Christine has *fangs*. A double set of them. Long, white, sharp fangs.

The Phantom clears his throat. "Could this dream of yours possibly have involved blood?"

She frowns. "What?"

He taps his lips, and Christine's hand goes to her mouth.

She prods the fangs. "Oh...shit." She sighs, shrugs, and looks helplessly at me. "Fine, I'm a vampire. He's a god. Get over it."

18

CHRISTINE

Raoul does not, in fact, get over it. He's still insisting he's fine in a high-pitched tone a couple hours later, when the Angel returns with breakfast.

We took turns in the Angel's well-appointed bathroom, after which he ordered our meal through a food delivery app and walked down the canal tunnel out of sight to fetch it. Apparently there's an exit somewhere along the canal route, a stairway that takes you up to street level and comes out by the riverfront.

I can't say I'm surprised by the existence of this place—after all, there are steam tunnels under Nashville, not to mention Civil War–era escape routes for enslaved people and Prohibition-era hideaways for bootleggers.

Like I told Raoul, the literal existence of the death god took me a minute to grasp, even when I have plenty of proof, like the Angel's shockingly addictive blood, his command of spirits, and his ability to wield mist and shadows. But now, with my mind refreshed by sleep, I'm remembering more of the mythos on which I was raised.

Wolfsheim's cult possesses a giant compendium of Celtic

mythology and history. They require each Progeny family to own a copy and read from it at night, so I grew up on alternate versions of the *Mabinogion*, the *Book of Taliesin*, and various historical texts. I still don't know which versions of the tales are correct—the ones readily available online or the secret tome revered by the Progeny. The Progeny compendium certainly contains a lot more details, including entire family trees for the ancient royal families and the Tuatha Dé Danann themselves, some of them spanning dozens of pages.

I share a few of the stories with Raoul while we eat. The Angel doesn't weigh in, but the unmasked half of his face looks contemplative, almost sad. Finally I ask, "These stories...are they accurate?"

His lips tighten, and he doesn't answer for a long moment. "I don't remember. The vampire who locked away my powers also suppressed most of my memories. My mind is often chaotic—fragments of recollection, whispers of memory, and the wails of the restless dead."

"That sounds awful," I murmur.

He meets my eyes, and for a second, I see it—the unending tempest, the torturous storm locked inside him. "Music quiets the noise."

"Then we should play together after we eat."

Raoul chokes on a bite of eggs. I pat him firmly on the back until he manages to wheeze, "Of course. What could be more normal? A jam session with a god, a vampire, and a—um..." He cuts himself off. "A human. A normal human."

The Angel gives Raoul a strange look, but he doesn't comment. He seems more at ease than he did last night—less prone to keep us captive. Perhaps he's feeling reassured because Raoul and I didn't leave while he was fetching the food.

After breakfast, Raoul gets up and begins poking around the instruments the Angel has collected. He pushes aside an afghan, uncovering a cherry-red Nord digital piano. "This is fantastic. Not cheap either. Where do you get your money? Do gods have some supernatural source of income?"

"The man who raised me left some funds in my possession," the Angel says.

"Cool, cool." Raoul locates a power strip into which the Angel has plugged a couple of lamps. Its cord runs all the way across the room, beneath the rugs, to an outlet in the wall.

I watch the Angel for a moment, marveling at his genius. From what he said, he's been in this body for about a year, maybe less... and in that time, he has absorbed a massive amount of information. He learned to use technology, then leveraged it to amass the skills and knowledge he needed to set up this place. And judging by the piles of notebooks beside one of the chairs, he's been writing music—tons of it.

When Raoul begins playing beats on the digital piano, the Angel rises, keen interest etched in every line of his body. He stands at Raoul's side, watching him manipulate the sound in different ways.

"Teach me," he says abruptly, and Raoul looks up at him.

My stomach flutters at the sight of them. Both shirtless, both gorgeous—the Angel with his broader, more powerful body and black hair, Raoul with his slim form and copper curls. Like the Devil and Cupid, bonding over music. I want to squeal with delight and smush them forcefully together, then wedge myself in between them and be the luckiest damn girl to ever exist.

But reality, that unrelenting bitch, crawls into my head and rips holes in the pretty picture I was painting.

None of this could ever work. Raoul is clearly freaked out about the vampire thing. Besides which, he has ongoing family trauma that apparently included some nasty abuse. The Angel is mentally disturbed on a number of levels. And I am more damaged than either of them could know.

That's not even accounting for the fact that the reason we're all here now together is that the Angel stalked me, decided to keep me here against my will, and threw Raoul in a torture chamber. Talk about a dysfunctional dynamic. There's no way a relationship among the three of us could be anything but toxic.

But it's hard not to smile as I watch Raoul teaching the Angel how to use the digital keyboard. He picks it up unbelievably fast, and before long, Raoul yields the piano to him, grabs a guitar, and begins strumming, singing in that light, golden tenor of his.

The Angel glances over at me and smiles—pure delight, pure joy. And suddenly I want to cry.

"Sing, Christine," he pleads softly, and Raoul echoes, "Sing for us."

I rise from the chair and take up a position on the other side of the digital piano, facing the Angel as he plays the intro to "As Long as You're Mine" from *Wicked*.

This time, even though I know the song and I understand how intimate singing it will be, I don't run. For the first time, I look at him while I sing. As I croon Elphaba's words, I watch the adoration blooming on his face, the tears gathering in his eyes. *I have the power to move him like this. Me.*

Then, eyes locked with his, I listen to the passionate rise and fall of his voice through Fiyero's stanza. And I know, with thrilling certainty, that no one has ever wanted me this badly before. No one has ever loved me this deeply.

Whatever he has been in the past, whatever he is now—this man, this *god*, adores me, body and soul.

Fuck reality. Fuck social norms and expectations, fuck guilt and fear. There's something I want from him, and I've decided to take it.

The Angel can see it in my face as we sing the final verse together. I know he understands what I crave, because the glow of worship in his eyes intensifies to a wicked hunger. He keeps playing, and I let all the reckless desire of my soul soar through my voice.

I glance at Raoul, and so does the Angel, both of us looking to him at the same moment, our hearts pulled by the same cord. Raoul's cheeks are red, his green eyes soft and bright. I don't see fear in his gaze. If it's there, desire has temporarily eclipsed it. Wherever we go right now, he'll go, too.

We end the song, and before the music has ceased vibrating in the air, the Angel steps around the keyboard and hauls me against him. I reach out one hand to Raoul, and when his fingers brush mine, I pull him close.

But I kiss the Angel first.

His lips have always belonged to me. They are firm and smooth, tender and rough all at once. He tastes of salt and pine trees…of wind, wilderness, and the darkness of long-forgotten tombs in a forest by the sea. My tongue explores the cave of his mouth, the lines of his teeth, the shape of his tongue.

Then, with the Angel's taste still on my lips, I kiss Raoul.

He's like coming home—the home I always wished for. Soft, warm, welcoming. There's a honeyed sweetness to him despite all the bitterness he has endured. Bullying at school, cruelty from his family—somehow none of it tarnished that pure, honest innocence. Affection for him wells up inside me as I press kiss after cherishing kiss to his precious mouth.

Then Raoul gasps, a fractured groan slipping from his lips. The Angel is rubbing his hand over Raoul's boxers, caressing the prominent shape of his dick.

I take advantage of their momentary distraction to remove my top. It's almost comical how quickly their attention snaps back to me, drawn by the sudden exposure of *boobs*. Mine aren't large, but that doesn't seem to matter to either Raoul or the Angel—they're equally entranced.

Slowly, I walk up the steps to the bed, pushing the curtains all the way back before climbing onto it.

Raoul and the Angel are both naked by the time they reach me. Raoul arrives first, and after he sets his glasses aside, I let him peel my leggings off. We sit together naked among the sheets, instinctively waiting for direction from the Angel.

He stands at the end of the bed, his hips tilted with the casual grace of a classic marble statue. He's fully erect and fully in control, the dominant one among the three of us.

I'm actually doing this. With *both* of them. We didn't discuss it, didn't lay down any rules. We simply decided.

The Angel glances down at his cock. It's a silent command

that Raoul obeys instantly, crawling to the end of the bed. Raoul has a lovely ass, round and perfect, and I can't resist following him, caressing those smooth cheeks as he circles the base of the Angel's cock with his hand and tucks the head into his mouth.

While he sucks the Angel's cock, I explore Raoul's body with my hands. He's lean and toned, but not as muscular as the Angel, softer in places. He quivers when I run my fingers through the groove between his ass cheeks. I tease the tight hole there, then stroke the sensitive skin beyond it, at the base of his balls.

Raoul turns from the Angel, his lips wet, and he lunges for me. We collide, kneeling upright on the bed, our bodies seamed together from thighs to lips. The hot, hard length of him slips into the space between my thighs, slotted against my pussy. He rocks his hips, and every glide is a tantalizing spiral of pleasure, pushing me higher, closer to the peak.

My head falls back, a gasp of exquisite bliss escaping my mouth. I glance at the Angel, half expecting jealousy, but instead he's grinning with a lustful malevolence that sends a tingling thrill through my lower belly.

"Lie down, Christine, and open yourself for him," commands the Angel.

I stretch out on the bed on my back, thighs open. The Angel walks around to the side of the bed, seats himself beside me, and reaches for my breast. When he touches me, the wondering bliss on his face sends another pulse of pleasure through my body.

He sweeps his palm over my breast, then squeezes lightly, almost experimentally. No wonder he's a little tentative. I doubt he's been with anyone since he was put into this human form, and before that, he was imprisoned for centuries. There's a cautious glee in his eyes as he explores my breasts, as he leans down to take one of my nipples in his mouth.

Raoul follows his example by burying his face between my legs. At the first strong flick of his tongue over my clit, I squeal breathlessly. "Shit! Oh, shit..."

"That's right, little poet," croons the Angel. "Use that clever mouth."

Two gorgeous men have their mouths on me. I've never experienced such unbearable heights of overstimulation. It's fucking exquisite, and it's a delicious kind of mental relief because I literally cannot think about anything else. No worries exist in my head. If there is an outside world, its problems cannot touch me. There is only the Angel's warm hand cupping the underside of my breast, feeding my nipple into his mouth, while Raoul's tongue dances and swirls through my pussy.

The delicious torture takes me to my limit faster than I expect. Every surge of pleasure builds on the next, and I gasp with each swelling pulse, sensing the oncoming explosion.

"I'm going to come," I whimper, my chest heaving beneath the Angel's tongue.

He lifts his head, slides his hand up my breastbone and around my throat, the lightest of holds. "Come for us, then," he murmurs. "Come for *me*."

Raoul hums against my sex, lashing his tongue deeper, faster, and I come with a violent arch of my spine and a shrill scream that echoes off the walls of the canal room. The Angel watches me, his eyes ravenous and demanding, his hand still clasping my throat. During the throes of the orgasm, my fangs emerge for a moment, but I manage to retract them. Much as I would love to mark both of these men with my fangs and take their blood into myself, I don't want to ruin our fun by introducing my monstrous side.

I don't want Raoul to be afraid of me.

As my breathing slows, the Angel leans down and kisses me with a firm possession that makes me shiver with delight.

"You came so fucking well," he whispers roughly. "While you recover, I'm going to play with the poet."

I nod, scooting backward and propping myself against the pillows for a better view.

Raoul sits back on his knees and wipes his mouth with the back of his hand. He looks infinitely pleased with himself, and rightfully so. He ate me out beautifully.

But he doesn't have more than a moment to enjoy his triumph, because the Angel catches him by the jaw and says, "Will you trust me?"

Raoul's throat jerks as he swallows. "Yes?"

"Do you remember what I said to you earlier? That I might tie you up and edge you until you scream?"

Faintly, Raoul says, "Yes."

"That is the game we will play." The Angel tilts his masked face aside like a raptor watching prey and trails his fingers down Raoul's chest. "You are safe. I will not harm you. If you want the game to end, simply say, 'I'm done.' Do you understand?"

I can hear Raoul's heartbeat, quick with fear...or perhaps excitement. People like us, who have endured terrible things, sometimes have darker needs. We crave something a little twisted, something to command our minds entirely, to pull us out of ourselves and set us free to enjoy the wildest heights of pleasure. My head holds so many fantasies I've never been able to realize, and perhaps these two beautiful men are the same way. I sense that this bondage game between Raoul and the Angel is something Raoul secretly craves, and somehow, the Angel knows it.

He makes Raoul stand between the posts at the end of the bed, then ties Raoul's wrists to the posts so his arms are stretched in a V shape. He fastens Raoul's ankles, too.

I slide off the sheets and come around to the end of the bed so I can see Raoul's face. He's not trapped in a small space, but he can't escape, and I'm concerned about him having another panic attack. But he seems all right—slightly nervous but mostly excited.

The Angel steps back, surveying his work. Then he goes to a drawer and extracts a small vibrator. It looks exactly like one of my favorites—the one I used the other night, when I suspected a naughty phantom might be watching me.

Raoul trembles when the tiny vibrator begins to buzz, and the Angel's mouth curves with a pleased smirk. He slides one hand along Raoul's dick, lifting it and setting the tip of the little vibrator to the underside. Raoul squirms and gasps, "Oh god, oh god," as the Angel strokes him with the device. After a few seconds of stimulation, the Angel backs off, and Raoul whimpers, his dick bobbing helplessly in midair.

The Angel sets the device aside and steps in, letting his own cock bump against the poet's. He runs both hands over Raoul's chest, pinching the nipples lightly, then sealing his mouth to Raoul's for a long kiss.

Reassured that Raoul is enjoying the experience, I arrange some pillows for myself and sit on the floor, watching them.

The Angel is merciless. He teases Raoul for a full hour, bringing him to the quivering edge of orgasm again and again, only to remove all stimulation and leave him straining for release. Raoul groans and pleads, but to my surprise, he doesn't speak the safe phrase. He knows how exquisite the relief will be when it finally comes.

I have to admit, he's beautiful like this. His skin gleams with sweat, and every abdominal muscle is taut with desperate need.

The Angel is still hard, too, still suffering, and I'm dripping with desire for them both. When the Angel moves in close to Raoul and wraps both their cocks in the tunnel of his large hand, I tuck my fingers between my legs, toying with my clit. My efforts produce a fresh surge of wetness, and both Raoul and the Angel look my way, nostrils flaring. Like they can smell it.

Oh god.

Raoul's eyes are lust-dazed, bleary, frantic with desire. But the Angel's gaze shocks me—it's the violent hunger of a predator who is beyond his own control.

He lunges at me, and I gasp in thrilled fervor, not terror. When he seizes my body and flips me facedown on the floor, among the scattered pillows, I don't tell him to stop.

It's like this with me and the Angel—a visceral, animal passion neither of us can resist. And I crave it more deeply than I can express.

I'm on my belly with him behind me, and he drags me closer, pulls my ass up so he can fit himself inside.

Then he begins to move. Not just move—he *pounds* into me so fast and hard that my whole body jerks with each thrust. It's the frenzied rut of a monster, a beast unleashed. My breath comes in little frantic bursts. My mind is being jarred loose, my thoughts melted and merged into one endless rhythm.

I'm being brutally fucked from behind by the masked god who stalked me, and I've never felt more alive.

Raoul moans, shrill and broken. "Oh god...I'm going to come..."

"Don't you dare," snarls the Angel, still fucking me so violently I can't do anything but make a faint, jagged, moaning sound.

He hitches me higher on his cock, and I gasp as the altered angle stimulates some delicate place deep inside me. I don't usually come just from penetration, but I'm about to, right now... I can feel the pleasure expanding, wider and wider, then tightening in a bright burst, a sparkling cataclysm through my whole body. The bliss bathes every nerve, every limb, my whole self. I have never experienced such supreme relief.

I'm sobbing, my pussy squeezing around his cock, and then I feel him come, too, a throbbing heat between my legs. The Angel groans, hauling my ass tighter against his hips and stomach, bottoming out inside me.

He urges every last drop from his body into mine, then drags his thick length out of my center. I collapse, panting, onto one of the pillows. Weak from ecstasy, I still manage to turn my face toward poor Raoul, who somehow managed to hold himself in check while the Angel finished with me.

The Angel walks toward him and touches the underside of Raoul's dick, right beneath the head. It's barely a second of contact, but Raoul is so sensitive that he lets out a choked sob.

"Please," he begs. "Please may I come?"

"Don't ask me," says the Angel coolly, tracing a fingertip up the side of Raoul's cock. "Ask *her*."

Raoul's gaze finds mine. I know he can see things at close

range without his glasses—it's the farther distance he has trouble with—but I move nearer just to be sure he can see me clearly. I'm wobbly on my legs, so I have to grip the bedpost to stay steady as I approach him.

"Poor Raoul," I murmur. "You've been so brave." I stroke his cheek.

He gives me a faint, exultant smile and whispers, "Please may I come?"

"You may."

The Angel looks at each of us in turn. Then he bows his masked head and sinks to his knees in front of Raoul.

There's something painfully intimate and submissive about the position, and I know by Raoul's sudden inhale that he recognizes it. This man was once an immortal god—he still possesses more hidden power than Raoul or I could ever imagine—and yet he's on his knees before the two of us. He gave Raoul's pleasure into my hands, and now he is yielding himself as the instrument of that pleasure.

With one hand on Raoul's shoulder, I place my other hand in the black, wavy hair of the Angel, guiding him.

The Angel wraps his lips around Raoul's cock, takes it deep in his throat. Raoul cries out, straining, sweating. I press myself close, my bare skin against his, holding him as he comes in the mouth of the Angel.

The Angel's throat moves, swallowing every drop Raoul gives him. Then he pulls his lips off Raoul's length and licks it clean, almost lovingly.

But Raoul shudders again, more strongly this time, and a rumbling sound issues from the center of his chest. Pressed against him, naked as I am, I can feel that rumble spreading through his whole frame, vibrating deep into his very bones. Startled, I pull back.

The Angel backs away, too, alarm in his eyes as Raoul wrenches against his restraints. The ropes snap like paper bands, one at a time, while Raoul's eyes flash a violent neon green.

A bloodcurdling snarl cracks through the air. Shadows and smoke exploding from Raoul's skin, and when they dissipate, instead of Raoul's lean male form, there's a huge, furry, four-legged shape.

A sleek, green-eyed wolf bigger than a Great Dane, with fur as black and glossy as the glimmering water of the canal.

19

RAOUL

I almost want to laugh. Perhaps I would if I weren't in this form.

It's deeply ironic that my family tortured me for years, believing that pain and fear were the key to unlocking my second form and getting me to shift for the first time, when in actuality, all it took was a threesome with a god and a vampire.

I should have been able to shift forms whenever I wanted to, starting as early as age five or as late as age twelve. But I haven't changed once, not in my twenty-two years of life, until now. I didn't even know what my form would be—wolf, raven, stag, cat, or some other creature. An unlucky third cousin transformed into a large black moth for the first time and was immediately burned to powder in a nearby candle.

Centuries ago, a full-blooded púca could take multiple forms and shift between them as needed. Now each púca has two shapes—one human, one creature. My second aspect is a wolf—the most respected form among the shifter hierarchy.

The Phantom and Christine are staring at me, but he approaches first, his hand outstretched. His eyebrow, the one not concealed by his half mask, is bent in a frown, but it's contemplative interest, not anger or fear.

"Not so long ago, I would have been able to easily discern what you were the moment I met you, but that power of mine is gone or suppressed," he says. "I knew you were hiding something, though. This is incredible."

"What the hell?" Christine's voice trembles.

"Our tender poet is a wolf shifter, probably descended from Laignech Fáelad, king of Ossory. You've heard of the werewolves of Ossory?"

Christine nods slowly, her face white.

The Phantom is partly right about my ancestry, though my family abandoned Ireland for France centuries ago and took up residence near the Mercoire Forest, in the region of Gévaudan. When one of our kind went mad and slaughtered scores of people in the area, my ancestors fled France and made their way to the Americas, arriving first in New Orleans and then spreading throughout the South, with several of the largest shifter families settling in the Nashville area.

I want to explain, to tell him those things, but now that I'm in this form, I'm uncertain how to leave it. And I can't speak as a wolf.

"Beautiful," murmurs the Phantom. His eyes gleam with admiration as he gently touches my neck.

I growl, a reflexive response, but he only grins wider and sinks his fingers into my fur.

"A shifter," Christine says slowly. "My parents told me there are shifters in the city, a close-knit, powerful pack. They said we should always steer clear of them. They're dangerous, ruthless, like the Mafia. And they hate vampires."

She's backing away, heedless of the steps leading down from the sleeping area. She's going to fall.

I bound forward, and she shrieks a little, teetering on the edge of a step. Quickly, I dart behind her, my bulk propping her up, keeping her from falling.

The next second, I'm back in human form, standing behind Christine, with her smooth body in my arms. I barely had to think about the shift. Now that I've done it once, the transformation was as smooth as blinking.

When Christine cringes away, it hurts me deeply. Mostly because everything she said is true.

"Did you know?" she asks, her voice quivering. "Did you know what I am? Could you smell it?"

"No," I assure her. "I had no idea. I noticed your scent would change occasionally, but I didn't understand why until I saw your fangs this morning. The alteration in your scent happened because you were drinking other people's blood. You would take on notes of their scent for a while afterward."

"What about your family?" she retorts. "Are you part of some huge pack here in Nashville?"

"We call it the Shifter Collective," I say. "It consists of five families. It's much smaller than it once was."

"I can't believe this." She's pulling on her clothes in an anxious frenzy while the Phantom looks on, his arms folded across his broad chest. "Shit...I just got out of one messed-up supernatural cult. I don't want any connection to another big, toxic family, especially not one that hates my kind. You should have told me, Raoul."

"I didn't know you were a vampire at first! And even after I found out—only a few hours ago, by the way—I didn't think it mattered, because until just now, I haven't been able to shift forms. This was my first time as a wolf."

She hesitates, staring at me.

"Being with both of you—it *fixed* me," I say quietly. "You unlocked something inside me that I've been struggling to resolve for years. I'm grateful."

For a second, her dark eyes soften. But she steels her expression again. "I'm sorry. I just can't handle this on top of everything else."

"Christine." The Phantom's voice is both caution and command.

She doesn't pay him any attention. Instead she runs past me, down the steps to the living area, where she snatches up her shoes. "I'm leaving. *You're* not going to stop me." She points to the Phantom. "And *you're* not going to follow me." She fixes me with a determined glare.

The Phantom swirls a velvety blanket around himself and stalks down the steps toward her, every inch of him radiating fierce power. Christine stands her ground, but I can tell she's trembling in his presence.

I came here to free her. And yet in this moment, I want him to make her stay, just long enough for me to help her understand, to reassure her.

But instead of a display of dominance, he only bends to kiss her softly on the mouth. When he straightens, he says, "I'll have one of the ghosts show you the way back to your room."

One of the ghosts? Right...because he's the god of the dead... or rather the *former* god of the dead.

At the Phantom's call, an honest-to-goodness ghost

materializes, its wispy form gliding ahead of Christine as she vanishes into the gloom.

She doesn't say goodbye.

With her gone, there's a gap between me and the Phantom. The three of us are a puzzle, and with Christine's piece missing, we're incomplete. I know he feels the same way—his broad shoulders sag, and his head hangs forward as he stands immobile where she left him.

"And you, poet," he says without turning around. "You will leave me, too?"

"I should go," I reply. "People will be wondering where I am."

"Of course." His voice is heavy, defeated.

I clear my throat. "Or you could give me my phone back, and I could text a few folks, make some excuses so I can stay a little longer. I could use some moral support while I practice shifting. And I have more to teach you about what you can do with the digital piano. There are a couple programs I want to show you as well, for composing and arranging music."

He turns around, his golden eyes bright. "I will fetch your phone."

When he passes me on the way to the sleeping area, I confess, "That was the best head I've ever gotten."

"I am pleased it was effective. I'm out of practice."

"Maybe you should practice more." I feel blood rising to my face.

He gives me a sidelong grin. "I think that can be arranged."

While he goes to one of the dressers in the sleeping area, I stare down at my body, my hands still trembling a little.

I'm struggling to believe this is real. In fact, it's harder for me to grasp than the Phantom being a god or Christine being a vampire. Her revelation shocked me, yes, but it explained a lot, too. I was relieved that my senses weren't going haywire—her changing scent had a reason behind it. But I worried that once she did find out about my shifter nature, she might hate me. Turns out I was right.

Maybe supernaturals have an innate perceptiveness, an instinct that draws them to others with mythical heritage. It can't be just *luck* that pulled me and Christine and the Phantom together. Somehow we felt the *otherness* we each possessed, an ineffable similarity, and we attracted each other like magnets.

I never expected that threesome to unlock my full potential as a shifter. Part of me is resentful, to be honest, because I suffered all those years at the hands of a family who thought I was broken. Maybe what I needed all along was kindness, touch, and intimacy—not the sexual kind, just the human kind. Maybe if my family had accepted me and loved me unconditionally, I could have shifted much sooner.

I can feel my wolf form in my head now, just beyond a filmy barrier. All I have to do is press through that barrier, and—

With a jolt, I land on all fours. I shake myself. The ripple of fur and canine muscle feels weirdly natural.

The Phantom returns with my phone in his hand and the blanket tied around his waist. He pauses at the sight of me.

"Good boy," he says with a faint smile. "You did it again."

Exuberance rushes through me from head to tail, and my jaws open, my tongue lolling out. He approaches slowly, extending his free hand.

"I never interacted much with animals," he says. "I'm more connected to plant life. But you're not really an animal, are you? And I must say you are rather intriguing in this form."

I stand stiff-legged and quaking with anticipation, trying to wait for his touch without letting my black plumed tail wag, doglike. Wolves don't wag their tails, do they? So why do I feel the strange urge to do so when his hand slides over the fur between my ears? He curls his fingers, scratching me lightly, and I push my head harder against his hand to show him how good it feels.

"There were dark tales of the púca when I walked the earth," he murmurs. "Some of them devoured humans, while others hunted vampires for their flesh."

I pull back from his hand. A whine escapes my throat.

"I do not believe you are a danger to Christine," he assures me.

That's a relief, I suppose.

I lean back through the mental veil, and my body reverts to human shape. It's not as if the pieces of me are rearranging. Instead, it feels like half of me is always waiting in another phase of reality, and I can simply switch back and forth depending on which body I want to inhabit in the physical world.

The moment I'm back in human form, the Phantom sets my phone on the arm of a leather chair.

Rather than picking it up, I wander to the upright piano and let my fingers run over the keys, picking out a sorrowful tune. "Once upon a time, I thought I might be able to unlock my other side with music," I murmur. "I wanted to try a gentler stimulus than the agony and terror my family used. Music was something I loved, and while it didn't bring out my second form, it became my refuge, my solace. I began to write songs, and through that, I realized that I wasn't bad at lyrics."

"Own your skill, poet," says the Phantom. "It is foolish for mastery to feign humility."

"I have never been the master of anything, least of all my own life."

He steps in beside me, takes my shoulders, and turns me toward him. His golden eyes blaze into mine.

"I've been trapped in the darkness, too. I know what it is to be reviled by a family—in my case, the deities who should have been my partners, who decided to reject and punish me. I had every choice wrenched away from me, every pleasure stolen. I thought I would go mad, there in the motionless dark."

He glances aside and hauls in a ragged, determined breath. I can't help being moved…and a little scared, because he seems to be on the verge of prying my soul open, perceiving me far more clearly than I thought anyone ever could. In revealing himself, he reveals me, because like it or not, we are linked, bound together not only by our shared affection and admiration for Christine but by our pasts, which are somehow both dramatically different and yet intrinsically similar.

"I broke out," he continues hoarsely, "through the efforts of a man who summoned me for his own ends, at great cost to those around him. I took possession of a body that wasn't mine. I intended harm, and I caused pain, all because I *refused* to descend into that confining prison again. I thought I wanted to reclaim my former status as god of the dead, but now I realize that role is superfluous, unnecessary. It isn't what I crave." He renews his grip on my shoulders, looks me in the eyes again. "You do not have to step into the role they have given you. You owe nothing to the family who made you suffer. Choose to be free, in this moment, and they can never control you again."

"My sister can," I whisper. "She controls everything—the family money, our home, my fucking life. She has connections throughout the city, so defying her would close a hundred doors for me. She uses guilt, manipulation, and threats to keep me in line. She's a wolf-aspect púca like me, descended from the purest bloodline still in existence in the southeastern United States. Her control isn't something I can escape."

I almost tell him about the way she can command me. As the leader of the Shifter Collective and the ascendant shifter in our home, she has the voice of the alpha. She can't use it on anyone who isn't in our immediate family, but if I had siblings, she would be able to control them, too. Like my father controlled both of us. He rarely used the alpha voice on Philippa, though—always on me. She *wanted* to obey. I was the one who had to be broken.

The Phantom is watching me. The confession is on the tip of my tongue, but I hold it in, because I don't want him to know how weak and helpless I truly am. He's right—I am proud, despite everything.

"All you want is freedom," he says, low. "You crave a world with no more darkness, no more cages. You need someone at your side to guide and guard you. I've done that for Christine—I can do it for you."

I shiver, partly from his touch and partly from the breeze wafting through the canal tunnel. After all, I'm still very naked.

"Think about it." He curls his hand beneath my jaw and

strokes his thumb over my lips. "This doesn't have to be a single occurrence. The three of us could join together in so many ways... not all of them sexual."

I vent a short, anxious laugh. "And what about Christine?"

"She will return to us."

"Will she?" I frown slightly, inspecting the visible half of his handsome face. "How can she trust either of us after all this? You won't even reveal your whole self to her, or to me."

He turns aside and bites his lip. "That's for your own safety. I will not endanger the people I love."

My breath catches. "The people you love?"

"I think this is love." He touches his chest. "Before, all I heard were the screams and moans of the dead, but now I have music inside me always, and it is louder when you or Christine are near. I suffer this violent need to be with you, against you, inside you— to protect you and seek the best for you. I will defy and destroy anyone who might threaten your well-being or your dreams. Is that love?"

I draw in a slow, purposeful breath, trying to calm my racing heart. "I'm fairly fucking sure that it is."

"I was afraid so." He says it despairingly and walks a few steps away, his shoulders sagging again. The glance he throws over his shoulder at me is flooded with so much pain that I feel it stab my own heart like a shard of mirrored glass. "It is the ultimate selfishness," he murmurs, "that I cannot remove myself from Christine's life and yours. But I cannot live without her, nor can I exist without you, poet, because she is my soul and you are my heart. I would give you both up if I could, but I am not strong enough to face that darkness again. Not alone."

His voice breaks on the last word, and that quiver of emotion finishes me. I stride forward and wrap both arms around him from behind, resting my cheek against his back. It's the tightest hug I've given anyone in a long time—maybe ever.

He stiffens. "What are you doing? Do you want to fuck again?"

"Not right now. I'm just giving you a hug."

"A hug," he repeats.

"Apparently you need one."

"I'm not sure I do."

Chuckling, I step back. "Turn around so we can do this properly. That's right, facing me. Lift your arms and wrap them around me as I hold you. There. And if it's a friend-type hug, you can grip the other person and then clap them on the back, like this."

"Hm." His arms tighten around me, and he whispers into my hair, "What if it's not a friend-type hug?"

My pulse kicks up again as I become suddenly hyperaware of his right hand, which is sliding down my back. His long, warm fingers cup my bare ass cheek, and he squeezes lightly, sending delicious tingles across my skin. I'm instantly hard, my dick throbbing against his through the blanket tied around his waist.

I clear my dry throat. "Well...if enough comfort has been provided, it can shift into a different kind of hug. Maybe something called a sword fight."

He rears back a little, frowning. But when I point out the swords in question, realization dawns on his face, along with a grin that belongs on the face of the Devil himself.

The blanket hits the floor, and it's my body against his, muscle and bone and skin and raw, pulsing desire. He speaks to me while we grind and stroke by turns. He calls me "poet" and "my brilliant darling" and "good fucking boy." He comes immediately after I do, sprinkling the muscles of my stomach while they're still tense from my own orgasm.

Afterward he brings me a robe and wraps himself in one as well. We explore the potential of his digital piano, plus a few apps and programs I wanted to show him. His capacity for learning seems limitless, and he grasps information much faster than a human could. We're deep in a conversation about music theory when a ghost pops out of his laptop screen, eliciting a sharp yell from me.

"Master," the ghost says to the Phantom, without apologizing for startling me. "You instructed Agnes to take the lady Christine back to her room, yes?"

"Of course." He frowns.

"Well, far be it from me to gossip," says the ghost with a smug expression on her round face, "but Christine never arrived at her room, and one of the other ghosts said they saw her stumbling through the northeast hallway, looking quite ill and faint."

"What?" The Phantom leaps up from his chair and bellows, "Agnes!" in a voice that shakes the concrete floor and the brick walls around us. Goose bumps erupt over every inch of my skin at the dreadful power of that voice.

A ghost appears instantly, conjured by his roar, apparently against her will. She coughs nervously and adjusts her flowered hat. "My lord?"

"Agnes," says the Phantom in a smooth, beautiful, menacing tone. "Did you lead Christine safely to her room?"

The ghost squirms, pinning her lips together as if struggling not to speak.

"Answer me," the Phantom commands. "Tell me what you have done."

With a painful writhe, the ghost bursts out, "I had to teach her a lesson. She doesn't appreciate you, sir. She doesn't respect you as she should. She occupies all your thoughts when she doesn't deserve—"

The Phantom lifts his hand and makes a sharp, dismissive gesture. The ghost explodes into scintillating fragments, each one like a glinting mote of dust. All that's left is the echo of a shriek.

"I wasn't sure I could still do that." He inspects his palm.

"Where did she go?"

"She has been dispelled. Annihilated. A little privilege of mine if a spirit is causing harm and havoc in the Afterworld—or here, apparently." He bends and kisses my forehead hastily. "My darling poet, as much as I have enjoyed our time together, I must find Christine."

"I'll go with you."

"I'm not sure she'll be ready to see you yet," he cautions. "Perhaps we should give her more time to acclimate to your secret."

Deflated, I nod. He's right. It has only been a few hours… Christine hasn't had time to come to terms with my heritage. She may never be able to accept it.

"Do you think she's all right?" I ask.

"We know she's alive. I'll make sure she remains that way," he assures me. "You may remain here or follow me to the main floor where I can point you to an exit."

"I'll follow you," I say morosely.

Much as I hate the thought of leaving this dreamlike place and returning to real life, I have no choice. My phone is blowing up with messages and email notifications. The cast and crew will accept that I was hungover or sick, but my sister will demand the truth. I'll have to give her the only piece of truth I can safely offer—that after hearing my musical performed before an audience for the first time, I was finally able to transform into a wolf. Once I share that news, she won't care about anything else.

"Text me and let me know how Christine is," I tell the Phantom. "Please."

"I swear it."

I smile a little at his dramatic vow, but part of me adores that about him—his overt, expressive manner, the old-fashioned turns of phrase. It's charming.

Once he gives me my clothes, I get dressed and follow him through the labyrinthine building to the upper floors. He points me down a hallway toward the exit, but I hesitate, my nostrils flaring when I catch a faint, familiar scent.

"That way." I point in the opposite direction, toward an area of the New Orpheum that's currently being renovated. "She's that way, and she's afraid or injured. I should go with you."

"Raoul!" He stops me, his palm against my chest. "Not now. I will care for her. I will text you once she is safe. And I will *ruin* anyone who has harmed her."

Teeth gritted, I consider defying him. But he looks nearly feral himself at the idea of Christine in pain. I can trust him to handle this.

"One more thing." I close my fingers over the hand he laid on my chest. "You called me by my name, and I want to know yours."

His features tighten, dark emotion flitting across them. "My old name is of no consequence. In this life, I wish to be called Erik."

"Erik." I press his hand to my heart for a second before releasing it. "Go. Find her. Help her."

With a vehement nod, he strides away.

It's the hardest thing I've ever done, staying away from Christine, letting him go to her alone. But I know he'll make sure she's well and happy. And I will do anything to prove to her that she can trust me.

20

CHRISTINE

The ghost leading me through the bowels of the New Orpheum is moving much too fast. The concrete floor is rough, littered with broken glass, shards of wood, and other detritus, and even with my vampire agility, I'm having trouble keeping up without hurting myself. Probably because I could use a fresh infusion of blood.

It was all I could do not to feed from Raoul or the Angel earlier. But Raoul already seemed unsettled, and I didn't want to make his trepidation worse. Now I realize that he wasn't concerned for the reasons I suspected. He wasn't being a normal human freaked out by the existence of supernaturals—he was a damn *werewolf* trying to cope with the fact that the girl he knew back in middle school is a vampire.

Damn it, I got distracted, and I can't see the ghost anymore. The faint light glowing around her body is gone, too, leaving me in darkness.

My night vision depends on some form of ambient or natural light, like starlight. In the complete absence of light, I can't really discern much.

I don't think the ghost led me the right way. Nothing I've seen has been recognizable. Although to be fair, when I first came down here, I was very distracted by the candles, the mist, and the Angel himself. I don't think I'd necessarily recognize the route back to the residence wing.

I try sniffing the air to determine the right direction, but my sense of smell has never been as acute as that of other vampires. A result of the way I was turned, maybe.

The way I was turned...

As soon as the memory hits, I shut it down. I can't afford to lose my shit.

"Ghost?" I call out. "Hello? You lost me. Can you come back?"

I'm not sure the ghost can even hear me, or that she would listen. True, she obeyed the Angel, but he's technically her boss, being the god of the dead and all. I'm just a random woman.

When no one answers my call, I move forward along the dark hallway. I stumble on a sliver of broken concrete, but I right myself and step forward again—only for my foot to plunge into a void.

A startled scream tears from my throat. I try to catch myself with my claws, but they only graze the edge of the pit as I fall. I'm not too concerned—I can climb like a cat, and once I hit the bottom, I'll just crawl back up—

But even as the plan flashes through my mind, my body *crunches* onto something, and horrific pain bursts through my torso as a spiked object punches through my chest cavity. I choke, unable to scream or breathe, skewered like a moth on a pin.

My fingers fumble around the circumference of the object. I think it's a large segment of broken pipe or a very thick piece of rebar. It's larger in girth than my arm, piercing my back to the right of my spine and emerging beneath my right breast. Blood flows from the wound—I can hear it dripping from my back onto the distant floor somewhere below.

I'm facing upward, arched in midair, drenched in pitch-blackness. My breath hisses through my teeth as I extend my arms, then my legs, trying to find a surface against which I can push or any type of leverage to get myself off this damn thing. I can't touch any walls, and it sounds like the floor of this pit is too far below me to be of help.

Tears slide from the corners of my eyes along my temples. Again I gingerly touch the thick piece of metal emerging from my torso. It's long, slick with blood. Maybe if I can get a grip on it, I can pull myself up and off the end. I grit my teeth and groan, straining to slide my body up the pipe, even a few inches. But my fingers slide in the blood, and I drop back, losing the ground I gained, letting out a hiss of pain.

If I can un-impale myself, I'll heal quickly. The greater danger lies in the blood loss I'm suffering while I'm stuck here. The pipe or rebar must have nicked something important, because my precious blood supply is pouring out of me much too fast.

I want to scream for help, but my lungs aren't working properly. Something is wrong with the right one, and I can't get enough air to really project my voice.

"Angel," I call out, but the word ends in a sob.

The only answer is silence and the quick drip-drip-dripping of my blood.

I haven't had to face my own mortality like this in a very long time. Vampires are a recent resurgence in the supernatural world, ever since a geneticist screwed around with a combination of terminal test subjects, animal DNA, and mythical relics. Theoretically, we should be able to live for centuries if we're careful. But we can be killed. My parents are proof of that. They joined Wolfsheim in a crusade against some new type of vampire, and the new vampires killed them. Tore off their heads, according to the Progeny member who gave me the news.

My parents gave up everything to become vampires and to please Wolfsheim. But before they ever gave their lives for him, they sacrificed their children.

Usually, a person's brain loses the distinct memory of a face over time, but I can still remember my siblings' faces, even though I never saw them again after my eighth birthday. My parents destroyed every photo of them. Wiped my brother and sister from existence. Yet I can still see Thomas and Edith in my head, as clearly as I did the day we were told about the change. Their faces appear to me now, floating in the dark, bright and clear as if they were being projected in high resolution.

I never see them happy and smiling. They appear to me as they were near the end, their faces contorted with violent agony, silent screams distending their mouths, blood vessels bursting in their eyes, trickles of dark liquid leaking from their nostrils.

The classic way of turning a human into a vampire through blood exchange is brutal. The transformation process is so hard on the body that only a small percentage of people survive it. Most people's bodies break down once their DNA starts rewriting itself. Others simply can't endure the agony of growing the new organs.

My parents survived the process together. Maybe they thought their bloodline was special, that their children would also survive. Whatever the reason, they decided to turn their offspring early on instead of waiting until they were teens or adults. Another member of the Progeny had turned his son at age five, and the boy grew and developed normally. What a gift, my parents thought, to acclimate to vampirism from an early age, to enjoy eternity as a family.

Progeny headquarters was far from Nashville, and my parents only visited a few times in person, but they listened to Wolfsheim's private podcast every week and applied his teachings with fervent devotion in their own twisted way.

Only once did they ever veer from his path. They didn't ask for his permission before turning all three of their children impulsively one night, when I was eight, Thomas was five, and Edith was four.

I don't think they had ever told the Progeny how many children they had. When it was over, they pretended like I was the only one.
The *Chosen*.

As a former band member, my father was skilled at keeping his personal life private. We had been an isolated and reclusive family unit for a long time, so when Thomas and Edith disappeared, no one questioned it. The week after they died, we moved to a new neighborhood and a new school district. If anyone ever did investigate further, I'm sure my father took care of it.

The way I feel right now, helpless and damaged, agonized and alone in a dark pit, is a dim reflection of my torment in the weeks and months after my siblings died. I will never be able to express the gut-twisting grief, the pain, and the horror of just *existing* with them gone. It fucked me up, tore wounds in my heart that will never heal.

From that point on, I feared everyone, even family, because the two people who were supposed to protect us essentially murdered my siblings and then acted like it was destiny. Like it was meant to be. Like I was the only child they were fated to have after all.

And I had to hide what I really felt, because they might turn on me and destroy me, too. That mistrust and terror, combined with the guilt I experienced whenever I started to enjoy something or express something—it's the root of my performance anxiety. The reason I couldn't sing for anyone for years.

I had to adapt to survive. I didn't forgive my parents exactly, but I had to find a way to cope with what they did, to reconcile the fact that somehow, they did love me. We had good times together—impromptu concerts, board games, movie nights, holidays, just like other families. My father read me dark fairy tales every night, and my mother would kiss my forehead and tuck me in. She and I would go shopping sometimes, enjoying a day at the outlets, laughing over smoothies and soft pretzels. And I would smile while somewhere deep in my soul, I mourned the ghosts of my siblings who should have been right there with us.

I loved my parents even while I despised them. Which is the most screwed-up part of it all.

In my mind, love is always entwined with violence.

Maybe that's why the Angel's dark, protective passion is appealing on such a visceral level. I think he might be one of the only people who could ever truly understand me.

I need time to get to know him. I can't just go and die right after meeting him. After everything I've been through, this *will not* be how it ends for me—hanging here, waiting to bleed out or be rescued.

I don't wait for help. That's not who I am. If there's a way out of this, I will find it myself.

If I can't climb off the pipe, I'll have to tear it out sideways, *through* my flesh.

"I'll heal," I whisper desperately to myself. "I'll heal, I'll heal, I'll heal. Okay, Christine. Do it. Stop being a coward and *just do this.*"

I extrude the claws of my right hand and slash at my side, ripping through skin and flesh. I have to work fast before it heals back up.

My faint, frantic screams echo back to me as I carve into my own body, working toward the pipe. Once I've gone far enough, I throw my weight to the left, as hard as I can. The metal tears through the rest of my decimated right side, and I fall, plummeting farther into the dark and crashing hard on my left shoulder.

My body has been severed partway through, right below my ribs. I can't move. I lie in the clammy dark on damp concrete, choking on my own blood and pain, waiting to heal.

My consciousness dips in and out while my organs, blood vessels, and muscles knit themselves back together. It's slower than usual, since my blood supply is so low.

I need to scale the side of the pit. I have to get back up to the main level and find someone to devour. Maybe I'll drink from the Angel again if I can find him.

Patting my side carefully, I discover that it's much more intact now. It's still sticky, since the muscles are forming, and there's no skin yet, but I'm whole enough to climb, and I must do it before blood loss sends me into convulsions.

At first, it's difficult to make headway up the wall. But my claws are strong, and I'm sure-footed, so I manage it, little by little, finding grooves and nooks for my toes and nails. Judging by the structure of the wall, I think I fell down a subterranean elevator shaft.

No city planner in their right mind would have approved this building as safe for use, not with so much of it in disrepair. I'm more convinced than ever that Firmin Richards and Gil Leveque bribed people to get approvals and pass their inspections. I've always gotten slimy vibes from them both, even more so since I ran into Mr. Richards that night in the residential wing. Not to mention the discovery that not only my room but several of the other apartments have two-way mirrors for walls. It's disturbing on a whole other level. Mr. Richards must have requested those mirrors, and Joe Buquet, the contractor, knows they exist, too. Those perverts set everything up and then lured in disadvantaged girls, offering them work and a cheap place to stay. And now Buquet, Mr. Richards, and probably Gil enjoy a free live peep show whenever they want. It's disgusting.

Fueled by rage, I drag myself over the edge of the pit and lie on the concrete floor for a moment to catch my breath while visions of lurid vengeance swirl through my mind. I should drink them both dry. But if I destroy Mr. Richards, what will happen to me, to Raoul's musical, to everyone who lives and works at the New Orpheum? Maybe lethal vengeance is too drastic an option. I need to figure out something else.

For now, all I can think about is drinking my fill of warm blood.

Where there's an elevator, there are probably stairs nearby. I fumble along the walls of the dark hallway until I locate a door, half-torn from its hinges. Cool air wafts through the space, and I know instinctively that I've found my way up.

Slowly, step by step, I climb out of the depths of the New Orpheum.

By the time I reach the upper floors and find familiar territory, I'm shaking all over. Thanks to the absence of prey and my nearly unconscious state, my body skipped right past the blood frenzy and into a state of weakened desperation. I'm not even sure I have the strength to overpower a human, much less the presence of mind to lure someone into a closet and make sure they stay quiet while I take what I need. There's no time to drug them, which means they'll remember everything, and that's a complication I don't need. But at this point, it's drink or die.

I shove my way through one of the doors with the construction tape on it, and I stagger into the hallway beyond.

There, in the buzzing light of the fluorescent fixtures overhead, stands a miracle in gray coveralls, wearing a hard hat and holding a measuring tape.

Joe Buquet, contractor.

At the sound of the door closing behind me, he turns.

I must be a sight, with my bloody shirt torn halfway off, blood drying on my leggings, more blood spotting my ballet flats. My hair is a wild tangle, and I know I'm pale as death.

Shock blazes across his whiskered face. He's got a big, frizzy neck beard and a red flush of alcohol across his cheeks. There's a beer bottle sitting near his feet.

So he's a little tipsy. That might help me. If I play my cards right, everyone will believe he got too drunk on the job and passed out. Even if he remembers what's about to happen, he won't talk about it for fear that people might think he's lost his mind.

I'm too weak to pounce on him, but if I can lure him in closer... if I can just get a taste of his blood, enough to revive me...

I stagger toward him.

Buquet's eyes widen at first, but there's an opportunistic glint in them, too.

"Hey, hey now," he drawls, hooking the measuring tape dispenser onto his work belt. "You're not supposed to be back here. It ain't safe. Did you get hurt? I don't see any cuts or nothing." His gaze slides along my body, lingering on the exposed part of my right breast.

Any decent man would be so alarmed by my bloody clothes that lusting for my body would be the furthest thing from his mind. Obviously, Joe Buquet is not a decent man.

"I'm fine," I manage. "I just need...a hug." It kills my pride to say it, but I have to get close enough to bite him, and I'm weakening fast. I don't think I can close the distance between us without help.

"Well then, c'mere, darlin'," he says in an oily tone that's probably supposed to be comforting. "You bump your pretty head back there? Head wounds can bleed like a sumbitch."

He approaches, and I collapse against him, clinging for support. At the scent of his thick body and the heated blood within it, my fangs slide out, so I turn my head away, letting my hair hang over my face so he doesn't see them yet.

I need to bite him now. Rise to my full height and latch on to his neck. Gulp down what I can, use the regained strength to push him down, then take everything he can safely spare. Maybe a little extra.

But a spasm passes through my whole frame, a hideous weakness washing over me.

Shit...I think I'm too late. I don't know if I can drink from him without help.

"Can you...hold me?" I whisper.

He chuckles with lecherous surprise. "You feelin' horny, little one? Come to see Daddy?"

He's pulling me closer, thank goodness. I turn my face toward his neck while his hands grope my ass.

But before I can bite him, he spins me around, shoves my front against the wall, and presses in behind me. "I dunno what kinky role-play shit you got goin' on, but I'm into it. Had my eye on you since the day you moved in." His hands fumble along the waistband of my leggings.

Sandwiched between him and the wall, my body racked with cold shivers and waves of nausea, I realize two things.

One, he's planning to fuck me. And two, I can't defend myself this time.

I am no longer the predator.

"Stop," I rasp with a faint attempt at struggling.

"Nah, you can't tease a man and then back out," he rumbles. "You take it like a good little slu—"

The last word cuts off, transformed into a garbled choking sound. Buquet is yanked off me. I slide down the wall and crumple to the floor, dizzy and fading.

A tall, black-clad figure in a white mask towers over him, seeming to fill the entire hallway. The Angel's jaw is hard as granite, and his gloved hands grip the long black rope he has flung around Buquet's neck. Is it a rope or a shadow? I can't tell. He draws it tighter while Buquet tears at the noose with both hands, kicking uselessly.

The Angel gives the shadowy rope a savage jerk, and Buquet sags, his eyes blank and bulging, his face brick-red stained with purple. He makes a sound I'll never forget...a choked burble, the last tiny bubbles of air escaping his constricted throat in a death gargle.

After several more seconds, the Angel lets the body fall to the floor. The noose vanishes instantly, confirming my suspicion that it was only a shadow all along. A shadow made real, a dream turned into sickening, tangible reality.

The Angel steps over Buquet's corpse and kneels beside me.

"One of my other ghosts told me that Agnes led you astray." Rage and sorrow mingle in his eyes. "I have destroyed her for good. She will never find rest, as she no longer exists in any plane of reality."

"You killed Joe Buquet," I murmur.

He cocks his head, eyes glittering behind the mask. "He touched you."

"But I need his blood. I got hurt, and—"

He tears his coat off one shoulder and pulls his shirt aside, baring his throat. "Take mine."

I try to make myself lean forward and drink from him, but I can't move a muscle. I'm finished. Dying.

"Help me." It's the barest whisper, and it's all I can manage.

"Fuck," says the Angel in a pained tone. Leaning forward, he grasps my head gently and pulls my face into the curve between his neck and shoulder. My fangs sink into his flesh, and instantly the blood flows, pulsing over my tongue.

His blood tastes as deliciously incandescent as the last time. Immediately, I'm awake, transported, whirled into a thrilling expanse where constellations dance behind my eyelids and meteors streak through my veins. After a few swallows, I'm invigorated enough to control my limp arms, curl them around the Angel's neck, and hold on tight while I drink my fill.

And yet amid the bliss of blood, a thought sticks in my mind like a splinter.

The Angel killed someone.

Killed him for *me*. Killed without a second thought, without a trace of guilt or regret. As if it was the most commonplace thing in the world to end the life of anyone who touches me with the wrong intentions.

I killed the men who cornered me in the alley. They had trapped me, and their intentions were clear. I was at full strength then, able to protect myself in a way that I couldn't today. If it hadn't been for the Angel, I'd probably be dying with Buquet's dick inside me.

I should be grateful, and I am. But horror churns in my heart.

Maybe it's hypocritical of me, but watching the Angel kill someone has shaken me to my core. It's the *way* he did it—so calm, so casual. Like he has done it a thousand times and would do it a thousand more. Like human life means nothing to him. He dropped Buquet's body as carelessly as I might pitch an empty bottle into a recycling bin.

It doesn't fit with the mental image I've had of him ever since I first heard his lovely voice. I wanted him to be someone beautiful, remote, and sacred—a paragon of artistic loveliness and moral rectitude. Maybe a bit of angelic weakness, just enough that I could tempt him.

I never pictured a dark, lonely, exiled god with a tormented past and a storm of lust in his heart. I never imagined a masked murderer whose gloved hands would press me close to his body while I sucked down his scintillating, powerful blood.

If the Angel and I were together, what horrors might wait in our future? Two killers, prone to violence by our very nature... we'd corrupt each other even further, sink into an abyss of gore and obsession.

And Raoul—sweet, kind Raoul—we'd drag him down, too. He's a wolf but not a hunter—a predator by blood but not by nature. We'd destroy the light inside him, entangle him in a trio of murderous monsters.

I can see the malevolent future, and to blot it out, I drink more deeply, inhaling the Angel's life into myself. His blood swirls through my lower belly, stirring other cravings in my body. It's an aphrodisiac, for sure, a fast-acting one that drowns my better judgment.

I'm starting to feel full, so I lean back, and with blood-wet lips, I kiss the Angel. I bite his mouth, and he groans, pain and need blended in blissful urgency. His fingers curl between my legs, and I gasp as tendrils of pleasure swirl through my body.

"I can't have sex with you right now," I exclaim breathlessly. "There's literally a body on the floor. No...no, I *can't*." I disentangle myself and climb off the Angel's lap before my willpower completely evaporates. "Thank you for...um...for everything. I need to change, and you need to get rid of Buquet somehow, or there will be an investigation, and Raoul's musical will be ruined."

"Yes." He nods thoughtfully, rising and pulling his clothes back into place. "My ghosts and I will handle it. After the issue with Agnes, I will need to question them all to be sure they are trustworthy. But first, I'll take you to your room." He catches me up in his arms, princess-style.

"You can't carry me through the halls like this!" I tap his arm furiously. "Put me down!"

"It's my responsibility to take care of you. I promised Raoul I would."

A pang flashes through my heart at Raoul's name. "I can get back to my room on my own. Please put me down."

His arms tense briefly, but to his credit, he respects my choice and sets me carefully on the floor again. "Very well. Shower and rest while I take care of this. No one will disturb you, I promise."

"Not even you?" I give him a faint smile.

"Not even me."

I hesitate, pressing a hand to my right side. The flesh is flawless again, but I feel as if there's a phantom wound there, a lingering pain.

"Is Raoul all right?" I ask.

"He and I spent some time together, and then he returned home." The Angel's voice is low, almost tender. "I should text him. He will be waiting for news, wanting to know that you are safe."

"Thank you for coming to find me."

"My heart is a compass," he replies softly. "It will always find you."

A chill passes over my body at those words. I can't tell if it's fear or pleasure. Perhaps with him, it will always be both.

The Angel must notice my shiver, because he says, "Never fear, my darling. This little incident"—he jerks his head toward the body—"will not affect Raoul's musical or your singing career. In fact, after last night's success, I suspect Gil Leveque will be far more amenable to the idea of making you the lead permanently."

"He won't." I shake my head. "Carlotta is too influential. Plus she's having her birthday party here next week...the masquerade thing. It represents a lot of money and prestige for the New Orpheum, so Gil and Richards won't risk offending her."

"So...*after* the party would be the ideal time for them to see reason," he muses.

I'm leaning against the wall, barely listening. I feel as if I've awakened from a long sleep that was part blissful dream and part nightmare. The music that twined softly around my soul in the Angel's lair, the bodies that slid against me, *into* me...the kisses and heartbeats we shared...those memories have faded, tainted by the terror that followed. Blissful violence, sex, and blood interwoven in a way that my mind can't reconcile right now.

I'm too exhausted to think clearly, and I need sleep, because tomorrow the New Orpheum is shifting into high gear for Carlotta Vanetti's birthday masquerade, and I'll be expected to carry twice my normal workload. That's what I get for being so fucking dependable.

"I have to go," I tell the Angel.

He nods absently, lost in his own thoughts. His expression makes me pause.

"You have scheming face," I accuse him. "You're plotting something. I can see it, even with the mask."

"You think you know me so well, so soon?" He gives me a dreary half smile.

"Yes," I reply, surprised by my own answer, but it's true. I feel like I've known him for years. Like the god of death has been in my life for ages instead of mere weeks. And right now, I can sense the darkness in him surging, braiding itself together in filaments of dreadful intent.

"Leave me to my scheming then," he says.

"What are you planning to do?"

"The idea is not quite formed. Not ready to be shared. Go,

blood queen, songstress, muse of mine, before I forget that you do not wish to be fucked in the miasma of death."

I leave him there with the corpse. But fear follows me, because if I can walk away so calmly from the scene of a murder, that must mean I'm already more of a monster than I want to believe.

21

THE PHANTOM

IN THE MISTY RECESSES OF MY MIND LINGERS THE MEMORY of an ancient revel...Imbolc, perhaps, or Samhain. Crude masks, painted bodies, rustic liquor brewed by farmers. I attended the gathering, my face concealed, my nude form painted scarlet. I was the most exquisite art they had ever seen. They desired me, worshipped me, plied me with drinks and stroked my skin with eager fingers. They did not know that Death walked among them.

That scrap of memory has frayed edges that taste of the grave. I can't recall if I was there to bear witness to a plague or a poisoning, but I know not a soul at that revel lived to see the red dawn.

The memory surfaces more clearly than ever as I prowl the edges of the party that fills the twin ballrooms of the New Orpheum Theatre. This party has kept Christine from me for a week, occupying her time and her thoughts. I have tried to be understanding, but I crave her skin, her mouth, and her voice every second I'm conscious. My patience can only last so long.

I promised I wouldn't watch her through the mirror. Instead I left notes on her bed, requesting to see her, and she left notes in return...excuses why we could not meet. Reasonable excuses, all of them, and yet I cannot help feeling that she has distanced herself on purpose, just like Raoul has. His texts have been sporadic at best—updates about his progress as he adjusts to his new form. His sister is thrilled that he can shift now. She has things to teach him, responsibilities to lay on his shoulders, and he is understandably preoccupied.

They both have lives beyond my domain. I understand that, I do. And yet it is maddening to be trapped in the darkness below while they move through circles I can never enter.

That is why I decided to attend Carlotta Vanetti's masquerade party. It provides the perfect opportunity for me to circulate among the humans without raising any suspicions. Both Raoul and Christine are here—one as an honored guest, the other begrudgingly invited as part of the *Sidewinder* cast.

Carlotta has been posting prolifically on all platforms about her status as the star of the show, clearly desperate to reclaim the attention the critics gave Christine after the preview performance. Tonight, she's dressed in a purple costume that screams to be noticed. And it appears to be working. She cannot walk more than a couple of steps without a guest begging to take her picture.

I step aside to avoid being bowled over by three of Carlotta's worshippers. One of them hesitates and gives me a wide-eyed look of admiration tinged with lust. I cock my masked head at her, and the girl blushes deeply before running after her friends.

I told Christine and Raoul I wouldn't be here. That I despised such gatherings. That I had ghostly business to which I must attend. Lies, of course. Humans seem to frown upon lying, especially to loved ones, but in this case, it's a necessity if I am to catch them both off guard.

I have waited long enough. It's time for my wolf boy and my blood queen to understand where their true destiny lies. I will not allow anything to rob me of the only two people I treasure in this cursed life—my poet and my muse.

If I had to wipe every other living thing off the face of the earth in order to be with them, I would do it gladly, without a shade of regret. I will end a thousand souls if I can claim theirs.

My costume is not flamboyant, but striking. It commands attention, so I stalk the edges of the room at first, lingering behind pillars, watching the guests dance and drink and laugh uproariously. The aroma of goat cheese, delicate herbs, and salmon wafts past me as a server hurries by with a platter. A garishly clad young man drops his drink, but the drinkware is acrylic, not glass, so there is no satisfying crash against the polished floor, only an impotent splatter.

Masked guests photograph themselves endlessly in front of brightly lit arches. Voices mutter and squeak and bellow in the cloying, perfume-scented air. Feet thump and tap and click against the floor. Bodies whirl past, so many bodies—heavy bodies and slender ones, tall forms and tiny figures, voluptuous curves and sensuous angles.

At a masquerade, faces are obscured but also magnified. Every mask demands attention; it steals a piece of its wearer's soul and holds it out, pulsing and bloody, for the other guests to see. *This is who I really am*, scream the masks. *This is what I wish I was, who I want to be.* The masks celebrate beauty, violence, creativity, lust, revulsion, humor. They are a twisted mirror of reality.

And in this fragmented reality, in this whirl of hidden faces and broken souls, the one truth is music. Vicious, panting, tremulous, thunderous music, changing every few minutes yet always the same, speaking the language of humanity, lacerating the soul, stirring the blood. I might have my musical preferences, but I am not immune to any of it. There's something in nearly every song that writhes in my veins, thrums along my bones, tries to wrench my heart from my chest. I have to hold myself inside, press that traitorous heart deeper behind my rib cage. I've been ripped out of a body before. I won't let it happen again. This body is mine, this life is mine, and I will have joy. I will have the one thing that music promises yet never delivers—happiness.

The incarnation of my future happiness is the two people standing on the opposite side of the room, so close to each other and so far from me. Raoul wears a sleek, tailored suit and a close-fitting domino mask. Christine's lacy black gown clings to her subtle curves. Her mask is heart-shaped—blood-red, glossy, and trimmed with pearls.

How do I know them with their faces covered? By their proximity, by the slant of their shoulders and the tilt of their heads, by the slope of their necks and the angle of their hips, by the color of their hair and the way Raoul reaches for Christine's arm, circling her wrist gently with his long fingers.

I know them by the surge of cruel adoration in my heart.

They appear to have made a tentative peace with each other, though I wasn't privy to that conversation. Jealousy, familiar and poisonous, coils against my ribs. Their supernatural heritage is complication enough—they do not need the corrosive influence of a damaged god. A better soul than mine would leave them alone.

For a moment, I imagine such unselfishness. I picture myself taking a few possessions, departing from this place, and finding another haven. But the only times I have ventured outside the New Orpheum were to follow Christine. Those excursions were fraught with purpose. The thought of leaving without her or Raoul sends a bolt of keen terror through my chest. I break into a chilled sweat, and my heart rate spikes, thundering in my throat.

The violence of the fear startles me. I hadn't anticipated that response within myself—hadn't questioned my aversion to being outside the New Orpheum. I thought I was simply yielding to my summoner's request that I stay hidden. I did not realize that I am terrified, down to my very core, of leaving this place alone.

The realization chokes me, sends a red haze to my brain, colors everything around me in the raging hue of blood.

I, the god of death, refuse to be afraid. I fear nothing, not *then*, not now, not ever again.

Never again will I be taken beyond my own control, suffocated and imprisoned. Never again will I be torn out of my refuge, whether it be body or lair. Never again will I lose what's most important to me.

To prevent such travesties, I will exert my remaining power, such as it is, over everyone here...especially Raoul and Christine. I can feel them slipping away, wriggling out of my grasp before I've had a chance to show them all that I am, everything I can offer. Only through my teaching can Christine rise to be the star she was always meant to be. Only with my assistance can Raoul fulfill his true potential. Only together can we turn this musical into a masterpiece that will captivate the world.

Then I will feel strong. I will have accolades; I will have reverence. I will have happiness and security.

This is my goal, and I will work to its end, manipulating this crowd, tugging their puppet strings, motivating first one, then another, until I achieve my purpose.

These puppets of mine are blithely ignorant of their fate. They do not know that Death walks among them, dressed in the color of blood.

22

RAOUL

Seeing Christine again is like breathing fresh air after being locked in a dark closet for days, yet I feel oddly awkward around her, and she seems a little withdrawn from me, too.

I wore contacts tonight to accommodate the mask. Contacts usually make my eyes feel dry and itchy, but the new brand I'm trying isn't too bad. Still, I keep touching the mask where the bridge of my nose would be, to push up the nonexistent glasses. A nervous habit I've developed, I guess.

"How did rehearsals go?" I ask Christine, and I want to bite my tongue for it, because just a week ago, my tongue was inside her, and now all I can do is ask about work. I blunder ahead without giving her the chance to reply. "Sorry I was absent. My family is excited that I finally unlocked my other form."

Alarm flares in her eyes, and she steps closer, shushing me.

She's right; I spoke too loudly. But we're masked, and everyone else is busy drinking, taking selfies, grinding, and dancing.

"Your family," she says tentatively. "They treated you so badly in the past."

"Because they wanted me to change on their timeline."

"And now?"

"Now..." I scoff bitterly. "Now, for the first time in my life, they value me. They're not embarrassed of me. I'm a wolf, one of the higher animals. A predator."

Her eyes harden behind her glossy mask. "If that's all they see, they don't really understand your worth."

"Yeah...they don't seem too concerned with anything except my wolf form," I admit. "My preferences and my consent aren't high priorities right now."

She actually growls, a threatening purr deep in her throat. Her anger isn't directed at me, though. She's furious with my family on my behalf. A sign that maybe, just maybe, she's coming to terms with this. Accepting me for who I am.

A slow thrill rolls through my stomach. Emboldened, I reach out and lightly grasp her wrist like I did the day she auditioned for me.

"Christine," I say softly.

She inhales, sharp and quick, then releases the breath gradually, yielding to my touch. "Do you want me to kill any of them for you?"

I laugh, but her echoing laugh is shaky, strained. She wasn't joking.

"I would, you know," she says, beneath the violent thrum of the music. "That's the horror of it all. *He* has already killed for me. I'd kill for you, and I'd kill for him—" She shudders. "The things we might do, Raoul. It's unthinkable. I never wanted to be part of any murderous, supernatural family. That's why I can't do this with either of you, much as I want to."

She withdraws her wrist, her cool fingers slipping through mine. She glides away, and I let her go.

I fucking *let* her go.

She drifts through the crowd, a graceful figure with sheathed claws and hidden fangs. Beauty and the beast in one elegant form.

Lyrics begin to unspool through my head, not married to a melody, just poetic phrases unfurling on their own. I take my phone from the inner pocket of my suit jacket and hurry toward an arched doorway, one that leads away from the polished floors and glittering chandeliers to the comparative gloom of a hallway.

I pass by restrooms and a couple closets, then duck into a half-open door. The room beyond is cluttered with folded tables and stacked chairs. Flicking the switch by the door, I spot a shabby, stiff-looking couch, the kind that might have been classy in the 1960s. I stretch out on the couch, take off my mask, and begin typing lyrics into my notes app. It's a compulsion I can't resist. Once the muse has been satisfied, I'll go after Christine.

I'm deep in the flow of the creative river when I smell him.

I don't have to look up. No one else carries that mystical forest scent, like the spicy earth and towering pines of a long-forgotten world, like death and life braided into one dark, delicious aroma.

His presence snaps my fragile connection to the muse and, along with it, my patience. Saving the note with a taut sigh, I sit up.

He's leaning in the doorway, one shoulder propped against the frame, his arms folded, gloved hands cupping his biceps. His suit is deep red—the darkest red I've ever seen—with a matching hooded cloak. His mask is satin black, with ridges along his cheekbones and hollows beneath them. The mask covers every bit of his face, featuring its own set of grim, full lips.

"I thought you weren't coming," I say.

The Phantom cocks his head.

"Did you think I wouldn't know you?" My laugh sounds a little breathless, even to me. "I can smell the cologne you used to mask your scent. But I'm connected to my wolf now. I would know your fragrance even if someone doused you in gasoline."

He tilts away from the doorframe and strides toward me, methodical and menacing. My blood roars at his approach.

It's about time I admit to myself that I have a mask kink.

"I was *writing*," I protest. "You interrupted me."

The Phantom reaches the couch. He towers over me, his belt at the level of my eyes. His gloved fingers grasp the buckle, ease the prong through the hole, and draw out the leather slowly, slowly. I swallow, licking my lips, mesmerized. He has some power to charm me, some charisma I can't resist. By the time he unzips his pants, my mouth is already watering.

His gloved hand cups my jaw, pulls it down. He strokes his leather-cloaked thumb over the flat of my tongue.

I'm trembling like a wounded animal, like a pet craving a treat. *Please, master.* My dick lifted the second I smelled him, and it's unbearably hard now, hot and straining against the inseam of my pants.

Holding my jaws open, he silently feeds me his cock. I take it so deep that I choke, my eyes wide and watering, fully conscious that anyone could walk into this room and see me gagging on the dick of a cloaked stranger. It would be all over social media within the hour.

The Phantom runs his gloved fingers over my hair, then clasps a handful and thrusts his cock into my mouth brutally, relentlessly. Tears stream from the corners of my eyes, but I don't try to pull away. I grip the vest he's wearing, two crimson handfuls, and I relax my throat even more, accepting the thick heat of his flesh gratefully.

I didn't even know I needed this from him, this assurance that no matter what my family believes, *they* don't control me. *He* does. Because I let him.

The Collective made me shift for them this week, over and over. I did it again and again for different groups of relatives and acquaintances, for every shifter in Nashville, or so it seemed. My sister didn't care that I was uncomfortable being naked in front of them all. "Get used to it," she said with a shrug. "This is who we are. Now that you've come into your birthright, we need witnesses. We need to secure our rank among the other families. No one can challenge us now."

By *us*, she always means herself.

She wants me to breed with a female shifter of good stock. She's already got a spreadsheet of "viable candidates."

She would hate it if she knew I was sitting on this couch, giving head to the god of death.

I gag, and the Phantom pulls back, letting me compose myself. I take only a second to control the reflex before I'm grabbing him, sliding his length back into my mouth, sucking him with such reckless enthusiasm that his breath goes ragged under his mask. He comes violently, with a harsh shudder that gives me a rush of wicked glee. His dick spurts over my tongue, and cum hits the back of my throat. I suck and swallow, welcoming the viscous heat.

The moment my lips slide off the wet head of his cock, he takes me by the throat and drags me upright. He lifts the lower edge of his mask and crushes his mouth to mine.

I think I've died, drowned in a blissful lake of liquid fire. His kiss sweeps me away, tears me out of myself, and yet I'm more *me* than I've ever been. With his mouth, he gives me all the power and glory I've craved for years.

"I love you," he says.

Three quiet words in the half-dark. Any other guy, I'd take that declaration with a grain of salt. Like *man, you just came in my mouth. Of course you think I'm your one and only*. But with him, it's different. The raw fragility of his tone tells me he means it.

"I love you, too." No poetry of mine has ever been deeper or more sincere.

He kisses me again, warm and fierce, then settles his mask in place. "Promise you won't hate me for what I'm going to do."

I frown, pulling back a little. "What are you going to do?"

"I am going to ruin your night. And save your musical."

23

CHRISTINE

I'm drinking more than usual. Pretty sure I've got a right to after everything I've gone through in the past month...the past year...no, the past decade. My entire fucking life.

On the stage at the end of the room, the band is shifting aside, making room for Carlotta, who will, of course, be singing at her own party. The gifts piled on tables in the lobby aren't enough for her—she needs the spotlight as well. Endless accolades. Her appetite for praise is voracious, but if I'm honest with myself, mine is, too. Much as I'd like to think I'm better than her, I wouldn't mind having millions of followers online and hundreds of adoring fans in person.

I think I've changed since I met the Angel. I'm hungrier now.

I throw back the rest of my drink, feeling the warm buzz along my veins.

When I told Raoul I couldn't be with either him or the Angel, he looked crestfallen. Like I sucked all the joy out of his existence.

None of us have said it aloud, but it's understood that he and the Angel are interwoven—a package deal. I can't have one without the other, couldn't be satisfied with one without dreaming of the other. I need them both, but it would be terrifying and toxic, so I have to tell myself *no*. Raoul and the Angel weren't part of the goddamn plan... Not that I had a particularly good plan for my life, but still...

Firmin Richards appears before me suddenly, sweat filming his forehead above his mask. "Christine! It is Christine, yes?"

When I lift my mask slightly and nod, he shoves a handful of sheet music in front of my face, asking desperately, "Do you know anything about this?" Behind him stands the conductor, looking equally perturbed.

"What is it?" I ask blankly, staring at the papers.

"New sheet music. The entire score of *Sidewinder* has been rewritten. I just received this from a messenger—a *messenger*! Who uses messengers these days? And there was a note with it—" He breaks off abruptly and clears his throat. "What I need to know is did Raoul send this?"

I shrug. "How should I know?"

"You're close with him. Both of you disappeared after the preview performance. There were rumors that you went off together. Did he mention rewriting the score?"

The conductor interjects. "The thing is, a composition on this scale would have taken weeks to complete, but Raoul didn't mention a rewrite. Not once!"

"Maybe someone else changed the score." I frown, confused by their panic. "You don't have to use the new music."

Richards's face reddens, and he splutters incoherently, while the conductor says faintly, "But we have to. If we don't, then—"

The two men glance at each other, as if startled by a shared secret. Or maybe I'm imagining it. I might be drunker than I thought.

"I can't help you, gentlemen," I tell them. "You'll have to discuss it with Raoul. He never said anything to me about rewriting the score. Good luck with all that. I'm off to hear our prima donna sing."

I saunter away from the two men. I can smell the fear on them. It's practically oozing out of their pores, and it gives me an odd sense of satisfaction to see them so unsettled. The predator in me rejoices when pompous, overbearing men are reduced to quivering mice.

As I wander toward the stage, Carlotta cups the microphone, nearly kissing it with her scarlet lips. She's boasting about having the lead role in *Sidewinder*. The cheers of the partygoers fill my ears, a vapid roar.

As a kid, I used to like watching the original *High School Musical*, and in this moment, Carlotta reminds me of Sharpay. Talented, sure, and devoted to her profession, yet annoyingly desperate to be the center of attention all the time. No one can say Carlotta doesn't work hard—she does—and yet the effort is minimal compared to the work others have to put in to get even a fraction of the opportunities that seem to fall into her lap.

The band swells, a boisterous intro to her first song, and Carlotta smiles through it all, picture-perfect teeth and glorious hair and flawless makeup. I don't hate her beauty, though. I hate the saucy curl of her lip when she notices me down below, among her worshipful peons. I hate the derisive droop of her fake lashes, the cocky flounce of her shoulders, like she's saying, *Hey, bitch, you had your one night of glory. The rest is mine.*

That's the part I hate. I want to bite her, and not in a sexy way. Let's see how well she performs without vocal cords...

Carlotta opens her mouth and sings the first line.

Or she tries to. But instead of lovely, soaring notes, she *croaks*.

A collective gasp breezes through the room, and the band falters. I glance around surreptitiously, half-certain, in my buzzed brain, that I somehow made it happen, like the universe heard my violent thoughts and decided to take Carlotta down a peg.

Carlotta's face freezes in a panicked smile. She holds up her hand, stops the music, and beckons for water. After gulping it down, she gives the guests an apologetic grin and tries singing a few notes.

Again, a horrible croaking sound emanates from her mouth—a dry, rasping horror instead of her beautiful voice.

"Oh, shit," exclaims a girl near me with a surprised giggle. She's been filming the whole time. "This is going straight to my socials. Carlotta Vanetti, croaking like a toad."

It's astounding how swiftly the current of the human heart can change. This girl is Carlotta's guest—supposedly a fan, if not a friend—and yet she's all too quick to gleefully capture Carlotta's embarrassment and use it for engagement.

Impulsively, I snatch the girl's phone and dash it against the ground. My heel descends instantly, grinding into the screen until it cracks.

"What the fuck?" squeaks the girl. "Are you crazy?"

I lean in, a hissing growl issuing from beneath my mask. The girl's eyes double in size, and she backs off, clutching her friends. They hurry away from me, toward one of the security guards by the doors.

I'm about to get in big trouble, so I slip through the churning crowd of shocked partygoers. A wheezing, weeping Carlotta is being hastily escorted offstage by a couple members of her entourage. I dart behind the stage and out the rear door.

The area I've just entered is a green room for the band, littered with instrument cases, chairs, extra amps, and other equipment, as well as personal belongings. Threading through the clutter, I step into the narrow hallway that connects this area with the rest of the building. It's dark here, and one of the overhead lamps is guttering like a flame in a high wind. In one of its brighter flashes, I spot a tall, hooded figure halfway down the hall.

My heart jumps, and my gut twists with fear. After the incident with the ghost and the assault by Joe Buquet, I've been jumpier than usual. I probably have mild PTSD from the Buquet incident, and it would probably be worse if I weren't already somewhat numb to the things that would horrify a normal human being. Nothing could ever be worse than watching my brother and sister die.

For a second, I imagine their silhouettes in the hallway, too, flanking the hooded figure. I blink, and they're gone. He's alone, and he's much closer to me now. The light flickers on the dark planes of his mask.

I sniff, trying to identify him by scent, but all I can smell is the heavy fragrance of cologne.

"Angel?" I venture.

"It's done." His smooth voice confirms my suspicions. "It's all settled now. I have fixed Raoul's music and given you the lead role."

"What...what are you talking about?"

"The first time I told them to make you the lead, they gave you the understudy part instead." His tone is tinged with frustration. "Even after I secured you the role for the preview performance, those boneheaded managers couldn't see reason—too blinded by Carlotta's status to recognize the value of pure, natural talent. I had to be more...persuasive. And now they have no other option. The role is yours, and the improved score will ensure that this musical makes headlines."

"Wait." I step back, staggering a little, bracing myself against the wall. "The *first* time? Did you try to force them to give me the lead?"

"I believe it's called blackmail. I have become quite adept at it. There's nothing quite so motivational as dark secrets."

By the sound of his voice, I can tell he's smiling under the mask, but I feel sick. Betrayed. "You didn't think I could do this on my own."

"I recognized the politics behind the arts," he counters. "As I said, there's more at play than talent."

"I never wanted you to *blackmail* people to further my singing career."

"I blackmailed them for other reasons, too," he says defensively. "You should be thanking me for that and for removing Carlotta from your path."

"Oh god." I close my eyes. "So *you* messed with her voice? Is it permanent?"

"I used a little death magic to damage her vocal cords. It's not permanent, but it will take her months to recover. I had to ensure she couldn't come back and take the role of Eugenie from you."

The horror of what he has done strikes deep in my soul. And yet he speaks about it so casually, as if his actions were the most rational thing in the world.

I struggle to keep my tone even. "You rewrote Raoul's entire score because you believed you could do it better. Do you understand how deeply that will hurt him?"

"He knew it wasn't perfect," replies the Angel.

"And your score is perfect?"

"Yes."

"God, you are unbearable." I seize my mask and toss it aside, losing all attempts at composure. My voice shrills and shakes with anger. "You complete narcissist. You self-absorbed piece of *shit*. You honestly believe you have the right to mess with people's lives like this? You think you're still a god? You're not. At best, you're a deeply disturbed man with a few supernatural powers."

He stands rigid, every line of his body tense and rock-hard.

"I don't want this." Tears slip from the corners of my eyes. "I'm screwed up enough, and you're going to break me even further. Maybe you honestly think you're helping, but you make everything worse. Can't you see that?"

The leather of his gloves creaks when his fists tighten. Beyond that, he doesn't move.

"Just leave me alone," I whisper.

When I push past him, he catches my arm and says, "Christine," in a voice like death.

I shake him off. "Don't you dare send one of your ghosts after me."

"Christine, please."

The *please* almost makes me hesitate. It sounds so unlike him—so desperate. But I keep running.

On the way to my room, I stop to grab a big cup of coffee from the employee break room near the New Orpheum lobby. I need caffeine for what I'm about to do.

The urge to run pounds through my head like a thunderous refrain. I need to go. I need to get away from the New Orpheum, from leering managers and groping hands, from murder and ghosts, from the death god who stalks the tunnels below. I need to run from the poet with the green eyes and gentle fingers, who also happens to be a wolf with a domineering family of shifters behind him.

I should never have stayed in Nashville after my parents died. I should have left, should have run somewhere, anywhere.

This city hates me. It has stolen everything from me—my siblings, my parents, my childhood home, my future, and my voice. After this, I doubt I'll have the heart to sing ever again.

I'm not even sure what I pack. It's not like I own much. I think I have all the essentials or most of them. I sling my dance bag over my shoulder and grab the handle of my suitcase, rolling it along as I hurry out the side door of the building and circle around to the parking lot.

My janky little car has never looked so wonderful. It's an escape, it's freedom, it's a portal out of this mess. Normally I wouldn't drive buzzed. For a human, it would be stupid and dangerous. But my vampire brain recovers from alcohol more quickly than a human's, and thanks to the coffee and my supernatural reflexes, I know I can handle the car safely.

As I'm loading my luggage into the trunk, I glance around the dark expanse of the parking lot, afraid that the Angel will emerge from the night. If I see him again, I think I might scream. I'm also afraid I won't have the strength to leave if I hear my name from his mouth one more time.

Run run run, get out, get away.

I slam the trunk, hop into the front seat, and start the engine. Then I twist around to check the back seat for phantoms.

Nothing.

I'm free.

But what does freedom actually mean?

I'm free to go somewhere else...probably a cheap, shabby motel, which is all I can afford. I'm free to do a job I will hate, like serving tables in some greasy diner for years until I know everyone's usual order.

Since the Angel came into my life, I've taken huge strides in confidence and skill. I've achieved things I never thought possible, turned dreams into reality. I've experienced dizzying heights of pleasure and felt the promise of love in the caresses of two beautiful men.

For a second, I think I might be a fool for throwing all that away.

But I'm trying to do the right thing. The healthy thing. The nontoxic thing.

I didn't choose to be a vampire or to have debilitating performance anxiety or to lose both my siblings.

But I can choose *this*.

I press my toes to the gas pedal, and I drive out of the New Orpheum parking lot.

I don't head straight out of town, though. Instead, I take a different route, to an eastern suburb of Nashville, and I follow familiar roads to a street I know all too well.

The fifth house on the left is the home I grew up in. Tall, imposing, beautiful. Red brick and white trim, surrounded by a fence of black wrought-iron bars.

I stop my car parallel to the gate, where I can see through the bars to the lawn and the house beyond.

I expected to see cars in the big driveway, maybe a lighted window or two. But the driveway is empty, and the only lights are the lanterns flanking the front entrance.

And then I spot something else, something I didn't notice at first, because from a certain angle, the mailbox half concealed it.

There's a "For Sale" sign in front of my family home.

Shock sears through me like acidic lightning.

The Progeny vampires are selling my parents' house. They fought so hard to keep me from having it, and now they are *selling* it.

Of course they wouldn't want to inhabit this place, not when there's such a strong shifter presence in Nashville. Of course they would take the money and let the house go.

For a moment, my rage paralyzes me.

But even if I had the money to buy this house outright, I don't think I would. My siblings didn't die in those rooms, but their ghosts haunt the halls all the same. I acclimated to my new physiology there. In the kitchen and the downstairs bathroom, I drank from the unconscious people my parents brought home. Sometimes, my parents took too much blood from those people, and the bodies of the victims ended up in the backyard, under the rhododendrons. In that house, I was taught the drug-and-drink process. In one of those bedrooms, I struggled with the doctrines of the Progeny and found my own kind of mental freedom long before I gained financial independence.

My rage gradually subsides, and a morbid peace filters into my heart.

Let the Progeny have it. Let them dispose of it as they please. I'm leaving this city, and I don't want my parents' blood-soaked mansion anyway.

I switch my foot from the brake to the gas and roll away from my childhood home, headed southwest, away from the City of Music.

24

THE PHANTOM

Raoul has been shouting at me for nearly an hour.

I have barely responded. This night was supposed to be triumphant. I was supposed to prove to myself, to all of them, that I am in control. That I have power. That I can shape this new life to suit my goals.

I succeeded, in a sense. Carlotta won't be performing for a long time, and thanks to the secrets I hold over them, Gil Leveque and the conductor are moving forward with the new score I composed.

But the only two people who matter to me are furious.

Raoul is walking back and forth along the edge of the canal, ranting about intellectual property and common decency and such things, while I sit disconsolate, staring at my hands. I've taken the gloves off, and I'm examining my own pale skin, the knuckles and flesh and fingernails of this body.

Despite my faulty memory, Christine's words are permanently etched in my brain. *You complete narcissist. You self-absorbed piece of shit. You honestly believe you have the right to mess with people's lives like this? You think you're still a god? You're not. At best, you're a deeply disturbed man with a few supernatural powers.*

I am death. I am ruin.

I ruin everything. For myself and for them.

Raoul has been berating me for so long that his voice has grown thin and strained. He stops in front of me, touching the bridge of his nose where his glasses usually rest. "Do you have anything to say for yourself?"

I was wrong. Forgive me. Simple words, and yet I cannot bring myself to say them. Pride will not allow it.

"What does Christine think about all this?" he asks. "You said you saw her and that she was angry. What else did she say?"

"Does it matter? She hates me, like you do."

"Stop." He sighs, exasperated. "I don't hate you. When you love someone and they do something wrong, you call them out on it. That's what I'm doing."

I look up, a vivid pulse of hope flaring through my chest. "You still love me?"

He kicks my foot lightly with his. "Yes, motherfucker."

"And what about Christine?"

"Well…" He runs a hand through his hair. "Might be a little more complicated with her. When I spoke to her at the party, she seemed pretty set against the idea of the three of us. I tried not to let it get to me. I figured she might just need some time to adjust. It's a lot to deal with. But then the thing with Carlotta happened, and I'm not gonna lie—that doesn't really help our cause. In fact, it probably just confirmed to her that a relationship with us would be toxic." He releases a long sigh. "Tell me everything she said to you, and tell me everything you've done."

We talk for another hour. Raoul tries not to yell again, but I see the judgment in his eyes, the unmistakable truth that I have broken humanity's moral code. I tell him about the blackmail, the secrets, my plans and goals.

His gaze softens by the end, and at last he says, "Yeah, it might take a while for Christine to forgive you. Instead of trusting her talent to take her where she needs to go, you tried to force people to give her the role. She's hurt. Your first step needs to be an apology. And I'm talking an apology with *groveling*."

"Gods do not grovel."

"You want her back? Because I sure as hell do."

I sigh. "Yes."

"Then, groveling."

"Fine." I rise, straightening my vest. "I suppose I should begin now. I can slip into her room through the mirror and—"

"No, don't do that. Go knock on her door like a normal person."

"Very well." I hesitate. "Will you come with me?"

He smiles, warm green eyes meeting mine. "Sure."

Carlotta's party is long over by now, ended in chaos and tears. I have ruined a woman's life, at least temporarily, and apparently I should feel remorseful about it. But though I try to summon regret, I cannot.

Raoul and I approach Christine's door together. It appears shut, but when I knock, it swings open, as if it was hastily closed and the latch did not click properly.

"Christine?" Raoul calls.

When she doesn't answer, Raoul pushes the door wider and steps inside.

Intimately acquainted with her room as I am, it takes me only a second to realize what has happened. Christine has packed up nearly all her possessions.

I thought this night could not get any worse. Obviously, I was wrong.

"She left," Raoul says blankly.

My limbs feel strangely hollow, as does my heart. I walk into the room and sit weakly on the bed. "Of course she did. She does not wish to be with us."

"Yeah, but I thought she'd come around to it. I didn't think she'd go this far." He plops down beside me, inhaling. "Goddamn it," he whispers brokenly. "I can smell her everywhere."

I place my bare hand on her pillow, my palm covering the indentation where her head usually rests. There's a long, dark hair curled on the pale pillowcase.

Raoul bends over, elbows propped on his knees, head sunk in his hands. His coppery hair falls over his forehead and temples in bright waves. "I love her," he whispers. "I can't stand losing her again."

Seeing him in pain hurts worse than the ache in my own heart. With a moment of lightning-sharp clarity, I realize that no goal of mine, no power I could ever achieve, no security or joy I could ever attain will mean anything if Raoul and Christine aren't happy.

I've caused them so much harm already that I'm not sure I can repair it. But there's one thing I never do, and that's yield to my fate. Even when I was trapped for centuries, cursed and bound, I did not fade into oblivion like some of the other gods. I held on. I struggled. I fought to rise, and I came back.

"Perhaps I have done everything wrong since my resurrection," I say. "Perhaps I've ruined any chance of Christine truly loving me. But I refuse to give up. I refuse to avoid the pain of trying to do better. If I have to sacrifice every shred of my remaining power, lie down at her feet, and yield my body to death, I will do it if the last sounds I hear on this earth are her words of forgiveness."

Raoul glances over at me. "Now that was some beautiful poetry. Dark, yes...but beautiful."

"We are going to follow her," I tell him.

"How?" He shakes his head, despondent. "We have no idea where she'll go."

"Your wolf's nose is sensitive, and the driver's side window of Christine's car does not close all the way," I tell him.

His eyes fill with a hopeful light. "I can track her by scent."

I nod, a smile tugging the corner of my mouth beneath my mask. "We can track her."

"Is it right to do that, though, if she wants to get away from us?" he asks doubtfully.

"Perhaps not. But both of us want the chance to speak to her again—me to apologize, you to persuade her. After that, if she wants to go her own way, we will not disturb her again."

"Stalking her for the right reasons," Raoul says with a smile of his own. "Okay then. Let's go after our girl."

25

CHRISTINE

I LIE ON THE DOUBLE BED IN THE MOTEL ROOM, STARING AT the ceiling above. It's cracked in one spot and bellied slightly, a pustule of plaster that sickens me whenever I look at it. The thin, scratchy blanket on the bed chafes against my outstretched arms. Despite the bold, sharp scent of cleaning fluid and room freshener, liberally sprayed to disguise the telltale odor, the stale reek of cigarettes clings to the walls.

I disliked my tiny studio apartment at the New Orpheum, but I *hate* this room. Walking in, I could practically feel the layers of filth saturating the carpet. But it's all I can afford.

Despite my intentions, I didn't drive far from Nashville. Couple hours southwest, maybe, past the Amish community of Ethridge, into farmland. By then, I was crying too hard to drive in the dark any longer, so I pulled off at the first shabby motel I found. I've been lying here, immobilized by doubt and anxiety, for longer than I care to admit.

Instead of trying to figure out my problems, I ran away. I can't decide if that was brave or stupid.

When my parents were killed, I didn't run from the estate

battle with the Progeny. I fought them, and I lost. That battle sapped all the fight out of me, and I'm tired, so tired I could cry, so tired I want to crawl into the dark gap under this bed and never move again.

Maybe I should have stayed in Nashville. But a relationship with a god and a werewolf, plus the lead in a musical, plus my secret vampire lifestyle, all felt like too much work. I'm not afraid of work, truly, but that kind of work—the work of relationships, of love, of *trust*—I'm too weak to take it on. I don't have enough hope to fuel that kind of energy.

Raoul and the Angel will be fine without me. Raoul is already softening, shifting into the morally gray space in which the Angel moves. He'll make excuses for the blackmail thing, or maybe he'll teach the Angel to do better. They'll forget me and be happy together while I start over. Again.

Tears trickle from my eyes because I want that elusive thing called "unconditional love." I want companionship, and I want family, but at the same time, I really, really don't. Family is a poison in the blood, one you can't escape, and there's no antidote except distance. Even then, the symptoms of the toxin persist, curdling your soul and shaking your resolve when you least expect it. If only I could—

Someone knocks at the door.

I remain absolutely still, frozen with apprehension.

The knock is repeated, and then a low, musical, masculine voice murmurs something I can't quite hear. A second voice, muffled and insistent, protests, "You can't just go in." But apparently he's overruled, because the next second, the electric lock beeps and clicks.

I sit up, dashing away my tears and pushing back my hair, torn between shock and anger. My body is already keyed up, and the defensive surprise I feel makes my fangs emerge.

Raoul enters first—a wise choice, because I'm less likely to kill him. He's wearing low-slung jeans and an unbuttoned shirt, like he threw it on in a hurry. He doesn't have his glasses; he's probably still wearing the contacts he wore to the party earlier.

His coppery hair is ruffled into a tangle that tempts my fingers. I want to separate the waves, arrange them, and massage his scalp while he relaxes and his eyes close.

"I tracked you by your scent," he says apologetically. "Don't be mad."

"Don't tell me how to feel," I snap.

"Fair enough." He holds up his hands in a placating gesture. "It was *his* idea." He steps aside, and the Angel enters my motel room.

He looks dramatically out of place here—tall, beautiful, and deadly serious, wearing a white mask over the right side of his face. His black hair is perfectly coiffed in glossy waves, his red suit immaculate. His eyes fix on me, their golden depths churning with blended resentment, hurt, and regret.

Raoul speaks again, his voice higher than usual, fragile with nerves. "Good news. Looks like my contacts stay in place when I switch forms, unlike my clothes. I guess I'll have to get used to wearing glasses less often."

I stare at him, unsmiling.

He clears his throat. "I had to run beside the truck in wolf form part of the time so I could track you. *He* drove. It's a miracle we made it without him crashing into a tree or running me over."

"I'm an excellent driver," replies the Angel, still holding my gaze. "I learn quickly. And tonight, Christine, I have learned that while you will accept my help in the form of lessons, you would prefer that any significant career goals are achieved on your own terms, without any hint of outside force or interference. Therefore, I apologize for using my influence in a way that made you uncomfortable."

I frown, trying to think of what to say. It's a decent apology, but I'm still angry. I still feel like he hasn't paid for what he did or fully realized how it hurt me.

At that moment, Raoul coughs and mutters, "Grovel," which pulls my attention away from the Angel.

"Don't think you're off the hook," I tell Raoul. "You had no right to track me down. Just because you're a wolf now doesn't mean you get to hunt down vampires."

"That's not at all what I—"

"And why are you even here?" I rise from the bed, shaking, trying to keep my voice steady. "You told me your family is already behaving in the same abusive, overbearing way they always have, ignoring your preferences and your consent, and yet you refuse to set boundaries. I won't be linked to a family like that again, Raoul. I *refuse*."

"You want me to break ties with them?" He plunges a hand through his hair, then shakes his head. "It's not that simple, Christine."

"It *is* that simple."

"It was easy for you. Your parents died."

His eyes flare wide the next second, like he realizes how horrible that sounded. But it's too late. In one tempestuous surge of grief and rage, I leap at him.

We crash against the wall, sliding to the floor in a tangle of limbs and claws. I snarl in his face, my fangs a bare inch from his nose.

"You're a fucking fool!" I yell. "Nothing has been easy for me. My parents *killed* my brother and sister. They turned us all, but only I survived the transformation process. They raised me as their Chosen—their one perfect vampire daughter. Survival of the fucking fittest. I hate my life, Raoul, do you understand? I hated my family—I still do. I miss them, and I despise them, and I live with that contradiction every day. I *hate* myself, and I hate both of you, because you want to drag me into that trap again, bind me with love and chains and shadows until I can't extricate myself from the knot we've become, no matter how much I might want to. I won't be trapped like that again—I won't."

"I'm so sorry," whispers Raoul. He lies quietly beneath me, his handsome face somehow strong and soft at the same time. His long fingers curl around my arms, not resisting, simply touching me. His warm green eyes sing so much love into mine that I can't bear it. I shove his face aside and graze my fangs along his beautiful throat.

A dizzying blaze of bloodlust rushes through my limbs, searing the inside of my skull. My fangs elongate farther, and my mouth waters for the taste of his blood. It will be warm and sweet, like him.

"I can end this," I breathe against his skin, against the hot thrum of his pulse. "I can kill you, and then you can't follow me anymore. I won't have to love you or leave you. I can kill the Angel, too. He'll let me, won't you?" Still crouched over Raoul like a cat over its prey, I turn my head briefly aside, looking to where the

Angel stands, tense and silent. "You hate yourself, too. That's why you wear the mask."

His lips part, and a flicker of pain crosses his face. "I don't know if I can die."

"Shall we find out?" I turn back to Raoul, inhaling the savory heat of his flesh. Widening my jaws for the bite.

"Kill me first," says the Angel calmly.

My head swerves toward him again.

"I mean it," he continues. "If you are so terrified of loving us that you have to eliminate us entirely, take me first. My end is long overdue. I should have perished under the ground and faded into oblivion centuries ago. You forget, my darling, that I know what it is to be trapped, bound to an existence I did not choose. I thought perhaps I had survived the long darkness for *this*—for you. For a chance at pleasure, creative joy, and true happiness. But I have ruined it all by my actions. I frightened you and hurt you instead of protecting and cherishing you." He comes swiftly forward and kneels beside me and Raoul, his face twisted with agonized passion. "Kill me first. I deserve death far more than I deserve your love...or his, though he gave it to me so willingly." He looks down at Raoul with pained affection, then returns his fierce golden gaze to me. "Kill me, darling, for failing you."

The monster in me assents greedily. I'm a split second away from lunging forward, ripping open his throat, and gulping down his rich blood.

Kill me, darling, for failing you.

He did ask for it.

But as my muscles twitch, preparing to pounce, Raoul whistles slowly and says, "Now *that's* how you grovel."

We both look at him, stunned.

"What?" He hooks an eyebrow, gives us a faint grin. "So dramatic, both of you. Fuck, we've all been trapped, torn apart, abused—we've all suffered. We get it. We understand each other. Christine, do you think I'm not terrified, too? You think I don't have trust issues so deep I could drown a mountain in them and have room to spare? Of course I do. But should we let our trauma *win*? Should we let it steal our future like it has already stolen our past? Hell no. I'll be damned if I'm going to give another second of my potential happiness to the people who took my childhood from me. You want the ties broken? I'll do it. I'll stand up to my sister, reject my birthright, throw myself out of the shifter pack. They might come after me, but fuck 'em. I've got a vampire girlfriend, and my boyfriend is a god."

A startled, hysterical laugh bubbles up inside me, slips out of my fanged mouth. Raoul's grin widens, his eyes crinkling at the corners.

I'm still broken inside, still wretched and hungry, but something has shifted into place. Me. I've shifted into place with the satisfying click of the last piece latching into a puzzle. The murderous pain in my heart eases, and relief floods into its place.

Whether he knows it or not, those words were exactly what I needed to hear.

I'll be damned if I'm going to give another second of my potential happiness to the people who took my childhood from me.

Fuck yes.

I duck my head, not to Raoul's neck this time, but to his mouth. With my fangs out, the kiss is messy, dangerous, but he growls in eager response, the most animalistic sound I've ever heard from him. When I pull away, his lower lip is bleeding. I lick the tiny cut, then turn to the Angel, drag him closer, and kiss him with Raoul's blood on my tongue.

He releases a ragged breath, an aching sigh that I feel right down to my bones.

Pulling back, I touch his half mask. "Raoul is giving up his family. What will you yield to me, besides your life?"

When I toy with the edge of the mask, dread pools in his eyes. "You don't know what you're asking. I can't control it."

"Show me," I whisper. "Show *us*."

Slowly, he reaches for the mask, tugs it away from his face, and sets it aside.

Beneath the mask, the right side of his face is striated with open gashes, red wounds that look fresh, though I know he must have carried them for a long time, ever since he gained this form.

As Raoul and I watch, tiny black tendrils poke out of the gashes and writhe in midair. A few of them sprout leaves as they extend and expand. It's as if a dark, deadly forest lives inside the Angel, ready to emerge and invade the world around him like a malevolent disease.

Part of me cringes at the sight of the vines, recoiling from the virulent magic I sense in them. But I force myself to reach out, to let one of the tendrils curl around my finger. With a twitch of my hand, the vine explodes into black ash. They're fragile, these vines of his. An echo of some greater power he used to possess.

Raoul shifts under me, and I scoot back to let him sit up. He strokes the wounded side of the Angel's face, and with each contact, more tendrils dissipate into black dust.

I want to erase the lost look from the Angel's eyes, to soothe

the ache I see there, to seal up the wounds of his heart. So I lean forward, and I kiss one of the open gashes.

Then, on impulse, I sweep my tongue along the wound.

There's a hum of reaction, a magical response to the enzymes in my saliva, so I lick the Angel's cheek again, another swipe over the ravine in his flesh.

When I lean back, the edges of the gash are coming together, sealing shut, forming a long, pale scar.

"Oh shit," whispers Raoul.

Heart pounding, I stroke the Angel's face with my tongue, bathing every cut, ignoring the twitch of the vines, the ashy burst of their tendrils when they contact my skin. Each gash closes, and when I'm finished, there are no more vines, no more raw red flesh. The Angel's face bears several white scars but no open wounds.

His fingertips drift wonderingly over his right cheek. I can see the realization dawning on his face—that if he had trusted me and bared himself to me, he could have been healed sooner. His suffering could have been alleviated, his fears allayed.

The symbolism of it penetrates my heart more deeply than Raoul's words.

If I open myself to loving these men, maybe I could heal, too. I won't have to work on these relationships alone; Raoul and the Angel will be there, too, working beside me. I know I can survive by myself, but maybe I don't have to. Maybe this trifold knot of ours isn't a snare at all but security. Strength. Relief. Maybe, instead of making each other worse, we can make each other *better*.

Days ago, I made the choice to share my body with them. This decision feels more important...monumental, in fact. And like that other choice, it happens softly, swiftly, in some deep place of my heart.

I thought choosing them would feel like a trap closing, but instead it feels like I've been released from torment. The bridge has been crossed, and it's burning behind me. I see the heat of the flames in the Angel's golden eyes, in the flash of Raoul's smile.

I look from the Angel to Raoul and back again. "If we're going to do this, I want to make one thing perfectly clear. I don't need a guide or a guardian. I don't belong to either of you." I pause, cupping Raoul's face with my left hand and the Angel's with my right. "You both belong to me."

"Hell yes," breathes Raoul.

Instead of answering, the Angel rises, drawing me to my feet as well. Once I'm standing, he drops to his knees and presses his face against me.

For a moment, he simply remains there with his arms wrapped around my hips and his cheek against my waist. My hands find their way into his hair instinctively, twining through the black curls.

The Angel inhales slowly, like he's savoring my scent, and then he nuzzles against my lower belly.

Arousal swirls through my body, every inch of me waking up to his nearness, his tenderness.

His fingers find the waistband of my dance shorts. Carefully, he drags them down my legs, along with the panties, inch by tantalizing inch, until they're loose and lax around my ankles.

Then he kisses my bare pussy, the tip of his tongue stroking my clit with an abject devotion that takes my breath away.

Raoul makes a sound of fervent enthusiasm and rises behind me on his knees, caressing my ass like it's his favorite thing. He lifts my shirt and begins planting kisses on my lower back, right over my spine.

The two of them kneel there, worshipping my body. They press their repentance into my flesh with their lips, trace their love on my skin with wet tongues.

And for the first time in my life, I begin to believe that I'm worthy of happiness.

Raoul trails his hands up my body, getting to his feet as he follows my curves upward. He slips both hands under my breasts and moves in until his body presses against my back and his lips brush my ear. The Angel remains at my feet, holding my thighs while he licks me softly, firmly, relentlessly.

When I whimper, Raoul kisses my temple and murmurs, "Come for him, sweetheart. Come on his tongue."

Raoul is cupping my breasts, his fingertips stimulating my nipples, and it's heaven, it's hell, it's more than I can take. The sensations spiraling through my body demand release, climbing in an irresistible crescendo toward the peak. And then, just when I'm writhing at the brink, the Angel's tongue *vibrates*.

I come with a hoarse scream, shuddering through the force of the ecstasy. My whole body shakes, and Raoul holds me steady, soothes me with whispers of wicked satisfaction until I go limp, my limbs turned to useless jelly. I sag in Raoul's arms while the Angel looks up, his mouth glistening. His scarred face is the loveliest thing I have ever seen.

"Oh my god," I gasp. "What you did at the end—what was that?"

"Something I thought I would try," he replies.

"You didn't think to do that last time we were together?"

He shrugs, a naughty smirk playing over his lips. "You don't expect me to reveal all my secrets at once, do you? I have to save a few surprises."

"Yes, but when you have a vibrating tongue—"

"Wait, what?" Raoul's tone is threaded with astonished envy.

"Would you like a turn, poet?" asks the Angel, his eyes hooded and lustful.

"Yes," says Raoul. "But if we're going to do this, I need to get something from my truck first."

He releases me and races out of the motel room. I sway on my feet, my shorts still around my ankles.

The Angel reaches past me and yanks back the covers of the bed, and I topple gratefully backward onto the sheets. They're cheap but much cleaner than the rest of the room, and I lie limply on them while the Angel removes my shoes and the rest of my clothes with methodical tenderness.

Raoul knocks at the door, and when the Angel lets him in, Raoul holds up a bottle of lube.

I hook an eyebrow at him. "You keep lube in your truck?"

Raoul flushes. "I picked some up the other day. You know... just in case." His gaze flicks to the Angel, who doesn't smile but gives Raoul the filthiest bedroom eyes I've ever witnessed. At first, I think Raoul might collapse under the dark intensity of that stare, but although his blush deepens, he manages to stay upright.

"Do you know what 'Raoul' means, little poet?" inquires the Angel, circling Raoul like a panther sizing up its prey.

"Wolf counsel," whispers Raoul.

"Very good. And do you vow, poet, to be our counsel? Our wolf, loyal to us alone?"

I spot a tremor of ingrained fear in Raoul's eyes—the soul scars of a lifetime. But there's courage in his gaze, too, and his voice is steady as he tells the Angel, "I do."

"You will seal that vow with us tonight," murmurs the Angel, sliding both hands along Raoul's waist beneath his open shirt. "You will come inside her while I come inside you."

Raoul shivers, his cheeks scarlet. "Yes."

"Good boy." With his hand in the auburn waves, the Angel pulls Raoul's head back for a long, passionate kiss.

My body is on fire, every inch of my skin glowing with violent need for them both. I watch the Angel disrobe Raoul, and then Raoul climbs onto the bed with me while the Angel discards his own clothing. Before he joins us, he takes his phone from his pants and opens a playlist of romantic instrumental music.

The unfurling melody changes the entire mood of the room, turns it into a place of sweet intimacy, adds a deeper layer of meaning and beauty to what we're doing. I've always loved how music can alter reality like that.

The Angel adjusts the volume, then turns to me and Raoul. He licks his lips and hesitates a moment before saying, "You can call me Erik. If you like."

He looks strangely, adorably nervous. Not at all like a monstrous, mythical figure with a capacity for the most diabolical of plans but a lonely soul, still unsure, still not convinced that he will ever be accepted completely or cherished entirely.

He doesn't yet believe that we love him.

"Erik," I repeat softly. "Come here."

He approaches, his body rigid. We pull him onto the creaking motel bed with us, into the symphony of our kisses and our naked bodies.

We writhe and shift and breathe, finding our places, our rhythm. I'm on my back, and Raoul's lovely cock has slipped inside my soaked pussy. Erik teases Raoul's asshole with his vibrating tongue for a few moments while Raoul pants heavily against me and I hold him tight, delighting in the expression of tortured bliss on his pretty face.

Then Erik applies the lube and eases himself inside Raoul, a little at a time, while I kiss Raoul's mouth and murmur encouraging words to him.

We move with the swell of the music, pleasure rippling through our joined bodies. There's a blissful anguish in our blended melody, in Raoul's faint moans and my whimpering pleas and Erik's shattered groans.

Raoul comes first, driven to the peak by the stimulation of my pussy and Erik's cock. He cries out, sobbing "Fuck" again and again while shivers run over his skin. The sensation of him throbbing inside me is more than I can take. I touch my clit while I surge against him, and I come in a rush of languid pleasure, like a warm tide foaming through my body.

We both feel it when Erik comes. It's violent, powerful, shaking all three of us, sending tremors through the bed, the room, maybe the entire motel. I have a momentary vision of the aftershocks thrumming through the realm of the dead, all the way into the deepest hollows of the universe.

Raoul collapses forward on me, his body still full of Erik, my body still full of him. He presses my face into the curve of his neck and whispers, "Drink."

At the invitation, my fangs emerge before I can think twice about it. I press the pointed tips against his hot flesh, puncture the skin, penetrate the muscle. His blood pumps into my mouth, hot and salty, rich and wild. I can taste the wolf, its ferocity and its loyalty, and I know, with a certainty beyond words, that Raoul's monster understands mine.

Raoul groans when Erik pulls out, a note of pain in the sound. I withdraw my fangs and lick the puncture wounds on his throat.

"Face down on the bed," I tell him. "Ass up."

Moments later, we're rearranged, with Erik cradling Raoul's head in his lap while I tend to the sore flesh between the cheeks of Raoul's perfect ass. I take long licks of the Angel's cum, which is slipping from Raoul's puckered hole, and then I press my tongue deep into Raoul so my vampire's saliva will soothe any lingering pain.

He breathes easier, relaxing, and I move alongside him so both our heads are in Erik's lap. When Erik grows hard again, Raoul and I take turns sucking on him until his cock is wet and glistening, swollen with need. Then we run our mouths along the length of it together until he comes.

Over and over, we pleasure each other, and between orgasms, I feed from them both until I'm so thoroughly sated I can't move. When we're straining for climax, we snarl the most wickedly erotic curses, and in the delirium of the afterglow, we murmur the most poetically ridiculous words of love.

I've never been happier. And this time, the sex is underpinned by confidence, by the commitment we each made tonight.

Erik has given us his whole self, unmasked.

Raoul has broken free of his past.

And I have embraced the family I never wanted—the family I desperately needed. The two people who know my secrets and love me recklessly, obsessively, worshipfully.

This time, I don't have to hide any part of myself, no matter how dark or unpalatable it may seem to me, because they accept it all, and I accept them in return.

It's the most naked, monstrous, indestructible kind of love.

26

RAOUL

The next day, none of us are quite ready to return to Nashville. Even once we're all awake, it takes us hours to get out of bed. I spend long, blissful minutes with Christine's breast in my mouth and Erik's vibrating tongue wrapped around my dick. When I come on his face, Christine licks my release off his cheeks while riding his cock.

An hour later, she's on all fours with his cock buried deep in her pussy and mine in her mouth. Erik reaches for my hand right before he comes. Holds it tight when his orgasm hits, and it makes my own climax so much sweeter.

Checkout is at eleven, though, so at last we clean up, pull on some clothes, and leave the room. We find a nearby diner and take a corner booth, all of us famished from hours of sex.

We talk about music mostly. Nobody mentions driving home. Back there, this new relationship of ours is going to be put to the test. Shit is going to get real, fast. I've got about two hundred emails and messages to deal with, Christine will have to step into Carlotta's role permanently, and we've got to figure out how to bring Erik into the light, so to speak. Honestly, just thinking about all the complications gives me a headache.

And that's not even counting the shitstorm that my sister will cause when I tell her I'm leaving the family, exiling myself from the Shifter Collective, and rejecting the entire list of potential mates she selected for me.

She'll probably kill me on the spot. And that's the best outcome I can envision.

I pledged myself to my muse and my god last night—made a vow with my body and my heart. I don't regret it, but I won't lie—in the harsh morning light, I'm scared of the consequences. I can't help it. I spent too many hours in the dark closet under the stairs or in the torture chair in the basement while my father, Jean-Luc, or other supernatural "specialists" tried to figure out how to trigger my shift. As a result, fear of my family is an automatic response, like blinking or swallowing.

"Look," says Christine suddenly, pointing to the wall of the restaurant. A bunch of flyers have been tacked up there. "A hoedown. Today. It's not far from here."

"Hoedown?" Erik frowns.

"Line dancing." Christine throws me a secretive, delighted grin. "You'll love it."

"I don't dance," Erik says.

"Of course you do," she counters. "Someone who adores music as much as you do *must* dance now and then. Raoul and I will teach you. Come on, it'll be fun."

And it will postpone our return to the city. She doesn't say it, but we all feel the unspoken thought. She's offering us a temporary escape, and I for one am ready to take it.

I nod to Erik. "Let's go."

Uncertain, he glances at Christine, who's sitting next to him. She scoots a little closer, touches his arm, and says softly, "Please."

Goddamn it, she's gorgeous. And of course, he can't say no to her any more than I can, so as soon as we've paid our check, we're out the door. We decide to take my vehicle to the hoedown, so we move Christine's things to the back of my truck, leaving her car in the diner lot. She seems anxious about the car being stolen, which I secretly think would be a mercy, but Erik reassures her that he'll buy her another one if that happens.

While I drive, I can't help mulling over our collective financial situation. Christine is practically broke, and once I sever ties with my family, I will be, too.

Erik is in better shape than both of us. He primarily relies on the bank account left to him by his summoner, but this morning, he told us that he also did some online gambling in the early days after his summoner left him. Erik says it was "easy" to outwit the games and make money. He has now been banned from a number of those apps and sites, but not before he collected a hefty payout from each one.

He also told us he intends to keep the blackmail money. Christine didn't protest, probably because it came from Firmin Richards, who's a pervert and an asshole.

Erik has put most of his money in a high-yield savings account, and he invested the rest of it in mutual funds. Both Christine and I nodded like we knew what the fuck he was talking about. Maybe she understood, but I've got only the vaguest idea what mutual funds are.

It's my own fault. I've avoided researching and learning some things. Maybe I didn't want to appear too savvy and tempt my sister to rope me into the financial side of the family affairs. Maybe I figured that after all the pain I've suffered, I deserved to focus only on the things that bring me pleasure, like musical theater and songwriting. But I'm starting to feel hungry for more. Erik's insatiable desire for knowledge is kind of contagious, I guess.

As it turns out, the event we're attending is more than a hoedown. It's part rodeo, part flea market, and part harvest festival. There's a big barn open to the afternoon air on three sides—clearly adapted for events, not cows. The second I jump out of the truck, the jaunty music coming from the barn teases my ears, filtering through the roar of trucks, the occasional lowing of a cow, the clanging bell of a strongman game somewhere among the festival tents, and the chatter of the people wandering among the booths and livestock pens. My sensitive wolf's nose picks up a hundred different scents—sunbaked straw, oiled leather, clay dirt, weathered wood, violin rosin, animal musk, sour sweat, hot spun sugar, furniture polish, cigarette smoke, and cheap cologne.

I circle the truck to see Christine hopping down without waiting for a hand. Erik climbs down more slowly. His face looks almost incomplete to me without the mask. I love that Christine was able to close those magical wounds of his, but it's going to take me a little time to get used to seeing all his features at once.

It's got to be hard for him, showing up here with his face exposed, especially when he's not used to being around people. His eyes are wide and hard, his jaw tight and his lips compressed. Taut discomfort shows in every line of his body.

Christine, on the other hand, is more keyed up than I've ever seen her. She's practically bouncing in place. "We need boots if we're going to dance. Mine are in the back with my stuff, but you two will have to buy some."

"Perhaps we should not dance at all," Erik suggests.

"Oh no." She waves a finger at him. "You're not getting out of this. It'll be good for you. You pushed me out of my comfort zone—I'm just returning the favor. Raoul, tell him we need boots."

Of course I have a couple pairs at home—I wouldn't be a true son of Nashville if I didn't. But they are inaccessible right now, and I know what Christine is trying to do isn't just about a particular style of footwear.

"We absolutely need cowboy boots," I confirm.

Erik looks at us both tragically but doesn't complain any further. After Christine finishes putting her own boots on, she leads us toward a big booth with several tables of beautifully crafted leather boots. She selects a black pair with silver thread for Erik and a brown pair with scarlet stitching for me.

"Hats next," she says.

I groan. "I don't do cowboy hats."

But when Erik picks up a black hat and sets it on his dark curls, I suddenly find myself losing my words and rethinking my aversion to cowboy headgear.

"Told you," Christine murmurs, nudging my arm with her elbow.

"How is he so fucking gorgeous in anything he wears?" I mutter.

Erik's mouth quirks in a half smile, and when he plops a cowboy hat onto my head, I leave it there.

The music from the barn had stopped temporarily—bands

switching places, maybe—but now it spills across the fields again, catchier and more compelling than ever, and I can't help tapping the toe of my new boot while Christine plants a crimson cowgirl hat on her head. When she turns to face us, her white skin, red lips, and black hair look more striking than ever. My brain immediately starts compiling sentimental couplets that compare her to Snow White.

Since we left the truck, she's been staying in the shadow of the tents, careful not to walk in the sun for too long. She doesn't make a big deal of it—the caution is natural for her, an instinct born from years as a vampire. From the little I know of vampires, they don't ignite in the sun, but they're sensitive to it. Sunshine can gradually poison them, like a terrible kind of sunstroke that eventually leads to death if the exposure is prolonged.

I remember Christine's confession—how her parents tried to transform all their children into vampires and ended up killing her siblings. Sometimes, I've wished Philippa dead. I'm not proud of it, but then again, she was never much of a sister to me. She was the favored one while my dad was alive, and then she became a manipulator, a dictator, a jailer in some sense. I can't remember ever actually loving her, and I'm not sure if that's her fault or mine.

Christine cared for her siblings, and their loss wrecked her. I can't imagine the pain of watching two loved ones die. When I think of her or Erik dying in front of me—

"What is it, my pet?" Erik's voice, cool and gentle, at my side. "You seem distressed."

A couple of guys in the boots tent glance over at us, their brows furrowed with disgust at the term of endearment he used for me.

"Don't call me 'pet' so loudly," I mutter. "Pay the vendor, and let's go."

With the purchase taken care of, I hurry Erik out of the tent. Christine follows us, then dances ahead toward the source of the fiddle music and the stomping feet.

"Why shouldn't I call you 'pet'?" Erik inquires.

"Not everyone is tolerant of all romantic relationships," I tell him. "Especially in the South or the Midwest, in some of these small towns and rural communities, it can be dangerous for people like us."

"People like us?" He flashes me a devastating grin. "There are no people like us. Let anyone try to deride or harm you. It will be the last word they speak, the last act they perform. There are ghosts in this place, too, spirits on whom I can call."

"While that's all very fucking hot, you really need to keep your voice down." I squeeze his arm briefly as we enter the big barn.

He scoffs a little, but he doesn't keep talking about his godly powers—mostly because Christine captures him immediately and begins teaching him the basic steps of a line dance.

"They have an area for beginners, see?" She points. "We'll start over there."

He's a natural dancer, because *of course* he is. With a nearly infinite intellect and a perfect body to match, how could he not be? The woman supervising the beginner's area seems astonished at how quickly he progresses. And that's how, not ten minutes after our arrival, Erik and Christine and I leave our hats on a table and take places on the main floor to dance Big & Rich's "Fake ID."

I can barely keep my mind on the steps half the time, because Christine is in her element. I've seen her moves onstage for *Sidewinder*; I know her sweet spot is somewhere between hip-hop and country with a dash of lyrical. But I couldn't have predicted the level of energy she's bringing to the floor today. Maybe it has something to do with all the orgasms we gave her—or the blood she drank from both of us—but she's dancing with a gleeful frenzy that makes me laugh aloud. Her hips swivel with a fluid grace I could never match. Her waist writhes and her spine curves like she's got no bones at all. She makes it look deceptively easy, but I'm already sweating, and I know just how much taut muscle it takes to move one's body so perfectly at that speed.

She's fucking amazing.

And then I look past her to Erik.

He dances with a furious power and a wicked freedom that make my heartbeat kick up even higher. His boots slam on the floor in perfect rhythm with hers. There are flames in his eyes and knives in his smile. His body swerves with virile ferocity I've never seen in a human being, and in that moment, I decide I need him in my show. I need him onstage, opposite Christine, in the role of the love interest. Hell, with their level of talent and chemistry, *Sidewinder* will be headed to Broadway in no time flat.

Their energy drives me, hauls me into the same hectic storm, and I dance harder than I ever have in my life. It's violence, it's wild joy, it's freedom—it's brutal on the body, but it feels almost as good as sex.

During the slower section, Erik and I move in on Christine, rolling our hips toward her in sync while she dances. We're riding the line of inappropriate, so after a few beats, I pull back, and Erik follows my lead. Still, even though we keep it PG the rest of the time, I'm pretty sure anyone watching can tell that we're both into Christine and that she welcomes our attention.

We dance through Belles's "I Hate Trucks" and Miranda Lambert's "Ain't in Kansas Anymore," and then I stagger off the floor, soaked and panting. I collapse into a chair at the table where we left our hats. Maybe I should spend more time working out and less time writing songs.

"Need a drink," I gasp out when the other two approach, and Christine hurries off to get me one. "So how'd it feel?" I ask Erik as he sits opposite me.

He smiles, the new scars across his right cheek pulling tight. "It felt like rebirth."

"Feels like death to me," I groan, and he laughs. His laugh, like his voice, is musical, beautiful. I crave the sound almost as much as I'm craving a glass of water right at this moment.

Christine returns with a couple waters and a couple beers. "Wasn't sure which kind of drink you wanted." She sets them on the table, then perches her butt on Erik's knee. His look of pleased astonishment is so cute, I can't help grinning as I open one of the water bottles.

A bulky shadow falls over our table, and I look up to see the same two guys who frowned at us in the booth earlier.

"Hey there, sugar. You wanna dance?" the bearded one says to Christine.

She lifts an eyebrow. "No, thanks. I'm here with someone— some people..." She blushes, looking disconcerted.

It doesn't bother me that she's a little flustered. After all, it's the first time she's had to explain our connection aloud to strangers.

"She's here with us," I clarify.

"But you and this guy are together, right?" says the bearded man to me. "So she's free to have a little fun on her own."

Christine has regained her composure, and she says firmly, "I'm here with both of them."

"You're shittin' me," says the man, and his friend whistles. "You're here with him?" He points to me, and Christine nods. "And with *him*?" He points to Erik, and Christine nods again.

"You seem capable of grasping simple facts," Erik says to the man, his voice a purring threat. "How delightful. Perhaps now you will take your unwanted attentions elsewhere and leave us in peace."

"Yeah..." The man scratches the back of his head. "See, y'all don't seem to realize that this ain't no place to show off your lifestyle. This is a family event. I'm sure you can understand why it's best if you move along."

"We're not showing off anything," Christine says. "And you don't run the event, so I don't think you have the authority to kick us out."

"I know the guy who runs it," replies the bearded man. "Y'all need to get gone, and I'm asking nicely. If you won't listen, Burt and I will go talk to some people who can make you move on."

"Look, man, we're just dancing and having some fun here, like everyone else," I tell him in my most placating tone. "Can't you just leave it be?"

"We gotta uphold the integrity of this event."

"Integrity," Erik says sardonically. "If she had agreed to dance with you, would you have left us alone?"

The man shifts his stance but avoids the question. "It's time for you three to go."

Erik's brows pull together, the golden brown of his eyes intensifying to a glowing yellow. At the same moment, the air around him seems to darken.

He's about to lose his shit and show off his supernatural side to everyone here. That can't happen.

Christine notices the change in him, too, and she rises from his lap. "Come on, Erik. Let's just go."

"That's right, honey, you tell him," says the second man. "How much do they pay you anyway? Do you give 'em a group rate? Two for the price of one?"

So much for keeping it family-friendly.

Erik rises, and I can practically smell the power rolling off him.

He's going to take these guys down, and it's going to be bloody. Unless I step in and do it first.

I'm not the kind to fight back. All my life, I've either taken my knocks or let someone else defend me—like Christine did when we were schoolmates. When I was locked up by my father, I stayed put. Defiance or rebellion only brought more pain or incited my father's alpha voice, so I just submitted, bowed my head, endured the agony.

But since last night, I'm different. I made a promise to the two people I adore, that I would summon the courage to break away from my family, to leave that toxic mess and cling to the ones who truly value me. Here's where I start exercising that courage muscle. It's gonna hurt, but if it saves Erik from outing himself, it's worth it.

I leap out of my chair so fast, it falls over, and I send my fist flying into the second man's jaw.

It's a good punch, better than I expected. He staggers back, trips over his friend's boot, and falls onto his butt. Pain flashes through my knuckles, but my adrenaline, already high from the dance and the confrontation, blurs the ache and swells my ego.

"Insult her one more time, motherfucker!" I roar at the man. "One more time!"

I've never yelled that loudly at anyone in my life. I came close when I was arguing with Erik, but this time, I'm bellowing the words with my whole chest. My face is probably beet red, and I feel invincible.

I'm not, though, which is probably why Christine grabs my hand and Erik's, dragging us both out of the barn while the guy I hit is still getting to his feet. He yells something like, "Get back here, you little bitch!" but we're already halfway down the slope, headed for the parking lot.

"I could go back and strangle him like Joe Buquet," offers Erik.

"Joe Buquet?" I exclaim. "What do you mean? Gil got a text from him the other day. Buquet took a job in Florida…left pretty suddenly…oh, shit…" My voice trails off as realization sets in. "Erik, did you send that text? You killed someone and didn't tell me? I thought all our secrets were out in the open!"

"It must have slipped my mind," says Erik coolly. "His death was well-deserved. Would you like me to drive? You seem agitated."

"Agitated? You bet your ass I'm fucking agitated!"

"Raoul, we'll talk when we're on the road," says Christine. "Not here, okay?"

"Fine." Grumbling, I climb into the truck, yielding the driver's seat to Erik.

Christine jumps in, too, and slams the door. "There's a bunch of guys headed down the hill toward us. Not that we couldn't take them, but it might get messy."

"Go, Erik," I urge him.

"One moment." He's fiddling with the radio. Only when Post Malone's "I Had Some Help" is blasting from the speakers does he pump the gas and send us out of the parking lot with a roar of the engine and a spray of gravel and dust. Christine whoops and waves to the oncoming men through the open window as we drive away.

"Back to Nashville?" inquires Erik.

"We're picking up my car first, and then…" Christine looks to me.

"Back to Nashville," I say resignedly. "I need to make a couple of casting changes to *Sidewinder*, and we've got a lot of rehearsing to do. But don't think I've forgotten about Joe Buquet. We're going to discuss this in detail."

"Of course." Erik gives me a sidelong look. "Does this mean you're accepting my changes to the score?"

"It means I'll look at them, and if I'll like them, we'll do it your way. But I'm still mad that you changed it without asking me first."

The smile he sheds over me is like sultry sunshine, designed to melt even the most resolved of hearts. My lips widen in an answering smile before I catch myself.

"Nope," I say firmly. "You can't fix this by flirting."

He frowns, looking deeply offended. "I never flirt."

"But I do," puts in Christine. I feel my zipper being dragged down by delicate fingers, and when I look at her, she smirks. "What can I say? Dancing and fighting make me horny. Scoot this way a bit. I'm going to sit on your lap."

I shift along the bench toward the passenger side, and she climbs on top of me, arranging her short skirt so it covers what we're doing. Her panties are already on the floor of the truck—I'm not sure when she took them off. Her fingers slide into my open jeans, bring out my dick, and nudge it into the slippery, warm center of her. I gasp when she seats herself fully on me.

"Eyes ahead," she tells Erik, and he reluctantly swerves his gaze back to the road.

With my left hand, I cup him between the legs, rubbing firmly even as Christine rides me, and my mind dissolves into bliss. My head tilts back against the seat. Slowly, the pain in my right hand submerges beneath the pleasure, and I allow myself a smile of satisfaction.

I defended Christine. Protected Erik from himself. Maybe I do have the strength I need to finally free myself from the Nashville pack. Maybe that's what my two lovers give me—the power to do the right thing.

Christine told us she left Nashville because she was afraid we might be toxic to each other—that combined in a trio, we might become capable of terrible things. But I suspect the opposite is true. Apart, we seem more prone to weakness, to fear, to evil. Together, we are stronger. We make better choices. We are healthier and more wholesome than ever.

I only hope our bond can withstand the pressure my family will exert on us once they find out why I'm leaving them.

27

CHRISTINE

Opening night. At last.

Shrouded in shadow, I wait offstage for my cue.

The merry voices of the chorus fill my ears, softly punctuated by a couple of terse whispers from the backstage crew. There's so much vibrant movement and glorious sound ahead of me, beneath the bright lights of the stage, yet the space around my body feels quiet, dark, and still.

My stomach flutters and rolls, the familiar pit of nausea tightening in my belly. My palms are sweating. But none of those symptoms deter me now, because I've been on that stage many times. I know that I can act, dance, and sing all at once. I was born to do this, and that certainty is a refuge in my heart, a cool, peaceful oasis that keeps me calm at my core no matter how anxiously my body may react. I've learned that if I endure the symptoms of stage fright without panicking about them, I can move through them.

When I step onstage, a different part of me takes over, unleashed from all the chains I've worn throughout my life and the barriers I set around myself—the walls that were meant to protect me from the world and the world from me.

A few months ago, I couldn't have imagined doing this. I couldn't have pictured singing in front of *one* person, let alone playing the lead for a musical. Not to mention costarring with the angel-voiced god of death.

The change in my confidence was mostly gradual, a slow transformation. But there were leaps in my growth, like the day I auditioned, the time Raoul sang with me at the Alouette, and the preview performance when I sang Eugenie for the first time.

I've always known the vampire side of me was an asset, but over the past few weeks, as we've rehearsed *Sidewinder* with its new score, I've realized just how useful vampirism is, how far it can propel me toward the new dreams that twirl through my brain at night when I'm lying in the lair below the theater, sharing the big bed with Erik and Raoul.

My nature as a vampire gives me the edge I need. It makes me faster, stronger, more graceful, more passionate. I'm less prone to injury and therefore less fearful of hurting myself, which spurs me to take greater risks with my dancing. My vocal cords recover quickly, so I can devote myself fully to belting out huge notes without worrying that I'll strain my voice.

Can it be that after so many years, I'm starting to move past the basic acceptance of my nature toward actually loving what I am?

Part of me still resists the idea of appreciating my vampire side, as if by being grateful for its benefits, I'm somehow betraying my siblings and forgiving my parents. I'm not sure how to fully get past that twinge of guilt and reluctance every time I feel pleased with myself.

One thing is certain, though—I'm healthier than ever, thanks to my two new blood sources. Both Erik and Raoul recover quickly after I drink from them, so I don't have to worry that I'm taking too much. Erik's blood gives me a hit of ecstatic power I've never gotten from anyone else, and Raoul's blood supplies a sensation of wholeness and strength that makes me feel like I could run across the entire continent without stopping. And the best part is I don't ever have to go hunting for strangers in bars again.

If I really am starting to love every part of myself, I owe a lot of that growth to Erik and Raoul.

Erik is still in his dressing room. He'll be here soon, ready to go onstage shortly after I do. Raoul managed to replace my former costar without too much fuss from the other directors, and even though I feel bad for Rune, I much prefer starring opposite Erik. He's naturally theatrical and lends a depth to the character that Rune just wasn't capable of.

Gil and Marj were curious about Erik, of course, demanding to know who he was and where he came from. Somehow, Erik concocted a brilliant backstory for himself, complete with online sources to back up his origins. It was enough to silence the directors, if not to completely allay Marj's suspicions. But at last she tapped her mouth with one shellacked fingernail and said sharply, "Well, he's easy on the eyes. Let's do it." And Erik proceeded to charm her and everyone else at each rehearsal after that.

I stretch my neck to one side, then the other, wondering how Raoul is doing in Box Five. He's probably up there worrying and tearing his program into tiny pieces. Erik and I have struggled to soothe Raoul's anxiety these past few weeks, ever since we returned from our road trip and he made the break with his family and the Shifter Collective.

Raoul refused to end things with his sister in person. I'm still not sure if that was the right choice, but it was his decision. He bribed one of the staff at the de Chagny house to pack up some of his things and bring them over to the New Orpheum, and then he sent his sister a long email explaining why he would no longer live in the house or assume any responsibilities with the pack.

Raoul was fully prepared for Philippa to retaliate. He thought she might withdraw funding from the musical, which Erik promised to supplement from his own investments. But the funding has held up, and there's been no response or retaliation at all.

As the weeks have passed, I've noticed Raoul relaxing more and more. Still, Erik insisted that we have extra security in place just in case Philippa decides that opening night is the perfect time to interfere with Raoul and his show.

So far, there's been no sign of anything wrong. But we've barely started the first act.

I need to stop fretting over things that aren't currently happening. I have to keep my mind clear and focused if I'm going to make Erik and Raoul proud tonight.

Closing my eyes, I mentally rehearse the first few bars I'll sing once I step onstage.

The music rises and crests. The chorus dancers shift to the left and right, making space for my entrance. *Three, two, one... here we go.*

And then it's over.

I'm standing with Erik, our clasped hands held high. We did it.

He performed his poignant solo in the second act—so much more hauntingly beautiful with its new orchestration. When I sang my final number to close out the last act, I hit the high note with more strength and clarity than ever before.

Each ensemble song, the bits of dialogue in between, the climactic fight, the passionate kiss—we did everything, and we did it beautifully. There were a couple of missteps and a fumble with a prop, but it didn't matter. We had the audience in the palm of our hand. I could feel their intensity, their attention. The roar of applause that greets us is proof of that, and so is the thunder of the audience leaving their seats, giving the entire cast a standing ovation.

When I look up at the tall, black-haired god beside me, I spot tears glittering in his eyes. I can't imagine what it must feel like to him, experiencing this praise. Finally, he is receiving the worship he deserves.

I peer at Box Five, but I can't see into its shadowed depths. Raoul was supposed to come down during the final song so he and the managers could walk onstage and receive their accolades, too. But when I glance offstage, he isn't waiting with Gil and Marj.

Where is he?

After a minute or two, during which the clapping starts to slacken, Gil and Marj walk out onstage without Raoul. Gil tries to take Marj's hand, but she shakes him off and waves to the crowd instead. We turn the audience's attention to the orchestra and the conductor, who performed a miracle by learning Erik's new score so quickly. After they've received their applause, we bow, and the curtain falls.

"Where is Raoul?" I whisper to Erik.

"Our poet may have been too emotional to appear before everyone."

I shake my head. "This is his dream come true. He would have wanted to be onstage, no matter how hard he was crying."

Cast members are crowding around, congratulating us and each other. Their faces shine with exuberant triumph, but a shadow of dread has fallen over my heart.

Erik pulls me close and bends down to speak in my ear. "I'll check Box Five and confer with my ghosts. Wait for me in your dressing room."

The grim look on his face tells me he's worried about the same thing I am. Despite the security in place throughout the theater, it's possible the shifters entered the building to reclaim the rogue member of their pack.

I head for my dressing room, removing pieces of my costume as I go—the gloves, the hat, the bow at my neck. I exchange congratulations and thanks with people along the way, but I manage not to get caught in conversation until a woman steps out in front of me. I recognize her as one of the wardrobe crew. She's carrying a large cup covered with quirky stickers.

I'm opening my mouth to say something like "Good work tonight!" but before I get the words out, she lunges forward, sending the icy, slushy contents of her cup all over my face, my hair, and the front of my dress.

"That's for Carlotta!" she yells, and she runs off, pursued by a security guard and two crew members.

For a second, I'm so shocked from the cold that I can't breathe. Then I'm seized with the violent urge to chase that woman, drag her down, and sink my fangs into her throat. It's all I can do to curb the hunting instinct that roars through my body.

I manage to accept the handfuls of paper towel that a

sympathetic cast member hands to me. She bobs at my elbow, cooing with soft concern, offering to escort me to my dressing room and help me clean up.

"I'm fine," I hear myself saying. "I'll just go take care of this in the bathroom."

After a moment's hesitation, she scurries away.

With the rage I currently feel, I don't trust myself in the communal bathroom, nor do I want to walk all the way to my dressing room with crimson slush dripping down my face. The last thing I want to do is answer questions about what happened or give Carlotta's rabid fan any further attention. Instead, I head for the broken-down bathroom I used before.

There's a burly security guard standing nearby, hands on his belt, keeping a watchful eye on this less-traveled backstage area. Even though I can defend myself easily, his presence is comforting.

I enter the bathroom and shut the door behind me. Leaning over the sink, I wipe off as much of the red slush as I can, along with some of my makeup. The mascara is waterproof, so at least I won't look like some sort of weeping clown when I emerge.

I'm picking bits of melting ice out of my hair when I spot something moving by the wall under the sink. My heart jumps, and I startle, but I don't scream.

It's a rat. Which is gross but nothing I can't handle. Of course I don't want the thing *on* me, but as a vampire, I have nothing to fear from any diseases its bite could communicate. Besides, it seems to be minding its own business, nosing along the edge of a broken tile.

Another shadow moves at the corner of my vision. This time, it's a slender black cat, stalking soundlessly from beneath one of the damaged stalls. Pursuing the rat, maybe.

Then, without warning, a scaly tubular thing rears up from the sink drain and writhes in midair. I muffle a startled cry with my hand as I stagger back against the wall.

The snake continues to emerge, coil after coil issuing from the drain until it's draped over the sink in striped loops. I'm no snake expert, but it looks like a death adder.

With a shudder and a burst of dark smoke, the snake transforms into a naked woman with tawny skin. The sink cracks free of the wall under her weight, and water begins dribbling from a pipe at the back. She hops down and stands before me.

Two more puffs of smoke, and the cat and the rat transform as well. The cat becomes an ebony-skinned man with a bald head, and the rat takes on the form of a huge, muscular man with freckled arms and a red face.

These three must be shifters from Philippa's pack. No use asking why they're here—it can't be for any good reason.

"Nice of you to make this easy for us." The woman speaks with a strong Australian accent.

I smile, letting my fangs slip from their sheaths as my claws emerge from my fingertips. "Who said anything about easy?"

When I swipe at her throat, she leaps back, and the two men charge me.

The only time I've had to fight was in the alley against those would-be rapists, and they were both inebriated and human. These people are shifters, and they are unexpectedly strong. My snarls and slashes don't seem to faze them at all. One of them strikes me skillfully with the side of his hand, once in the kidney and once on the neck, rendering me temporarily immobile with pain.

The two men grip my arms, pinning me against the wall, and

the big man collars my throat with his huge hand so I can't bite or breathe.

The snake shifter darts in, grinning with daggerlike teeth. "You're not the only one with fangs, honey," she hisses.

She bites my shoulder so deeply that her teeth scrape bone. I choke out a strangled groan.

Instantly, a feeling like liquid cold spreads from the bite. Ice travels along my veins, locking up my muscles and joints. I try to struggle, but I can't move, not even when the two men release me. I drop to the floor, stiff and motionless.

"She's a vampire, so the paralytic venom won't last long," the snake shifter tells her companions. "Be ready." Stepping over to the bathroom door, she opens it a crack and calls to the security guard. "Can you come over here? Miss Daaé just collapsed. I think she's really sick."

When the guard rushes in, the cat shifter darts forward, wraps a lean arm around the guard's throat, and throttles him into unconsciousness. The big guy, whose build and skin tone resemble the guard's, strips off the victim's uniform and puts it on himself.

"I'll carry her to the side door," he says. "Meet me there." He picks me up, and the snake shifter flicks my eyelids shut with her finger.

I can't open my eyes. Can't move a muscle.

The death adder shifter said that her venom won't last long for a vampire. How long? A few minutes? An hour? What will have happened to me by then? Where are they taking me, and where is Raoul?

Though I try desperately to speak, my lips feel too thick and heavy to move. I can feel myself being carried out of the bathroom, through the backstage area, and then down a hall.

"Oh my god, is she okay?" It's Meg's voice, and right on the heels of her exclamation, I hear Gabriella exclaim, "What happened?"

Fuck, if only I could send them some kind of signal that I'm in trouble…

"She hit her head," says the shifter carrying me. "There's an ambulance on the way to check her out."

"Should you have moved her?" Gabriella sounds doubtful, her tone bordering on rebuke.

"They told me to take her out into the fresh air," replies the man.

"We'll come with you," Meg says. "If she needs to go to the hospital, we'll go along. And I'll text her…um…her boyfriend… boyfriends?"

I don't blame her for hesitating. Raoul, Erik, and I decided not to formally announce our relationship, since it might bring up questions that would distract from the musical. But I know rumors have been circulating through the cast and crew—some more favorable or accurate than others.

Guilt flickers through me, because a real best friend would have told Meg everything as soon as I got back to Nashville. Okay, maybe I wouldn't have launched into a spiel about how myths are real and supernatural beings exist, but I could have explained the throuple I'm now a part of. I didn't. And to her credit, her concern for me outweighs any lingering hurt she might feel because I didn't confide in her.

I love Meg for wanting to go with me and make sure I'm okay. After everything I've failed to do as a friend, it means a lot. But I also want to scream at her to run, because who knows what the other two will do to her and Gabriella once they meet up with this brute outside.

"Sure, come along," says the big shifter genially. "I'm sure she'll be happy to see you when she wakes up."

They ask him a few more questions, and he lies easily and convincingly until I hear the squeak of the outside door and feel the cool air hit my face. There's a gasp and a faint shriek, immediately stifled, then a scuffling sound and the familiar squelch of fangs puncturing flesh. One bite, then another, followed by the sound of two bodies thumping limply onto the concrete.

"Just leave them here. They'll recover in a few hours. We have to go." It's the snake shifter, the woman. "Ollie, once we get to the van, give Ms. de Chagny an update and our ETA. Brit will take care of any camera footage, and then she'll join us at the rendezvous point."

I'm bundled ungraciously into a vehicle and dumped on the floor. At first, I'm hopeful because my fingers and toes are beginning to tingle as feeling returns to them, but the next second, cold metal presses against the skin of my wrists, then my ankles. A chilly metal band clicks shut around my throat, and a chain clanks. I feel the death adder's breath on my face right before her fangs sink into my cheek.

They've shackled and paralyzed me. They're not taking any chance that I might get loose.

Did they do something to Raoul? If anyone has hurt him or traumatized him even more, I swear I'll claw their hearts out.

The drive feels interminable, especially with my head lolling and my body tumbling every time the vehicle veers around a turn. The driver seems to like braking sharply, which makes me slide across the floor of what seems to be a work van of some kind.

For a while, I try memorizing the turns and counting the seconds, but eventually I lose track and give up. To amuse myself, I contemplate what I'll do to each of these shifters when I get my mobility back.

Eventually, I'm able to open my eyes and twitch my fingers. The two men are up front while the snake woman sits in the back with me, fully clothed now, holding the end of the chain that's fastened to the collar around my neck. She doesn't bite me again, but I'm sure she will if I make the wrong move.

Looking down, I discover that my handcuffed wrists and shackled ankles are connected to each other by a short chain, probably just long enough to allow me to walk. The restraints look thicker and stronger than anything I've seen on TV. They're probably designed to hold creatures with supernatural strength.

When the van finally stops, the two men drag me out. We're at the back of a long brick structure—an ugly, serviceable kind of building. Brown, brittle weeds sprout thigh-high from cracks in the concrete.

The shifters escort me up several steps and through a grimy back door. I dislike the slow, shuffling pace I have to maintain thanks to the chains, but at least it gives me a few minutes to look around.

This building used to be a high school, judging by the dingy hallways, the rows of graffiti-splattered lockers, and the mildewed posters congealed to the walls. In several places, squares of the drop ceiling have rotted away, but the electricity must still work, because a few watery fluorescent bulbs glimmer here and there to illuminate our path.

While his friend waits out in the hall, the big shifter shoves me into an empty room with a single chair. The dust-coated plaques on the wall hint that this room might once have been a school official's office—maybe even the office of the principal. Despite my anxiety for Raoul and for my own safety, I almost laugh at the irony of it.

When I was in school, I was particularly careful not to do anything that might get me in trouble. As a vampire, I couldn't risk any additional attention, so I stayed low and kept quiet. I wasn't popular or unpopular—I just floated along in the middle, being unremarkable, average. Not worth a second glance.

When I got older and boys started to notice me in spite of myself, I dressed in baggier clothes and avoided contact most days. I interacted with them just enough to ensure that I got invited to parties where I might be able to sneak a few swallows of blood from people who were too drunk or high to notice.

Being brought here feels odd, not only because of the rush of unbidden high school memories, but because this decrepit place doesn't fit with the bits of information I've gleaned about Raoul's sister. By all accounts, Philippa de Chagny should be operating out of a gorgeous office building with elegantly villainesque decor. A grungy abandoned high school doesn't seem like her thing.

But apparently it is, because a moment after I'm forced into the battered chair, a woman walks in who can't be anyone but Philippa de Chagny.

Her sleek bob is auburn, darker than Raoul's hair, but she has the same pale green eyes, along with the same delicate, angular jawline and crisp features. Except wherever there's softness in Raoul's face, there is only hardness in Philippa's.

She wears a blouse, tailored slacks, and a pair of heels that I'm fairly sure are Louboutins.

"Let's get right to the point," she says. "I'm a busy woman, Christine Daaé, and you've made me waste entirely too much time on you as it is."

"If you're going to try to bribe me to stay away from Raoul, save your breath," I tell her. "Where is he? If you hurt him, I swear—"

"Hurt him?" Her green eyes flash. "He's my brother. He's family. No, Christine, you're the one hurting him. In his email, he wasn't specific about *why* he suddenly decided to leave the family and the Collective, but I knew it had to be a lover. I had my people ask around, and they discovered *you*. You're the girl who's been messing with his head, with his life."

"All I've done is encourage him to be himself."

She scoffs lightly. "You know, when I first heard your name from my sources, I thought it sounded familiar. Imagine my surprise when I discovered who your parents were." Philippa's merciless eyes never leave my face, like she's reading me in spite of my silence. "The Shifter Collective keeps tabs on all the supernaturals in Nashville. We're rather territorial, you might say. Any supernatural who isn't a shifter has to register with the Collective and pay an annual tax in order to remain within our territory. Your parents paid their dues without fail, for all three of you."

Yet another thing my parents did without my knowledge or input. Why am I not surprised?

"Since their deaths, you haven't paid your dues." Philippa takes a slim smartphone from the pocket of her pants. "It slipped our notice, but we would have discovered the issue during our next audit. As it is, you owe two years' worth of fees to the Collective."

"Add that to the debts I can't pay," I say dryly.

Her icy gaze holds mine. "And you're hoping Raoul is your way out of a financial hole?"

"No, of course not! And I didn't know about the tax. My parents never discussed it with me."

I'm guessing they never talked about it because they thought I'd be under the protection of the Progeny after their death. If anything happened to them, they thought I would leave Nashville and go to a Progeny commune, or that Progeny representatives would come to Nashville to take care of me. Somehow, they never imagined that I'd try to do life on my own.

"Ignorance is no excuse," says Philippa.

"So you kidnapped me because I owe you money?" I vent a disbelieving laugh.

"In part, yes," she says coolly. "The Collective takes debts very seriously, and when someone is in default, an example must be made, or other supernaturals will begin to test our good graces. But you're correct—the mere existence of the debt is not enough. To dispose of you completely, I knew I would need more." She touches her phone a few times, then holds it out so I can see the screen.

It's security camera footage of me in an alley, slaughtering the men who were planning to rape me. Killing them in the most messy, violent way imaginable. The scene is dark, but she's had the footage enhanced, and when I leave the alley, there's a shot of my face. A little blurry, but it would probably hold up in court.

"The Collective hushed up these murders when they

occurred," says Philippa. "Truthfully, we thought it was one of our own who'd gone rogue around the same time. The two of you look rather alike. But once my people started digging to find information on you, we realized the truth. And that's not all we found."

She swipes through several more clips and images of me with my various victims, leaving bars or going into motels. With each successive piece of evidence, the sense of nauseating dread builds in my stomach.

This is my worst nightmare. I thought I'd been so careful.

When I glance up, Philippa is watching me with a shrewd, triumphant smile. "You've committed assault against at least five men that we could find—probably dozens more. You're a danger to the people of this city. And the way you operate, you could easily expose the supernatural world to the humans."

I want to tell her I don't do that anymore. But I can't risk confessing to those crimes aloud, and mentioning that I frequently drink from her brother probably isn't the best move here.

"Most of all, you're a danger to Raoul," Philippa continues. "I don't know what kind of sick hold you've got over him, but the Raoul I know would never reject his family. He knows his place and what's expected of him."

"You expect him to stay with the Collective and let himself be used," I lash out. "That's why you want him—because his status as a wolf shifter cements your control of the pack. You don't care if he'd be happier elsewhere, away from all this political shit. That's so typical of supernaturals. You're so obsessed with yourself and with power that you're ready to sacrifice your own family to attain your goals." I spit, and the foam hits her left Louboutin. "I despise people like you."

She quirks her right forefinger, and the big shifter who escorted me in kneels meekly and wipes my spit off her shoe with the cuff of his shirtsleeve.

"You won't have to despise me long," Philippa says. "Once you're out of the picture, Raoul will come to his senses."

"And how exactly are you going to take me out of the picture?"

"Use your imagination." Her smile is a thin, malevolent line. "You said it yourself—we can't bribe you. We could give this evidence to the human authorities, but I doubt their prisons would hold you, and the Collective doesn't keep prisoners. So there's only one practical solution."

They're going to kill me. That's what she's saying.

Dying at the hands of my boyfriend's sister was definitely not on my to-do list for opening night.

"Go ahead then," I say with a bravado I don't feel. "Have your guy shoot me. Raoul will hate you for it."

"Shoot you? And have you pop right back up again the second we leave? I don't think so." Her smile widens. "I know all about the healing power of vampires. We're going to make sure the job is done properly. Another thing you may have learned about the supernatural community—we love a good ritual. I've already invited the Collective to witness your death. I like to hold these little executions from time to time to remind everyone of the importance of paying their dues and following the rules. It's just good business."

My mouth is dry, and though I refuse to beg for my life, I need to know what timeframe I'm working with. So far, Philippa has given no indication that she knows about Erik, which could play in my favor, if only he has enough *time* to locate me and Raoul.

"When?" I ask quietly. "When am I going to die?"

She glances at her phone. "In an hour or two if all goes well." She gives the burly shifter a tight nod. "Keep the girl here until I text you. Don't underestimate her."

"Yes, ma'am," he replies.

Philippa meets my gaze again, her eyes like mint-green ice. "It's been a pleasure, Christine. And now, if you'll excuse me, I need to have a conversation with my little brother."

28

THE PHANTOM

"Who's going to tell me what the fuck happened?" My voice reverberates like thunder through my lair, echoing across the canal, bouncing off the concrete walls. The gathered ghosts retreat slightly, shifting and murmuring among themselves. Ever since I destroyed Agnes, they've been more obsequious around me, more eager to please, with the unfortunate result that no one wants to be the one to deliver bad news.

"You have nothing to fear from me," I growl, trying not to sound too threatening. "My lovers have disappeared from this place, and I need to know exactly how it happened and who took them. I have spoken with a few of you, but none of those spirits witnessed anything suspicious. That is why I have called this meeting. If any of you have information, come forward."

With a faint squeak of anxiety, a tiny ghost drifts forward—a little girl who somehow managed to bring the ghost of a dilapidated stuffed rabbit with her into the afterlife. It floats behind her, towed by one ragged ear.

I modulate my tone still more, trying to be gentle despite the rage and fear churning through my chest. "What did you see, little one?"

"I was playing in one of the bathrooms," she says in a voice so high and faint I can barely hear her. "I saw the pretty singer, Christine, washing her face. Then three animals entered the room, and they changed. They turned into people. She fought, but one of them bit her, and then she stopped fighting. The big one carried her away."

My teeth clench so hard they hurt. That must have happened to Christine while I was searching for Raoul. I failed them both tonight.

"Thank you, my dear. You've done well." With a twitch of my fingers, I transform the ghostly stuffed rabbit, mending its threadbare appearance and frayed edges, giving it a bow and replacing its missing eye. The child coos with delight and clutches it to her chest.

"And the poet with the reddish-gold hair?" I demand of the other ghosts. "What news of him?"

Gradually, gathering bits of information from one ghost and another, I piece together the sequence of events. Near the end of the performance, a woman made her way past the security guards, none of whom stopped her. She entered Box Five and spoke to Raoul. He got up and went with her quietly—no sign of force or reluctance. They walked out of the theater, got in a black car, and drove away.

I do a quick online search for a photo of Philippa de Chagny and present it to the ghosts who saw the pair at various points during their exit from the theater. "Was this the woman?"

All of them affirm that it was. Which means Raoul left with his sister, apparently of his own free will, while Christine was kidnapped by three shifters, probably on Philippa de Chagny's orders.

I only know Philippa de Chagny through Raoul's brief mentions of her. Overbearing, dominant, exacting. A ruthless leader determined to maintain control and accumulate more power. At one time, I might have admired her, but her behavior toward Raoul and her actions tonight have made us mortal enemies.

These events are partly my fault. I let my guard down. I saw Raoul becoming more relaxed, believing that his sister had accepted his decision, and I failed to recognize the true threat posed by the Shifter Collective. Though Raoul seems to have left the theater of his own free will, I can't shake the sense that he is in just as much danger as Christine.

Wherever they are being taken or held, I can expect to encounter significant resistance when I go to fetch them. If I ever manage to find them again.

For a moment, I feel wretched, helpless, lost. An acidic sense of failure eats away at my soul, turning my stomach bilious. Heat rushes through me, and I run to the edge of the canal, bending over while my body heaves vomit into the black water.

I have never vomited before. I never wish to experience it again.

I rush to the bathroom and brush my teeth until all I can taste is mint toothpaste. During that process, my sense of helplessness shifts, transforming into a murderous intent, an all-consuming rage.

Philippa de Chagny thought she could take my darlings from me and suffer no consequences. She will soon discover just how wrong she is. Raoul does not belong to her anymore—he is *mine*. Christine is *mine*. And I will decimate this city, raze it to the ground if I must, but I will get both of them back.

I stride out again, back to the place where my ghosts wait for my orders. They are many yet not enough. I will need more.

After a moment's consideration, I sweep my black coat around my shoulders and snatch up my favorite mask, the white one that conceals every part of my face except my mouth and jawline. I fit it into place, feeling oddly comforted by its presence. It's no longer a necessity, but for the task that lies ahead, it gives me the edge I need.

"Follow me," I command the ghosts. They obey, trailing after me as I leave the lair and head for the stairway where I first heard Christine sing.

Since I met her, the wailing of the city's dead has been fainter and farther away—a distant whisper in my mind. Whenever their laments grew too loud, I remembered her voice and let it fill my head, dispelling all unwanted sounds. But now, I turn my attention to that ghostly chorus, and I coax it forward in my consciousness. Louder and louder it grows with every flight of steps that I mount until I throw open the door at the very top of the stairway and step out onto the roof of the New Orpheum.

It's a black night blistered with stars, and a brisk October wind rushes through my hair, catching my unbuttoned coat and billowing it behind me.

There's a small building on the rooftop, probably constructed to protect equipment. I climb the iron ladder to its roof and stand there, gripping the lightning rod, looking out over the entire New Orpheum property and the river beyond. The lights of the city glitter like scattered diamond flecks on dark velvet.

Violence swells within me, a tide of magic surging deep in

my psyche. As it rises, I hear the voice of the blond vampire who suppressed my powers. Her words are a law to my magic, a dam separating me from the flood of my true potential. I know why she closed me off from my powers—to protect human life from my destructive potential. But I need that magic now.

I strain against the insistent compulsion of her voice. I struggle until cold sweat breaks out over my entire body, but it's no use. I can't access the powers she sealed away.

To her credit, she left me with some magic, including my vocal abilities. Since I was put into this body, I've used my ventriloquism many times, thrown my voice at various distances and volumes. But I've never tested how far I can project or how loud I can be.

Whipped by the wind, standing beneath the arch of the star-flecked void, I let the consciousness of every ghost in the city fill my mind. Then I call to them, out loud.

It's the language of my heart, the one I spoke on the Isle long ago, in ancient times—a tongue that few living humans would recognize or comprehend. Yet I know the ghosts will understand me. I am their lord, and my call has a power beyond the shape of words.

Magic floods out of me, spurring the sound of my voice to every corner of the city, to every churchyard and graveyard and morgue, every alley and attic and tunnel. It reverberates across bridges and thunders through homes, resonates with a sonorous threat and an irresistible command. It is a summons to every last ghost in the City of Music.

The effect is immediate. I can sense the pull, the onrush of hundreds of restless spirits straight toward the peak of the New Orpheum Theatre.

If I must fight to retrieve the people I love, the ghosts will be useful to distract and terrorize any shifters I may encounter. But I do not possess sufficient magic to make the ghosts corporeal enough to fight, which worries me. I wield limited shadows and mist, and I have godlike strength, but there is only one of me. I need more bodies on my side.

I briefly consider calling upon the people I've blackmailed, but I quickly discard that notion. None of them are fighters. Besides, Christine and Raoul would be disappointed in me if I fed hapless humans to the jaws of the Shifter Collective.

Searching the corners of my mind, I recall one presence I've suppressed even more deeply than the ghosts. One voice that spews hatred and resentment with particular force.

The voice of the sea god, Manannan, the only other god in our former pantheon who now moves through the modern world.

In the past, all the Tuatha Dé Danann were able to communicate mentally. We could press against each other's thoughts, requesting entrance, and be granted access for a telepathic dialogue even over great distance. But discord among our race and the changes in the world of mortals made such conversations less and less common.

Manannan hates me more than the other Tuatha Dé Danann for reasons that are blurred in my memories. The last thing I want to do is ask for his help. But it can't be denied that with proximity to him, my powers would likely grow, and vice versa. That was the way of things among us. We were a family of sorts, albeit a dysfunctional one. We could bolster each other's power. The more of us who were connected, the greater the feats we could achieve.

Tentatively, I reach for Manannan's consciousness.

Brother, I would speak with you.

He replies instantly, violently, a shout blazing through my mind with such force that I gasp and stagger, holding my head.

You are no brother of mine! Bastard, traitor, outcast, most hated of all the gods...

The list of insults continues for a while until I find a gap and push through. *Whatever you feel about me, I need your help. I may be forced to battle against a pack of shifters, and if you fight beside me, I will grant you anything you ask in exchange.*

He hesitates. *What could you possibly have that I would want?*

Tell me what you most desire, and I will attempt to achieve it.

For several moments, he doesn't reply. Then he snarls, *I have been wandering the oceans of the world for more than a year. With your resurrection, I regained some of my power, but the ocean is clogged with human waste and debris. I am miserable, mired in their shit. The one who raised me promised me a glorious awakening of other gods, as many as he could find. He swore we would have power again, that we would reign supreme and cure the evils of humanity.*

I try to keep my mind on his words, but I'm also surveying the growing multitude of ghosts around me, all of them congregating on the rooftop of the New Orpheum and in the skies above. They're waiting for my command, and the sound of their mutters and wails is nearly deafening.

Frowning beneath my mask, I concentrate on Manannán's growling voice in my head. *My summoner has abandoned me, left me rudderless and nearly impotent. This is not the existence he promised. He has not communicated with me in many months. I want to speak with him and demand an explanation. I wish to know if his great plan is still in motion or if he raised me up only to leave me in misery.*

He abandoned me as well, I say. *But I have some information that could help you contact him. If you assist me tonight in my battle against the shifters of Nashville, I will give you everything I have that could help you speak with our summoner. And...* A pang dashes through me at the incentive I'm about to offer, the sacrifice I intend to make...but I forge ahead. *I will give you my lair, the refuge I have built, to be your own. There is a canal within it that runs to the river and then to the sea, so you can take your aqueous form or your human form as you please. I assume you have a human form?*

I do, he replies. *I do not prefer it.*

In physical form, you will be able to take greater advantage of the resources the humans possess, I tell him. *They are wasteful, to be sure, but they can also be very entertaining. You might find your existence more bearable if you acclimate to their ways and technology. Will you come?*

His voice in my mind darkens. *Why are you in conflict with this pack of shifters?*

They took my lovers from me.

It's a sensitive point with him. I remember that much. My relationship with the Morrigan in times past caused a great rift among the Tuatha Dé Danann. With half a dozen words, I may have ensured that Manannan will never help me.

But to my surprise, he responds within a few minutes. *I sense your location. Prepare for my arrival.*

In his aqueous form, he can move from place to place almost instantly, as long as there are adjoining bodies of water between him and his destination. I have only moments before he surfaces in the canal beneath the New Orpheum.

I turn my attention to the assembly of ghosts. Though they are invisible to humans, to my eyes, they seem to fill the sky.

"I'm searching for two people," I call out. "You can perceive their images through your connection to me. Their names are Raoul de Chagny and Christine Daaé. Fly through the city, search every building. Go down to the steam tunnels and the sewers. Fly into the suburbs and the warehouses. Search everywhere, and when you find their location, tell me at once. Go!"

The ghosts whirl away, soaring through the night to do my bidding. Bodiless and soundless, they can rush through walls, searching places I could never access, and with their numbers, they're sure to locate Christine and Raoul quickly.

I descend the stairs, trying to decipher my feelings about the impending encounter with Manannan. There's a strange quiver of anticipation in my stomach, yet every muscle in my body is tight with caution. He has always been one of the most volatile and aggressive gods. Not that I can remember specific instances of his volatility—it's more of a vague impression.

When I reach the lair, I only have to wait for a few seconds before the water of the canal churns like black ichor in a cauldron. Its bubbles explode into spray as a broad, sinewy form leaps out of the water onto the walkway beside the canal. He rises, water streaming from his naked body and his big red beard.

"You're looking at me as if you don't remember me, Cernunnos," he growls.

"When I was put into this body, someone tampered with my memories," I tell him. "You look vaguely familiar, but my recollections of our past are blurred."

His nostrils widen and his eyes burn with barely suppressed rage. "You should remember that I hate you. That I despise all your offspring, from generation to generation."

"Offspring?" I give a rueful laugh. "I don't remember any of them, although I know the line of banshees came from me and from..." I hesitate.

"Say it," he presses. "Say her name."

"The Morrigan."

"Do you remember that I loved her?" His Irish accent is thicker than when he spoke in my mind, perhaps due to his mounting emotion. "Do you recall that you stole her from me?"

"I recall that she made her own choices," I reply. "But I do not remember the specifics of what happened, nor do I carry any lingering love or desire for her. If she were raised today, perhaps she would be yours."

"And that was the agreement I had with our summoner." His huge fists clench. "He promised to bring forth Fate herself, in a body I could touch, with a voice I could hear. Where is he? Has he decided to break all his promises?"

"I do not know. But I have a phone number for him."

Manannan stares at me.

"A phone is human technology used for communication. How long have you been at sea?"

"I know what a phone is!" He scoffs, then mutters a series of curses.

"Good. And there is much more I can teach you. I swear, if you help me now, I will help you find Lloyd-Henry so you can ask him about his promise to raise the Morrigan."

"I'll not be taught by the likes of you," he growls. "Nor do I want this poppet's parlor you call your 'lair.' But you'll contact Lloyd-Henry for me. You'll find him, and I'll make him fulfill his word."

"Yes."

"Very well. Where are these shifters we need to kill?"

"I'll have their location soon. And we may not need to kill all the shifters—only enough to free their captives. My lovers prefer it when I choose less violent paths." I give him a grim smile. "In the meantime…let's find you some clothes."

29

RAOUL

"Well," says my sister. "You've fucked up. As usual."

I've been standing behind a high-backed chair in the library, but at those words, I march around the chair toward her. I'm not sure what I intend to do—attack her? Dart out the door and run?

But she lifts her chin, cool and imperious, and says, "*Sit.*"

It's her alpha voice, a command I can't resist. Teeth gritted, I sink down into the chair.

Part of me wasn't surprised when she appeared in Box Five at the end of the musical. I'd asked the security guards not to let her into the New Orpheum, but I'm sure she bribed or threatened her way past them. Or maybe Gil, being an ally of hers, overruled my order to the security personnel.

He and I have never discussed my sister, not since we began working together on *Sidewinder*. In the weeks since I broke ties with the Collective, the closest he came to mentioning it was to clap me on the shoulder and say, "You've done well, Raoul. Doing your own thing, standing on your own two feet like a man should. It suits you."

I've never liked him, but those words of praise put me off my guard a bit where he's concerned. I assumed he was on my side, more or less, and I didn't look at him as a threat. I should have kept a closer eye on him, should have realized that he was probably there to spy on me for Philippa, even while he looked out for his own interests.

I should have been more careful, and I should have told Erik and Christine about Philippa's influence over me. Why didn't I warn them? Maybe because her control is limited by proximity, and I thought I could stay away. Maybe because her commands have no power once I've left her presence. Maybe because I didn't want Erik to go and kill her immediately. Maybe because I didn't want the two people I admire most to realize how fucking weak I really am.

In spite of all that, I should have swallowed my pride and told them about the danger. I should have known that my sister's silence was anything but an admission of defeat.

I should have known she would never let me go.

Of course, I realized it all too late, the moment Philippa sat down beside me in Box Five.

I went for my phone immediately, but she said, "No phones. Come with me, now. Quietly."

I've never fought so hard to resist a command, not even when my father was the one giving the orders. But it was no use. My body obeyed her, leaving the box calmly and walking beside her to the car. She dropped me off at our house, where several shifters were waiting to make sure I went inside and stayed in the library, per Philippa's orders. They remained with me until she got back a few minutes ago. I don't know where she was or what she was doing, but it can't have been anything good.

Now she's standing in the door of the library, looking at me like I'm a wayward pet who has disappointed her for the last time.

The library is one of my least favorite rooms in the house. Not a novel in sight; my father disapproved of fiction. No poetry either. It was contraband for me, smuggled in from the public library, inhaled during my lunch breaks at school, downloaded on my phone and kept in a folder I titled "social studies test notes" so my father would overlook it during his periodic checks of my phone's contents. Only when I finally made it into college did I have free rein to indulge my passion for poetry and lyricism.

Philippa paces slowly toward one of the bookcases, traces a finger along one shelf, and inspects her fingertip for dust. Apparently she finds none, which is good news for the maid.

"When you came back from college, I supported you," Philippa says. "I let you pursue your music. I didn't immediately summon Jean-Luc and try to bring out your wolf like Dad did."

She pauses, glances at me. She's positioning our father as a common enemy, trying to put herself on my side.

I scoff loudly. "Don't act like you're better than him. You were at his elbow the whole time, all those years he was tormenting me. You fucking *worshipped* him."

"I was *loyal* to him. To this family. A concept that seems too difficult for you to grasp. Do you understand where we came from? What our parents and grandparents built? Do you realize how many people crave the level of power and influence that comes with the de Chagny name, not to mention the financial assets?"

"I'm aware that we're a bunch of billionaire assholes," I reply. "Wait…*supernatural* billionaire assholes. Does that make it better or worse?"

Philippa gives me a vicious sneer. A single lock of her hair flops over her eyebrow, brushing her cheek. "You act as if you're not one of us. Like you're better than everyone else in the Collective. Better than me." She shakes her head, venting a sharp chuckle. "Where do you get the audacity, the hubris? It's new, and it doesn't look good on you. Wait...I know where you got it. From *her*."

She means Christine, and she's not wrong.

"You didn't mention a lover's name in your email." Philippa captures the stray lock of hair and smooths it into place. "But it wasn't hard to figure out who she is. The entire cast and crew of your musical know you're sleeping with Christine Daaé. Or you *were*. That won't be happening again."

"You can't keep me away from her." I try to rise from the chair, but her command to *sit* still grinds against my bones, holding me in place.

"I realize that," she says more calmly. "You'd figure out a way to get to her. Temporarily removing her influence won't work. There has to be a permanent uncoupling."

I twist in the chair, fear flaring through my veins like molten metal. "What does that mean?"

She continues her walk along the bookshelves. "It's beyond frustrating, the way you gobbled up the money I gave you. The way you act like you deserve the funding for your precious musical—like it's your *right*. It's not. It's a fucking *privilege*. A privilege afforded to loyal members of this family. Now that you can shift—"

"Yes, I can shift now. So what?" I exclaim. "Why can't I keep living my life as I choose? Keep the money. I don't want it."

"But you need it," she counters, eyes narrowing.

I want to tell her that no, I don't need it, because Erik has promised to support my musical career. But I hold back the retort. I can't tell her anything about him. She and the others would consider him a threat. The Collective would hunt him down, and none of his voice tricks would save him from all those teeth and claws.

I keep silent, and she takes that as an admission of need.

"Privileges are earned."

Her tone, her inflection, and her expression have never reminded me so much of our father. Acid inches up my throat. I can feel flashbacks quivering at the back of my brain, ready to leap forward and crush my consciousness or send me into a sweating panic.

Philippa's voice continues, hard as bulletproof glass. "You really expect me to hold on to this empire myself, don't you? And I could, I suppose. But it may surprise you to learn, little brother, that I'm not a robot. I get tired. Do you hear me? I get fucking tired of managing everything, dialoguing with everyone, settling disputes and maintaining alliances so we can stay at the top. You don't know how easily it could all fall apart. You don't want to know. You just want to keep drinking from the family tit until you're glutted without lifting a finger to—"

"I don't want the money," I cut in. "I want to be free. No more Collective, no more supernatural shifter Mafia or whatever the hell we are. I just want out. You could get out, too. You could leave."

She freezes midstep and turns her shocked gaze on me.

Even on the day when I first showed her my wolf form, I never saw her look like this. Utterly stupefied.

"Leave?" Her voice is breathless with anger...and maybe a touch of panic. "You have no idea what you're saying. You know only a fraction of the influence the Collective wields in this city—the power we have. And I rule the Collective. *I* do. Why in the hell would I ever give that up? What else would I do?"

I shrug. "Go live in Colorado with Conri?"

Her laugh is nearly hysterical. "He'd *leave* me, you idiot. We are engaged because of the Collective, because an alliance makes sense and we fit perfectly as mates. That's our duty, yours and mine—to mate within the shifter lines and keep our blood strong. But you don't care. You ran off with someone completely inappropriate for you. Not just some unknown dancer, but a fucking *vampire*."

Ice trickles down my spine. Until now, I was sure she thought Christine was human. Not much of a threat.

But if she knows Christine is a vampire...

Fuck. Oh *fuck*.

Philippa shakes her head at me. "You're thinking about denying it. Don't bother. I have proof. She was cautious with her feedings, but her caution was no match for the people who work for me. I imagine she's fretting about her mistakes right now, thinking about everything she could have done differently. Thinking about how this ends."

"Where is she?" I try to stay calm, but I'm not as coolheaded as Erik or as clever as Christine, so my voice trembles. "If you touch her..."

"What will you do, Raoul?" Philippa steps in front of me, one hand on her hip, bending slightly to look me in the face. "Kill me? I'm your family. Oh wait...I forgot. Family means nothing to you."

"There's more than one kind of family."

"You didn't answer my question. What will you do if I hurt Christine?"

I stare into her eyes—the eyes of the person I opened Christmas presents with. The one who made the same *ew* face as I did when we were served asparagus at dinner. The person who watched quietly while our father shoved me into the closet under the stairs.

I remember how she looked in those moments—pity mixed with cool interest and a touch of rebuke. I remember what she would say to me afterward. *Just shift next time, and everything will be all right. Just obey him, and he'll be nicer to you.* As if I were purposefully resisting the change somehow.

I remember watching her young wolf form gamboling on the back lawn after dark. I remember the first time she fought a member of the pack over an offense I can't recall. My father made me stand with him that night and witness the event. I remember how the other shifter's blood looked black against the yellow grass under the floodlights.

She was merciless even then, and she is ruthless now.

Her stare penetrates mine. "I know what you'll do," she says quietly. "You'll do exactly as I say." She straightens, smoothing her blouse. "Father was right. The only way to accomplish anything with you is to break you. You have to keep being broken until you're finally pliant enough to fill the role you were born to assume."

From what Philippa has said, Christine is already in her hands. I don't know where Erik is, and I pray he won't be foolish enough to come after us and get himself killed.

"Please, Philippa." I force the words out. "Just let me go. Let Christine go. You have Conri to support you. You don't need me."

"Conri isn't family, Raoul. You were taught the same lessons I was, in a bloodier font. I don't understand why you still can't grasp it." She sighs. "I gave you as much freedom as I could, but you abused it and forfeited my trust. You did this to yourself, little brother."

"No, Philippa—"

"You're going to come with me now. Christine has broken several laws of the Collective. She owes a two-year debt, she has murdered several humans, and she has taken blood from humans who were not on the index of approved prey. We can't have a rogue vampire running around. Exiling her would only distract you— you'd want to chase after her. So for your own good as well as the good of our city, her sentence is death. And you will carry it out."

30

CHRISTINE

I'VE BEEN WAITING FOR TWO HOURS.

I tried talking to the big shifter. I had some vague idea of charming him into helping me, but he gave me *nothing*. Not a word, not a glance.

For a while, I strained against my handcuffs, just to test them, but I only ended up causing myself pain. As I suspected, they're too strong to break.

When I started moving around too much in the chair, my guard went out into the hall and came back with a fucking cattle prod, so I decided to stay still. It's tough, though, as worked up as I am about Raoul and my own impending death.

At last, three more shifters enter the room. I guess they're my escort to my execution. When they drag me to my feet, I struggle—a last-ditch effort. But with the restraints, I can't get the range of motion I need to attack successfully. The most damage I do is a few cuts with my claws and a good hard bite to a shifter's shoulder. He groans, shudders, then staggers back, allowing the other shifters to handle me.

The taste of him explodes on my tongue, a revolting wave of acidic corrosion that I wasn't expecting. I choke and spit out as much as I can, but the metallic horror of that blood clings to the inside of my mouth like a liquid plague. It's ancient, like the blood of the Angel, and wild, like Raoul's blood, but it has turned utterly foul, sickeningly wrong.

I spit again and gag at the taste. The other shifters glance from me to the man I bit, surprise on their faces.

"What the hell are you?" I gasp.

He retreats farther, gripping his wounded shoulder. He has brown wavy hair that almost brushes his shoulders, a short beard, neatly groomed, and a pair of tragic eyes…the kind of eyes you see in paintings of the Christ. Not that I'm religious by any means, but when you're a vampire, you tend to be somewhat fascinated by religions that focus heavily on the importance of blood.

The haunted desperation in the man's eyes makes me stop struggling for a second.

"You're not just a shifter," I say. "You're something else. And you're sick. Dying."

"Lloyd, what is she talking about?" asks one of the shifters.

"Fuck if I know," the man replies, holding my gaze. "I told you I'm having trouble with my shifting. That's why I'm here. Philippa said she could help me—ah, fuck—"

He doubles over as if he's in agony. Smoke leaks from him, and he flashes into a new form—a black stag much too tall for this room. His antlers rip through the ceiling tiles. Another burst of smoke, and he's a black owl with silver eyes. He utters a half-choked shriek before he transforms yet again into a night-dark panther whose muscled shoulder gleams wet with blood.

The startled exclamations from the other shifters let me know that this isn't a normal occurrence.

"You can take multiple forms?" exclaims a shifter next to me.

The panther snarls at him, then bounds out of the office.

"What was that?" mutters the burly shifter, and another replies, "Let Philippa sort it out. She let him into the pack. Let's just get this one to the gym."

They escort me to the gymnasium, a big one by high school standards. Moss cloaks the cracks in the walls, and the once-glossy flooring is stained by water damage...or maybe blood. There are tiers of stadium chairs, the hard plastic ones that you have to fold down so you can sit on them.

Many of those seats are filled by people in hooded coats. Some of them wear masks, which makes sense. I can see why people in a murderous supernatural collective might not want their identities to be common knowledge. There are probably factions here, rival groups with opposing interests. And Raoul's sister has to keep them all loyal, docile, and cooperative.

I don't envy the bitch.

As I'm dragged across the floor of the stadium, I scan the place for exits. The few I can see have clusters of people nearby—guards probably. Even if I could break loose, getting *out* would be a challenge.

A wave of panic weakens my limbs and blazes a red-hot warning in my mind. I want to shout at the crowd and beg them to understand that I'm not just a vampire—I'm a dancer, a singer, someone with dreams on the cusp of coming true. I want to ask them for mercy. I want to scream with all my might, "Please, *please*, don't do this. Please let me go!"

My brother and sister screamed. They begged me to help them, but I was suffering through my own transition. Their voices rise in my memory, a cacophony in my head, far louder than the murmuring of the crowd in the stadium.

I don't scream, because some dark part of me believes that I have no right to, that if this is my end, it's only fair. My death was delayed by a trick of fate, but it should have happened in that bedroom all those years ago. I should have died with my siblings and left my parents childless, with no Chosen daughter to lighten the guilt of the choice they made.

What hurts the most is that I never saw true guilt from either of them.

The spectators point at me and lean toward each other, whispering. I must look so strange to them, dressed in my sexy bounty huntress costume from *Sidewinder*, with my hair disheveled and my makeup smeared. I can feel the panther shifter's rotten blood around my mouth. I don't want to lick it off, and no one wipes it away for me.

My handlers drag me over to a tall metal post bolted to a small rolling platform on wheels. It's like a stake that can be moved from place to place for convenient burning of witches or, in my case, vampires.

I'm forced to stand on the low platform, and I'm held in place by powerful hands. They lift my arms high above my head and lock the handcuffs to a bracket on the post.

My handlers back away, yielding space as three people approach.

One is Gil Leveque, one of the directors of *Sidewinder*. Raoul never talks much about him except to call him a misogynistic ass, but I remember hearing someone say that he and Raoul are distantly related. It never really clicked with me until this moment that as a relative of Raoul's, he must also be a shifter.

He's carrying a large, shallow wooden box covered with intricate engravings. His eyes rove my body, and an oily smirk spreads across his face. He likes seeing me in this state, with my arms bound above my head and my body stretched taut against the pole. Dickhead.

In the center of the trio is Philippa de Chagny, and at her other side is Raoul.

He's visibly shaking. Each step drags as if he's struggling not to move forward, as though his limbs are being forced to advance against his will.

"Raoul," I say desperately. "Raoul, did she hurt you?"

His face contorts as if he's trying to speak, but not a word passes his lips.

"We can fight them together," I say, even though I know it's a lie. He doesn't seem like himself—Philippa has done something to him. And even if he was fine, the two of us against the Collective is really bad odds.

Someone reads a statement over the gym's PA system. It's a recap of the "crimes" I'm guilty of, with a couple false accusations thrown in for good measure.

"That's not true!" I shout, jerking against the handcuffs. But it's mostly true. I did kill the men in the alley—slaughtered them brutally when I could have just injured them and walked away. I did fail to pay my dues to the Collective. And I did lure, drug, and drink from dozens of human men.

No one pays attention to my protest anyway. The announcer

declares that my sentence is a trifold death, which apparently means I'll be stabbed through the heart, decapitated, and then burned for good measure. Talk about overkill. Decapitation or burning would do the trick, but I suppose they like to be thorough when dealing with vampires.

"Raoul de Chagny, brother of our esteemed leader, will carry out the sentence," declares the announcer.

"The fuck he will," I gasp. "Raoul?"

Again, his face twists with agony, but he can't seem to speak. She's controlling him somehow. A shifter thing maybe, some power related to their pack dynamic.

Philippa nods to Gil, who opens the lid of the box he's carrying. Philippa lifts out a curved silver dagger and hands it to Raoul. "Perform the first death."

"No." I twist and buck against the chains, panic thrilling through my body. "No, Raoul, don't do this. Fight it, for fuck's sake. Fight *her*."

But his fingers close mechanically around the hilt, and he walks forward with wooden steps. Looking into his eyes, I can see that he's dying with the agony of what he's being forced to do. She's not just killing me—she's killing him, too.

His face is a mask of stricken anguish. His eyes drop to my chest, and he sets the tip of the knife against my left breast.

"Raoul, look at me," I whisper frantically. "You have to delay this somehow. Erik is going to come save us, you know he will. Please…please just wait, Raoul. Don't, please, don't…"

His hand, his arm, his whole body is shaking, and a smothered groan grates through his chest, like a stone being dragged over his ribs from the inside. The knife pushes through the fabric of my dress and pierces the first layer of my skin, a prick of blood-red pain.

My lips tremble, and my eyes fill with tears until I can barely see him. "It's all right. I know you're trying. Please—"

I snatch a pained breath as the knife sinks deeper, scraping against the left edge of my breastbone. Raoul angles it and pushes harder. It's the most horrific sensation as the blade slowly cleaves my skin, viscera, and tendons, then pierces the thumping muscle of my first heart, the one I was born with.

If it's damaged, my body can repair it, thanks to the second, smaller heart situated behind my right lung. I can survive being stabbed like this.

But I can't regrow my head. If Raoul goes that far, the damage will be irreversible.

My cheeks are burning, wet with tears. "Raoul, I need you to try harder. For me. For him."

"Deeper," says Philippa, and Raoul shoves against the hilt of the knife.

I choke, feeling the cascade of adrenaline and panic as my body reacts to this cataclysmic threat. When the first heart slows and stutters, my second heartbeat increases to a frenzied pace. My fangs emerge from my gaping jaws, and the crowd utters a collective exclamation of interest and horror.

Raoul jerks the dagger out of my chest. His fingers uncurl from the hilt, and it falls to the floor.

Another shifter walks forward, carrying an ax—yes, a fucking ax—just as ornate as the ceremonial box Gil is holding. She hands it to Raoul, then withdraws.

"Now the head, Raoul," commands Philippa. "Cut it off."

I can see his pupils, blown so wide his green eyes are nearly black. They widen a little more when she speaks to him.

I struggle for control, for words. Blood spills over my lower lip as I force my voice to work, just one more time. I won't waste precious seconds pleading for the mercy he can't give me. There's something more important I need to say.

"Don't hate yourself for this. I love you."

At my words, Raoul's pupils contract slightly. He stands motionless, gripping the ax.

"Now, Raoul!" orders Philippa.

Through blood and fangs, I speak a line from the lyrics he wrote—the language of his soul poured into music. "Love is a cruel angel, a thorny rose that blooms and bleeds in this rotten void, that whispers relentless hope into the wicked universe."

The black dot in the center of Raoul's iris shrinks, and the band of pale green widens suddenly, gloriously.

He whirls and slings the ax at his sister.

One second, the ax is spinning toward her, and the next she's a huge white wolf, leaping aside out of harm's way, shadows curling and melting around her while the ax clangs against the floor.

Raoul reaches for my chained hands, but before he can attempt to free me, my restraints spring open of their own accord.

Magic like that can only mean one thing.

The god of death and his ghosts have arrived.

I shake off my chains and stumble forward, but my primary heart still isn't working. Raoul catches me in his arms as I collapse.

"Christine." He's crying, kissing my face with heartbroken penitence. "Christine, precious, I'm so sorry—"

Philippa's wolf soars past him, and her jaws latch around my throat.

She bears me down to the floor, teeth gnawing into my flesh like she's determined to chew off my head.

A howl rips through the stadium, and a furry weight slams into the white wolf. Raoul's black wolf is a demented devil, tearing into his sister's side with all the fury of a rabid beast. With an agonized whine, she releases my neck and turns to attack him. He meets her onslaught with a storm of snarls and the flash of lightning-white teeth.

The stadium erupts into chaos, shifters shedding their human forms and diving toward us, all of them bent on defending their leader. But the stands also fill with misty shapes moaning in ghostly voices, rendered visible and audible by the will of their master. The ghosts can't stop the shifters, but they're disorienting and distracting them, preventing them all from descending on Raoul and me at once.

I claw my way across the floor, gaining a little distance from the battling wolves. Much as I want to leap into the fray and help Raoul, I can't. In addition to the heart wound, my neck has been chewed up. Thankfully, Raoul stopped his sister before she gnawed too deep, but I'm bleeding copiously, and I need to refuel.

My frenzied gaze lands on Gil Leveque, who hasn't shifted and stands motionless, mouth agape, watching Raoul and Philippa tear into each other.

In wolf form, Philippa can't give her brother commands. But can she exert her power over him nonverbally? Did he break her control for only a moment, or is he free forever? I need to know… need to help him…need to drink…

Half-conscious, my vision fading, I pull myself toward Gil, already salivating for his blood. Why hasn't he shifted? Maybe his other shape is something small and defenseless, not ideal for a fight like this one.

I never feel more like an animal than when I'm desperate for blood. The craving steals my reasoning and my higher thought processes, leaving only blind instinct and a visceral, all-consuming need.

Gil must spot my approach out of the corner of his eye because he glances my way, then dives to grab the ax Raoul threw. "Might as well finish you off," he mutters, hefting it.

I want to close the distance between us and pounce on him, but without my primary heart in play, I don't have the strength.

Gil lifts the ax over his head, ready for a killing blow.

A whip of shadow snakes through midair and coils around his throat. It yanks him backward, then lashes around his body in endless loops of darkness, tightening relentlessly.

Erik strides into my view, masked, wearing a black coat. Even in this dire moment, his theatricality makes me smile a little.

"You need this one, sweetheart?" he asks me casually.

I nod, and the shadow ropes snap tight around Gil's body before rolling him in my direction. I crawl forward, push Gil's head to the side, and sink my fangs gratefully into his throat.

"If you'll excuse me for a moment, I am going to deal with our enemies," Erik says.

I murmur my assent through my mouthful of Gil's neck, and he stalks toward Raoul and Philippa.

As I drink, pleasure rolls through me, a sensation beyond the comfort of blood. Erik is here. He's with us. I'm not sure he and

Raoul and I can fight off the entire Shifter Collective, but at least if we die, we'll be together.

Gil Leveque whimpers under my teeth. His blood flows over my tongue in small, warm floods, pumped straight from his artery. He tastes a little like Raoul, but instead of the wildness, there's an earthy flavor to his blood, something grounded and slimy and vulnerable. Like a worm.

God, how miserable would it be to have a *worm* as your second form?

Out of pity, I give his wound a cursory lick when I'm done.

By now, the other shifters have realized the ghosts aren't a threat to them, and they're reaching the floor, bounding toward Raoul and Philippa. Some of them head for Erik, recognizing him as an enemy.

The first one to reach Erik is a huge dog, possibly a wolfhound. At the same time, a giant vulture swoops down toward Erik's head, talons extended.

I leap to my feet, horror galvanizing my heart and kicking it awake, but I know I can't make it to Erik in time. Those talons will rip him apart.

A black stag leaps from the stands, giant hooves crashing on the wooden floor as it lands between Erik and the dog. It rears up and, with a jerk of its head, catches the vulture's wing on the tips of its antlers.

The vulture screams as the stag slings it to the floor and tramples its body beneath merciless hooves. The stag charges the dog next, head down, antlers whipping through the air.

I watch, dumbfounded. Why the hell is one of the shifters protecting Erik?

A pained whine seizes my attention, and I turn toward Raoul and Philippa. She has him pinned down, and several other shifters are closing in—two foxes, a boar, and a handful of coyotes. None of the shifters look quite like normal animals—they're larger, darker in color, gifted with longer claws, bulkier muscles, and wickedly sharp teeth. They might be able to pass as normal when glimpsed alone or in the shadows, but as a group, they're unmistakably supernatural, denizens of the uncanny valley, wakening a faint sense of wrongness and horror.

Erik has been warding them off with bursts of energy, whips of shadow, and blasts of mist, but I have no idea how long his magic will last. As the shifters tighten the circle, I spring to Erik's side and take up a fighting stance. Claws extended, I snarl through my fangs, daring any of them to approach. They hesitate, probably a little shocked that I'm up for combat so soon after being stabbed in the heart.

"Help Raoul," Erik says tightly. "I'll hold them off."

I'm all too glad to pounce on Philippa's back and sink my claws deep into her body. Her howls ring in my ears as I lift her off Raoul and throw her as far as I can—which isn't far, since I'm not quite at full strength.

Wolf-Raoul struggles to his feet, panting and bleeding. Erik's breathing is strained—he's tiring quickly from using so much of his magic. And it's going to be a few minutes before I'm fully healed—minutes we don't have, judging by the sheer number of beasts prowling around us. Their growls, shrieks, chitters, and unearthly cries fill my ears, and their claws screech against the gym floor until I think I might go mad.

The stag who protected Erik changes form, turning into a

panther, and I realize it's the man I bit earlier—the one with the hideous blood.

But my surprise is nothing compared to Erik's reaction. He recoils from the panther, eyes wide. "Lloyd-Henry?"

The panther ignores him and snarls at one of the other shifters.

"Have you been in the city this whole time? With *them*?" Erik says to the panther, his voice sharp with anger. "Why haven't you—oh fuck, I forgot he's in my head. He knows you're here now. He's coming."

"Who's coming? And who is Lloyd-Henry?" I exclaim.

Erik is staring past me, toward the double doors at the end of the gymnasium. "Lloyd-Henry is the man who resurrected me. As for the one who's coming…I made an ally of sorts. He was supposed to wait for my signal, but he is too angry now. Stay close. Be ready."

"You and Raoul need to quit keeping secrets," I snap, but I turn to face the same direction as Erik. Wolf-Raoul stands beside me. I curl my fingers into the thick fur along his neck, and he moves closer, each of us instinctively seeking support from the other.

Thunder shakes the floor of the gym, drawing the attention of the shifters. The sound intensifies, vibrating the rows of seats, rattling the old scoreboard against the wall, eliciting growls of fear from the beasts.

Lightning flickers around the edges of the double doors, and more thunder rolls through the building. With a concussive blast, the doors burst open, and a tsunami crashes in.

The water leaps in foaming waves across the floor of the gym, almost as if it has a mind of its own. And perhaps it does, because through the spray and lightning and thunder strides a massive figure, bigger than any man I've ever seen. His huge red beard conceals the lower half of his face, but I don't need to see his mouth to know that he's absolutely enraged.

"Erik." I grab his coat. "You tell me who that is right now, or I swear I'll drain you within an inch of your life."

"That's Manannan, the sea god," he replies.

Raoul makes a sound between a whine and growl, and I press my hand reassuringly to his neck. "Sea god. Right. Is he angry at you, or them, or..."

"As I said, he is a temporary ally of mine. His rage is primarily directed at *him*." He points to the panther, who bristles and delivers a silent snarl.

I have more questions, but it's impossible to speak over the onrushing waves and the crack of more thunder. Water flows across the gym floor, soaking my shoes, but the huge waves seem to avoid us, chasing down the shifters instead. One giant wave swallows two dogs and traps them, keeping them submerged until their frantic struggles cease.

It's hard to watch, even though I know what the animals really are and the fate they intended for me and Raoul. I look down at the water sliding past my feet...and then I notice swirls of blood leaking from the body of Gil Leveque not far away. His skull is partly caved in. One of the shifters with hooves must have trampled him while trying to outrun a wave.

It's all coming true—the violence I feared would result from any relationship I might have with Erik and Raoul. But it wasn't our fault. We didn't instigate this. All we wanted—all Raoul wanted—was to live peacefully and happily together.

And his fucking sister screwed it up.

I glance at the spot where I threw her. She's gone.

Frantically, I scan the bleachers, which are full of shifters trying to escape the flood. Some of them have switched back to human form and are clambering over the rows of seats naked, screaming, out of their minds with panic. Pity surges in me in spite of myself.

Maybe I'm not heartless yet.

I touch Erik's arm. "It's too much. They're on the run already, no need to massacre them all. Can you tell him to stop drowning them?"

"I can try." He sounds doubtful.

"Good." Then I spot what I've been looking for—a white wolf slinking up the steps. She's nearing the top of the stadium seats, where there's an emergency exit door. "I'm going after Philippa."

I run toward the steps too quickly, and my foot slips on the wet floor. Vampiric balance kicks in, and I right myself quickly, but not before I feel Raoul's wolf at my side, ready to provide support if I need it. When I start up the steps, he follows me.

I look back at him, wincing. "You shouldn't come. She might still have power over you."

He whines.

"You know what I have to do, Raoul. You shouldn't be there to see it."

With a frustrated growl, he bounds up the bleachers ahead of me.

I guess I won't be chasing his sister alone after all.

After reaching the top of the bleachers, Raoul and I rush through the exit door into the hallway. I look in both directions, but I don't see the white wolf. My nose isn't as finely tuned as Raoul's, and all I can smell is wet fur and mildew.

I glance over at him. His green eyes meet mine, and I know he understands the request I won't voice.

I need my sweet wolf boyfriend to track his sister down so I can kill her.

31

THE PHANTOM

I WANT TO FOLLOW CHRISTINE AND RAOUL. THEY NEED ME to be with them, protecting them. They require my constant oversight and guidance.

Or perhaps it is time to recognize that what I call protection is often obsession. They are both powerful beings with scores of their own to settle. And I have a directive from Christine to ensure that Manannan's attack on the shifters does not become a slaughter.

Her conscience and Raoul's must guide me from now on.

It is enough, I tell Manannan in my mind. *You've killed enough of them.*

You summoned me to your side for vengeance, he retorts. *Would you abandon the task half done?*

Watching the shifters thrash and struggle for their lives is disturbing. The pity unfurling in my heart is a new sensation for me. I think perhaps Christine's sympathy for them is contagious and has infected me.

I cast aside my mask. "Stop," I call aloud to Manannan.

He remains near the doors by which he entered, both of his

huge hands lifted, his brow bent in concentration as he wields the water he summoned from the nearby river.

I do not have the power to stop him. He will continue killing, beyond reason, beyond need. Once, I would have gloried in all the death, in the influx of souls to my realm.

But I am not the being I once was.

When more waves rush into the building, the panther crouches down at my side, muscles coiled tight. Lloyd-Henry is getting ready to spring away, to change forms…to leave us again.

I won't allow it.

The limited magic I possess is nearly depleted, and I keep mentally colliding with the barriers the blond vampire erected in my mind. But I scrape together the remaining power I can access, and when the panther leaps away from me, I throw a coil of shadow rope around his body.

He transforms into a raven, and I quickly tighten the magical lasso, managing to keep it cinched around his foot. He shifts into a stag, snapping my grip, but I hurl the shadows around his midsection as he's bounding toward the rows of seats. I jerk him backward with all my might.

With a cry of rage that sounds both human and monstrous, he whirls to face me, changing into the shape of a huge black dog. I tighten my shadows again, preventing his escape, and he snarls, a demonic threat.

"You protected me," I say. "Why? Why would you care about my life when you cast me aside as worse than useless?"

A voice emerges from the dog—a voice so hollow and distorted that even I feel a chill at the sound of it. No shifter should be able to speak while in beast form. The fact that Lloyd-Henry can is a grotesque distortion of everything I know to be true.

"I don't enjoy watching the destruction of something I worked to create," he says. "Even if it was, in the end, a deformed and impotent failure." His head turns, watching Manannan's waves continue to pursue and drown the shifters.

Anger coils around my heart. "Why do you consider me a failure?"

"Because you could not eliminate one small band of vampires at Wicklow. They defeated you. You, a *god*."

"I was not yet at my full strength. And there was the girl, the blond vampire."

"Little Daisy." The wretched voice croaks from the dog's throat. "I did not expect her to be there."

"Her power surprised me. So much has changed since I was forced into sleep beneath the earth," I say. "Something she told me has remained in my mind ever since that day. She said, 'In this world, we are the new gods.' And I believe she may have been right."

He growls, tugging against my shadows.

"This crusade of yours, this endeavor to raise the old gods—it was doomed from the beginning," I tell him. "The world changed, yes, and so have we. Manannan's control over water and storms is impressive, but it's nothing like the power he used to wield. And I am...something else. Something new."

"You're a mistake," he snarls.

"Face me, man to man, and tell me that," I reply.

For a moment, the dog's lips only pull back farther, exposing jagged yellow teeth and purple gums. Then, with a whirl of smoke, the creature transforms, and there he is. Lloyd-Henry Woodson, as he called himself during the time we spent traveling and residing together. What his true name is, I may never know.

My shadow rope has slipped away, and when I cast it again, he raises his hand to the level of his eyes so that when the lasso drops, it tightens around both his neck and his hand. Wrapping his fingers around the rope, he pushes outward, easing the pressure of the noose, loosening it until he can toss it away.

I don't attempt to recapture him.

"Ever since you resurrected me, I have struggled with my old memories," I say. "But I can recall millions of new things. I have accumulated knowledge, experienced music, and composed my own songs. I have delighted in the talents of others, particularly Christine—a vampire, as it happens, like those who defeated me at Wicklow. I became obsessed with her, but my obsession changed as well. I have grown to love two precious souls with all my heart."

I step closer while he eyes me warily.

"I have made mistakes," I continue. "I will make more, and I will keep learning from them. But I was meant to be here, just as I was meant to meet Christine and Raoul. I firmly believe that Fate, wherever she is, has blessed me with this existence. So tell me again. Tell me I'm a mistake. Tell me I'm useless, worthless, and a failure."

He backs away as I advance. I'm smiling, flooded with a confidence and triumph I've never felt before.

It feels like I have won a battle I never acknowledged I was fighting—a war within myself.

"I do not need to be a god or even the shadow of one," I tell him. "I can let every part of that existence go, release my past, and fully embrace my new role in this world. If only you could see how freeing it is—how beautiful life can be when you are at home within yourself. I swear, it's better than magic."

"You don't understand," Lloyd-Henry seethes. "This is my great plan. All the pieces—I've been setting them up for decades, for centuries."

"So you said."

"I want to conquer death. Rule the world. Be worshipped as the savior of humanity."

"Modest goals, to be sure," I say dryly. "Wouldn't you be happier if you released yourself from the pressure of such cosmic ambition?"

"I can't. All that work—all the lives I destroyed along the way—to abandon it all?" His voice shrills. "To say my life's work was useless, no longer worth pursuing—it's unthinkable!"

"I have done terrible things, too," I say. "I fully acknowledge that part of myself, and if I need to do terrible things again to protect those I love, I will. But peace will come when you accept the past rather than excusing it. It should not be the guide for your future."

"You're a fucking imbecile, and you talk like my therapist," he snarls. His naked body shudders, and I notice lumps writhing beneath his skin, as if his flesh is corrupted by worms. He bends over, a groan bursting from him as a stronger spasm racks his frame.

"What is happening to you?" I ask.

He looks up, features contorted with pain. "I tried to cheat death one too many times. But it won't get me, I swear. I will defeat it. Someday, there will be no more death, and I will be the one who ushers in that utopian world."

"From what I've read of human fiction and philosophy, attempts at a utopian world rarely meet one's expectations," I reply.

"Death is the great enemy," he rasps. "The only one worth fighting."

Abruptly, I realize that the waves have ceased and that Manannan has drawn closer to us. He has been listening to our conversation.

"I ruled over death once," I say quietly. "I came to realize there are worse things. Confinement. Loss of choices. Imprisonment within a cage of twisted ideals. The belief that your own existence is the most important thing in the world."

"Then you no longer fear death?" Lloyd-Henry scoffs. "If it came for you, you would succumb without resisting?"

"I fear the end of possibilities, of choices. I will strive to remain in this world as long as I can to be with those I adore and to contribute something beautiful. Yes, I fear the end. It is only natural… only human. But I will not let the terror of death control me or steal the joy from the experience of living."

Manannan's deep voice speaks on my left. "Joy? How can there be joy when the one you crave is beyond your reach?" He glares at Lloyd-Henry. "You promised you would raise the Morrigan for me."

"And I looked for her," Lloyd-Henry gasps, grimacing through another spasm. "She has no grave, no prison. There is no physical trace of her to be found. She was never bound like the rest of you."

Startled, I glance at Manannan. He looks just as shocked as I am.

"That's impossible," he says. "We trapped her just as we trapped *him*." He jerks his bearded chin toward me.

"And I looked in the place where you told me to search," replies Lloyd-Henry. "There was nothing. No trace of the divine or other supernatural influence. The ritual you and the other gods performed was either temporary or it did not work at all. Perhaps she fooled you into thinking it did."

A laugh surges up inside me, and I can't resist letting it out. "She tricked you." I grin at Manannan. "Of course she did. She's been free this whole time, weaving her threads through the tapestry of the world."

"Meddling, you mean," growls Manannan. "Well...fuck."

Lloyd-Henry vents a rasping chuckle. "I suppose your plan won't work now, eh?" When I throw him a confused glance, he explains. "Manannan asked me to raise the Morrigan, and then he planned to tell her that her new existence was all thanks to him. He hoped that in her gratitude for the resurrection, she would forgive him for scheming with the other gods to confine her."

Manannan swears loudly and sends a great fist of water smashing into the bleachers. Metal snaps and plastic chairs crumple. But in the wake of the damage, his shoulders slump. I recognize that posture, that loss of purpose. A sense of helplessness, feeding his external fury.

"There is a word I've learned recently," I muse. "Might be useful if you ever do encounter the Morrigan."

"And what is that?" growls Manannan.

"Grovel," I say simply.

"Grovel? The fuck does that mean?"

"You can look it up when we get back to my lair," I tell him. "I can give you some tips."

"You're both fools." Lloyd-Henry's voice is a thread on

the verge of snapping. "Talking of moving on, of accepting death—trapped by sentimentality, with no sense of vision—it is insufferable!"

He falls to his knees, releasing a cry of anguish before shifting into stag form. The shift doesn't seem to offer him relief, however. He stamps and tosses his head, screaming as only a deer can. The stag morphs into a crow, then a dog, then a panther, each form becoming more frenzied than the last, until he is switching forms too fast for me to perceive any of them.

Manannan and I instinctively back away. No power that either of us possess can help him. We listen to his garbled shrieks and stare at the amorphous whirl of limbs, antlers, mouths, and tails that was once our summoner until, with one final unearthly whimper, the matter of which he was composed loses all integrity and plops to earth, a steaming pile of red flesh and black ichor.

If he could have found peace within himself, if he could have accepted his defeat, he might have survived. Or perhaps, as he said, he had cheated death once too often, and Fate herself decided to snip the cord of his life one final time.

I tilt my head, surveying the mass, wondering if he's really gone. Wondering how I should feel. I think I am experiencing gratitude and sympathy, both of which seem appropriate for the man who was instrumental in my resurrection.

"I am going to find Christine and Raoul," I tell Manannan. "You can come with me or wait here."

Without waiting for his decision, I take the steps of the bleachers three at a time. My conversation with Lloyd-Henry was one I needed to have, but now that it's over, the urgency to be with my singer and my poet is back, full force.

I only hope I was right to trust their strength and cunning, to let them pursue Raoul's sister on their own, injured as they both were.

When I reach the top of the stairway, I encounter two of my ghosts drifting aimlessly in midair.

"Where did the wolf and the girl go?" I ask.

"That way," replies one. "They climbed up to the roof. Two wolves and a woman, but one wolf is dying. Can you smell it, my lord? The sweet aroma of death?" The ghost giggles, and her companion joins in with a wailing laugh.

I rush past them, a curse on my lips. I feel as if, like Christine, I have two hearts—except they are both outside my body, beyond the shelter of my ribs.

All I care about is reaching them in time.

32

RAOUL

Shifters do not heal as quickly as vampires. For us, it's a matter of hours, not minutes.

My joints ache from being slammed against the ground by my sister. Philippa also tore into my right flank at one point, and the pain of those torn muscles hampers my ability to track her as quickly as I want to. But I do my best.

I don't attempt to return to my human form. When we find my sister, she will likely still be in wolf form, so it would be foolish to switch. And I'm not ready to have the power of speech again. Not ready to talk about what happened, how I drove a dagger into the heart of one of the people I love best, the girl who defended me all those years ago, who trusted me enough to sing with me that night at the Alouette. The girl who came so beautifully on my tongue.

What if Christine hadn't spoken my own lyrics to me at the right moment? What if I hadn't found the strength to break the control of Philippa's voice? What if I had killed the woman that Erik and I adore? I don't think he would have been able to forgive me. I couldn't have forgiven myself.

But I *did* find the strength. I broke through Philippa's compulsion. Could I do it again? Am I a coward who only manages a few trembling moments of courage, or am I a brave person who occasionally gives in to fear?

What am I so afraid of?

I bound up a flight of steps and put my nose to the crack of the door. There's fresh air beyond, and the scent of my sister's blood.

When Christine reaches past me to open the door, I pace cautiously onto the rooftop. The area before me is bathed in sickly yellow light from a couple of cloudy exterior lamps, probably illuminated at night to keep vandals away from the abandoned building. Sections of the rooftop are shadowed, inky black voids in which anything might be hiding. The air has the cracked cold of late October, a few hours after midnight.

The sharpness of that cold air confuses my sense of smell for a moment. Philippa is out here, but I can't pinpoint her location.

A battering ram of fur and jaws crashes against my shoulder. I skid to the side, howling with pain. Philippa clambers over me in an attempt to pin me down, but I thrash, trying to keep her from sinking her teeth into my flesh. If she gets a good grip, she'll slam me against the concrete again. It's her signature move when fighting in this form.

I've had no training in either of my forms. My father wouldn't let me learn martial arts, and my wolf form is too new. All I can do is kick, bite, and wriggle away as my sister tries to secure a throat hold.

But I'm not alone in this fight. Christine dives into the fray, careless of injury to herself, fangs bared, voicing a hissing scream that startles even me. Philippa is thrown off guard for a second, and Christine slashes at her with razor claws, aiming to cut my sister's throat.

But Philippa rears backward just in time. She twists, springs away, and lands on her feet, braced and ready, her head lowered. Her white fur looks yellow in the hideous light.

Christine faces off against her. "I can't let you live. You know that."

A growl ripples from Philippa's throat.

It's always been strange to me, seeing her like this. In human form, she is so composed, so crisp and controlled, every hair in place. Yet in wolf form, she is violence incarnate. Two personalities. Or perhaps one is merely a mask for the other.

I circle Philippa, working my way behind her. She eyes me but continues facing Christine, whom she apparently considers the real threat. Perhaps she's right. I'm not sure I'm on board with Christine's plan to kill Philippa. I should be, after what Philippa made me do. What is this fucking hold my family has on my psyche, even after everything they've done to show me they're *not* worthy of my love or loyalty? Why can't I incinerate the bridge entirely so I can't even think about crossing it again?

I was strong enough to send Philippa that email, breaking my ties with the Collective. And I was strong enough to fling the ax at my sister instead of chopping off Christine's head. In that moment, I truly *wanted* to kill Philippa. I simply need to summon that anger again, because now Christine is the one hesitating.

I can see the torment on her face. She's a mess—ripped dress, wild hair, makeup in ruins—but her beauty is more powerful than any of it. It's the striking beauty of the girl from middle school, the avenging angel with a heart full of so much kindness the world couldn't suck it all out of her, though it has tried to drain her dry.

Christine might have killed people, but she isn't a murderer, and my sister realizes it the same moment I do.

Philippa rockets forward at a speed impossible for any normal wolf. Christine's vampiric reflexes should save her, but she's weary, still healing. She dodges, but not far enough. Philippa's teeth seize her shoulder instead of her throat.

My sister's weight knocks Christine over. She rips her teeth free of Christine's shoulder and goes in for the throat hold.

A cry of agony wrenches out of Christine. She plunges all her claws into the white wolf's body, but Philippa hangs on, determined as a bulldog, grinding deeper every second.

I'm already leaping in, jaws wide. I clamp down on the back of Philippa's neck and chew into the hide and muscle with all my might, but she's not letting go. My sister bucks upward and rams Christine down. Christine's skull hits the concrete with a sickening thud. I swear I hear bone crack.

I clamp my jaws around Philippa's back leg and wrench backward with violent jerks until I hear the hip joint pop. Philippa whines through her mouthful of Christine's neck, but she still won't let go.

Fuck you, I sob inwardly. *Fuck you for everything*.

And with all my strength, I pull.

Fur and flesh rip, and I'm left holding my sister's back right leg between my teeth.

Philippa howls, a murderous, bloodcurdling shriek to the blurred half-moon.

I don't give her a moment to recover. I leap onto her, pinning her in place. Finding my own throat hold. Grasping the tender flesh beneath her muzzle, clamping my jaws in place, crushing ever deeper.

All I can think about is that my father was also a white wolf. The color of the moon, he said. A reflection of light.

He would have been disappointed that my wolf is the color of darkness. But what else would it be after he gave me to the dark over and over for so many years?

And the darkness welcomed me, nurtured me. I'm not afraid of it now.

Philippa goes limp beneath me, but I hold on. I taste her blood, feel it cooling in my mouth, and still I hold until I'm sure. Until her body transforms beneath me into human shape, and I know it's done.

I withdraw on trembling paws, my sensitive nose clogged with the rank smell of death.

I don't want to see her. I don't want to look.

Darkness is kind to me once again. As I retreat, a cloud passes over the moon, and my sister's body is swathed in shadow.

I shift to my human form, a shiver racking my bones. The midnight cold pierces my fragile human skin, but I ignore the chill and rush over to Christine.

Her condition is as bad as I feared. Looking at her ruined throat makes me retch. I have no idea how she can possibly swallow any blood with her esophagus in tatters.

"Oh god...Christine," I whisper.

The door to the stairs bangs open, and Erik rushes onto the roof with my name on his lips. When he sees me, his shoulders sag with relief. "Thank Fate, you're alive."

"Yes, but…Christine…"

Alarm floods his face, and he rushes forward, dropping to his knees on the other side of her body.

Behind him, framed in the doorway, is the big man with the red beard, the one who wielded waves and drowned so many shifters of the Collective. He stands with his arms folded, surveying us.

Erik tears off his coat and hands it to me. "Put this on, or you'll freeze."

Slowly, I obey while he strokes Christine's hair back from her forehead. The ends of her dark curls are soaked with red.

"She needs blood," he says.

"She can't drink blood, Erik."

"I'll pour it into her," he says desperately, tearing at his wrist with his fingernails. "Come on, Raoul. Both of us. We can save her."

His urgency spurs my own desperate hope, and I bite my own wrist until it bleeds. We hold our forearms above her body, our blood dripping onto her parted lips, slipping into her mouth, running in rivulets along the terrible wounds in her throat. We clasp each other's hands over her, and we bleed.

I'm weeping. So is he. When he kisses me, I taste his tears.

And still we bleed.

The man with the red beard doesn't move. He doesn't try to help us—not that anyone could—but neither does he move to leave. He witnesses our grief in silence, with his head bowed.

When our bodies begin to heal, Erik and I open the wounds again. There's so much of our blood and hers cloaking her throat that we can't tell if it's working.

We weep, and we bleed until I feel dizzy. I'm not sure if it's from grief or blood loss.

At last, I venture a question. "Will we see her ghost, do you think, if she..."

"Don't," he snaps. "Don't say it."

"Can you see every ghost, though?" I know it's risky to push him on this point, but I'm reckless and sick with loss. I need to know.

"Only the ones who could not find rest. Would you wish that on her?"

I ponder for a moment. "Yes, if I could see her again."

He stares at me. "I do believe that is the most selfish thought you've ever had."

"I *am* selfish." I gather her limp hand in mine. Her fingers feel so fragile, so breakable. "I *want* her, Erik."

"I would cut out my own heart and place it in her chest if I thought it would do any good," he says. "For your sake and hers. I would die if I believed the two of you could be happy."

"Stop it," I whisper, tears stinging my eyes again. "Not without you."

He smiles a little, his scarred face incandescent under the moon.

"Her voice, Raoul," he says quietly. "If this works, do you think it will be the same, after..."

"After my sister tore apart her larynx?" My tone is dull, dead. "I don't know."

"It won't matter to me," he murmurs. "I will love her the same. How fortunate are we, to have heard that beautiful voice in our lifetimes?"

33

CHRISTINE

Mirrors. I'm in a maze of mirrors, broken pieces of my own reflection staring at me for miles. Beyond the mirrors, there is darkness, and behind me…something. A powerful connection, drawing me back into a body stricken with pain.

Something flickers in the dark, a misty shape. A ghost. I've seen one before. It's approaching me, sailing out of the sea of nothing. Its image isn't repeated in the mirrors.

"Dad?" I whisper.

The ghost halts before me, close enough to touch yet so blurred I can't discern its features. Then it splits into two forms, and my mind goes blank with shock.

Thomas. And Edith. My little brother and sister.

"Oh my god," I whisper. "Oh my god. You're here."

"Just for a minute," says Thomas. "We can only stay for a minute."

"I love you," I choke out. "I love you so much, and I've missed you…and I'm so sorry."

Edith reaches for my face. I feel her touch like a cool mist.

"You didn't do this to us," she says. "It wasn't your fault."

"But I lived," I sob. "I should have died, too."

"Oh, no," says Thomas. "The Lady spared you because she knew one day he would need you, and you would need him."

"What does that even mean? Where are we? Am I dead?"

"No."

"But I'm here with you."

"Only for a minute," repeats Thomas. "We have to go."

"It's peaceful where we go," says Edith. "But you can't come with us. Not yet. She's sending you back."

"She?"

"The Lady," they say in unison. "The Morrigan."

"We love you," whispers Edith, and Thomas echoes, "We've always loved you."

They're drifting, and I reach out my hand…but I don't scream or sob for them to return. This moment is consolation, not desperation. I won't ruin it for myself or for them.

I saw them once, and once will do.

A sound like a plucked string echoes through the mirrored space, and my reflections shiver, like reflections on rippling water. Everything blurs, and I blink, trying to clear my vision.

My eyes open to two faces hovering above me. One is pale, scarred, and anxious, framed by wavy black hair. The other is flushed, ice-green eyes shining, a riot of coppery curls tumbling over his forehead.

"Christine," says Erik. As if my name is the one word essential to his happiness.

Raoul kisses me on the forehead, and the warmth of his lips brings me fully back to life.

I touch my throat, remembering the teeth. My skin is smooth, unblemished, though still sticky with blood.

"Where is she?" I murmur, lifting my head.

"Philippa is gone." Raoul's voice thickens. "I got her off you, but if I'd been faster, you...you wouldn't have..."

I sit up and put both arms around his neck. He's wearing Erik's coat and nothing else, and his skin is ice-cold. "Thank you," I whisper. As I'm hugging him, I spot the sea god Manannan, standing in the doorway that leads to the stairs. Then I see Philippa's naked body and her right leg lying a few paces beyond her corpse. My arms tighten around Raoul. "We need to get you warm. And I think we could all use a good meal."

Raoul lifts me to my feet. I hang on to him, mostly to keep his attention focused on me so he won't have to look toward Philippa's body.

Manannan shifts his bulky form aside for three of us to access the stairs, then he takes up the rear as we descend them.

While Raoul and I were pursuing Philippa, we saw many of the shifters fleeing, escaping Manannan's waves. I'm not sure how many got away, but I know the death toll must have been high. It's a small relief that there are no bodies in the hallway when we reach it.

"A lot of people died here tonight," I say. "What do you think the cops will make of it? Can we be connected to this?"

"No," says Manannan gruffly before Erik can reply. "All the bodies will be transported out to sea, and I will wash the place clean."

"And then you'll join us at my lair," Erik says. "It's yours now, since you helped us."

"What?" I exclaim, and Raoul says, "Fuck no."

"I made the bargain," Erik says calmly. "I'm happy to fulfill it."

"But what about all your things?" I protest.

"I have the only two treasures that matter to me right here."

"You sicken me, Cernunnos," Manannan growls. "And I decline your offer. I have no use for a drafty basement full of human garbage. You may keep the lair, as you call it. Now be off with you. I have work to do."

"Call me if you ever want to learn a few things," Erik replies.

Manannan scoffs. "Not likely."

We circumvent the gym, which judging by the smell is full of river water and dead shifters, and make our way outside by an alternate route. Once we reach the fresh air again, I turn around to see the building where we spent the most harrowing night of my life. A handful of huge letters still cling to the brick exterior, but I have no idea what they're supposed to spell and no mental capacity for playing hangman at the moment.

"What's the plan?" asks Raoul. "I have literally nothing, not even my clothes. And my phone is probably still in Box Five."

"Mine is in my dressing room." I shiver, rubbing my arms.

We turn to look at Erik, who's unusually silent, his face illuminated by the light from his phone. He taps his thumb twice and glances up. "Our ride is on the way. We'll meet him at the street corner two blocks east of here. We should get moving."

One Year Later

The standing ovation is thunderous. So loud, in fact, that my mind goes back to that night in the abandoned gym when Manannan crashed through the doors and sent his waves in to drown the shifters of the Collective.

A knot of panic twists my stomach. It's tiny, but it could get worse fast.

I squeeze Erik's fingers tighter as we lift our hands, bow, and bow again.

His warm fingers hold mine securely, squeezing three times. *I love you.*

Then it's over—we're retreating, and the curtain is coming down. I didn't have a panic attack. I made it through.

Erik leans down to murmur in my ear, "Are you all right?"

"Yes." I kiss him lightly, but he's never satisfied with that. He pulls me close to his body and seals his mouth over mine with a sigh of decadent satisfaction.

"You sang like an angel tonight, my darling," he murmurs against my lips.

"It might have been my best performance since we took this show on the road."

"Such humility. So charming."

I poke him in the ribs, and he laughs. He laughs so much more now, and though I enjoy his darker moods, I'm delighted by the fact that he's happy—that *this life* makes him happy.

By the time *Sidewinder* ended its run at the New Orpheum Theatre, it had garnered such accolades that theaters across the country were begging for us to come and perform. At the time, Nashville was coping with the mysterious disappearance of multiple prominent citizens, including Philippa de Chagny and Gil Leveque, all of whom vanished overnight without a trace. Neither

Raoul nor I were considered suspects, and Erik kept a low profile, making himself invisible except for performances.

But within a week, Carlotta Vanetti and her followers stirred up rumors online, questioning why Raoul would choose to keep the musical running in light of his sister's and his manager's disappearance.

With Marj's coaching, Raoul made a public statement praising his sister for her support of his dream and dedicating the remaining performances to her. After his emotional speech, the rumors and reporters only fed the hype surrounding our musical. The mystery associated with *Sidewinder* was nothing less than publicity gold.

But those same rumors and reporters also made it difficult for the three of us to enjoy life in Nashville, so the idea of taking the show on the road could not have come at a better time. Besides, none of us were comfortable with the idea that a pervert like Firmin Richards might get rich off our work. So Raoul sold his family home, liquidated the assets, and took *Sidewinder* on tour. It was the true severance we all needed from the city that brought us together.

The day after we left, Erik leaked what he had on Firmin Richards. From what I've heard, he's divorced now, and he sold the New Orpheum to none other than Carlotta Vanetti herself, whose voice—and ego—have returned with a vengeance.

Manannan agreed to watch over the lair for Erik. He grumbled about how inconvenient it was for him, but he also paid very close attention when Erik taught him how to use the technology in the lair. Judging by Erik's mental check-ins with Manannan, the sea god is adapting well to modern conveniences—just as Erik,

Raoul, and I are adapting well to a life of travel, music, fine cuisine, and indulgent sex in luxurious hotels. We're headed back to one such hotel tonight.

Erik has become an expert at guiding me through clusters of people, whether it's our friends in the cast and crew, fans eager for autographs, critics looking to ruin our day, or reporters in the guise of show enthusiasts. He's quite skilled at deploying a bit of mist here, a few shadows there, or a ghostly distraction at just the right moment so we can slip away for some much-needed privacy.

A handful of the Nashville ghosts came along for the tour—the ones whose loyalty to the former death god outweighed their postmortem connection to the city. The cast and crew are all comfortable with the idea of the ghosts now, whether they've actually seen one or not. If a prop falls or a glass breaks, it's always "the *Sidewinder* ghost" who's to blame. Sometimes the *Sidewinder* ghost is to blame when people arrive late to rehearsal, run into traffic, or forget their lines. It irritates Marj, who maintains that ghosts are not real and should not be used as excuses.

As Erik ushers me through the backstage hallways toward the rear exit, I glance into one of the dressing rooms. Meg is there, accepting a bouquet from Gabriella. I whistle at them, and they both look my way, faces flushed with happiness. Gabriella, as it turns out, is not only a talented violinist but also an excellent social media manager. I'm determined to make them a part of our success for as long as it lasts. I will never forget how they tried to look after me when I was being smuggled out of the theater by that shifter in disguise.

"Where are you off to, Christine?" calls Meg.

"Back to the hotel. Hey, is your mom still coming next week?"

Her face falls a little. Ever since she found out about her mom's affair with the student, they haven't been on good terms.

"Yeah," she says without enthusiasm.

"We'll be sure to get her a good seat for the show," I say. "Gotta run. I'm starving."

"Same. We're going out to dinner." Meg brightens.

From just behind her, Gabriella waggles an eyebrow and touches the third finger of her left hand. Which means it's proposal night, and Meg is about to be sporting a gorgeous diamond during rehearsals.

I almost squeal, but I manage to keep a straight face so as not to reveal the surprise. "Call me tomorrow?"

"You know it. Bye, Erik." Meg nods politely. She still has question marks in her mind about him, and I don't blame her. It's not like I can fully explain his quirks, like *Oh yeah, well, he used to be the god of the dead, so that's why he talks the way he does and has weird knowledge gaps and seems to enjoy morbid topics far too much*.

"Raoul is waiting," Erik says with just enough dark desire in his tone to make me hurry down the hall with him.

Raoul didn't come to the show tonight. He was struck by inspiration this morning and plunged into a creative rabbit hole, so we let his inspiration flow uninterrupted while we went to the venue to perform.

Every time he finishes writing a new song, he's hyper, hungry, and horny, and tonight is no exception. He's naked when Erik and I walk into the suite, and he's had room service delivered already—steak and salad for Erik, shrimp carbonara for me, a quarter chicken with a side of roasted corn for himself.

I kick off my heels with an eager groan, pulling off my blouse as I race for the huge bed. I take a seat on the edge of the mattress to strip off the leggings, then fling myself onto the sheets in my underwear.

"There is nothing like having bare feet after dancing all night," I mumble against the mattress.

Raoul smacks my ass lightly, then squeezes it. "Want a foot massage?"

"I want all the kinds of massage."

"Eat something first, naughty girl. Then we'll play."

Erik picks up a cherry tomato and pops it into his mouth. "I'm going to shower."

"I'll join you," Raoul and I say at the same time, both of us eager as puppies.

Erik grins—cocky bastard—and heads into the bathroom, unbuttoning his shirt as he goes.

Showers are slick, heated affairs now—all three of us gleaming, dripping, sliding against one another. One of us usually ends up kneeling on the tiles with a cock in their mouth and their fingers in a hole while the other two kiss.

For us, sex has no real beginning and no definitive end. We stroke each other while we towel off, then roll around on the sheets naked while nibbling bits of delicious dinner. Then the lube comes out, and Erik gets on all fours, lifting his ass while Raoul eases inside.

"I need your help on the new song," Raoul says. His eyes roll back as he sinks deeper. "This is truly a divine asshole."

Erik chuckles, then groans when Raoul begins to thrust inside him. "Fuck, this is exactly what I needed. Only one thing would make it better." His golden eyes meet mine.

I smirk and take another sip of wine before crawling over,

sliding under him, and tracing my finger along his straining cock. "I'm guessing *this* is what you want?" I take the plump head in my mouth, savoring the salty bit of precum along the slit.

Erik groans again. "Yes, angel."

I let him pop out of my mouth. "Hey. That's my name for you."

"I stole it. You should punish me—ahhh—" He gasps as I shift my position and take him deeper.

Raoul and I love the way he is with us—the way he always seems overcome by the sensations of us with him, around him, inside him. I suck on him luxuriously, like he's the sweetest treat I've ever tasted, until his breathing quickens and his abs go taut.

"Our pretty god is about to come, Raoul," I say with a flick of my tongue to the sensitive tip of Erik's cock.

"Yes," moans Raoul. "Make him come...god, I'm coming now...f-u-u-u-ck..."

I close my lips over Erik just in time to feel the jetting of his cum into my cheek. The taste of these two men is better than any human male, and I don't mind swallowing every last bit.

Erik is groaning, the broken, blissful groans of a man who just had one of the best orgasms of his life. Still inside, Raoul strokes Erik's bare back, murmuring incoherent endearments. Gradually, he pulls out, and they both go to clean up while I relax against the pillows, anticipating the bliss that I know is coming.

Both of them get hard again faster than a normal man could, and they last longer when they've already come once, which is why I don't mind waiting my turn.

They return with their arms wound around each other's shoulders, and I nearly pass out from the delight of knowing that both these gorgeous men are *mine*.

First, Raoul savors my pussy. He has a special liking for it—he says my scent is strongest there, and he enjoys simply hanging out between my legs, lapping at my clit while Erik massages my feet or my shoulders.

Erik works on my feet this time, tending to every sore muscle so skillfully that I can't decide whether I'm enjoying his ministrations or Raoul's tongue more.

But Raoul's tongue…it's as lovely as his poetry, and there's a fervent enthusiasm about the way he sucks and licks me that sends warm, glittering spirals up through my belly.

"I'm going to come," I gasp out. "Oh shit…not yet, not yet. I want you inside when I come."

Raoul stops immediately. "Double or single tonight?"

I usually prefer just one cock inside me, but sometimes, when I'm feeling especially wild or frustrated, I'll ask for two. I'm not usually a fan of anal, though. Even with the lube and with practice, it can hurt, so I save it for the times when I need a little pain with my pleasure.

"Double," I tell him.

Erik kisses my foot and then moves onto the bed, stretching out to his full length, on his back with his perfect cock jutting up, as if it's begging to be stroked.

I climb on top of him, kissing him softly while I position his tip at my entrance.

Raoul is on his knees behind me. His warm hand takes over, circling both his cock and Erik's, squishing the heads together and nudging them inside my pussy. He adds lube, the kind that leaves you tingly and warm, applying it in long, practiced strokes.

While Raoul feeds their cocks into me, I shift slowly backward onto them. We know each other's bodies intimately now—it's smooth, easy, flawless. Even the stretch of taking them both is familiar—challenging but not daunting. It's the trust we share that makes it so perfect. We have complete faith in each other. Much as Raoul and Erik love rubbing against each other, skin to skin, while inside me, I know they would never force it or take the fun beyond my comfort level. That's why I can relax, and breathe, and shift my hips backward to take them both deeper.

Raoul is nearly sobbing, out of his mind with pleasure. He craves this more than anything else—the friction of Erik's cock along the sensitive underside of his own, all while they're both gliding inside me, welcomed in my heat.

Erik reaches for him, and they clasp hands. Raoul holds my hip, bracing me, and my hand twines in my angel's black hair. We move together, silken skin and slick need and thundering hearts, until Erik's cock thrums with a light vibration. At that extra stimulation, a golden burst of exquisite pleasure shatters inside me.

I'm beautifully, thoroughly whole, packed full, coming with exquisite intensity on the thick cocks of two beautiful men. My pussy quivers around them, and they come with me, Erik's deeper cries blending with Raoul's lighter ones. The heat is intense, magnetic, dizzying. I can feel their cum pulsing into me, spilling warm around the edges of my stretched hole.

Raoul pulls out first, panting, and flings himself down beside Erik. Cum pours out of me, a creamy flood. I stay on top of Erik, my head resting on his chest, until we've recovered our breath and our sanity.

"I think we need another shower," I murmur, running my

hand along Erik's side. Then I lift my head and look over at Raoul. "You need a run through the park later?"

He enjoys a night run in wolf form, and we've developed a system where one of us runs with him, carrying a leash in case we're questioned. We've been stopped a couple times, and in both cases were able to convince the curious passerby that Wolf-Raoul was actually a large dog, some cross between a malamute and a black Lab. Raoul prefers it when I run with him, since my vampire speed makes me faster than Erik.

"I think I've had enough exercise for one night," Raoul replies with a yawn. "But tomorrow night, for sure."

"Get us a towel, won't you, pet?" asks Erik. "The princess won't sleep unless she's clean."

It's true. I hate sticky, dried cum on my thighs.

Raoul fetches a damp towel, and we clean up before snuggling together among the sheets.

Our wolf boyfriend brings a tiny golden nightlight with him everywhere we go, even though he claims to "love the darkness." Neither Erik nor I ever tease him about it. Nor do we mention it when one of our hotels has a smaller shower than usual and he refuses to enter the confined space with both of us.

We all have scars. Most of them are deeper and less noticeable than the white lines along the right side of Erik's face.

He dreams sometimes, our recovering death god. He'll wake up in a dark panic and start pacing the room with thunder in his eyes and shadows leaking from his body—shadows in the shape of leafy vines. When that happens, Raoul switches from our "Night Music" playlist to the "Dream Recovery" playlist, and I sing quietly until the frenzy fades from Erik's gaze and we can lead him back to bed.

Music continues to be his passion. He listens to it, performs it, or composes it during nearly every waking hour of his life. And he can't fall asleep without it softly playing in the room.

It's one of the things I love best about him.

Music forged Raoul's path away from his family. Dance helped me cope with the tragedies of my childhood, and singing gave me my freedom. The musical we created together enabled us to live the dream we're enjoying right now.

And as for Erik…well, he has often said that music woke him from a living death, and Raoul's poetry opened his heart.

But my voice made him an angel.

BONUS FEATURES

You are cordially invited to step into the world of *Cruel Angel*, containing exclusive bonus content including:

Christine, Raoul, and Erik's Playlist

A bonus scene of the 1800s Christine, Raoul, and Erik

CHRISTINE, RAOUL, AND ERIK'S PLAYLIST

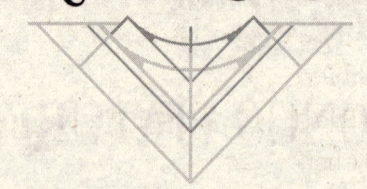

"The Phantom of the Opera"—HAUSER's version

"Dreamweaver" (Epic Trailer Version)—J2, feat. Keeley Bumford

"(Don't Fear) The Reaper"—cover by Keep Shelly in Athens

"Black Velvet"—Alannah Myles

"Rush E," Piano Solo Version—Kassia

"Green Finch and Linnet Bird" from *Sweeney Todd*—Jayne Wisener

"Breakfast"—Dove Cameron

"I Saw Him Once" from *Les Misérables*—Caitlin Finnie, Abdiel Iriarte

"Make Me Wanna Die"—The Pretty Reckless

"Show Me Where It Hurts"—Skylar Grey

"The Fighter"—Keith Urban, feat. Carrie Underwood

"Shallow"—cover by The Hound + The Fox
"Nothing Breaks Like a Heart"—Mark Ronson, feat. Miley Cyrus
"As Long as You're Mine" from *Wicked*—Idina Menzel and Norbert Leo Butz
"Kill For You"—Gigi Perez
"Devil Side"—Foxes
"Highway Don't Care"—Tim McGraw, feat. Taylor Swift and Keith Urban
"No One Will Ever Love You" from *Nashville*—Connie Britton and Charles Esten
"Fake ID"—Big & Rich, feat. Gretchen Wilson
"I Hate Trucks"—Belles
"Ain't in Kansas Anymore" from *Twisters*—Miranda Lambert
"I Had Some Help"—Post Malone, feat. Morgan Wallen
"The Devil Inside"—Daniel Murphy, Anthony Sanudo, and Erick Serna
"I Could Use a Love Song"—Maren Morris

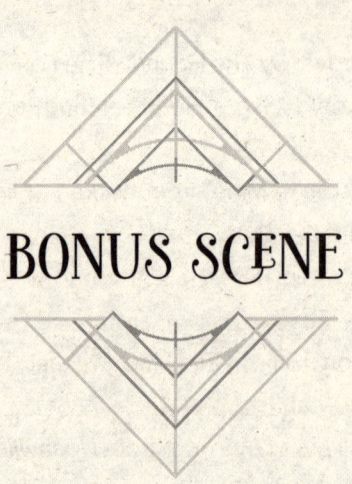

BONUS SCENE

Trigger warning: suicide ideation
A Burning Theater in Paris
1880

Christine left with him.

She pressed the ring I gave her into my hand, her mournful eyes begging for my forgiveness, and she followed Raoul down the passage to freedom...

I wish I could say that I'm happy for Christine and the young viscount. But I hate them for the life they will have, and I hate them for leaving me here, and I hate myself for driving them to it.

It's all crumbling now, falling down around me in the most literal sense. The place that has been my playground and my sanctuary for years is burning, as hot as the wretched anger that inflames my heart.

I could run. I know at least two other ways out of the cellars of the opera house. Neither route is certain, and neither leads to any kind of life I want to live.

Remaining here could bring one of two ends. I could die, devoured by the flames or crushed by the collapsing walls. Or perhaps the police will reach me first, drag me into the light, question me in ugly rooms, and parade my disfigured face before the high courts of Paris for the grim pleasure of the people.

None of those ends appeal to me. I do not wish to escape if I can't have her. It is better to perish here, to feed myself wholly to the flames. It is a poetic end, one I deserve for the torment that I forced Christine and Raoul to endure.

Even as I pinned him to the water gate, threatened to choke out his life, and demanded Christine's devotion, I could not help but admire Raoul's defiance. I'd thought him weak, the spoiled offspring of nobility, but he let me glimpse the fire within him when we fought in the graveyard. Tonight he showed me that rebellious spirit again when he came to save Christine from my grasp.

I can see him now, his profile a breath from mine, water gleaming along the hard line of his jaw and slicking his white shirt to his chest. His lips were wet and soft, parted over his clenched teeth, and his eyes burned into mine.

In that moment, I understood why she wanted him.

But she wanted me, too. She did. When we sang together this evening, the very air vibrated with desire, with passion. Society dictates that she cannot have both Raoul and me, and even if she were willing to defy its customs, my pride and cruelty ruined every chance of that.

The fire has reached the edges of my lair. It licks at the farthest curtains, at the armchair, at the rug. I will go and lie down in its hellish embrace. It is better than existing in the inferno of my own head.

I take a step toward the greedy flames.

Thin fingers wrap around my wrist, and I glance down, startled to see Christine's white face. There's determination in the set of her mouth, a bright violence in her eyes.

"Come, Angel," she says.

I lift my gaze to the passage. Raoul stands at the entrance, his forearm braced against the stone. There's a soft heat in his gaze—mercy and something more.

"What are you waiting for, Ghost?" he says crisply. "*Dépêche-toi.*"

"He's offering you sanctuary," Christine explains. "I suggest you accept." She coughs on the hazy, heated air, and for her sake, I don't linger any longer. I'm not sure what *sanctuary* means in this case, but it can't be worse than the other fates I envisioned for myself.

As we run down the stone tunnel, five words repeat over and over in my head.

They came back for me.

That truth transforms the burning pain of my heart into a new kind of heat, something warm and hopeful.

We emerge from the tunnel smoke scented and wheezing. Raoul has lost his coat, his walking stick, his papers, and his money, but he has his rings and a certain aristocratic air that cannot be learned, only ingrained from birth. Despite the disheveled state of our trio, he secures a cab for us easily.

Christine sits on the rear seat with me, while Raoul faces us. I don't have my cloak or my mask. Without them, I feel naked and vulnerable, especially since Raoul won't stop staring at me.

"What?" I snap at him.

His stare eases, and he gives me a wry half smile. "You're so rude. No manners at all."

"Forgive me if I wasn't born to a life of silk sheets and silver spoons," I growl. "Everything I ever possessed I had to take. Every item I cherished belonged to someone else and had to be stolen. That's why—" I break off the sentence, my throat too tight to speak.

"That's why you took me," Christine says softly.

"Forgive me." The words crack from my parched lips.

"I came back, didn't I?" She lifts her hand and sweeps the black hair back from the disfigured side of my face. "What happened here? They look like burn scars."

"I don't know. I've looked like this ever since I can remember," I reply. "As I told you, I do not recall any moments of kindness or love from my childhood, only disgust and rejection. I had to wear a mask—or a bag over my head—whenever my mother was around."

"The cruelty of that," Christine whispers. "I can't imagine it."

"Am I to be a pet for the two of you now?" A caustic bitterness tinges my words. "The object of your pity, kept behind walls and stared at occasionally when you want a bit of novelty in your lives?"

"I don't pity you," Raoul says bluntly. "Many people have horror in their past, and yet they choose to be good anyway. You suffered, but you made bad choices, and they led you here. What I want to know is, are you ready to follow a different path in the future?"

"Who are you to instruct me, pup?" I snarl.

Raoul leans forward with a grin more wicked than I've yet seen from him. "So your pride isn't entirely gone, then. Your spirit is not yet broken. It's incredible, really…the resilience of you."

It feels like a compliment. I'm overwhelmed by it all—his smile, the heat in his eyes, the touch of Christine's fingers, the soft push of her breast against my bicep.

"I propose an arrangement," Raoul says. "The two of you will live with me. My ancestral home is solely mine, and there is no one to interfere if I choose to bring a friend or two within its walls. You will be safe, and you will have anything you want—supplies for music, for writing, for invention."

"And in exchange for this generosity?"

Raoul's tongue traces his lips, and he glances at Christine. She nods, her hand moving from my hair to my chest. My shirt, like Raoul's, is still damp, and I feel the heat of her palm like a scorching sun through the fabric.

"There is no obligation," Raoul says carefully. "You could remain safely at my house for years and never see either of us, unless you wish to. But as Christine and I were leaving your lair, we both paused, as if our minds were synchronized, and we confessed a certain discomfort with leaving you to your fate."

"I told Raoul that although I love him, I love you, too." Christine presses her hand over my heart. "You frighten me, Angel, but I understand you. I want you."

My breath catches, and my heart thunders beneath her palm. My eyes meet Raoul's.

"She loves us both," he says simply. "You and I have done nothing but fight over her, and I must admit that I've enjoyed our conflict. It's the most excitement I've had in a long time. That swordplay in the graveyard—I'd like to do it again. What do you say, Ghost? How would you feel about crossing our swords?"

There's no mistaking the seductive suggestion in his voice, the beautiful depravity in his eyes.

My cock was hard when I fought him in the graveyard. I thought it was simply the rush of battle, but perhaps it wasn't. I'm certainly reacting now, both to Christine's caresses and the lecherous suggestion in Raoul's gaze.

"No obligation," he says again. "You will be safe and cared for either way. But as far as Christine goes—you must learn to share or never see her at all."

"And is *she* willing to share as well?" I ask, turning to her.

Christine's cheeks are flushed rosy, her lips curved in a coy smile. "I don't have much experience with…certain things," she says. "But I think perhaps I could share and be shared. I propose an experiment—a test, if you will, to see if this could work." She leans back against the cushioned seat of the cab. "Give each other a kiss."

A growl of protest rumbles in my chest, and Raoul turns crimson.

"He won't do it," I say with a gruff, mocking laugh.

"Who says I won't?" he exclaims, bristling.

"You're such a stiff, proper, straitlaced lord, you could never—"

He lunges for me, grabbing the back of my neck and yanking me forward until our lips meet in a swift crush.

His mouth is as soft as it looks. His breath is tobacco scented, hints of whisky and honey. I open for him out of sheer surprise, and his tongue slips inside me, tentative and sweet.

I haven't kissed anyone except Christine, though I've watched many couples take each other's mouths in various ways. Perhaps kissing Raoul should feel awkward to me, but it seems like the most natural thing in the world.

My hands move up to clasp both sides of his face. I invade his mouth, my tongue swirling between his teeth. Jaws stretched wide, we empty hidden desires into each other, spilling sinful breaths into the sweet darkness of our throats.

My cock swells in my trousers. They were already tight, and the added pressure is both a delight and a torture.

Raoul's mouth parts from mine with a gasp, and I hold his face a moment longer, examining his expression before I let him go. He sits back, breathless and flushed, his eyes shining. There's a startled euphoria in his gaze, an understanding that I share—the conviction that he and I are indeed linked by something more than our mutual desire for Christine.

Silken fingers touch my face, and my darling muse angles my face toward hers. When I meet her eyes, I melt.

I'm not the ruler or the master here, no matter what I've been pretending. She is the queen before whom I will always bow in willing obedience. I took her and claimed her, but she owns me, body, mind, and soul.

"Let me taste him in your mouth," she whispers.

"Naughty words for a virgin ballet girl," I whisper back.

"I've heard plenty of licentious talk at the opera," she retorts. "And I suspect you're a virgin, too. Aren't you, Angel?"

I swallow hard, and she chuckles lightly, her breath drifting over my lips.

"Am I the only one who isn't a virgin?" Raoul cocks an eyebrow, a naughty smirk curling his lips. "Do I get to give both of you lessons?"

"It appears so," Christine murmurs against my mouth.

"How exciting!" he crows. "I saw a naughty painting once, something truly debauched that I've always wanted to try. I shall put a leather collar around that thick, strong neck of yours, Ghost, and have you naked on all fours while I flick your ass with my riding crop—"

"Pace yourself, darling," Christine admonishes. "You're scaring him. I can feel how fast his heart is beating." She sinks her lips onto mine, a soft and soothing pressure. The tip of her tongue explores the twisted corner of my mouth, the part that's tugged a bit sideways by my scars. The sensitive questing of that little tongue is the most erotic thing I've ever felt, and my cock hardens still more.

"You're about to burst from those trousers, Ghost," Raoul comments.

Christine looks down at my crotch. Her hand floats tentatively above the bulge before settling there, light as a butterfly, warm as the sun.

I can't suppress a groan, and her pupils dilate with pleasure at the sound. She rubs her palm over me confidently, triggering sensations more intense and exquisite than anything I've felt from my own hand.

"Take him out, Christine," Raoul says. "I want to see him."

She glances up at me, questioning, and when I nod, she undoes the buttons on either side of my trousers and folds down the flap. My cock springs out, monstrously erect, leaking helpless desire from the tip.

The sight of my own nakedness, when my scarred face is already so exposed, is almost too much for me to bear. I feel a surge of panic, of violence. I want to hurt them both, make them bleed and scream before they have the chance to laugh and mock me. Once I've crushed them, I will flee into the darkness and hide myself in some deep hole, in some forgotten tunnel of the city.

I picture myself seizing Christine's tender throat in my hand and crushing the voice box that produces such heavenly sounds. I imagine smashing Raoul's skull against the frame of the cab, knocking the light from his eyes. My shaking hands curl into powerful fists as I struggle to restrain the brutal impulses that have guided and protected me for so many years.

"My god," breathes Raoul. "That is a magnificent cock."

"Beautiful," Christine agrees, tracing a delicate finger along my length. She looks up at me to see my reaction, and the sweetness of her expression tears my soul apart. She *wants* me to feel good. She craves my pleasure. And that gentle selflessness breaks me, dismantles me, dissipates all the anger in my body.

Raoul slips off the opposite seat, dropping to his knees between my thighs. "May I try something?" he asks. "I've done it twice for friends of mine at parties, but they weren't nearly this big."

I suspect what he might be planning to do, and with a harsh swallow, I nod.

Raoul wraps a hand around my length and dips the head between his lips. Christine lets out a soft, excited gasp, clinging to my shoulder, her fingers finding my breast and toying with the nipple while the Viscount de Chagny sucks my cock.

The easy, nonchalant way Raoul took me struck a chord in my heart, vibrating the very strings of my soul. As if tasting my cock is the natural progression of the fervent rivalry between us.

The cab rattles over a particularly rough stretch of

cobblestones, and Raoul is thrown forward. He chokes on me, then pulls off, laughing. "Perhaps this should wait until we reach my house."

"Perhaps," I agree.

Christine buttons me up again and kisses my face several times before joining Raoul on his side of the cab. She kisses his mouth, then looks at me, as if checking to see if I'm able to handle witnessing their intimacy. There's a familiar surge of jealousy in my heart, but it's not an overwhelming tide—merely a small ripple. I am beginning to understand that her heart is big enough for both of us. Raoul having her doesn't mean that I'm left alone in the darkness—I can be part of their union, too.

And what is more holy than a trinity?

When we reach the de Chagny estate, Raoul escorts us inside while his butler pays the cab driver. I scan our surroundings—fine carpets, rich tapestries, and heavy, glossy furniture laden with delicate vases, relics of exotic travel, statuary, and cigar boxes. Raoul appears to collect the boxes; there is one on nearly every surface, including the bookshelves.

Mentally, I begin to design one for him—part music box, part puzzle box, with a place for the finest of cigars at the center. It shall be my gift to him someday—a token to show my gratitude.

I'm not skilled at showing gratitude. I've never had much to be grateful for. But I feel thankful to Raoul with an intensity that borders on the obsessive. Ever since he took my mouth and then my cock, looking at him feels like the early days I spent watching Christine. It's as if I'm truly seeing him for the first time.

But I can't look at him for very long without feeling a restless ache in my soul, a yearning as familiar to me as breathing. I need

Christine. I must seek out her face, her voice, her skin. Whatever I might find with Raoul, she remains my beauty, my angel, my muse. I'm addicted to her very existence, and the greatest joy of this new situation is that at last I will be able to *touch* her, taste her, and sink myself inside her, as I've longed to do so many times.

For the first months of my acquaintance with Christine, I wouldn't allow myself to think about my physical attraction to her. She was a lofty ideal, and it felt sacrilegious to imagine sex with her. But as I came to know her better, I realized that her sexuality was part of her nature. Her desires fueled much of her singing. Her passion guided her body through each dance she performed for the opera. She is a creature of light, beauty, and talent, but she has every right to be earthly, sensual, and naughty as she pleases. She is a human being, not just a goddess for me to worship, and I came to view her as both.

Her fingers lace through mine as we follow Raoul deeper into his enormous house. This grandeur is as unfamiliar and unexpected to her as it is to me. She has lived at the opera since her father's death, and the dormitories for the ballet girls provide only the basic accommodations—certainly not luxuries on this level.

While Christine may have entertained thoughts of living at Raoul's estate someday, I know she wasn't planning to come here so soon—certainly not on the very night that was supposed to end in my capture by the Paris police.

The thought strikes doubt into my heart. What if this is part of a game these two are playing, an elaborate ruse to lull me into submission before they betray me? What if there are policemen or guards hiding behind the doors we pass, lurking between the curtains, slinking in alcoves, ready to leap out and clap me in irons?

My steps slow as my breathing escalates.

Christine looks at me questioningly. "Angel?"

My chest heaves, yet I can't seem to draw a full breath. My eyes dart from side to side, watching for traps, for tricks, for tormentors. If I am not the one setting the snares and causing the torment, I must be a target. I can't let my guard down, or I will be cornered, captured, and *seen* for what I really am.

I can't breathe. I let go of Christine's hand and bend over, grasping my thighs.

"Raoul, wait," Christine calls. Her fingers press between my shoulder blades, rubbing in comforting circles.

Raoul comes back to us. "Is he all right?"

"It's too much," Christine says quietly. "It's been a difficult night for all of us."

"Tell me I won't be caged," I rasp out. "Tell me you don't have men waiting to seize me, like you did at the theater."

Raoul's voice is shadowed with regret. "I did work with the police to apprehend you, yes. We used Christine as bait and performed your opera to coax you out. But I had misgivings the whole time, especially when I saw you onstage with her. The way you sang together—the way you *loved* her and ached for her so openly out there, for everyone to see—I wept. I hated you, and I admired you, and I wept."

I squeeze my eyes shut, feeling the pull of the scars on my right temple. I still can't breathe, but I hold on to his voice like a tether, like a promise.

"I changed, Ghost," Raoul says softly. "Or perhaps I merely released what was inside me all along. I came to your lair for *her*, yes, but for you as well. I wanted to see who you really were—if there remained any goodness or mercy in your heart. I craved the violence of our mutual conflict. I wanted to taste your anger and your passion. And then, when you let us go, I saw your brokenness."

He drops to one knee on the carpet in front of me, cups my face like I held his, and forces me to meet his eyes. "I have been broken, too. In a different way, but no less deeply and wretchedly. I *see* you. I care about you. And that means I will never try to entrap you again."

"Each of us are broken," Christine murmurs. "I broke when my mother passed and again when my father died. I broke a little more each time a man squeezed my breast or my ass, seeing me only for my body and not for my talents. You, sweet Angel—you saw my soul and adored my voice long before you craved my body. I loved you for that, even when I feared you. I swear that I will not betray you, and if you treat me with the respect I deserve, I will never leave your side."

Air rushes deep into my lungs, a full and satisfying breath. The tension eases from my neck and shoulders. My heart rate is slowing.

"To be unmasked and loved openly," I whisper. "I suppose that is what we all crave."

I let them lead me upstairs, our path illuminated by lamps in ornate sconces. Raoul rings for the servants to prepare hot water, and we each bathe luxuriously in the decadent rooms of his home.

When I am clean, I wrap myself in one of his dressing gowns. It's too tight in the shoulders and upper arms, but I manage. A servant leads me down the upstairs hallway to a small parlor where Christine sits on a sofa, wearing a lacy white nightdress beneath her own robe. Raoul stands by the fireplace, his hand braced on the mantel. They both look up when I enter, but they do not speak until the servant has left the room.

"Your people must wonder who we are and why we're here," I comment.

"They understand discretion," Raoul says. "When my brother ran this household, there were many parties and dalliances. Compared to his debauchery, a couple of late-night guests are of little consequence."

"Even one like me?" I gesture to the scarred half of my face.

"They will not speak of it," he insists. "They are paid handsomely, and they have well-appointed rooms and plenty of days off. I treat my staff better than anyone else in the city. None of them will risk losing their place in this house by indulging in foolish gossip."

His reassurance soothes me, but I'm more impressed by his evident care for his employees. He is effectively sharing his wealth with them, which speaks well of his character. Not that I'm one to judge a nobleman for how he runs his house, but the revelation of Raoul's generosity pleases me.

I've never been generous myself. As I told Christine, I'm used to theft, blackmail, and trickery as the only means of getting what I want, and I do not regret it. Why should other people have wealth, beauty, homes, and families, while I was deprived of all that? I was only taking what I deserved, claiming what Fate withheld from me.

For all her previous vagaries, Fate is smiling on me tonight. I'm standing in a comfortable room, amid plush furnishings. The man and woman I've been chasing around the opera house are watching me with mingled caution and desire. They're still both a little afraid of me, and I find a dark pleasure in the knowledge. My cock stiffens beneath the heavy folds of the dressing gown.

"This is my private suite." Raoul clears his throat. "I can show you to your room if you'd prefer to rest."

"I prefer to remain here," I say.

Christine gives Raoul a secret little smile of pure delight. "Perhaps we should continue our game then?"

"The one where I put the Opera Ghost's cock down my throat?" Raoul says casually, though his cheeks redden. "That game?"

"Yes," she breathes. "Or a variation thereof."

Raoul walks through a set of open double doors, and we follow him into his bedroom, toward the immense four-poster bed. He drops his dressing gown on the floor, and I do the same. Christine sheds her robe, but she doesn't remove her nightgown. She stares at my body and Raoul's, her cheeks a hearty shade of crimson.

Raoul goes over to a tray laden with decanters and glasses. He pours us each two fingers of whisky. I'm no stranger to alcohol, though I take it in moderation, and I throw back the offered drink quickly, enjoying the heated buzz of the liquor in my throat and stomach.

Christine coughs a bit on the first sip, but she seems to like the taste, or perhaps she simply enjoys the transgressive indulgence of drinking the Viscount de Chagny's whisky in his bedroom. She swallows a bit more of the liquor while Raoul and I approach each other cautiously, like a pair of lions contemplating a challenge.

When his cock touches mine, it's like a jolt of lightning, a white-hot burn along my nerves. I have never felt anything like it, and yet my body understands the sensation on an instinctive level. It's as if I already know this language of searing skin and taut muscle, of thick veins and burning fingers.

I grasp Raoul's lean hip with one hand and his throat with the other, crowding in, feeling the grind of our two rods between our bellies. He's breathing hard, his throat flexing against my grip as he swallows, but though I can sense his fear, he doesn't ask me to release him.

Christine makes a soft sound, a whimper that draws our attention. Her face is scarlet, her eyes wide. She's clearly pleased by what she's seeing, and yet she seems overwhelmed. She is a virgin, after all. I am, too, but in this moment, I don't feel like one. There is no hesitation in my heart. I ache for them both.

I start toward her, drawn by her whimper, eager to show her that in this, as in our voice lessons, I can be her guide and her comfort.

"You revealed your soul to me already," I murmur. "Bare the rest, and let me worship you."

"Angel," she whispers. "Touch me like you did when we sang tonight."

I move behind her, pulling her back against my chest, wrapping both arms around her. One of my hands shifts to cup her breast, squeezing lightly, my thumb tracing over her nipple. Only the thinnest of soft lace separates her skin from mine.

Christine sighs in my arms, relinquishing her fears and becoming a creature of passion and fire, like she did onstage, before I was betrayed. Before the theater burned.

With her back to me, she takes both my hands and guides them firmly down her body, over her stomach, shoving them between her legs. She prompts my left hand to gather up the material of the nightgown, then shifts my right fingers into the delicate, bare cleft between her thighs.

I can feel her—the soft lips of her sex, the bits of tender flesh between them. Touching that part of her drives my brain into bright delirium, incites a deep groan from my very soul.

Raoul kneels in front of us, his eyes on Christine's sex. With both hands, I part her legs wider, revealing her to him. When he puts out his tongue and licks between her sensitive folds, she shivers against my chest.

With a surge of strength, I gather her, carry her to the bed just as she is, and sit naked on the edge of the mattress with her on my lap. In this position, I can open her wider for Raoul. I hold back her thighs and splay her dripping center to his view.

Christine winds her arms around my biceps, clinging to me while I present her to the viscount. He's on his knees, eyes mad with desire. At the stroke of his tongue, she writhes, panting.

"Yes, yes," she gasps. "How does that feel so delicious?"

"Sin is always delicious," I murmur against her temple.

Raoul has done this before, that much is clear. I watch him carefully, memorizing his use of pressure, his little coaxing nips and kisses, the way he suckles at the apex of her thighs and then laps at that spot with a swift rhythm.

"I don't know what's happening," Christine gasps out, twisting in my arms again. "I feel...I feel...ah..." She squeals faintly and jerks her hips against Raoul's mouth. Her body convulses once, and then she's panting, easing, relaxing.

"Look how beautifully you came for me," croons Raoul, sliding two fingers against her sopping flesh. "Now you're ready for him. Lift her, Ghost, and she'll slip smoothly onto your cock."

"May I?" I whisper in her ear, and Christine nods eagerly.

I feel Raoul's fingers wrap around my length as I lift Christine. He guides the tip of my cock to her center and pokes it inside as I lower her body onto me.

The viscount's eyes meet mine as our beautiful Christine begins to take my cock, and I understand that this is her choice, yes, but it's also his gift to me. He wants me to have her first, so I will know his sincerity and believe in his love.

Christine cries out softly, and Raoul presses his mouth to her sex, licking the peak of her folds where the pleasure seems most intense, soothing her while she takes a little more of me. She is soaked and slippery, but my cock is large and long, so it takes time for her to acclimate. I hold her suspended in place, my biceps swelling. Despite the strain, I refuse to seat her fully on my length until she is ready.

Gradually I ease her down, lowering her bit by bit, while Raoul teases her toward another climax.

"Lift her again," he says, glancing up at me with wet, scarlet lips. "Raise and lower her body. Gently now, a steady rhythm."

I slide Christine up my cock, then down again. The slick gloving of my length by her tight heat is more than I can bear. I've never felt the inside of a woman before, and it's exquisite as heaven.

Christine seems to enjoy the movement. Her breath catches and she begins making sharp, eager little sounds as I move her up and down on my cock, pushing inside her more deeply each time. Raoul follows our progress with long licks of my shaft and her opening, while his hand jerks rapidly along his own cock.

He rises, bending to kiss first me, then Christine. When his mouth meets hers, he comes with a ragged gasp. I feel his hot cum fly against the place where Christine and I are joined, drops of his release slicking my length and her pussy.

With his thumb against the peak of her sex and my arms pumping her faster on my length, Christine comes, shrieking her bliss. She throws her head back while her body convulses around my cock.

The stimulation of her climax is more than I can take. I release the full force of my desire inside her, my cock throbbing. Raoul strokes the base of my length with his fingers, then cups my balls in his hand, grinning as he feels them tighten.

"You are both so beautiful." Emotion thickens his voice as he leans forward to kiss each of us again. "My darling friend and my passionate enemy."

When we've recovered a little, Raoul gives Christine some wine to blur the slight soreness between her legs. We settle her on fluffy pillows in the center of the bed, and I slide in beside her, between silky sheets. Raoul drapes a duvet over us, blows out the candles, and crawls in on Christine's other side.

Sleep comes softly, pressing my eyelids like a lover's touch, seducing me like a strain of whispered melody. For the first time, there are no schemes in my head, no violent torment of love unsatisfied, no wretched jealousy, no molten resentment. Here in this grand house, in this richly appointed room, in this comfortable bed, I am at peace. I am with the woman I have loved for what feels like ages—the sweet, fiery, gentle soul I adore. With us lies the man who has been her friend since childhood, who loves her dearly, and whose generous heart is open to me as well.

What secrets will we learn from each other? What joys will we experience, and what desires will unfurl in this very room? What heights of music and beautiful madness will we reach?

I cannot be certain, and yet I am not afraid.

I listen to their soft breathing, and it is the loveliest music to ever grace the night.

ACKNOWLEDGMENTS

Thank you to my wonderful editor, Mary Altman, for giving me the chance to write the Phantom retelling of my dreams as part of this series. Thank you to everyone at Sourcebooks who helped to polish and prepare it. Thank you, as always, to Eva Scalzo, my amazing agent, my map through the wilderness of the publishing world. And thank you to my incredible readers who went feral when they found out I was writing this story—you give me life, and I love you.

ABOUT THE AUTHOR

Rebecca Kenney writes spicy contemporary and fantasy romance about sassy, strong women and hot guys with tragic backstories. She is the author of the Wicked Darlings series (spicy Fae retellings of the Nutcracker, Wonderland, and Oz), the Dark Rulers series (stand-alone fantasy romances in a shared world), and the For the Love of the Villain series. Rebecca is represented by Eva Scalzo of Speilburg Literary. She lives in upstate South Carolina with her handsome blue-eyed husband and two smart, energetic kids. For updates and information about upcoming novels, follow her on:

Instagram: @rebeccafkenneybooks
TikTok: @rebeccafkenney